A Cinderella Story

MAUREEN CHILD
ELIZABETH BEVARLY
ANNA DePALO

MILLS & BOON

First Published in Great Britain 2018
by Mills & Boon, an imprint of HarperCollins*Publishers*
1 London Bridge Street, London, SE1 9GF

A CINDERELLA STORY © 2018 Harlequin Books S. A.

Maid Under The Mistletoe © 2016 Maureen Child
My Fair Billionaire © 2014 Elizabeth Bevarly
Second Chance With The CEO © 2016 Anna DePalo

ISBN: 978-0-263-27465-3

1118

MIX
Paper from
responsible sources
FSC™ C007454

FSC
www.fsc.org

Printed and bound in Spain
by CPI, Barcelona

MAID UNDER THE MISTLETOE

MAUREEN CHILD

To all the mums who are out there right now,
making magic

One

Sam Henry hated December.

The days were too short, making the nights seem an eternity. It was cold and dark—and then there was the incessant Christmas badgering. Lights, trees, carols and an ever-increasing barrage of commercials urging you to shop, spend, buy. And every reminder of the holiday season ate at the edges of his soul and heart like drops of acid.

He scowled at the roaring fire in the hearth, slapped one hand on the mantel and rubbed his fingers over the polished edge of the wood. With his gaze locked on the flames, he told himself that if he could, he'd wipe the month of December from the calendar.

"You can't stick your head in the snow and pretend Christmas isn't happening."

Sam flicked a glance at the woman in the open doorway. His housekeeper/cook/nag, Kaye Porter, stood there glaring at him through narrowed blue eyes. Hands at her wide hips, her gray-streaked black hair pulled back into a single thick braid that hung down over one shoulder, she shook her head. "There's not enough snow to do it anyway, and whether you like it or not, Christmas is coming."

"I don't and it's only coming if I acknowledge it," Sam told her.

"Well, you're going to have to pay attention because I'm out of here tomorrow."

"I'll give you a raise if you cancel your trip," he said, willing to bargain to avoid the hassle of losing the woman who ran his house so he didn't have to.

A short bark of laughter shot from her throat. "Not a chance. My friend Ruthie and I do this every year, as you well know. We've got our rooms booked and there's no way we're canceling."

He'd known that—he just hadn't wanted to think about it. Another reason to hate December. Every year, Kaye and Ruthie took a month-long vacation. A cruise to the Bahamas, then a stay at a splashy beachside hotel, followed by another cruise home. Kaye liked to say it was her therapy to get her through the rest of the year living with a crank like himself.

"If you love Christmas so much, why do you run to a beach every year?"

She sighed heavily. "Christmas is everywhere, you know. Even in hot, sandy places! We buy little trees, decorate them for our rooms. And the hotel lights up all the palm trees…" She sighed again, but this time, it was with delight. "It's gorgeous."

"Fine." He pushed away from the hearth, tucked both

hands into the pockets of his jeans and stared at her. Every year he tried to talk her out of leaving and every year he lost. Surrendering to the inevitable, he asked, "You need a ride to the airport?"

A small smile curved her mouth at the offer. "No, but thanks. Ruthie's going to pick me up at the crack of dawn tomorrow. She'll leave her car there so when we come back we don't have to worry about taking one of those damn shuttles."

"Okay then." He took a breath and muttered, "Have a great time."

"The enthusiasm in that suggestion is just one of the reasons I need this trip." One dark eyebrow lifted. "You worry me, Sam. All locked away on this mountain hardly talking to anyone but me—"

She kept going, but Sam tuned out. He'd heard it all before. Kaye was determined to see him "start living" again. Didn't seem to matter that he had no interest in that. While she talked, he glanced around the main room of what Kaye liked to call his personal prison.

It was a log home, the wood the color of warm honey, with lots of glass to spotlight the view that was breathtaking from every room. Pine forest surrounded the house, and a wide, private lake stretched out beyond a narrow slice of beach. He had a huge garage and several outbuildings, including a custom-designed workshop where Sam wished he was right at that moment.

This house, this *sanctuary*, was just what he'd been looking for when he'd come to Idaho five years ago. It was isolated, with a small town—Franklin—just fifteen minutes away when he needed supplies. A big city, with the airport and all manner of other distractions, was just an hour from there, not that he ever went. What he needed, he had Kaye pick up in Franklin and only rarely went to town himself.

The whole point of moving here had been to find quiet. Peace. *Solitude.* Hell, he could go weeks and never talk to anyone but Kaye. Thoughts of her brought him back to the conversation at hand.

"...Anyway," she was saying, "my friend Joy will be here about ten tomorrow morning to fill in for me while I'm gone."

He nodded. At least Kaye had done what she always did, arranged for one of her friends to come and stay for the month she'd be gone. Sam wouldn't have to worry about cooking, cleaning or pretty much anything but keeping his distance from whatever busybody she'd found this year.

He folded his arms over his chest. "I'm not going to catch this one rifling through my desk, right?"

Kaye winced. "I will admit that having Betty come last year was a bad idea…"

"Yeah," he agreed. She'd seemed nice enough, but the woman had poked her head into everything she could find. Within a week, Sam had sent her home and had spent the following three weeks eating grilled cheese sandwiches, canned soup and frozen pizza. "I'd say so."

"She's the curious sort."

"She's nosy."

"Yes, well." Kaye cleared her throat. "That was my mistake, I know. But my friend Joy isn't a snoop. I think you'll like her."

"Not necessary," he assured her. He didn't want to like Joy. Hell, he didn't want to *talk* to her if he could avoid it.

"Of course not." Kaye shook her head again and gave him the kind of look teachers used to reserve for the kid acting up in class. "Wouldn't want to be human or anything. Might set a nasty precedent."

"Kaye…"

The woman had worked for him since he'd moved to Idaho five years ago. And since then, she'd muscled her way much deeper into his life than he'd planned on allowing. Not only did she take care of the house, but she looked after *him* despite the fact that he didn't want her to. But Kaye was a force of nature, and it seemed her friends were a lot like her.

"Never mind. Anyway, to what I was saying, Joy already knows that you're cranky and want to be left alone—"

He frowned at her. "Thanks."

"Am I wrong?" When he didn't answer, she nodded. "She's a good cook and runs her own business on the internet."

"You told me all of this already," he pointed out. Though she hadn't said what *kind* of business the amazing Joy ran. Still, how many different things could a woman in her fifties or sixties do online? Give knitting lessons? Run a babysitting service? Dog sitting? Hell, his own mother sold handmade dresses online, so there was just no telling.

"I know, I know." Kaye waved away his interruption. "She'll stay out of your way because she needs this time here. The contractor says they won't have the fire damage at her house repaired until January, so being able to stay and work here was a godsend."

"You told me this, too," he reminded her. In fact, he'd heard more than enough about Joy the Wonder Friend. According to Kaye, she was smart, clever, a hard worker, had a wonderful sense of humor and did apparently everything just short of walking on water. "But how did the fire in her house start again? Is she a closet arsonist? A terrible cook who set fire to the stove?"

"Of course not!" Kaye sniffed audibly and stiffened as if someone had shoved a pole down the back of her sweatshirt. "I told you, there was a short in the wiring. The house she's renting is just ancient and something was bound to go at some point. The owner of the house is having all the wiring redone, though, so it should be safe now."

"I'm relieved to hear it," he said. And relieved he didn't have to worry that Kaye's friend was so old she'd forgotten to turn off an oven or something.

"I'm only trying to tell you—" she broke off to give him a small smile of understanding "—like I do every year, that you'll survive the month of December just like you do every year."

He ground his teeth together at the flash of sympathy that stirred and then vanished from her eyes. This was the problem with people getting to know too much about him. They felt as if they had the right to offer comfort where none was wanted—or needed. Sam liked Kaye fine, but there were parts of his life that were closed off. For a reason.

He'd get through the holidays his way. Which meant ignoring the forced cheer and the never-ending lineup of "feel good" holiday-themed movies where the hard-hearted hero does a turnaround and opens himself to love and the spirit of Christmas.

Hearts should never be open. Left them too vulnerable to being shattered.

And he'd never set himself up for that kind of pain again.

* * *

Early the following day Kaye was off on her vacation, and a few hours later Sam was swamped by the empty silence. He reminded himself that it was how he liked his life best. No one bothering him. No one talking at him. One of the reasons he and Kaye got along so well was that she respected his need to be left the hell alone. So now that he was by himself in the big house, why did he feel an itch along his spine?

"It's December," he muttered aloud. That was enough to explain the sense of discomfort that clung to him.

Hell, every year, this one damn month made life damn near unlivable. He pushed a hand through his hair, then scraped that hand across the stubble on his jaw. He couldn't settle. Hadn't even spent any time out in his workshop, and usually being out there eased his mind and kept him too busy to think about—

He put the brakes on that thought fast because he couldn't risk opening doors that were better off sealed shut.

Scowling, he stared out the front window at the cold, dark day. The steel-gray clouds hung low enough that it looked as though they were actually skimming across the tops of the pines. The lake, in summer a brilliant sapphire blue, stretched out in front of him like a sheet of frozen pewter. The whole damn world seemed bleak and bitter, which only fed into what he felt every damn minute.

Memories rose up in the back of his mind, but he squelched them flat, as he always did. He'd worked too hard for too damn long to get beyond his past, to live and breathe—and hell, *survive*—to lose it all now. He'd beaten back his demons, and damned if he'd release them long enough to take a bite out of him now.

Resolve set firmly, Sam frowned again when an old blue four-door sedan barreled along his drive, kicking up gravel as it came to a stop in front of the house. For a second, he thought it must be Kaye's friend Joy arriving. Then the driver stepped out of the car and that thought went out the window.

The driver was too young, for one thing. Every other friend Kaye had enlisted to help out had been her age or older. This woman was in her late twenties, he figured, gaze locked on her as she turned her face to stare up at the house. One look at her and Sam felt a punch of lust that stole his breath. Everything in him fisted tightly as he continued to watch her. He couldn't take his eyes off her as she stood on the drive studying his house. Hell, she was like a ray of sunlight in the gray.

Her short curly hair was bright blond and flew about her face in the sharp wind that slapped rosy color into her cheeks. Her blue eyes swept the exterior of the house even as she moved around the car to the rear passenger side. Her black jeans hugged long legs, and her hiking boots looked scarred and well-worn. The cardinal-red parka she wore over a cream-colored sweater was a burst of color in a black-and-white world.

She was beautiful and moved with a kind of easy grace that made a man's gaze follow her every movement. And even while he admitted that silently, Sam resented it. He wasn't interested in women. Didn't want to feel what she was making him feel. What he had to do was find out why the hell she was there and get her gone as fast as possible.

She had to be lost. His drive wasn't that easy to find—purposely. He rarely got visitors, and those were mainly his family when he couldn't stave off his parents or sister any longer.

Well, if she'd lost her way, he'd go out and give her directions to town, and then she'd be gone and he could get back to—whatever.

"Damn." The single word slipped from his throat as she opened the car's back door and a little girl jumped out. The eager anticipation stamped on the child's face was like a dagger to the heart for Sam. He took a breath that fought its way into his chest and forced himself to look away from the kid. He didn't do kids. Not for a long time now. Their voices. Their laughter. They were too small. Too vulnerable.

Too breakable.

What felt like darkness opened up in the center of his chest. Turning his back on the window, he left the room and headed for the front door. The faster he got rid of the gorgeous woman and her child, the better.

"It's a fairy castle, Mommy!"

Joy Curran glanced at the rearview mirror and smiled at the excitement shining on her daughter's face. At five years old, Holly was crazy about princesses, fairies and everyday magic she seemed to find wherever she looked.

Still smiling, Joy shifted her gaze from her daughter to the big house in front of her. Through the windshield, she scanned the front of the place and had to agree with Holly on this one. It did look like a castle.

Two stories, it spread across the land, pine trees spearing up all around it like sentries prepared to stand in defense. The smooth, glassy logs were the color of warm honey, and the wide, tall windows gave glimpses of the interior. A wraparound porch held chairs and gliders that invited visitors to sit and get comfortable. The house faced a private lake where a long dock jutted out into the water that was frozen over for winter. There was a wide deck studded with furniture draped in tarps for winter and a brick fire pit.

It would probably take her a half hour to look at everything, and it was way too cold to simply sit in her car and take it all in. So instead, she turned the engine off, then walked around to get Holly out of her car seat. While the little girl jumped up and down in excitement, pigtails flying, Joy grabbed her purse and headed for the front door. The cold wrapped itself around them and Joy shivered. There hadn't been much snow so far this winter, but the cold sliced right down to the bone. All around her, the pines were green but the grass was brown, dotted with shrinking patches of snow. Holly kept hoping to make snow angels and snowmen, but so far, Mother Nature wasn't cooperating.

The palatial house looked as if it had grown right out of the woods surrounding it. The place was gorgeous, but a little intimidating. And from everything she'd heard, so was the man who lived here. Oh, Kaye was crazy about him, but then Kaye took in stray dogs, cats, wounded birds and any lonely soul she happened across. But there was plenty of speculation about Sam Henry in town.

Joy knew he used to be a painter, and she'd actually seen a few of his paintings online. Judging by the art he created, she would have guessed him to be warm, optimistic and, well, *nice*. According to Kaye, though, the man was quiet, reclusive to the point of being a hermit, and she thought he was lonely at the bottom of it. But to

Joy's way of thinking, if you didn't want to be lonely, you got out and met people. Heck, it was so rare to see Sam Henry in town, spotting him was the equivalent of a Bigfoot sighting. She'd caught only the occasional rare glimpse of the man herself.

But none of that mattered at the moment, Joy told herself. She and Holly needed a place to stay for the month, and this housesitting/cooking/cleaning job had turned up at just the right time. Taking Holly's hand, she headed for the front door, the little girl skipping alongside her, chattering about princesses and castles the whole way.

For just a second, Joy envied her little girl's simpler outlook on life. For Holly, this was an adventure in a magical castle. For Joy, it was moving into a big, secluded house with a secretive and, according to Kaye, cranky man. Okay, now she was making it sound like she was living in a Gothic novel. Kaye lived here year-round, right? And had for years. Surely Joy could survive a month. Determined now to get off on the right foot, she plastered a smile on her face, climbed up to the wide front porch and knocked on the double doors.

She was still smiling a moment later when the door was thrown open and she looked up into a pair of suspicious brown eyes. An instant snap of attraction slapped at Joy, surprising her with its force. His black hair was long, hitting past the collar of his dark red shirt, and the thick mass lifted slightly as another cold wind trickled past. His jaws were shadowed by whiskers and his mouth was a grim straight line. He was tall, with broad shoulders, narrow hips and long legs currently encased in worn, faded denim that stacked on the tops of a pair of weathered brown cowboy boots.

If it wasn't for the narrowed eyes and the grim expression on his face, he would have been the star of any number of Joy's personal fantasies. Then he spoke and the already tattered remnants of said fantasy drifted away.

"This is private property," he said in a voice that was more of a growl. "If you're looking for town, go back to the main road and turn left. Stay on the road and you'll get there in about twenty minutes."

Well, this was starting off well.

"Thanks," she said, desperately trying to hang on to the smile curving her mouth as well as her optimistic attitude. "But I'm not lost. I've just come from town."

If anything, his frown deepened. "Then why're you here?"

"Nice to meet you, too," Joy said, half tugging Holly behind her. Not that she was afraid of him—but why subject her little girl to a man who looked like he'd rather slam the door in their faces than let them in?

"I repeat," he said, "who are you?"

"I'm Joy. Kaye's friend?" It came out as a question though she hadn't meant it as one.

"You're kidding." His eyes went wide as his gaze swept her up and down in a fast yet thorough examination.

She didn't know whether to be flattered or insulted. But when his features remained stiff and cold, she went for insulted.

"Is there a problem?" she asked. "Kaye told me you'd be expecting me and—"

"You're not old."

She blinked at him. "Thank you for noticing, though I've got to say, if Kaye ever hears you call her 'old,' it won't be pretty."

"That's not—" He stopped and started again. "I was expecting a woman Kaye's age," he continued. "Not someone like you. Or," he added with a brief glance at Holly, "a child."

Why hadn't Kaye told him about Holly? For a split second, Joy worried over that and wondered if he'd try to back out of their deal now. But an instant later she assured herself that no matter what happened, she was going to hold him to his word. She needed to be here and she wasn't about to leave.

She took a breath and ignored the cool chill in his eyes. "Well, that's a lovely welcome, thanks. Look, it's cold out here. If you don't mind, I'd like to come in and get settled."

He shook his head, opened his mouth to speak, but Holly cut him off.

"Are you the prince?" She stepped out from behind her mother, tipped her head back and studied him.

"The what?"

Joy tensed. She didn't want to stop Holly from talking—wasn't entirely sure she *could*—but she was more than willing to intervene if the quietly hostile man said something she didn't like.

"The prince," Holly repeated, the tiny lisp that defined her voice tugging at Joy's heart. "Princes live in castles."

Joy caught the barest glimmer of a smile brush across his face before it was gone again. Somehow, though, that ghost of real emotion made her feel better.

"No," he said and his voice was softer than it had been. "I'm not a prince."

Joy could have said something to that, and judging by the glance he shot her, he half expected her to. But irritating him further wasn't going to get her and Holly into the house and out of the cold.

"But he looks like a prince, doesn't he, Mommy?"

A prince with a lousy attitude. A dark prince, maybe.

"Sure, honey," she said with a smile for the little girl shifting from foot to foot in her eagerness to get inside the "castle."

Turning back to the man who still stood like an immovable object in the doorway, Joy said reasonably, "Look, I'm sorry we aren't what you were expecting. But here we are. Kaye told you about the fire at our house, right?"

"The firemen came and let me sit in the big truck with the lights going and it was really bright and blinking."

"Is that right?" That vanishing smile of his came and went again in a blink.

"And it smelled really bad," Holly put in, tugging her hand free so she could pinch her own nose.

"It did," Joy agreed, running one hand over the back of Holly's head. "And," she continued, "it did enough damage that we can't stay there while they're fixing it—" She broke off and said, "Can we finish this inside? It's cold out here."

For a second, she wasn't sure he'd agree, but then he nodded, moved back and opened the wide, heavy door. Heat rushed forward to greet them, and Joy nearly sighed in pleasure. She gave a quick look around at the entry hall. The gleaming, honey-colored logs shone in the overhead light. The entry floor was made up of huge square tiles in mottled earth tones. Probably way easier to clean up melting snow from tile floors instead of wood, she told herself and let her gaze quickly move over what she could see of the rest of the house.

It seemed even bigger on the inside, which was hard to believe, and with the lights on against the dark of winter, the whole place practically glowed. A long hallway led off to the back of the house, and on the right was a stairway leading to the second floor. Near the front door, there was a handmade coat tree boasting a half-dozen brass hooks and a padded bench attached.

Shrugging out of her parka, Joy hung it on one of the hooks, then turned and pulled Holly's jacket off as well, hanging it alongside hers. The warmth of the house surrounded her and all Joy could think was, she really wanted to stay. She and Holly needed a place and this house with its soft glow was…welcoming, in spite of its owner.

She glanced at the man watching her, and one look told her that he really wanted her gone. But she wasn't going to allow that.

The house was gigantic, plenty of room for her and Holly to live and still stay out of Sam Henry's way. There was enough land around the house so that her little girl could play. One man to cook and clean for, which would leave her plenty of time to work on her laptop. And oh, if he made them leave, she and her daughter would end up staying in a hotel in town for a month. Just the thought of trying to keep a five-year-old happy when she was trapped in a small, single room for weeks made Joy tired.

"Okay, we're inside," he said. "Let's talk."

"Right. It's a beautiful house." She walked past him, forcing the man to follow her as she walked to the first doorway and peeked in. A great room—that really lived up to the name.

Floor-to-ceiling windows provided a sweeping view

of the frozen lake, a wide lawn and a battalion of pines that looked to be scraping the underside of the low-hanging gray clouds. There was a massive hearth on one wall, where a wood fire burned merrily. A big-screen TV took up most of another wall, and there were brown leather couches and chairs sprinkled around the room, sitting on brightly colored area rugs. Handcrafted wood tables held lamps and books, with more books tucked onto shelves lining yet another wall.

"I love reading, too, and what a terrific spot for it," Joy said, watching Holly as the girl wandered the room, then headed straight to the windows where she peered out, both hands flat against the glass.

"Yeah, it works for me." He came up beside her, crossed his arms over his chest and said, "Anyway..."

"You won't even know we're here," Joy spoke up quickly. "And it'll be a pleasure to take care of this place. Kaye loves working here, so I'm sure Holly and I will be just as happy."

"Yeah, but—"

She ignored his frown and the interruption. On a roll, she had no intention of stopping. "I'm going to take a look around. You don't have to worry about giving me a tour. I'll find my own way—"

"About that—"

Irritation flashed across his features and Joy almost felt sorry for him. Not sorry enough to stop, though. "What time do you want dinner tonight?"

Before he could answer, she said, "How about six? If that works for you, we'll keep it that way for the month. Otherwise, we can change it."

"I didn't agree—"

"Kaye said Holly and I should use her suite of rooms

off the kitchen, so we'll just go get settled in and you can get back to what you were doing when we got here." A bright smile on her face, she called, "Holly, come with me now." She looked at him. "Once I've got our things put away, I'll look through your supplies and get dinner started, if it's all right with you." *And even if it isn't*, she added silently.

"Talking too fast to be interrupted doesn't mean this is settled," he told her flatly.

The grim slash of his mouth matched the iciness in his tone. But Joy wasn't going to give up easily. "There's nothing to settle. We agreed to be here for the month and that's what we're going to do."

He shook his head. "I don't think this is going to work out."

"You can't know that, and I think you're wrong," she said, stiffening her spine as she faced him down. She needed this job. This place. For one month. And she wouldn't let him take it from her. Keeping her voice low so Holly wouldn't overhear, she said, "I'm holding you to the deal we made."

"*We* didn't make a deal."

"You did with Kaye."

"Kaye's not here."

"Which is why we are." *One point to me.* Joy grinned and met his gaze, deliberately glaring right into those shuttered brown eyes of his.

"Are there fairies in the woods?" Holly wondered aloud.

"I don't know, honey," Joy said.

"No," Sam told her.

Holly's face fell and Joy gave him a stony glare. He could be as nasty and unfriendly with her as he wanted to be. But he wouldn't be mean to her daughter. "He means he's never seen any fairies, sweetie."

"Oh." The little girl's smile lit up her face. "Me either. But maybe I can sometime, Mommy says."

With a single look, Joy silently dared the man to pop her daughter's balloon again. But he didn't.

"Then you'll have to look harder, won't you?" he said instead, then lifted his gaze to Joy's. With what looked like regret glittering in his eyes, he added, "You'll have a whole month to look for them."

Two

A few hours in the workshop didn't improve Sam's mood. Not a big surprise. How the hell could he clear his mind when it was full of images of Joy Curran and her daughter?

As her name floated through his mind *again*, Sam deliberately pushed it away, though he knew damn well she'd be sliding back in. Slowly, methodically, he ran the hand sander across the top of the table he was currently building. The satin feel of the wood beneath his hands fed the artist inside him as nothing else could.

It had been six years since he'd picked up a paint-brush, faced a blank canvas and brought the images in his mind to life. And even now, that loss tore at him and his fingers wanted to curl around a slim wand of walnut and surround himself with the familiar scents of turpentine and linseed oil. He wouldn't—but the desire was always there, humming through his blood, through his dreams.

But though he couldn't paint, he also couldn't simply sit in the big house staring out windows, either.

So he'd turned his need for creativity, for creation, toward the woodworking that had always been a hobby. In this workshop, he built tables, chairs, small whimsical backyard lawn ornaments, and lost himself in the doing. He didn't have to think. Didn't have to remember.

Yet, today, his mind continuously drifted from the project at hand to the main house, where the woman was. It had been a long time since he'd had an attractive woman around for longer than an evening. And the prospect of Joy being in his house for the next month didn't make Sam happy. But damned if he could think of a way out of it. Sure, he could toss her and the girl out, but then what?

Memories of last December when he'd been on his own and damn near starved to death rushed into his brain. He didn't want to repeat that, but could he stand having a kid around all the time?

That thought brought him up short. He dropped the block sander onto the table, turned and looked out the nearest window to the house. The lights in the kitchen were on and he caught a quick glimpse of Joy moving through the room. Joy. Even her name went against everything he'd become. She was too much, he thought. Too beautiful. Too cheerful. Too tempting.

Well, hell. Recognizing the temptation she represented was only half the issue. Resisting her and what she made him want was the other half. She'd be right there, in his house, for a month. And he was still feeling that buzz of desire that had pumped into him from the moment he first saw her getting out of her car. He didn't want that buzz but couldn't ignore it, either.

When his cell phone rang, he dug it out of his pocket and looked at the screen. His mother. "Perfect. This day just keeps getting better."

Sam thought about not answering it, but he knew that Catherine Henry wouldn't be put off for long. She'd simply keep calling until he answered. Might as well get it over with.

"Hi, Mom."

"There's my favorite son," she said.

"Your *only* son," he pointed out.

"Hence the favorite," his mother countered. "You didn't want to answer, did you?"

He smiled to himself. The woman was practically psychic. Leaning one hip against the workbench, he said, "I did, though, didn't I?"

"Only because you knew I'd harangue you."

He rolled his eyes and started sanding again, slowly, carefully moving along the grain. "What's up, Mom?"

"Kaye texted me to say she was off on her trip," his mother said. "And I wanted to see if Joy and Holly arrived all right."

He stopped, dropped the sander and stared out at the house where the woman and her daughter were busily taking over. "You knew?"

"Well, of course I knew," Catherine said with a laugh. "Kaye keeps me up to date on what's happening there since my favorite son tends to be a hermit and uncommunicative."

He took a deep breath and told himself that temper would be wasted on his mother. It would roll right on by, so there was no point in it. "You should have warned me."

"About what? Joy? Kaye tells me she's wonderful."

"About her daughter," he ground out, reminding himself to keep it calm and cool. He felt a sting of betrayal because his mother should have understood how having a child around would affect him.

There was a long pause before his mother said, "Honey, you can't avoid all children for the rest of your life."

He flinched at the direct hit. "I didn't say I was."

"Sweetie, you didn't have to. I know it's hard, but Holly isn't Eli."

He winced at the sound of the name he never allowed himself to so much as think. His hand tightened around the phone as if it were a lifeline. "I know that."

"Good." Her voice was brisk again, with that clipped tone that told him she was arranging everything in her mind. "Now that that's settled, you be nice. Kaye and I think you and Joy will get along very well."

He went completely still. "Is that right?"

"Joy's very independent and according to Kaye, she's friendly, outgoing—just what you need, sweetie. Someone to wake you up again."

Sam smelled a setup. Every instinct he possessed jumped up and shouted a warning even though it was too late to avoid what was already happening. Scraping one hand down his face, he shook his head and told himself he should have been expecting this. For years now, his mother had been nagging at him to move on. To accept the pain and to pick up the threads of his life.

She wanted him happy, and he understood that. What

she didn't understand was that he'd already lost his shot at happiness. "I'm not interested, Mom."

"Sure you are, you just don't know it," his mother said in her crisp, no-nonsense tone. "And it's not like I've booked a church or expect you to sweep Joy off her feet, for heaven's sake. But would it kill you to be nice? Honestly, sweetie, you've become a hermit, and that's just not healthy."

Sam sighed heavily as his anger drained away. He didn't like knowing that his family was worried about him. The last few years had been hard. On everyone. And he knew they'd all feel better about him if he could just pick up the threads of his life and get back to some sort of "normal." But a magical wave of his hands wasn't going to accomplish that.

The best he could do was try to convince his mother to leave him be. To let him deal with his own past in his own way. The chances of that, though, were slim. That was the burden of family. When you tried to keep them at bay for their own sake, they simply refused to go. Evidence: she and Kaye trying to play matchmaker.

But just because they thought they were setting him up with Joy didn't mean he had to go along. Which he wouldn't. Sure, he remembered that instant attraction he'd felt for Joy. That slam of heat, lust, that let him know he was alive even when he hated to acknowledge it. But it didn't change anything. He didn't want another woman in his life. Not even one with hair like sunlight and eyes the color of a summer sky.

And he for damn sure didn't want another child in his life.

What he had to do, then, was to make it through December, then let his world settle back into place. When nothing happened between him and Joy, his mother and Kaye would have to give up on the whole Cupid thing. A relief for all of them.

"Sam?" His mother's voice prompted a reaction from him. "Have you slipped into a coma? Do I need to call someone?"

He laughed in spite of everything then told himself to focus. When dealing with Catherine Henry, a smart man paid attention. "No. I'm here."

"Well, good. I wondered." Another long pause before she said, "Just do me a favor, honey, and don't scare Joy off. If she's willing to put up with you for a month, she must really need the job."

Insulting, but true. Wryly, he said, "Thanks, Mom."

"You know what I mean." Laughing a little, she added, "That didn't come out right, but still. Hermits are *not* attractive, Sam. They grow their beards and stop taking showers and mutter under their breath all the time."

"Unbelievable," he muttered, then caught himself and sighed.

"It's already started," his mother said. "But seriously. People in those mountains are going to start telling their kids scary stories about the weird man who never leaves his house."

"I'm not weird," he argued. And he didn't have a beard. Just whiskers he hadn't felt like shaving in a few days. As far as muttering went, that usually happened only when his mother called.

"Not yet, but if things don't change, it's coming."

Scowling now, he turned away from the view of the house and stared unseeing at the wall opposite him. "Mom, you mean well. I know that."

"I do, sweetie, and you've got to—"

He cut her off, because really, it was the only way. "I'm already doing what I have to do, Mom. I've had enough change in my life already, thanks."

Then she was quiet for a few seconds as if she was remembering the pain of that major change. "I know. Sweetie, I know. I just don't want you to lose the rest of your life, okay?"

Sam wondered if it was all mothers or just his who refused to see the truth when it was right in front of them. He had nothing left to lose. How the hell could he have a life when he'd already lost everything that mattered? Was he supposed to forget? To pretend none of it had happened? How could he when every empty day reminded him of what was missing?

But saying any of that to his mother was a waste of time. She wouldn't get it. Couldn't possibly understand what it cost him every morning just to open his eyes and move through the day. They tried, he told himself. His whole family tried to be there for him, but the bottom line was, he was alone in this. Always would be.

And that thought told Sam he'd reached the end of his patience. "Okay, look, Mom, good talking to you, but I've got a project to finish."

"All right then. Just, think about what I said, okay?"

Hard not to when she said it every time she talked to him.

"Sure." A moment later he hung up and stuffed the phone back into his pocket. He shouldn't have answered it. Should have turned the damn thing off and forced her to leave a message. Then he wouldn't feel twisted up inside over things that could never be put right. It was better his way. Better to bury those memories, that pain, so deeply that they couldn't nibble away at him every waking moment.

A glance at the clock on the wall told him it was six and time for the dinner Joy had promised. Well, he was in no mood for company. He came and went when he liked and just because his temporary housekeeper made dinner didn't mean he had to show up. He scowled, then deliberately, he picked up the sander again and turned his focus to the wood. Sanding over the last coat of stain and varnish was meticulous work. He could laser in on the task at hand and hope it would be enough to ease the tension rippling through him.

It was late by the time he finally forced himself to stop working for the day. Darkness was absolute as he closed up the shop and headed for the house. He paused in the cold to glance up at the cloud-covered sky and wondered when the snow would start. Then he shifted his gaze to the house where a single light burned softly against the dark. He'd avoided the house until he was sure the woman and her daughter would be locked away in Kaye's rooms. For a second, he felt a sting of guilt for blowing off whatever dinner it was she'd made. Then again, he hadn't asked her to cook, had he? Hell, he hadn't even wanted her to stay. Yet somehow, she was.

Tomorrow, he told himself, he'd deal with her and lay out a few rules. If she was going to stay then she had to understand that it was the *house* she was supposed to take care of. Not him. Except for cooking—which he would eat whenever he damn well pleased—he didn't want to see her. For now, he wanted a shower and a sandwich. He was prepared for a can of soup and some grilled cheese.

Later, Sam told himself he should have known better.

He opened the kitchen door and stopped in the doorway. Joy was sitting at the table with a glass of wine in front of her and turned her head to look at him when he walked in. "You're late."

That niggle of guilt popped up again and was just as quickly squashed. He closed and locked the door behind him. "I don't punch a clock."

"I don't expect you to. But when we say dinner's at six, it'd be nice if you showed up." She shrugged. "Maybe it's just me, but most people would call that 'polite.'"

The light over the stove was the only illumination and in the dimness, he saw her eyes, locked on him, the soft blond curls falling about her face. Most women he knew would have been furious with him for missing a dinner after he'd agreed to be there. But she wasn't angry, and that made him feel the twinge of guilt even deeper than he might have otherwise. But at the bottom of it, he didn't answer to her and it was just as well she learned that early on.

"Yeah," he said, "I got involved with a project and forgot the time." A polite lie that would go down better than admitting *I was avoiding you.* "Don't worry about it. I'll fix myself something."

"No you won't." She got up and walked to the oven. "I've kept it on warm. Why don't you wash up and have dinner?"

He wanted to say no. But damned if whatever she'd made didn't smell amazing. His stomach overruled his head and Sam surrendered. He washed his hands at the sink then sat down opposite her spot at the table.

"Did you want a glass of your wine?" she asked. "It's really good."

One eyebrow lifted. Wryly, he said, "Glad you approve."

"Oh, I like wine," she said, disregarding his tone. "Nothing better than ending your day with a glass and just relaxing before bed."

Bed. Not a word he should be thinking about when she was so close and looking so...edible. "Yeah. I'll get a beer."

"I'll get it," she said, as she set a plate of pasta in a thick red meat sauce in front of him.

The scent of it wafted to him and Sam nearly groaned. "What is that?"

"Baked mostaccioli with mozzarella and parmesan in my grandmother's meat sauce." She opened the fridge, grabbed a beer then walked back to the table. Handing it to him, she sat down, picked up her wineglass and had a sip.

"It smells great," he said grudgingly.

"Tastes even better," she assured him. Drawing one knee up, she propped her foot on her chair and looked at him. "Just so you know, I won't be waiting on you every night. I mean getting you a beer and stuff."

He snorted. "I'll make a note."

Then Sam took a bite and sighed. Whatever else Joy Curran was, the woman could *cook*. Whatever they had to talk about could wait, he thought, while he concentrated on the unexpected prize of a really great meal. So he said nothing else for a few bites, but finally sat back, took a drink of his beer and looked at her.

"Good?"

"Oh, yeah," he said. "Great."

She smiled and her face just—lit up. Sam's breath caught in his chest as he looked at her. That flash of something hot, something staggering, hit him again and he desperately tried to fight it off. Even while that strong buzz swept through him, remnants of the phone call with his mother rose up in his mind and he wondered if Joy had been in on whatever his mother and Kaye had cooking between them.

Made sense, didn't it? Young, pretty woman. Single mother. Why not try to find a rich husband?

Speculatively, he looked at her and saw sharp blue eyes without the slightest hint of guile. So maybe she wasn't in on it. He'd reserve judgment. For now. But whether she was or not, he had to set down some rules. If they were going to be living together for the next month, better that they both knew where they stood.

And, as he took another bite of her spectacular pasta, he admitted that he was going to let her stay—if only for the sake of his stomach.

"Okay," he said in between bites, "you can stay for the month."

She grinned at him and took another sip of her wine to celebrate. "That's great, thanks. Although, I wasn't really going to leave."

Amused, he picked up his beer. "Is that right?"

"It is." She nodded sharply. "You should know that I'm pretty stubborn when I want something, and I really wanted to stay here for the month."

He leaned back in his chair. The pale wash of the stove light reached across the room to spill across her, making that blond hair shine and her eyes gleam with amusement and determination. The house was quiet, and the darkness crouched just outside the window made the light and warmth inside seem almost intimate. Not a word he wanted to think about at the moment.

"Can you imagine trying to keep a five-year-old entertained in a tiny hotel room for a month?" She shivered and shook her head. "Besides being a living nightmare for me, it wouldn't be fair to Holly. Kids need room to run. Play."

He remembered. A succession of images flashed across his mind before he could stop them. As if the memories had been crouched in a corner, just waiting for the chance to escape, he saw pictures of another child. Running. Laughing. Brown eyes shining as he looked over his shoulder and—

Sam's grip on the beer bottle tightened until a part of him wondered why it didn't simply shatter in his hand. The images in his mind blurred, as if fingers of fog were reaching for them, dragging them back into the past where they belonged. Taking a slow, deep breath, he lifted the beer for a sip and swallowed the pain with it.

"Besides," she continued while he was still being dogged by memories, "this kitchen is amazing." Shaking her head, she looked around the massive room, and he knew what she was seeing. Pale oak cabinets, dark blue granite counters with flecks of what looked like abalone shells in them. Stainless steel appliances and sink and an island big enough to float to Ireland on. And the only things Sam ever really used on his own were the double-wide fridge and the microwave.

"Cooking in here was a treat. There's so much space." Joy took another sip of wine. "Our house is so tiny, the kitchen just a smudge on the floor plan. Holly and I can't be in there together without knocking each other down. Plus there's the ancient plumbing and the cabinet doors that don't close all the way...but it's just a rental. One of these days, we'll get our own house.

Nothing like this one of course, but a little bigger with a terrific kitchen and a table like this one where Holly can sit and do her homework while I make dinner—"

Briskly, he got back to business. It was either that or let her go far enough to sketch out her dream kitchen. "Okay, I get it. You need to be here, and for food like this, I'm willing to go along."

She laughed shortly.

He paid zero attention to the musical sound of that laugh or how it made her eyes sparkle in the low light. "So here's the deal. You can stay the month like we agreed."

"But?" she asked. "I hear a *but* in there."

"But." He nodded at her. "We steer clear of each other and you keep your daughter out of my way."

Her eyebrows arched. "Not a fan of kids, are you?"

"Not for a long time."

"Holly won't bother you," she said, lifting her wine-glass for another sip.

"All right. Good. Then we'll get along fine." He finished off the pasta, savoring that last bite before taking one more pull on his beer. "You cook and clean. I spend most of my days out in the workshop, so we probably won't see much of each other anyway."

She studied him for several long seconds before a small smile curved her mouth and a tiny dimple appeared in her right cheek. "You're sort of mysterious, aren't you?"

Once again, she'd caught him off guard. And why did she look so pleased when he'd basically told her he didn't want her kid around and didn't particularly want to spend any time with *her*, either?

"No mystery. I just like my privacy is all."

"Privacy's one thing," she mused, tipping her head to one side to study him. "Hiding out's another."

"Who says I'm hiding?"

"Kaye."

He rolled his eyes. Kaye talked to his mother. To Joy. Who the hell *wasn't* she talking to? "Kaye doesn't know everything."

"She comes close, though," Joy said. "She worries about you. For the record, she says you're lonely, but private. Nice, but shut down."

He shifted in the chair, suddenly uncomfortable with the way she was watching him. As if she could look inside him and dig out all of his secrets.

"She wouldn't tell me why you've locked yourself away up here on the mountain—"

"That's something," he muttered, then remembered his mother's warning about hermits and muttering. Scowling, he took another drink of his beer.

"People do wonder, though," she mused. "Why you keep to yourself so much. Why you almost never go into town. I mean, it's beautiful here, but don't you miss talking to people?"

"Not a bit," he told her, hoping that statement would get her to back off.

"I really would."

"Big surprise," he muttered and then inwardly winced. Hell, he'd talked more in the last ten minutes than he had in the last year. Still, for some reason, he felt the need to defend himself and the way he lived. "I have Kaye to talk to if I desperately need conversation—which I don't. And I do get into town now and then." Practically never, though, he thought.

Hell, why should he go into Franklin and put up

with being stared at and whispered over when he could order whatever he wanted online and have it shipped overnight? If nothing else, the twenty-first century was perfect for a man who wanted to be left the hell alone.

"Yeah, that doesn't happen often," she was saying. "There was actually a pool in town last summer—people were taking bets on if you'd come in at all before fall."

Stunned, he stared at her. "They were betting on me?"

"You're surprised?" Joy laughed and the sound of it filled the kitchen. "It's a tiny mountain town with not a lot going on, except for the flood of tourists. Of course they're going to place bets on the local hermit."

"I'm starting to resent that word." Sam hadn't really considered that he might be the subject of so much speculation, and he didn't much care for it. What was he supposed to do now? Go into town more often? Or less?

"Oh," she said, waving one hand at him, "don't look so grumpy about it. If it makes you feel better, when you came into Franklin and picked up those new tools at the hardware store, at the end of August, Jim Bowers won nearly two hundred dollars."

"Good for him," Sam muttered, not sure how he felt about all of this. He'd moved to this small mountain town for the solitude. For the fact that no one would give a damn about him. And after five years here, he found out the town was paying close enough attention to him to actually lay money on his comings and goings. Shaking his head, he asked only, "Who's Jim Bowers?"

"He and his wife own the bakery."

"There's a bakery in Franklin?"

She sighed, shaking her head slowly. "It's so sad that you didn't know that."

A short laugh shot from his throat, surprising them both.

"You should do that more often," she said quietly.

"What?"

"Smile. Laugh. Lose the etched-in-stone-grumble expression."

"Do you have an opinion on everything?" he asked.

"Don't you?" she countered.

Yeah, he did. And his considered opinion on this particular situation was that he might have made a mistake in letting Joy and her daughter stay here for the next month.

But damned if he could regret it at the moment.

Three

By the following morning, Joy had decided the man needed to be pushed into getting outside himself. Sitting in the kitchen with him the night before had been interesting and more revealing than he would have liked, she was sure. Though he had a gruff, cold exterior, Joy had seen enough in his eyes to convince her that the real man was hidden somewhere beneath that hard shell he carried around with him.

She had known he'd been trying to avoid seeing her again by staying late in his workshop. Which was why she'd been waiting for him in the kitchen. Joy had always believed that it was better to face a problem head-on rather than dance around it and hope it would get better. So she'd been prepared to argue and bargain with him to make sure she and Holly could stay for the month.

And she'd known the moment he tasted her baked

mostaccioli that arguments would not be necessary. He might not want her there, but her cooking had won him over. Clearly, he didn't like it, but he'd put up with her for a month if it meant he wouldn't starve. Joy could live with that.

What she might not be able to live with was her body's response to being near him. She hadn't expected that. Hadn't felt anything remotely like awareness since splitting with Holly's father before the little girl was born. And she wasn't looking for it now. She had a good life, a growing business and a daughter who made her heart sing. Who could ask for more than that?

But the man...intrigued her. She could admit, at least to herself, that sitting with him in the shadow-filled night had made her feel things she'd be better off forgetting. It wasn't her fault, of course. Just look at the man. Tall, dark and crabby. What woman wouldn't have a few fantasies about a man who looked like he did? Okay, normally she wouldn't enjoy the surly attitude—God knew she'd had enough "bad boys" in her life. But the shadows of old pain in his eyes told Joy that Sam hadn't always been so closed off.

So there was interest even when she knew there shouldn't be. His cold detachment was annoying, but the haunted look in his eyes drew her in. Made her want to comfort. Care. Dangerous feelings to have.

"Mommy, is it gonna snow today?"

Grateful for that sweet voice pulling her out of her circling thoughts, Joy walked to the kitchen table, bent down and kissed the top of her daughter's head.

"I don't think so, baby. Eat your pancakes now. And then we'll take a walk down to the lake."

"And skate?" Holly's eyes went bright with excitement at the idea. She forked up a bite of pancake and chewed quickly, eager now to get outside.

"We'll see if the lake's frozen enough, all right?" She'd brought their ice skates along since she'd known about the lake. And though she was no future competitor, Holly loved skating almost as much as she loved fairy princesses.

Humming, Holly nodded to herself and kept eating, pausing now and then for a sip of her milk. Her heels thumped against the chair rungs and sounded like a steady heartbeat in the quiet morning. Her little girl couldn't have been contained in a hotel room for a month. She had enough energy for three healthy kids and needed the room to run and play.

This house, this place, with its wide yard and homey warmth, was just what she needed. Simple as that. As for what Sam Henry made Joy feel? That would remain her own little secret.

"Hi, Sam!" Holly called out. "Mommy made pancakes. We're cellbrating."

"Celebrating," Joy corrected automatically, before she turned to look at the man standing in the open doorway. And darn it, she felt that buzz of awareness again the minute her gaze hit his. So tall, she thought with approval. He wore faded jeans and the scarred boots again, but today he wore a long-sleeved green thermal shirt with a gray flannel shirt over it. His too-long hair framed his face, and his eyes still carried the secrets that she'd seen in them the night before. They stared at each other as the seconds ticked past, and Joy wondered what he was thinking.

Probably trying to figure out the best way to get her and Holly to leave, she thought.

Well, that wasn't going to happen. She turned to the coffeemaker and poured him a cup. "Black?"

He accepted it. "How'd you guess?"

She smiled. "You look like the no-frills kind of man to me. Just can't imagine you ordering a half-caf, vanilla bean cappuccino."

He snorted, but took a long drink and sighed at the rush of caffeine in his system. Joy could appreciate that, since she usually got up a half hour before Holly just so she could have the time to enjoy that first, blissful cup of coffee.

"What're you celebrating?" he asked.

Joy flushed a little. "Staying here in the 'castle.'"

Holly's heels continued to thump as she hummed her way through breakfast. "We're having pancakes and then we're going skating on the lake and—"

"I said we'll see," Joy reminded her.

"Stay away from the lake."

Joy looked at him. His voice was low, brusque, and his tone brooked no argument. All trace of amusement was gone from eyes that looked as deep and dark as the night itself. "What?"

"The lake," he said, making an obvious effort to soften the hard note in his voice. "It's not solid enough. Too dangerous for either of you to be on it."

"Are you sure?" Joy asked, glancing out the kitchen window at the frigid world beyond the glass. Sure, it hadn't snowed much so far, but it had been below freezing every night for the last couple of weeks, so the lake should be frozen over completely by now.

"No point in taking the chance, is there? If it stays this cold, maybe you could try it in a week or two…"

Well, she thought, at least he'd accepted that she and

Holly would still be there in two weeks. That was a step in the right direction, anyway. His gaze fixed on hers, deliberately avoiding looking at Holly, though the little girl was practically vibrating with barely concealed excitement. In his eyes, Joy saw real worry and a shadow of something darker, something older.

"Okay," she said, going with her instinct to ease whatever it was that was driving him. Reaching out, she laid one hand on his forearm and felt the tension gripping him before he slowly, deliberately pulled away. "Okay. No skating today."

"Moooommmmmyyyyy…"

How her daughter managed to put ten or more syllables into a single word was beyond her.

"We'll skate another day, okay, sweetie? How about today we take a walk in the forest and look for pinecones?" She kept her gaze locked on Sam's, so she actually saw relief flash across his eyes. What was it in his past that had him still tied into knots?

"Can we paint 'em for Christmas?"

"Sure we can, baby. We'll go after we clean the kitchen, so eat up." Then to Sam, she said, "How about some pancakes?"

"No, thanks." He turned to go.

"One cup of coffee and that's it?"

He looked back at her. "You're here to take care of the house. Not me."

"Not true. I'm also here to cook. For you." She smiled a little. "You should try the pancakes. They're really good, even if I do say so myself."

"Mommy makes the *best* pancakes," Holly tossed in.

"I'm sure she does," he said, still not looking at the girl.

Joy frowned and wondered why he disliked kids so much, but she didn't ask.

"Look, while you're here, don't worry about breakfast for me. I don't usually bother and if I change my mind I can take care of it myself."

"You're a very stubborn man, aren't you?"

He took another sip of coffee. "I've got a project to finish and I'm going out to get started on it."

"Well, you can at least take a muffin." Joy walked to the counter and picked a muffin—one of the batch she'd made just an hour ago—out of a ceramic blue bowl.

He sighed. "If I do, will you let me go?"

"If I do, will you come back?"

"I live here."

Joy smiled again and handed it over to him. "Then you are released. Go. Fly free."

His mouth twitched and he shook his head. "People think I'm weird."

"I don't." She said it quickly and wasn't sure why she had until she saw a quick gleam of pleasure in his eyes.

"Be sure to tell Kaye," he said, and left, still shaking his head.

"'Bye, Sam!" Holly's voice followed him and Joy was pretty sure he quickened his steps as if trying to outrun it.

Three hours later, Sam was still wishing he'd eaten those damn pancakes. He remembered the scent of them in the air, and his stomach rumbled in complaint. Pouring another cup of coffee from his workshop pot, he stared down at the small pile of blueberry muffin crumbs and wished he had another one. Damn it.

Wasn't it enough that Joy's face kept surfacing in

his mind? Did she have to be such a good cook, too? And who asked her to make him breakfast? Kaye never did. Usually he made do with coffee and a power bar of some kind, and that was fine. Always had been anyway. But now he still had the lingering taste of that muffin in his mouth, and his stomach was still whining over missing out on pancakes.

But to eat them, he'd have had to take a seat at the table beside a chattering little girl. And all that sunshine and sweet innocence was just too much for Sam to take. He took a gulp of hot coffee and let the blistering liquid burn its way to the pit of his sadly empty stomach. And as hungry as he was, at least he'd completed his project. He leaned back against the workbench, crossed his feet at the ankles, stared at the finished table and gave himself a silent pat on the back.

In the overhead shop light, the wood gleamed and shone like a mirror in the sun. Every slender grain of the wood was displayed beautifully under the fresh coat of varnish, and the finish was smooth as glass. The thick pedestal was gnarled and twisted, yet it, too, had been methodically sanded until all the rough edges were gone as if they'd never been.

Taking a deadfall tree limb and turning it into the graceful pedestal of a table had taken some time, but it had been worth it. The piece was truly one of a kind, and he knew the people he'd made it for would approve. It was satisfying, seeing something in your head and creating it in the physical world. He used to do that with paint and canvas, bringing imaginary places to life, making them real.

Sam frowned at the memories, because remembering the passion he'd had for painting, the rush of starting something new and pushing himself to make it all perfect, was something he couldn't know now. Maybe he never would again. And that thought opened up a black pit at the bottom of his soul. But there was nothing he could do about it. Nothing that could ease that need, that bone-deep craving.

At least he had this, he told himself. Woodworking had given him, if not completion, then satisfaction. It filled his days and helped to ease the pain of missing the passion that had once driven his life. But then, he thought, once upon a time, his entire world had been different. The shame was, he hadn't really appreciated what he'd had while he had it. At least, he told himself, not enough to keep it.

He was still leaning against the workbench, studying the table, when a soft voice with a slight lisp asked, "Is it a fairy table?"

He swiveled his head to the child in the doorway. Her blond hair was in pigtails, she wore blue jeans, tiny pink-and-white sneakers with princesses stamped all over them and a pink parka that made her look impossibly small.

He went completely still even while his heart raced, and his mind searched for a way out of there. Her appearance, on top of old memories that continued to dog him, hit him so hard he could barely take a breath. Sam looked into blue eyes the exact shade of her mother's and told himself that it was damned cowardly to be spooked by a kid. He had his reasons, but it was lowering to admit, even to himself, that his first instinct when faced with a child was to bolt.

Since she was still watching him, waiting for an answer, Sam took another sip of coffee in the hopes of steadying himself. "No. It's just a table."

"It looks like a tree." Moving warily, she edged a little farther into the workshop and let the door close behind her, shutting out the cold.

"It used to be," he said shortly.

"Did you make it?"

"Yes." She was looking up at him with those big blue eyes, and Sam was still trying to breathe. But his "issues" weren't her fault. He was being an ass, and even he could tell. He had no reason to be so short with the girl. How was she supposed to know that he didn't do kids anymore?

"Can I touch it?" she asked, giving him a winsome smile that made Sam wonder if females were *born* knowing how to do it.

"No," he said again and once more, he heard the sharp brusqueness in his tone and winced.

"Are you crabby?" She tilted her head to one side and looked up at him in all seriousness.

"What?"

Gloomy sunlight spilled through the windows that allowed views of the pines, the lake and the leaden sky that loomed threateningly over it all. The little girl, much like her mother, looked like a ray of sunlight in the gray, and he suddenly wished that she were anywhere but there. Her innocence, her easy smile and curiosity were too hard to take. Yet, her fearlessness at facing down an irritable man made her, to Sam's mind, braver than him.

"Mommy says when I'm crabby I need a nap." She nodded solemnly. "Maybe you need a nap, too."

Sam sighed. Also, like her mother, a bad mood wasn't

going to chase her off. Accepting the inevitable, that he wouldn't be able to get rid of her by giving her one-word, bit-off answers, he said, "I don't need a nap, I'm just busy."

She walked into the workshop, less tentative now. Clearly oblivious to the fact that he didn't want her there, she wandered the shop, looking over the benches with tools, the stacks of reclaimed wood and the three tree trunks he had lined up along a wall. He should tell her to go back to the house. Wasn't it part of their bargain that the girl wouldn't bother him?

Hell.

"You don't look busy."

"Well, I am."

"Doing what?"

Sam sighed. Irritating, but that was a good question. Now that he'd finished the table, he needed to start something else. It wasn't only his hands he needed to keep busy. It was his mind. If he wasn't focusing on *something*, his thoughts would invariably track over to memories. Of another child who'd also had unending questions and bright, curious eyes. Sam cut that thought off and turned his attention to the tiny girl still exploring his workshop. Why hadn't he told her to leave? Why hadn't he taken her back to the house and told Joy to keep her away from him? Hell, why was he just standing there like a glowering statue?

"What's this do?"

The slight lisp brought a reluctant smile even as he moved toward her. She'd stopped in front of a vise that probably looked both interesting and scary to a kid.

"It's a wood vise," he said. "It holds a piece of wood steady so I can work on it."

She chewed her bottom lip and thought about it for a minute. "Like if I put my doll between my knees so I can brush her hair."

"Yeah," he said grudgingly. Smart kid. "It's sort of like that. Shouldn't you be with your mom?"

"She's cleaning and she said I could play in the yard if I stayed in the yard so I am but I wish it would snow and we could make angels and snowballs and a big snowman and—"

Amazed, Sam could only stare in awe as the little girl talked without seeming to breathe. Thoughts and words tumbled out of her in a rush that tangled together and yet somehow made sense.

Desperate now to stop the flood of high-pitched sounds, he asked, "Shouldn't you be in school?"

She laughed and shook her head so hard her pigtails flew back and forth across her eyes. "I go to pre-K cuz I'm too little for Big-K cuz my birthday comes too late cuz it's the day after Christmas and I can probably get a puppy if I ask Santa and Mommy's gonna get me a fairy doll for my birthday cuz Christmas is for the puppy and he'll be all white like a snowball and he'll play with me and lick me like Lizzie's puppy does when I get to play there and—"

So…instead of halting the rush of words and noise, he'd simply given her more to talk about. Sam took another long gulp of his coffee and hoped the caffeine would give him enough clarity to follow the kid's twisty thought patterns.

She picked up a scrap piece of wood and turned it over in her tiny hands.

"What can we make out of this?" she asked, holding it up to him, an interested gleam in her eye and an eager smile on her face.

Well, hell. He had nothing else to work on. It wasn't as though he was being drawn to the kid or anything. All he was doing was killing time. Keeping busy. Frowning to himself, Sam took the piece of wood from her and said, "If you're staying, take your jacket off and put it over there."

Her smile widened, her eyes sparkled and she hurried to do just what he told her. Shaking his head, Sam asked himself what he was doing. He should be dragging her back to the house. Telling her mother to keep the kid away from him. Instead, he was getting deeper.

"I wanna make a fairy house!"

He winced a little at the high pitch of that tiny voice and told himself that this didn't matter. He could back off again later.

Joy looked through the window of Sam's workshop and watched her daughter work alongside the man who had insisted he wanted nothing to do with her. Her heart filled when Holly turned a wide, delighted smile on the man. Then a twinge of guilt pinged inside her. Her little girl was happy and well-adjusted, but she was lacking a male role model in her life. God knew her father hadn't been interested in the job.

She'd told herself at the time that Holly would be better off without him than with a man who clearly didn't want to be a father. Yet here was another man who had claimed to want nothing to do with kids—her daughter in particular—and instead of complaining about her presence, he was working with her. Showing the little girl how to build...*something*. And Holly was loving it.

The little girl knelt on a stool at the workbench, following Sam's orders, and though she couldn't see what they were working on from her vantage point, Joy didn't think it mattered. Her daughter's happiness was evident, and whether he knew it or not, after only one day around Holly, Sam was opening up. She wondered what kind of man that opening would release.

The wind whipped past her, bringing the scent of snow, and Joy shivered deeper into her parka before walking into the warmth of the shop. With the blast of cold air announcing her presence, both Sam and Holly turned to look at her. One of them grinned. One of them scowled.

Of course.

"Mommy! Come and see, come and see!"

There was no invitation in Sam's eyes, but Joy ignored that and went to them anyway.

"It's a fairy house!" Holly squealed it, and Joy couldn't help but laugh. Everything these days was fairy. Fairy princesses. Fairy houses.

"We're gonna put it outside and the fairies can come and live in it and I can watch from the windows."

"That's a great idea."

"Sam says if I get too close to the fairies I'll scare 'em away," Holly continued, with an earnest look on her face. "But I wouldn't. I would be really quiet and they wouldn't see me or anything…"

"Sam says?" she repeated to the man standing there pretending he was somewhere else.

"Yeah," he muttered, rubbing the back of his neck. "If she watches through the window, she won't be out in the forest or—I don't know."

He was embarrassed. She could see it. And for some

reason, knowing that touched her heart. The man who didn't want a child anywhere near him just spent two hours helping a little girl build a house for fairies. There was so much more to him than the face he showed to the world. And the more Joy discovered, the more she wanted to know.

Oh, boy.

"It's beautiful, baby." And it was. Small, but sturdy, it was made from mismatched pieces of wood and the roof was scalloped by layering what looked like Popsicle sticks.

"I glued it and everything, but Sam helped and he says I can put stuff in it for the fairies like cookies and stuff that they'll like and I can watch them..."

He shrugged. "She wanted to make something. I had some scrap wood. That's all."

"Thank you."

Impatience flashed across his face. "Not a big deal. And not going to be happening all the time, either," he added as a warning.

"Got it," Joy said, nodding. If he wanted to cling to that grumpy, don't-like-people attitude, she wouldn't fight him on it. Especially since she now knew it was all a front.

Joy took a moment to look around the big room. Plenty of windows would let in sunlight should the clouds ever drift away. A wide, concrete floor, scrupulously swept clean. Every kind of tool imaginable hung on the pegboards that covered most of two walls. There were stacks of lumber, most of it looking ragged and old—reclaimed wood—and there were deadfall tree trunks waiting for who knew what to be done to them.

Then she spotted the table and was amazed she

hadn't noticed it immediately. Walking toward it, she sighed with pleasure as she examined it carefully, from the shining surface to the twisted tree limb base. "This is gorgeous," she whispered and whipped her head around to look at him. "You made this?"

He scowled again. Seemed to be his go-to expression. "Yeah."

"It's amazing, really."

"It's also still wet, so be careful. The varnish has to cure for a couple of days yet."

"I'm not touching."

"I didn't either, Mommy, did I, Sam?"

"Almost but not quite," he said.

Joy's fingers itched to stroke that smooth, sleek tabletop, so she curled her hands into fists to resist the urge. "I've seen some of your things in the gallery in town, and I loved them, too, by the way. But this." She shook her head and felt a real tug of possessiveness. "This I love."

"Thanks."

She thought the shadows in his eyes lightened a bit, but a second later, they were back so she couldn't be sure. "What are you working on next?"

"Like mother like daughter," he muttered.

"Curious?" she asked. "You bet. What are you going to do with those tree trunks?" The smallest of them was three feet around and two feet high.

"Work on them when I get a minute to myself." That leave-me-alone tone was back, and Joy decided not to push her luck any further. She'd gotten more than a few words out of him today and maybe they'd reached his limit.

"He's not mad, Mommy, he's just crabby."

Joy laughed.

Holly patted Sam's arm. "You could sing to him like you sing to me when I'm crabby and need a nap."

The look on Sam's face was priceless. Like he was torn between laughter and shouting and couldn't decide which way to go.

"What's that old saying?" Joy asked. "Out of the mouths of babes…"

Sam rolled his eyes and frowned. "That's it. Everybody out."

Still laughing, Joy said, "Come on, Holly, let's have some lunch. I made soup. Seemed like a good, cold day for it."

"You *made* soup?" he asked.

"Uh-huh. Beef and barley." She helped Holly get her jacket on, then zipped it closed against the cold wind. "Oh, and I made some beer bread, too."

"You made bread." He said it with a tinge of disbelief, and Joy couldn't blame him. Kaye didn't really believe in baking from scratch. Said it seemed like a waste when someone went to all the trouble to bake for her and package the bread in those nice plastic bags.

"Just beer bread. It's quick. Anyway," she said with a grin, "if you want lunch after your nap, I'll leave it on the stove for you."

"Funny."

Still smiling to herself, Joy took Holly's hand and led her out of the shop. She felt him watching her as they left and told herself that the heat swamping her was caused by her parka. And even she didn't believe it.

Four

Late at night, the big house was quiet, but not scary at all.

That thought made Joy smile to herself. She had assumed that a place this huge, with so many windows opening out onto darkness, would feel sort of like a horror movie. *Intrepid heroine wandering the halls of spooky house, alone, with nothing but a flashlight—until the battery dies.*

She shook her head and laughed at her own imagination. Instead of scary, the house felt like a safe haven against the night outside. Maybe it was the warmth of the honey-toned logs or maybe it was something else entirely. But one thing she was sure of was that she already loved it. Big, but not imposing, it was a happy house. Or would be if its owner wasn't frowning constantly.

But he'd smiled with Holly, Joy reminded herself as she headed down the long hallway toward the great room. He might have wished to be anywhere else, but he had been patient and kind to her little girl, and for Joy, nothing could have touched her more.

Her steps were quiet, her thoughts less so. She hadn't seen much of Sam since leaving him in the workshop. He'd deliberately kept his distance and Joy hadn't pushed. He'd had dinner, alone, in the dining room, then he'd disappeared again, barricading himself in the great room. She hadn't bothered him, had given him his space, and even now wouldn't be sneaking around his house if she didn't need something to read.

Holly was long since tucked in and Joy simply couldn't concentrate on the television, so she wanted to lose herself in a book. Keep her brain too busy to think about Sam. Wondering what his secrets were. Wondering what it would be like to kiss him. Wondering what the heck she was doing.

She threw a glance at the staircase and the upper floor, where the bedrooms were—where *Sam* was— and told herself to not think about it. Joy had spent the day cleaning the upstairs, though she had to admit that the man was so tidy, there wasn't much to straighten up.

But vacuuming and dusting gave her the chance to see where he slept, how he lived. His bedroom was huge, offering a wide view of the lake and the army of pine trees that surrounded it. His bed was big enough for a family of four to sleep comfortably, and the room was decorated in soothing shades of slate blue and forest green. The attached bath had had her sighing in imagined pleasure.

A sea of pale green marble, from the floors to the counters, to the gigantic shower and the soaker whirlpool tub that sat in front of a bay window with a view of the treetops. He lived well, but so solitarily it broke her heart. There were no pieces of *him* in the room. No photos, no art on the wall, nothing to point to this being his *home*. As beautiful as it all was, it was still impersonal, as if even after living there for five years he hadn't left his own impression on the place.

He made her curious. Gorgeous recluse with a sexuality that made her want to drool whenever he was nearby. Of course, the logical explanation for her zip of reaction every time she saw the man was her self-imposed Man Fast. It had been so long since she'd been on a date, been kissed…heck, been *touched*, that her body was clearly having a breakdown. A shame that she seemed to be enjoying it so much.

Sighing a little, she turned, slipped into the great room, then came to a dead stop. Sam sat in one of the leather chairs in front of the stone fireplace, where flames danced across wood and tossed flickering shadows around the room.

Joy thought about leaving before he saw her. Yes, cowardly, but understandable, considering where her imaginings had been only a second or two ago. But even as she considered sneaking out, Sam turned his head and pinned her with a long, steady look.

"What do you need?"

Not exactly friendly, but not a snarl, either. Progress? She'd take it.

"A book." With little choice, Joy walked into the room and took a quick look around. This room was gorgeous during the day, but at night, with flickering shadows floating around…amazing. Really, was there anything prettier than firelight? When she shifted her gaze back to him, she realized the glow from the fire shining in his dark brown eyes was nearly hypnotic. Which was a silly thought to have, so she pushed it away fast. "Would you mind if I borrow a book? TV is just so boring and—"

He held up one hand to cut her off. "Help yourself."

"Ever gracious," she said with a quick grin. When he didn't return it, she said, "Okay, thanks."

She walked closer, surreptitiously sliding her gaze over him. His booted feet were crossed at the ankle, propped on the stone edge of the hearth. He was staring into the fire as if looking for something. The flickering light danced across his features, and she recognized the scowl that she was beginning to think was etched into his bones. "Everything okay?"

"Fine." He didn't look at her. Never took his gaze from the wavering flames.

"Okay. You've got a lot of books." She looked through a short stack of hardbacks on the table closest to him. A mix of mysteries, sci-fi and thrillers, mostly. Her favorites, too.

"Yeah. Pick one."

"I'm looking," she assured him, but didn't hurry as he clearly wanted her to. Funny, but the gruffer and shorter he became, the more intrigued she was.

Joy had seen him with Holly. She knew there were smiles inside him and a softness under the cold, hard facade. Yet he seemed determined to shut everyone out.

"Ew," she said as she quickly set one book aside. "Don't like horror. Too scary. I can't even watch scary movies. I get too involved."

"Yeah."

She smiled to herself at the one-word answer. He hadn't told her to get out, so she'd just keep talking and see what happened. "I tried, once. Went to the movies with a friend and got so scared and so tense I had to go sit in the lobby for a half hour."

She caught him give her a quick look. Interest. It was a start.

"I didn't go back into the theater until I convinced an usher to tell me who else died so I could relax."

He snorted.

Joy smiled, but didn't let him see it. "So I finally went back in to sit with my friend, and even though I knew how it would end, I still kept my hands over my eyes through the rest of the movie."

"Uh-huh."

"But," she said, moving over to the next stack of books, "that doesn't mean I'm just a romantic comedy kind of girl. I like adventure movies, too. Where lots of things blow up."

"Is that right?"

Just a murmur, but he wasn't ignoring her.

"And the Avengers movies? Love those. But maybe it's just Robert Downey Jr. I like." She paused. "What about you? Do you like those movies?"

"Haven't seen them."

"Seriously?" She picked up a mystery she'd never read but instead of leaving with the book, she sat down in the chair beside his. "I think you're the first person I've ever met who hasn't seen those movies."

He spared her one long look. "I don't get out much."

"And isn't that a shame?"

"If I thought so," he told her, "I'd go out more."

Joy laughed at the logic. "Okay, you're right. Still. Heard of DVDs? Netflix?"

"You're just going to keep talking, aren't you?"

"Probably." She settled into her chair as if getting comfy for a long visit.

He shook his head and shifted his gaze back to the fire as if that little discouragement would send her on her way.

"But back to movies," she said, leaning toward him over the arm of her chair. "This time of year I like all the Christmas ones. The gushier the better."

"Gushy."

It wasn't a question, but she answered anyway. "You know, the happy cry ones. Heck, I even tear up when the Grinch's heart grows at the end of that little cartoon." She sighed. "But to be fair, I've been known to get teary at a heart-tugging commercial at Christmastime."

"Yeah, I don't do Christmas."

"I noticed," she said, tipping her head to one side to study him. If anything, his features had tightened, his eyes had grown darker. Just the mention of the holiday had been enough to close him up tight. And still, she couldn't resist trying to reach him.

"When we're at home," she said, "Holly and I put up the Christmas decorations the day after Thanksgiving. You have to have a little restraint, don't you think? I mean this year, I actually saw Christmas wreaths for sale in *September*. That's going a little far for me and I love Christmas."

He swiveled a look at her. "If you don't mind, I don't really feel like talking."

"Oh, you don't have to. I like talking."

"No kidding."

She smiled and thought she saw a flicker of a response in his eyes, but if she had, it wasn't much of one because it faded away fast. "You can't get to know people unless you talk to them."

He scraped one hand across his face. "Yeah, maybe I don't want to get to know people."

"I think you do, you just don't want to want it."

"What?"

"I saw you today with Holly."

He shifted in his chair and frowned into the fire. "A one-time thing."

"So you said," Joy agreed, getting more comfortable in the chair, letting him know she wasn't going anywhere. "But I have to tell you how excited Holly was. She couldn't stop talking about the fairy house she built with you." A smile curved Joy's mouth. "She fell asleep in the middle of telling me about the fairy family that will move into it."

Surprisingly, the frown on his face deepened, as if hearing that he'd given a child happiness made him angry.

"It was a small thing, but it meant a lot to her. And to me. I wanted you to know that."

"Fine. You told me."

Outside, the wind kicked up, sliding beneath the eaves of the house with a sighing moan that sounded otherworldly. She glanced toward the front window at the night beyond, then turned back to the man with darkness in his eyes. She wondered what he was thinking, what he was seeing as he stared into the flames. Leaning toward him, she locked her hands around her up-drawn knees and said, "That wide front window is a perfect place for a Christmas tree, you know. The glass would reflect all the lights…"

His gaze shot to hers. "I already told you, I don't do Christmas."

"Sure, I get it," she said, though she really didn't. "But if you don't want to, Holly and I will take care of decorating and—"

He stood up, grabbed a fireplace poker and determinedly stabbed at the logs, causing sparks to fly and sizzle on their wild flight up the chimney. When he was finished, he turned a cold look on her and said, "No tree. No decorations. No Christmas."

"Wow. Speak of the Grinch."

He blew out a breath and glared at her, but it just didn't work. It was too late for him to try to convince her that he was an ogre or something. Joy had seen him with Holly. His patience. His kindness. Even though he hadn't wanted to be around the girl, he'd given her the gift of his time. Joy'd had a glimpse of the man behind the mask now and wouldn't be fooled again. Crabby? Yes. Mean? No.

"You're not here to celebrate the holidays," he reminded her in a voice just short of a growl. "You're here to take care of the house."

"I know. But, if you change your mind, I'm an excellent multitasker." She got to her feet and held on to the book she'd chosen from the stack. Staring up into his eyes, she said, "I'll do my job, but just so you know? You don't scare me, Sam, so you might as well quit trying so hard."

Every night, she came to the great room. Every night, Sam told himself not to be there. And every night, he was sitting by the fire, waiting for her.

Not like he was talking to her. But apparently *noth-*

ing stopped *her* from talking. Not even his seeming disinterest in her presence. He'd heard about her business, about the house fire that had brought her to his place and about every moment of Holly's life up until this point. Her voice in the dark was both frustrating and seductive. Firelight created a cocoon of shadows and light, making it seem as if the two of them were alone in the world. Sam's days stretched out interminably, but the nights with Joy flew past, ending long before he wanted them to.

And that was an irritation, as well. Sam had been here for five years and in that time he hadn't wanted company. Hadn't wanted anyone around. Hell, he put up with Kaye because the woman kept his house running and meals on the table—but she also kept her distance. Usually. Now, here he was, sitting in the dark, waiting, *hoping* Joy would show up in the great room and shatter the solitude he'd fought so hard for.

But the days were different. During the day, Joy stayed out of his way and made sure her daughter did the same. They were like ghosts in the house. Once in a while, he would catch a little girl's laughter, quickly silenced. Everything was clean, sheets on his bed changed, meals appeared in the dining room, but Joy herself was not to be seen. How she managed it, he wasn't sure.

Why it bothered him was even more of a mystery.

Hell, he hadn't wanted them to stay in the first place. Yet now that he wasn't being bothered, wasn't seeing either of them, he found himself always on guard. Expecting one or both of them to jump out from behind a door every time he walked through a room. Which was stupid, but kept him on edge. Something he didn't like.

Hell, he hadn't even managed to get started on his next project yet because thoughts of Joy and Holly kept him from concentrating on anything else. Today, he had the place to himself because Joy and Holly had gone into Franklin. He knew that because there'd been a sticky note on the table beside his blueberry muffin and travel mug of coffee that Joy routinely left out in the dining room every morning.

Strange. The first morning they were here, it was *him* avoiding having breakfast with them. Now, it seemed that Joy was perfectly happy shuffling him off without even seeing him. Why that bothered him, Sam didn't even ask himself. There was no damn answer anyway.

So now, instead of working, he found himself glancing out the window repeatedly, watching for Joy's beat-up car to pull into the drive. All right, fine, it wasn't a broken-down heap, but her car was too old and, he thought, too unreliable for driving in the kind of snow they could get this high up the mountain. Frowning, he noted the fitful flurries of snowflakes drifting from the sky. Hardly a storm, more like the skies were teasing them with just enough snow to make things cold and slick.

So naturally, Sam's mind went to the road into town and the possible ice patches that dotted it. If Joy hit one of them, lost control of the car...his hands fisted. He should have driven them. But he hadn't really known they were going anywhere until it was too late. And that was because he wasn't spending any time with her except for those late-night sessions in the library.

Maybe if he'd opened his mouth the night before, she might have told him about this trip into town and he could have offered to drive them. Or at the very least, she could have driven his truck. Then he wouldn't be standing here wondering if her damn car had spun out.

Why the hell was he watching? Why did he care if she was safe or not? Why did he even bother to ask himself why? He knew damn well that his own past was feeding the sense of disquiet that clung to him. So despite resenting his own need to do it, he stayed where he was, watching. Waiting.

Which was why he was in place to see Ken Taylor when he arrived. Taylor and his wife, Emma, ran the gallery/gift shop in Franklin that mostly catered to tourists who came up the mountain for snow skiing in winter and boating on the lake in summer. Their shop, Crafty, sold local artisans' work—everything from paintings to jewelry to candles to the hand-made furniture and decor that Sam made.

Grateful for the distraction, Sam shrugged into his black leather jacket and headed out of the workshop into the cold bite of the wind and swirl of snowflakes. Tugging the collar up around his neck, Sam squinted into the wind and walked over to meet the man as he climbed out of his truck.

"Hey, Sam." Ken held out one hand and Sam shook it.

"Thanks for coming out to get the table," Sam said. "Appreciate it."

"Hey, you keep building them, I'll drive up the mountain to pick them up." Ken grinned. About forty, he had pulled his black hair into a ponytail at the base of his neck. He wore a heavy brown coat over a flannel shirt, blue jeans and black work boots. He opened the gate at the back of his truck, then grinned at Sam. "One of these times, though, you should come into town yourself so you can see the reactions of the people who buy your stuff." Shaking his head, he mused, "I mean, they all but applaud when we bring in new stock."

"Good to know," Sam said. It was odd, he thought, that he'd taken what had once been a hobby—woodworking—and turned it into an outlet for the creativity that had been choked off years ago. He liked knowing that his work was appreciated.

Once upon a time, he'd been lauded in magazines and newspapers. Reporters had badgered him for interviews, and one or two of his paintings actually hung in European palaces. He'd been the darling of the art world, and he'd enjoyed it all. He'd poured his heart and soul into his work and drank in the adulation as his due. Sam had so loved his work, he'd buried himself in it to the detriment of everything else. His life outside the art world had drifted past without him even realizing it.

Sam hadn't paid attention to what should have been most important, and before he could learn his lesson and make changes, he'd lost it and all he had left was the art. The paintings. The name he'd carved for himself. Left alone, it was only when he had been broken that he realized how empty it all was. How much he'd sacrificed for the glory.

So he wasn't interested in applause. Not anymore.

"No thanks," he said, forcing a smile in spite of his dark thoughts. He couldn't explain why he didn't want to meet prospective customers, why he didn't care about hearing praise, so he said, "I figure being the hermit on the mountain probably adds to the mystique. Why ruin that by showing up in town?"

Ken looked at him, as if he were trying to figure him out, but a second later, shook his head. "Up to you, man. But anytime you change your mind, Emma would love to have you as the star of our next Meet the Artist night."

Sam laughed shortly. "Well, that sounds hideous."

Ken laughed, too. "I'll admit that it really is. Emma drives me nuts planning the snacks to get from Nibbles, putting out press releases, and the last time, she even bought some radio ads in Boise…" He trailed off and sighed. "And the artist managed to insult almost everyone in town. Don't understand these artsy types, but I'm happy enough to sell their stuff." He stopped, winced. "No offense."

"None taken," Sam assured him. "Believe me." He'd known plenty of the kind of artists Ken was describing. Those who so believed in their own press no one could stand to be around them.

"But, Emma loves doing it, of course, and I have to give it to her, we do big business on those nights."

Imagining being in the center of a crowd hungering to be close to an artist, to ask him questions, hang on everything he said, talk about the "art"… It all gave Sam cold chills and he realized just how far he'd come from the man he'd once been. "Yeah, like I said, awful."

"I even have to wear a suit. What's up with that?" Ken shook his head glumly and followed after Sam when he headed for the workshop door. "The only thing I like about it is the food, really. Nibbles has so many great things. My favorite's those tiny grilled cheese sandwiches. I can eat a dozen of 'em and still come back for more…"

Sam was hardly listening. He'd done so many of those "artist meets the public" nights years ago that he had zero interest in hearing about them now. His life, his *world*, had changed so much since then, he couldn't even imagine being a part of that scene anymore.

Ken was still talking. "Speaking of food, I saw Joy and Holly at the restaurant as I was leaving town."

Sam turned to look at him.

Ken shrugged. "Deb Casey and her husband, Sean, own Nibbles, and Deb and Joy are tight. She was probably in there visiting since they haven't seen each other in a while. How's it going with the two of them living here?"

"It's fine." What the hell else could he say? That Joy was driving him crazy? That he missed Holly coming into the workshop? That as much as he didn't want them there, he didn't want them gone even more? Made him sound like a lunatic. Hell, maybe he was.

Sam walked up to the table and drew off the heavy tarp he'd had protecting the finished table. Watery gray light washed through the windows and seemed to make the tabletop shine.

"Whoa." Ken's voice went soft and awe-filled. "Man, you've got some kind of talent. This piece is amazing. We're going to have customers outbidding each other trying to get it." He bent down, examined the twisted, gnarled branch pedestal, then stood again to admire the flash of the wood grain beneath the layers of varnish. "Dude, you could be in an art gallery with this kind of work."

Sam stiffened. He'd been in enough art galleries for a lifetime, he thought, and had no desire to do it again. That life had ultimately brought him nothing but pain, and it was best left buried in the past.

"Your shop works for me," he finally said.

Ken glanced at him. The steady look in his eyes told Sam that he was wondering about him. But that was nothing new. Everyone in the town of Franklin had no doubt been wondering about him since he first arrived and holed up in this house on the mountain. He had no answers to give any of them, because the man he used to be was a man even Sam didn't know anymore. And that's just the way he liked it.

"Well, maybe one day you'll explain to me what's behind you hiding out up here." Ken gave him a slap on the back. "Until then, though, I'd be a fool to complain when you're creating things like this for me to sell—and I'm no fool."

Sam liked Ken. The man was the closest thing to a friend Sam had had in years. And still, he couldn't bring himself to tell Ken about the past. About the mess he'd made of his life before finding this house on the mountain. So Sam concentrated instead on securing a tarp over the table and making sure it was tied down against the wind and dampness of the snow and rain. Ken helped him cover that with another tarp, wrapping this one all the way down and under the foot of the pedestal. Double protection since Sam really hated the idea of having the finish on the table ruined before it even made it into the shop. It took both of them to carry the table to the truck and secure it with bungee cords in the bed. Once it was done, Sam stuffed his hands into the pockets of his jacket and nodded to Ken as the man climbed behind the wheel.

"Y'know, I'm going to say this—just like I do every time I come out here—even knowing you'll say 'no, thanks.'"

Sam gave him a half smile, because he was ready for what was coming next. How could he not be? As Ken said, he made the suggestion every time he was here.

"Why don't you come into town some night?" the other man asked, forearm braced on the car door. "We'll get a couple beers, tell some lies…"

"No, thanks," Sam said and almost laughed at the knowing smile creasing Ken's face. If, for the first time, he was almost tempted to take the man up on it, he'd keep that to himself.

"Yeah, that's what I thought." Ken nodded and gave him a rueful smile. "But if you change your mind…"

"I'll let you know. Thanks for coming out to pick up the table."

"I'll let you know as soon as we sell it."

"I trust you," Sam said.

"Yeah, I wish that was true," Ken told him with another long, thoughtful look.

"It is."

"About the work, sure, I get that," Ken said. "But I want you to know, you can trust me beyond that, too. Whether you actually do or not."

Sam had known Ken and Emma for four years, and if he was looking for friendships, he couldn't do any better and he knew it. But getting close to people—be it Ken or Joy—meant allowing them close enough to know about his past. And the fewer people who knew, the less pity he had to deal with. So he'd be alone.

"Appreciate it." He slapped the side of the truck and took a step back.

"I'll see you, then."

Ken drove off and when the roar of his engine died away, Sam was left in the cold with only the sigh of the wind through the trees for company. Just the way he liked it.

Right?

Five

"Oh, God, look at her with that puppy," Joy said on a sigh.

Her heart filled and ached as she watched Holly laughing at the black Lab puppy jumping at her legs. How could one little girl mean so much? Joy wondered.

When she'd first found herself pregnant, Joy remembered the rush of pleasure, excitement that she'd felt. It hadn't mattered to her that she was single and not exactly financially stable. All she'd been able to think was, she would finally have her own family. Her child.

Joy had been living in Boise back then, starting up her virtual assistant business and working with several of the small businesses in town. One of those was Mike's Bikes, a custom motorcycle shop owned by Mike Davis.

Mike was charming, handsome and had the whole

bad-boy thing going for him, and Joy fell hard and fast. Swept off her feet, she gave herself up to her first real love affair and thought it would be forever. It lasted until the day she told Mike she was pregnant, expecting to see the same happiness in him that she was feeling. Mike, though, had no interest in being anyone's father—or husband, if it came to that. He told her they were through. She was a good time for a while, but the good time was over. He signed a paper relinquishing all future rights to the child he'd created and Joy walked away.

When she was a kid, she'd come to Franklin with a foster family for a long weekend in the woods and she'd never forgotten it. So when she needed a fresh start for her and her baby, Joy had come here, to this tiny mountain town. And here is where she'd made friends, built her family and, at long last, had finally felt as though she belonged.

And of all the things she'd been gifted with since moving here, Deb Casey, her best friend, was at the top of the list.

Deb Casey walked to Joy and looked out the window at the two little girls rolling around on the winter brown grass with a fat black puppy. Their laughter and the puppy's yips of excitement brought a quick smile. "She's as crazy about that puppy as my Lizzie."

"I know." Joy sighed a little and leaned on her friend's kitchen counter. "Holly's telling everyone she's getting a puppy of her own for Christmas."

"A white one," Deb supplied.

Rolling her eyes, Joy shook her head. "I've even been into Boise looking for a white puppy, and no one has any. I guess I'm going to have to start preparing her for the fact that Santa can't always bring you what you want."

"Oh, I hate that." Deb turned back to the wide kitchen island and the tray of tiny brownies she was finishing off with swirls of white chocolate icing. "You've still got a few weeks till Christmas. You might find one."

"I'll keep looking, sure. But," Joy said, resigned, "she might have to wait."

"Because kids wait so well," Deb said with a snort of laughter.

"You're not helping."

"Have a brownie. That's the kind of help you need."

"Sold." Joy leaned in and grabbed one of the tiny brownies that was no more than two bites of chocolate heaven.

The brownies, along with miniature lemon meringue pies, tiny chocolate chip cookies and miniscule Napoleons, would be filling the glass cases at Nibbles by this afternoon. The restaurant had been open for only a couple of years, but it had been a hit from the first day. Who wouldn't love going for lunch where you could try four or five different types of sandwiches—none of them bigger than a bite or two? Gourmet flavors, a fun atmosphere and desserts that could bring a grown woman to tears of joy, Nibbles had it all.

"Oh, God, this should be illegal," Joy said around a mouthful of amazing brownie.

"Ah, then I couldn't sell them." Deb swirled white chocolate on a few more of the brownies. "So, how's it going up there with the Old Man of the Mountain?"

"He's not old."

"No kidding." Deb grinned. "I saw him sneaking into the gallery last summer, and I couldn't believe it.

It was like catching a glimpse of a unicorn. A gorgeous unicorn, I've got to say."

Joy took another brownie and bit into it. *Gorgeous* covered it. Of course, there was also *intriguing*, *desirable*, *fascinating*, and as yummy as this brownie. "Yeah, he is."

"Still." Deb looked up at Joy. "Could he be more antisocial? I mean, I get why and all, but aren't you going nuts up there with no one to talk to?"

"I talk to him," Joy argued.

"Yes, but does he talk back?"

"Not really, though in his defense, I do talk a lot." Joy shrugged. "Maybe it's hard for him to get a word in."

"Not that hard for me."

"We're women. Nothing's that hard for us."

"Okay, granted." Deb smiled, put the frosting back down and planted both hands on the counter. "But what's really going on with you? I notice you're awful quick to defend him. Your protective streak is coming out."

That was the only problem with a best friend, Joy thought. Sometimes they saw too much. Deb knew that Joy hadn't dated anyone in years. That she hadn't had any interest in sparking a relationship—since her last one had ended so memorably. So of course she would pick up on the fact that Joy was suddenly very interested in one particular man.

"It's nothing."

"Sure," Deb said with a snort of derision. "I believe that."

"Fine, it's *something*," Joy admitted. "I'm not sure what, though."

"But he's so not the kind of guy I would expect you to be interested in. He's so—cold."

Oh, there was plenty of heat inside Sam Henry. He just kept it all tamped down. Maybe that's what drew her to him, Joy thought. The mystery of him. Most men were fairly transparent, but Sam had hidden depths that practically demanded she unearth them. She couldn't get the image of the shadows in his eyes out of her mind. She wanted to know why he was so shut down. Wanted to know how to open him up.

Smiling now, she said, "Holly keeps telling me he's not mean, he's just crabby."

Deb laughed. "Is he?"

"Oh, definitely. But I don't know why."

"I might."

"What?"

Deb sighed heavily. "Okay, I admit that when you went to stay up there, I was a little worried that maybe he was some crazed weirdo with a closet full of women's bones or something."

"I keep telling you, stop watching those horror movies."

Deb grinned. "Can't. Love 'em." She picked up the frosting bag as if she needed to be doing something while she told the story. "Anyway, I spent a lot of time online, researching the local hermit and—"

"What?" And why hadn't Joy done the same thing? Well, she knew why. It had felt like a major intrusion on his privacy. She'd wanted to get him to actually *tell* her about himself. Yet here she was now, ready to pump Deb for the information she herself hadn't wanted to look for.

"You know he used to be a painter."

"Yes, that much I knew." Joy took a seat at one of the counter stools and kept her gaze fixed on Deb's blue eyes.

"He was famous. I mean *famous*." She paused for emphasis. "Then about five years ago, he just stopped painting entirely. Walked away from his career and the fame and fortune and moved to the mountains to hide out."

"You're not telling me anything I didn't know so far."

"I'm getting there." Sighing, Deb said softly, "His wife and three-year-old son died in a car wreck five years ago."

Joy felt as though she'd been punched in the stomach. The air left her lungs as sympathetic pain tore at her. Tears welled in her eyes as she tried to imagine that kind of hell. That kind of devastation. "Oh, my God."

"Yeah, I know," Deb said with a wince. Laying down the pastry bag, she added, "When I found out, I felt so bad for him."

Joy did, too. She couldn't even conceive the level of pain Sam had experienced. Even the thought of such a loss was shattering. Remembering the darkness in his eyes, Joy's heart hurt for him and ached to somehow ease the grief that even five years later still held him in a tight fist. Now at least she could understand a little better why he'd closed himself off from the world.

He'd hidden himself away on a mountaintop to escape the pain that was stalking him. She saw it in his eyes every time she looked at him. Those shadows that were a part of him were really just reflections of the pain that was in his heart. Of *course* he was still feeling the soul-crushing pain of losing his family. God, just the thought of losing Holly was enough to bring her to her knees.

Instinctively, she moved to Deb's kitchen window and looked out at two little girls playing with a puppy.

Her gaze locked on her daughter, Joy had to blink a sheen of tears from her eyes. So small. So innocent. To have that…*magic* winked out like a blown-out match? She couldn't imagine it. Didn't want to try.

"God, this explains so much," she whispered.

Deb walked to her side. "It does. But Joy, before you start riding to the rescue, think about it. It's been five years since he lost his family, and as far as I know, he's never talked about it. I don't think anyone in town even knows about his past."

"Probably not," she said, "unless they took the time to do an internet search on him."

Deb winced again. "Maybe I shouldn't have. Sort of feels like intruding on his privacy, now that I know."

"No, I'm glad you did. Glad you told me," Joy said, with a firm shake of her head. "I just wish I'd thought of doing it myself. Heck, I'm on the internet all the time, just working."

"That's why it didn't occur to you," Deb told her. "The internet is work for you. For the rest of us, it's a vast pool of unsubstantiated information."

She had a point. "Well, then I'm glad I came by today to get your updates for your website."

As a virtual assistant, Joy designed and managed websites for most of the shops in town, plus the medical clinic, plus she worked for a few mystery authors who lived all over the country. It was the perfect job for her, since she was very good at computer programming and it allowed her to work at home and be with Holly instead of sending the little girl out to day care.

But, because she spent so much time online for her job, she rarely took the time to browse sites for fun.

Which was why it hadn't even occurred to her to look up Sam Henry.

Heart heavy, Joy looked through the window and watched as Holly fell back onto the dry grass, laughing as the puppy lunged up to lavish kisses on her face. Holly. God, Joy thought, now she knew why Sam had demanded she keep her daughter away from him. Seeing another child so close to the age of his lost son must be like a knife to the heart.

And yet...she remembered how kind he'd been with Holly in the workshop that first day. How he'd helped her, how Holly had helped *him*.

Sam hadn't thrown Holly out. He'd spent time with her. Made her feel important and gave her the satisfaction of building something. He had closed himself off, true, but there was clearly a part of him looking for a way out.

She just had to help him find it.

Except for her nightly monologues in the great room, Joy had been giving him the space he claimed to want. But now she thought maybe it wasn't space he needed... but less of it. He'd been alone too long, she thought. He'd wrapped himself up in his pain and had been that way so long now, it probably felt normal to him. So, Joy told herself, if he wouldn't go into the world, then the world would just have to go to him.

"You're a born nurturer," Deb whispered, shaking her head.

Joy looked at her.

"I can see it on your face. You're going to try to 'save' him."

"I didn't say that."

"Oh, honey," Deb said, "you didn't have to."

"It's annoying to be read so easily."

"Only because I love you." Deb smiled. "But Joy, before you jump feetfirst into this, maybe you should consider that Sam might not *want* to be saved."

She was sure Deb was right. He didn't want to come out of the darkness. It had become his world. His, in a weird way, comfort zone. That didn't make it right.

"Even if he doesn't want it," Joy murmured, "he needs it."

"What *exactly* are you thinking?" Deb asked.

Too many things, Joy realized. Protecting Holly, reaching Sam, preparing for Christmas, keeping up with all of the holiday work she had to do for her clients... Oh, whom was she kidding? At the moment, Sam was uppermost in her mind. She was going to drag him back into the land of the living, and she had the distinct feeling he was going to put up a fight.

"I'm thinking that maybe I'm in way over my head."

Deb sighed a little. "How deep is the pool?"

"Pretty deep," Joy mused, thinking about her reaction to him, the late-night talks in the great room where it was just the two of them and the haunted look in his eyes that pulled at her.

Deb bumped her hip against Joy's. "I see that look in your eyes. You're already attached."

She was. Pointless to deny it, especially to Deb of all people, since she could read Joy so easily.

"Yes," she said and heard the worry in her own voice, "but like I said, it's pretty deep waters."

"I'm not worried," Deb told her with a grin. "You're a good swimmer."

That night, things were different.

When Sam came to dinner in the dining room, Joy

and Holly were already seated, waiting for him. Since every other night, the two of them were in the kitchen, he looked thrown for a second. She gave him a smile even as Holly called out, "Hi, Sam!"

If anything, he looked warier than just a moment before. "What's this?"

"It's called a communal meal," Joy told him, serving up a bowl of stew with dumplings. She set the bowl down at his usual seat, poured them both a glass of wine, then checked to make sure Holly was settled beside her.

"Mommy made dumplings. They're really good," the little girl said.

"I'm sure." Reluctantly, he took a seat then looked at Joy. "This is not part of our agreement."

He looked, she thought, as if he were cornered. Well, good, because he was. Dragging him out of the darkness was going to be a step-by-step journey—and it started now.

"Actually…" she told him, spooning up a bite of her own stew, then sighing dramatically at the taste. Okay, yes she was a good cook, but she was putting it on for his benefit. And it was working. She saw him glance at the steaming bowl in front of his chair, even though he hadn't taken a bite yet. "…our agreement was that I clean and cook. We never agreed to not eat together."

"It was implied," he said tightly.

"Huh." She tipped her head to one side and studied the ceiling briefly as if looking for an answer there. "I didn't get that implication at all. But why don't you eat your dinner and we can talk about it."

"It's good, Sam," Holly said again, reaching for her glass of milk.

He took a breath and exhaled on a sigh. "Fine. But this doesn't mean anything."

"Of course not," Joy said, hiding the smile blossoming inside her. "You're still the crabby man we all know. No worries about your reputation."

His lips twitched as he tasted the stew. She waited for his reaction and didn't have to wait long. "It's good."

"Told ya!" Holly's voice was a crow of pleasure.

"Yeah," he said, flicking the girl an amused glance. "You did."

Joy saw that quick look and smiled inside at the warmth of it.

"When we went to town today I played with Lizzie's puppy," Holly said, taking another bite and wolfing it down so she could keep talking. "He licked me in the face again and I laughed and Lizzie and me ran and he chased us and he made Lizzie fall but she didn't cry…"

Joy smiled at her daughter, loving how the girl could launch into a conversation that didn't need a partner, commas or periods. She was so thrilled by life, so eager to experience everything, just watching her made Joy's life better in every possible way. From the corner of her eye, she stole a look at Sam and saw the flicker of pain in his eyes. It had to be hard for him to listen to a child's laughter and have to grieve for the loss of his own child. But he couldn't avoid children forever. He'd end up a miserable old man, and that would be a waste, she told herself.

"And when I get my puppy, Lizzie can come and play with it, too, and it will chase us and mine will be white cuz Lizzie's is black and it would be fun to have puppies like that…"

"She's really counting on that puppy," Joy murmured.

"So?" Sam dipped into his stew steadily as if he was hurrying to finish so he could escape the dining room—and their company.

Deliberately, Joy refilled his bowl over his complaints.

"So, there aren't any white puppies to be had," she whispered, her own voice covered by the rattle of Holly's excited chatter.

"Santa's going to bring him, remember, Mommy?" Holly asked, proving that her hearing was not affected by the rush of words tumbling from her own mouth.

"That's right, baby," Joy said with a wince at Sam's smirk. "But you know, sometimes Santa can't bring everything you want—"

"If you're not a good girl," Holly said, nodding sharply. "But I am a good girl, right, Mommy?"

"Right, baby." She was really stuck now. Joy was going to have to go into Boise and look for a puppy or she was going to have a heartbroken daughter on Christmas morning, and that she couldn't allow.

Too many of Joy's childhood Christmases had been empty, lonely. She never wanted Holly to feel the kind of disappointment Joy had known all too often.

"I told Lizzie about the fairy house we made, Sam, and she said she has fairies at her house, but I don't think so cuz you need lots of trees for fairies and there's not any at Lizzie's..."

"The kid never shuts up," Sam said, awe in his voice.

"She's excited." Joy shrugged. "Christmas is coming."

His features froze over and Joy could have kicked herself. Sure, she planned on waking him up to life, but she couldn't just toss him into the middle of a fire, could she? She had to ease him closer to the warmth a little at a time.

"Yeah."

"I know you said no decorations or—"

His gaze snapped to hers, cold. Hard. "That's right."

"In the great room," she continued as if he hadn't said a word, as if she hadn't gotten a quick chill from the ice in his eyes, "but Holly and I are here for the whole month and a little girl needs Christmas. So we'll keep the decorations to a minimum."

His mouth worked as if he wanted to argue and couldn't find a way to do it without being a complete jerk. "Fine."

She reached out and gave his forearm a quick pat. Even with removing her hand almost instantly, that swift buzz of something amazing tingled her fingers. Joy took a breath, smiled and said, "Don't worry, we won't be too happy around you, either. Wouldn't want you upset by the holiday spirit."

He shot her a wry look. "Thanks."

"No problem." Joy grinned at him. "You have to be careful or you could catch some stray laugh and maybe even try to join in only to have your face break."

Holly laughed. "Mommy, that's silly. Faces can't break, can they, Sam?"

His brown eyes were lit with suppressed laughter, and Joy considered that a win for her. "You're right, Holly. Faces can't break."

"Just freeze?" Joy asked, her lips curving.

"Yeah. I'm good at freezing," he said, gaze meeting hers in a steady stare.

"That's cuz it's cold," Holly said, then added, "Can I be done now, Mommy?"

Joy tore her gaze from his long enough to check that her daughter had eaten most of her dinner. "Yes, sweetie. Why don't you go get the pinecones we found today and put them on the kitchen counter? We'll paint them after I clean up."

"Okay!" The little girl scooted off the chair, ran around the table and stopped beside Sam. "You wanna paint with me? We got glitter, too, to put on the pinecones and we get to use glue to stick it."

Joy watched him, saw his eyes soften, then saw him take a deliberate, emotional step back. Her heart hurt, remembering what she now knew about his past. And with the sound of her daughter's high-pitched, excited voice ringing in the room, Joy wondered again how he'd survived such a tremendous loss. But even as she thought it, Joy realized that he was like a survivor of a disaster.

He'd lived through it but he wasn't *living*. He was still existing in that half world of shock and pain, and it looked to her as though he'd been there so long he didn't have a clue how to get out. And that's where Joy came in. She wouldn't leave him in the dark. Couldn't watch him let his life slide past.

"No, thanks." Sam gave the little girl a tight smile. "You go ahead. I've got some things I've got to do."

Well, at least he didn't say anything about hating Christmas. "Go ahead, sweetie. I'll be there in a few minutes."

"Okay, Mommy. 'Bye, Sam!" Holly waved, turned and raced toward the kitchen, eager to get started on those pinecones.

When they were alone again, Joy looked at the man opposite her and smiled. "Thanks for not popping her Christmas balloon."

He scowled at her and pushed his empty bowl to one side. "I'm not a monster."

"No," she said, thoughtfully. "You're not."

He ignored that. "Look, I agreed to you and Holly doing Christmas stuff in your part of the house. Just don't try to drag me into it. Deal?"

She held out one hand and left it there until he took it in his and gave it a firm shake. Of course, she had no intention of keeping to that "deal." Instead, she was going to wake him up whether he liked it or not. By the time she was finished, Joy assured herself, he'd be roasting chestnuts in the fireplace and stringing lights on a Christmas tree.

His eyes met hers and in those dark depths she saw... everything. A tingling buzz shot up her arm and ricocheted around in the center of her chest like a Ping-Pong ball in a box. Her heartbeat quickened and her mouth went dry. Those eyes of his gazed into hers, and Joy took a breath and held it. Finally, he let go of her hand and took a single step back as if to keep a measure of safe distance between them.

"Well," she said when she was sure her voice would work again, "I'm going to straighten out the kitchen then paint pinecones with my daughter."

"Right." He scrubbed one hand across his face. "I'll be in the great room."

She stood up, gathered the bowls together and said, "Earlier today, Holly and I made some Christmas cookies. I'll bring you a few with your coffee."

"Not necessary—"

She held up one hand. "You can call them winter cookies if it makes you feel better."

He choked off a laugh, shook his head and started

out of the room. Before he left, he turned to look back at her. "You don't stop, do you?"

"Nope." He took another step and paused when she asked, "The real question is, do you want me to?"

He didn't speak, just gave her a long look out of thoughtful, chocolate-brown eyes, then left the room. Joy smiled to herself, because that nonanswer told her everything she wanted to know.

Six

Sam used to hate the night.

The quiet. The feeling of being alone in the world. The seemingly endless hours of darkness. It had given him too much time to think. To remember. To torture himself with what-might-have-beens. He couldn't sleep because memories became dreams that jolted him awake—or worse, lulled him into believing the last several years had never really happened. Then waking up became the misery, and so the cycle went.

Until nearly a week ago. Until Joy.

He had a fire blazing in the hearth as he waited for her. Night was now something he looked forward to. Being with her, hearing her voice, her laughter, had become the best part of his days. He enjoyed her quick mind, and her sense of humor—even when it was directed at him. He liked hearing her talk about what was happening in town, even though he didn't know any of the people she told him about. He liked seeing her with her daughter, watching the love between them, even though it was like a knife to his heart.

Sam hadn't expected this, hadn't thought he wanted it. He rubbed his palms together, remembering the flash of heat that enveloped him when he'd taken her hand to seal their latest deal. He could see the flash in her eyes that told him she'd felt the same damn thing. And with the desire gripping him, guilt speared through Sam, as well. Everything he'd lost swam in his mind, reminding him that *feeling*, *wanting*, was a steep and slippery road to loss.

He stared into the fire, listened to the hiss and snap of flame on wood, and for the first time in years, he *tried* to bring those long-abandoned memories to the surface. Watching the play of light and shadow, the dance of flames, Sam fought to draw his dead wife's face into his mind. But the memory was indistinct, as if a fog had settled between them, making it almost impossible for him to remember just the exact shade of her brown eyes. The way her mouth curved in a smile. The fall of her hair and the set of her jaw when she was angry.

It was all...hazy, and as he battled to remember Dani, it was Joy's face that swam to the surface of his mind. The sound of *her* laughter. The scent of her. And he wanted to know the taste of her. What the hell was happening to him and why was he allowing it? Sam told himself to leave. To not be there when Joy came into the room. But as much as he knew he should, he also knew he wouldn't.

"I brought more cookies."

He turned in his chair to look at her, and even from across the room, he felt that now-familiar punch of awareness. Of heat. And he knew it was too late to leave.

At her smile, one eyebrow lifted and he asked, "More reindeer and Santas?"

That smile widened until it sparkled in her eyes. She walked toward him, carrying a tray that held the plate of cookies and two glasses of golden wine.

"This time we have snowmen and wreaths and—" she paused "—*winter* trees."

He shook his head and sighed. It seemed she was determined to shove Christmas down his throat whether he liked it or not. "You're relentless."

Why did he like that about her?

"That's been said before," she told him and took her usual seat in the chair beside his. Setting the tray down on the table between them, she took a cookie then lifted her glass for a sip of wine.

"Really. Cookies and wine."

"Separately, they're both good," she said, waving her cookie at the plate, challenging him to join her. "Together, they're amazing."

The cookies were good, Sam thought, reaching out to pick one up and bite in. All he'd had to do was close his eyes so he wasn't faced with iced, sprinkled Santas and they were just cookies. "Good."

"Thanks." She sat back in the chair. "That wasn't so hard, was it?"

"What?"

"Talking to me." She folded her legs up beneath her, took another sip of her wine and continued. "We've been sitting in this room together for five nights now and usually, the only voice I hear is my own."

He frowned, took the wine and drank. Gave him an excuse for not addressing that remark. Of course, it was true, but that wasn't the point. He hadn't asked her to join him every night, had he? When she only looked at him, waiting, he finally said, "Didn't seem to bother you any."

"Oh, I don't mind talking to myself—"

"No kidding."

She grinned. "But it's more fun talking to other people."

Sam told himself not to notice how her hair shined golden in the firelight. How her eyes gleamed and her mouth curved as if she were always caught on the verge of a smile. His gaze dropped to the plain blue shirt she wore and how the buttons pulled across her chest. Her jeans were faded and soft, clinging to her legs as she curled up and got comfortable. Red polish decorated her toes. Why that gave him a quick, hot jolt, he couldn't have said.

Everything in him wanted to pull her out of that chair, wrap his arms around her and take her tantalizing mouth in a kiss that would sear both of them. And *why*, he asked himself, did he suddenly feel like a cheating husband? Because since Dani, no other woman had pulled at him like this. And even as he wanted Joy, he hated that he wanted her. The cookie turned to chalk in his mouth and he took a sip of wine to wash it down.

"Okay, someone just had a dark thought," she mused.

"Stay out of my head," Sam said, slanting her a look.

Feeling desire didn't mean that he welcomed it. Life had been—not easier—but more clear before Joy walked into his house. He'd known who he was then. A widower. A father without a child. And he'd wrapped himself up in memories designed to keep him separate from a world he wasn't interested in anyway.

Yet now, after less than a week, he could feel those layers of insulation peeling away and he wasn't sure how to stop it or even if he wanted to. The shredding of his cloak of invisibility was painful and still he couldn't stop it.

Dinner with Joy and Holly had tripped him up, too, and he had a feeling she'd known it would. If he'd been smart, he would have walked out of the room as soon as he'd seen them at the table. But one look into Joy's and Holly's eyes had ended that idea before it could begin. So instead of having his solitary meal, he'd been part of a unit—and for a few minutes, he'd enjoyed it. Listening to Holly's excited chatter, sharing knowing looks with Joy. Then, of course, he remembered that Joy and Holly weren't *his*. And that was what he had to keep in mind.

Taking another drink of the icy wine, he shifted his gaze to the fire. Safer to look into the flames than to stare at the deep blue of her eyes. "Yeah," he said, finally responding to her last statement, "I don't really talk to people anymore."

"No kidding." She threw his earlier words back at him, and Sam nodded at the jab.

"Kaye tends to steer clear of me most of the time."

"Kaye doesn't like talking to people, either," Joy said, laughing. "You two are a match made in heaven."

"There's a thought," he muttered.

She laughed again, and the sound of it filled every empty corner of the room. It was both balm and torture to hear it, to know he *wanted* to hear it. How was it possible that she'd made such an impact on him in such a short time? He hadn't even noticed her worming her way past his defenses until it was impossible to block her.

"So," she asked suddenly, pulling him from his thoughts, "any idea where I can find a puppy?"

"No," he said shortly, then decided there was no reason to bark at her because he was having trouble dealing with her. He looked at her. "I don't know people around here."

"See, you should," she said, tipping her head to one side to look at him. "You've lived here five years, Sam."

"I didn't move here for friends." He came to the mountains to find the peace that still eluded him.

"Doesn't mean you can't make some." Sighing, she turned her head to the flames. "If you did know people, you could help me on the puppy situation." Shaking her head, she added, "I've got her princess dolls and a fairy princess dress and the other small things she asked for. The puppy worries me."

He didn't want to think about children's Christmas dreams. Sam remembered another child dictating letters to Santa and waking to the splendor of Christmas morning. And through the pain he also recalled how he and his wife had worked to make those dreams come true for their little boy. So, though he hated it, he said, "You could get her a stuffed puppy with a note that Santa will bring her the real thing as soon as the puppy's ready for a new home."

She tipped her head to one side and studied him, a wide smile on her face. God, when she smiled, her eyes shone and something inside him fisted into knots.

"A note from Santa himself? That's a good idea. I think Holly would love that he's going to make a special trip just for her." Clearly getting into it, she continued, "I could make up a certificate or something. You know—" she deepened her voice for dramatic effect "—*this is to certify that Holly Curran will be receiving a puppy from Santa as soon as the puppy is ready for a home.*" Wrinkling her brow, she added thoughtfully, "Maybe I could draw a Christmas border on the paper and we could frame it for her—you know, with Santa's signature—and hang it in her bedroom. It could become an heirloom, something she passes down to her kids."

He shrugged, as if it meant nothing, but in his head, he could see Holly's excitement at a special visit from Santa *after* Christmas. But once December was done, he wouldn't be seeing Joy or Holly again, so he wouldn't know how the Santa promise went, would he? Frowning to himself, he tried to ignore the ripple of regret that swept through him.

"Okay, I am not responsible for your latest frown."

"What?" He turned his head to look at her again.

She laughed shortly. "Nothing. So, what'd you work on today?"

"Seriously?" Usually she just launched into a monologue.

"Well, you're actually speaking tonight," she said with a shrug, "so I thought I'd ask a question that wasn't rhetorical."

"Right." Shaking his head, he said, "I'm starting a new project."

"Another table?"

"No."

"Talking," she acknowledged, "but still far from chatty."

"Men are not chatty."

"Some men you can't shut up," she argued. "If it's not a table you're working on, what is it?"

"Haven't decided yet."

"You know, in theory, a job like that sounds wonderful." She took a sip of wine. "But I do better with a schedule all laid out in front of me. I like knowing that website updates are due on Monday and newsletters have to go out on Tuesday, like that."

"I don't like schedules."

She watched him carefully, and his internal radar went on alert. When a woman got that particular look in her eye—curiosity—it never ended well for a man.

"Well," she said softly, "if you haven't decided on a project yet, you could give me some help with the Santa certificate."

"What do you mean?" He heard the wariness in his own voice.

"I mean, you could draw Christmassy things around the borders, make it look beautiful." She paused and when she spoke again, the words came so softly they were almost lost in the hiss and snap of the fire in front of them. "You used to paint."

And in spite of those flames less than three feet from him, Sam went cold right down to the bone. "I used to."

She nodded. "I saw some of your paintings online. They were beautiful."

He took a long drink of wine, hoping to ease the hard knot lodged in his throat. It didn't help. She'd looked him up online. Seen his paintings. Had she seen the rest, as well? Newspaper articles on the accident? Pictures of his dead wife and son? Pictures of him at their fu-neral, desperate, grieving, throwing a punch at a photographer? God he hated that private pain was treated as public entertainment.

"That was a long time ago," he spoke and silently congratulated himself on squeezing the words from a dry, tight throat.

"Almost six years."

He snapped a hard look at her. "Yeah. I *know*. What is it you're looking for here? Digging for information? Pointless. The world already knows the whole story."

"Talking," she told him. "Not digging."

"Well," he said, pushing to his feet, "I'm done talking."

"Big surprise," Joy said, shaking her head slowly.

"What's that supposed to mean?" Damn it, had he really just been thinking that spending time with her was a good thing? He looked down into those summer-blue eyes and saw irritation sparking there. Well, what the hell did *she* have to be mad about? It wasn't *her* life being picked over.

"It means, I knew you wouldn't want to talk about any of this."

"Yet, you brought it up anyway." Hell, Kaye knew the whole story about Sam's life and the tragedy he'd survived, but at least she never threw it at him. "What the hell? Did some reporter call you asking for a behind-the-scenes exclusive? Haven't they done enough articles on me yet? Or maybe you want to write a tell-all book, is that it?"

"Wow." That irritation in her eyes sparked from mild to barely suppressed fury in an instant. "You really think I would do that? To you? I would never sell out a friend."

"Oh," he snapped, refusing to be moved by the statement, "we're friends now?"

"We could be, if you would stop looking at everyone around you like a potential enemy."

"I told you I didn't come here for friends," he reminded her. Damn it, the fire was heating the air. That had to be why breathing was so hard. Why his chest felt tight.

"You've made that clear." Joy took a breath that he couldn't seem to manage, and he watched as the fury in her eyes softened to a glimmer. "Look, I only said something because it seemed ridiculous to pretend I didn't know who you were."

He rubbed the heel of his hand at the center of his chest, trying to ease the ball of ice lodged there. "Fine. Don't pretend. Just ignore it."

"What good will that do?" She set her wine down on the table and stood up to face him. "I'm sorry but—"

"Don't. God, don't say you're sorry. I've had more than enough of that, thanks. I don't want your sympathy." He pushed one hand through his hair and felt the heat of the fire on his back.

This place had been his refuge. He'd buried his past back east and come here to get away from not only the press, but also the constant barrage of memories assaulting him at every familiar scene. He'd left his family because their pity had been thick enough to choke him. He'd left *himself* behind when he came to the mountains. The man he'd once been. The man who'd been so wrapped up in creating beauty that he hadn't noticed the beauty in his own life until it had been snatched away.

"Well, you've got it anyway," Joy told him and reached out to lay one hand on his forearm.

Her touch fired everything in him, heat erupting with a rush that jolted his body to life in a way he hadn't experienced in too many long, empty years. And he resented the hell out of it.

He pulled away from her, and his voice dripped ice as he said, "Whatever it is you're after, you should know I don't want another woman in my life. Another child. Another loss."

Her gaze never left his, and those big blue pools of sympathy and irritation threatened to drown him.

"Everybody loses, Sam," she said quietly. "Houses, jobs, people they love. You can't insulate yourself from that. Protect yourself from pain. It's how you respond to the losses you experience that defines who you are."

He sneered at her. She had no idea. "And you don't like how I responded? Is that it? Well, get in line."

"Loss doesn't go away just because you're hiding from it."

Darkness beyond the windows seemed to creep closer, as if it were finding a way to slip right inside him. This room with its bright wood and soft lights and fire-lit shadows felt as if it were the last stand against the dark, and the light was losing.

Sam took a deep breath, looked down at her and said tightly, "You don't know what you're talking about."

Her head tipped to one side and blond curls fell against her neck. "You think you're the only one with pain?"

Of course not. But his own was too deep, too ingrained to allow him to give a flying damn what someone else might be suffering. "Just drop it. I'm done with this."

"Oh no. This you don't get to ignore. You think I don't know loss?" She moved in closer, tipped her head back and sent a steely-blue stare into his eyes. "My parents died when I was eight. I grew up in foster homes because I wasn't young enough or cute enough to be adopted."

"Damn it, Joy—" He'd seen pain reflected in his own eyes often enough to recognize the ghosts of it in hers. And he felt like the bastard he was for practically insisting that she dredge up her own past to do battle with his.

"As a foster kid I was never 'real' in any of the families I lived with. Always the outsider. Never fitting in. I didn't have friends, either, so I went out and made some."

"Good for you."

"Not finished. I had to build everything I have for myself *by* myself. I wanted to belong. I wanted family, you know?"

He started to speak, but she held up one hand for silence, and damned if it didn't work on him. He couldn't take his eyes off her as he watched her dip into the past to defend her present.

"I met Holly's father when I was designing his website. He was exciting and he loved me, and I thought it was forever—it lasted until I told him about Holly."

And though Sam felt bad, hearing it, watching it, knowing she'd had a tough time of it, he couldn't help but ask, "Yeah? Did he die? Did he take Holly away from you, so that you knew you'd never see her again?"

She huffed out a breath. "No, but—"

"Then you don't know," Sam interrupted, not caring now if he sounded like an unfeeling jerk. He wouldn't feel bad for the child she'd once been. *She* was the one who had dragged the ugly past into the present. "You can't possibly *know*, and I'm not going to stand here defending myself and my choices to you."

"Great," she said, nodding sharply as her temper once again rose to meet his. "So you'll just keep hiding yourself away until the rest of your life slides past?"

Sam snapped, throwing both hands high. "Why the hell do you care if I do?"

"Because I *saw* you with Holly," Joy said, moving in on him again, flavoring every breath he took with the scent of summer flowers that clung to her. "I saw your kindness. She needed that. Needs a male role model in her life and—"

"Oh, stop. Role models. For God's sake, I'm no one's father figure."

"Really?" She jammed both hands on her hips. "Better to shut yourself down? Pretend you're alone on a rock somewhere?"

"For me, yeah."

"You're lying."

"You don't know me."

"You'd like to think so," Joy said. "But you're not that hard to read, Sam."

Sam shook his head. "You're here to run the house, not psychoanalyze me."

"Multitasker, remember?" She smiled and he resented her for it. Resented knowing that he wanted her in spite of the tempers spiking between them. Hell, maybe *because* of it. He hated knowing that maybe she had a point. He really hated realizing that whatever secrets he thought he'd been keeping were no more private than the closest computer with an internet connection.

And man, it bugged him that she could go from anger to smiles in a blink.

"This isn't analysis, Sam." She met his gaze coolly, steadily, firelight dancing in her eyes. "It's called conversation."

"It's called my *family*," he said tightly, watching the reflection of flame and shadow in the blue of her eyes.

"I know. And—"

"Don't say you're sorry."

"I have to," she said simply. "And I am."

"Great. Thanks." God he wanted to get out of there. She was too close to him. He could smell her shampoo and the scent of flowers—Jasmine? Lilies?—fired a bolt of desire through him.

"But that's not all I am," she continued. "I'm also a little furious at you."

"Yeah? Right back at you."

"Good," she said, surprising him. "If you're angry at least you're *feeling* something." She moved in closer, kept her gaze locked with his and said, "If you love making furniture and working with wood, great. You're really good at it."

He nodded, hardly listening, his gaze shifting to the open doorway across the room. It—and the chance of escape—seemed miles away.

"But you shouldn't stop painting," she added fiercely. "The worlds you created were beautiful. Magical."

That magic was gone now, and it was better that way, he assured himself. But Sam couldn't remember a time when anyone had talked to him like this. Forcing him to remember. To face the darkness. To face himself. One reason he'd moved so far from his parents, his sister, was that they had been so careful. So cautious in everything they'd said as if they were all walking a tightrope, afraid to make the wrong move, say the wrong thing.

Their…*caution* had been like knives, jabbing at him constantly. Creating tiny nicks that festered and ached with every passing minute. So he'd moved here, where no one knew him. Where no one would offer sympathy he didn't want or advice he wouldn't take. He'd never counted on Joy.

"Why?" she asked. "Why would you give that up?"

It had been personal. So deeply personal he'd never talked about it with anyone, and he wasn't about to start now. Chest tight, mouth dry, he looked at her and said, "I'm not talking about this with you."

With anyone.

He took a step or two away from her, then spun back and around to glare down at her. In spite of the quick burst of fury inside him, sizzling around and between them, she didn't seem the least bit intimidated. Another thing to admire about her, damn it. She was sure of herself even when she was wrong.

"I already told you, Sam. You don't scare me."

"That's a damn shame," he muttered, trying not to remember that his mother had warned him about lonely old recluses muttering to themselves. He turned from her again, and this time she reached out and grabbed his arm as he moved away from her.

"Just stop," she demanded. "Stop and talk to me."

He glanced down at her hand on his arm and tried not to relish the heat sliding from her body into his. Tried not to notice that every cell inside him was waking up with a jolt. "Already told you I'm not talking about this."

"Then don't. Just stay. Talk to me." She took a deep breath, gave his arm a squeeze, then let him go. "Look, I didn't mean to bring any of this up tonight."

"Then why the hell did you?" He felt the loss of her touch and wanted it back.

"I don't like lying."

Scowling now, he asked, "What's that got to do with anything?"

Joy folded both arms in front of her and unconsciously lifted them until his gaze couldn't keep from admiring the pull of her shirt and the curve of those breasts. He shook his head and attempted to focus when she started talking again.

"I found out today about your family and not saying something would have felt like I was lying to you."

Convoluted, but in a weird way, she made sense. He wasn't much for lies, either, except for the ones he told his mother every time he assured her that he was fine. And truth be told, he would have been fine with Joy pretending she knew nothing about his past. But it was too late now for pretense.

"Okay, great. Conscience clear. Now let's move on." He started walking again and this time, when Joy tugged on his arm to get him to stop, he whirled around to face her.

Her blue eyes went wide, her mouth opened and he pulled her into him. It was instinct, pure, raw instinct, that had him grabbing her close. He speared his fingers through those blond curls, pulled her head back and kissed her with all the pent-up frustration, desire and, yeah, even temper that was clawing at him.

Surprised, it took her only a second or two to react. Joy wrapped her arms around his waist and moved in even closer. Sam's head exploded at the first, incredible taste of her. And then he wanted more. A groan slid from her throat, and that sound fed the flames enveloping him. God, he'd had no idea what kissing her would do to him. He'd been thinking about this for days, and having her in his arms made him want the feel of her skin beneath his hands. The heat of her body surrounding his.

All he could think was to get her clothes off her. To cup her breasts, to take each of her nipples into his mouth and listen to the whimpering sounds of pleasure she would make as he took her. He wanted to look down into blue eyes and watch them go blind with passion. He wanted to feel her hands sliding across his skin, holding him tightly to her.

His kiss deepened farther, his tongue tangling with hers in a frenzied dance of desire that pumped through him with the force and rush of a wildfire screaming across the hillsides.

Joy clung to him, letting him know in the most primal way that she felt the same. That her own needs and desires were pushing at her. He took her deeper, held her tighter and spun her around toward the closest couch. Heart pounding, breath slamming in and out of his lungs, he kept his mouth fused to hers as he laid her down on the wide, soft cushions and followed after, keeping her close to his side. She arched up, back bowing as he ran one hand up and down the length of her. All he could think about was touching her skin, feeling the heat of her. He flipped the button of her jeans open, pulled down the zipper, then slid his hand down, across her abdomen, feeling her shiver with every inch of flesh he claimed. His fingers slipped beneath the band of her panties and she lifted her hips as he moved to cup her heat.

She gasped, tore her mouth from his and clutched at

his shoulders when he stroked her for the first time. He loved the feel of her—slick, wet, hot. His body tightened painfully as he stared into her eyes. His mind fuzzed out and his body ached. He touched her, again and again, stroking, pushing into her heat, caressing her inside and out, driving them both to the edge of insanity.

"Sam—" She breathed his name and that soft, whispered sound rattled him.

When had she become so important? When had touching her become imperative? He took her mouth, tangling his tongue with hers, taking the taste of her deep inside him as he felt her body coil tighter with the need swamping her. She rocked into his hand, her hips pumping as he pushed her higher, faster. He pulled his head back, wanting, needing to see her eyes glaze with passion when the orgasm hit her.

He wasn't disappointed. She jolted in his arms when his thumb stroked across that one small nub of sensation at the heart of her. Everything she was feeling flashed through her eyes, across her features. He was caught up, unable to tear his gaze from hers. Joy Curran was a surprise to him on so many levels, he felt as though he'd never really learn them all. And at the moment, he didn't have to. Right now, he wanted only to hold her as she shattered.

She called his name again and he clutched her to him as her body trembled and shivered in his grasp. Her climax rolled on and on, leaving her breathless and Sam more needy than ever.

His body ached to join hers. His heart pounded in a fast gallop that left him damn near shaking with the want clawing at him.

"Sam," she whispered, reaching up to cup his face with her palms. "Sam, I need—"

He knew just what she needed because he needed it too. He shifted, pulled his hand free of her body and thought only about stripping them both out of their clothes.

In one small, rational corner of his mind, Sam admitted to himself that he'd never known anything like this before. This pulsing, blinding, overpowering sense of need and pleasure and craving to be part of a woman. To be locked inside her body and lose himself in her. Never.

Not even with Dani.

That thought broke him. He pulled back abruptly and stared down at Joy like a blind man seeing the light for the first time. Both exhilarated and terrified. A bucket full of ice water dumped on his head wouldn't have shocked him more.

He fought for breath, for balance, but there wasn't any to be had. His own mind was shouting at him, telling him he was a bastard for feeling more for Joy than he had for his wife. Telling him to deny it, even to himself. To bury these new emotions and go back to feeling nothing. It was safer.

"That's it," he said, shaking his head, rolling off the couch, then taking a step, then another, away from her. "I can't do this."

"Sure you can," Joy assured him, a confused half smile on her face as her breath came in short, hard gasps. She pushed herself up to her elbows on the couch. Her hair was a wild tumble of curls and her jeans still lay open, invitingly. "You were doing great."

"I *won't* do this." His eyes narrowed on her. "Not again."

"Sam, we should talk—"

He actually laughed, though to him it sounded harsh, strained as it scraped against his throat. "Talking doesn't solve everything and it won't solve this. I'm going out to the workshop."

Joy watched him go, her lips still buzzing from that kiss. Her heart still pounding like a bass drum. She might even have gone after him if her legs weren't trembling so badly she was forced to drop into the closest chair.

What the hell had just happened?

And how could she make it happen again?

Seven

Joy didn't see Sam at all the next morning, and maybe that was just as well.

She'd lain awake most of the night, reliving the whole scene, though she could admit to herself she spent more time reliving the kiss and the feel of his amazingly talented fingers on her body than the argument that had prompted it. Even now, though, she cringed a little remembering how she'd thrown the truth of his past at him out of nowhere. Honestly, what had she been thinking, just blurting out the fact that she knew about his family? She hadn't been thinking at all—that was the problem.

She'd stared into those amazing eyes of his and had seen him shuttered away, closing himself off, and it had just made her so angry, she'd confronted him without considering what it might do to the tenuous relationship they already had.

In Kaye's two-bedroom suite off the kitchen, there had been quiet in Joy's room and innocent dreams in Holly's. The house seemed to sigh with a cold wind that whipped through the pines and rattled glass panes. And Joy hadn't been able to shut off her brain. Or her body. But once she'd gotten past the buzz running rampant through her veins, all she'd been able to think about was the look in his eyes when she'd brought up his lost family.

Lying there in the dark, she'd assured herself that once she'd said the words, opened a door into his past, there'd been no going back. She could still see the shock in his eyes when she'd brought it up, and a twinge of guilt wrapped itself around her heart. But it was no match for the ribbon of anger that was there as well.

Not only had he walked away from his talent, but he'd shut himself off from life. From any kind of future or happiness. Why? His suffering wouldn't bring them back. Wouldn't restore the family he'd lost.

"Mommy, are you all done now?"

Joy came out of her thoughts and looked at her daughter, beside her at the kitchen table. Behind them, the outside world was gray and the pines bent nearly in half from that wind sweeping in off the lake. Still no snow and Joy was beginning to think they wouldn't have a white Christmas after all.

But for now, in the golden lamplight, she looked at Holly, doing her alphabet and numbers on her electronic tablet. The little girl was squirming in her seat, clearly ready to be done with the whole sit-down-and-work thing.

"Not yet, baby," Joy said, and knew that if her brain hadn't been filled with images of Sam, she'd have been finished with the website update a half hour ago. But no, all she could think of was the firelight in his eyes. The taste of his mouth. The feel of his hard body pressed to hers. And the slick glide of his fingers.

Oh, boy.

"Almost, honey," she said, clearing her throat and focusing again on the comments section of her client's website. For some reason people who read books felt it was okay to go on the author's website and list the many ways the author could have made the book better. Even when they loved it, they managed to sneak in a couple of jabs. It was part of Joy's job to remove the comments that went above and beyond a review and deep into the realm of harsh criticism.

"Mommy," Holly said, her heels kicking against the rungs of the kitchen chair, "when can we gooooooo?"

A one-syllable word now six syllables.

"As soon as I'm finished, sweetie," Joy promised, focusing on her laptop screen rather than the never-ending loop of her time with Sam. Once the comment section was cleaned up, Joy posted her client's holiday letter to her fans, then closed up the site and opened the next one.

Another holiday letter to post and a few pictures the author had taken at the latest writers' conference she'd attended.

"How much longer, though?" Holly asked, just a touch of a wheedling whine in her voice. "If we don't go soon all the Christmas trees will be *gone*."

Drama, thy name is Holly, Joy thought with a smile. Reaching out, she gave one of the girl's pigtails a tug. "Promise, there will be lots of trees when we get into town. But remember, we're getting a little one this year,

okay?" Because of the Grinch and his aversion to all
things festive.

"I know! It's like a fairy tree cuz it's tiny and can
go on a table to put in our room cuz Sam doesn't like
Christmas." Her head tipped to one side. "How come
he doesn't, Mommy? Everybody likes presents."

"I don't know, baby." She wasn't about to try to explain Sam's penchant for burying himself in a loveless,
emotionless well. "You should ask him sometime."

"I'll ask him now!" She scrambled off her chair and
Joy thought about calling her back as she raced to get
her jacket. But why should she? Joy had already seen
Sam with Holly. He was kind. Patient. And she knew
darn well that even if the man was furious with *her*, he
wouldn't take it out on Holly.

And maybe it would be good for him to be faced with
all that cheerful optimism. All that innocence shining
around her girl.

In seconds, Holly was back, dancing in place on the
toes of her pink princess sneakers. Joy zipped up the
jacket, pulled up Holly's hood and tied it at the neck.
Then she took a moment to just look at the little girl
who was really the light of her life. Love welled up inside her, thick and rich, and she heard Sam's voice in
her mind again.

*Did he take Holly away from you, so that you knew
you'd never see her again?*

That thought had Joy grabbing her daughter and pulling her in close for a tight hug that had Holly wriggling
for freedom. He was right, she couldn't really *know*
what he'd survived. She didn't even want to imagine it.

"You're squishing me, Mommy!"

"Sorry, baby." She swallowed the knot in her throat

and gave her girl a smile. "You go ahead and play with Sam. I'll come get you when it's time to go. As soon as I finish doing the updates on this website. Promise."

"Okay!" Holly turned to go and stopped when Joy spoke up again.

"No wandering off, Holly. Right to the workshop."

"Can't I look at my fairy house Sam helped me make? There might be fairies there now."

Boy, she was really going to miss this imaginative age when Holly grew out of it. But, though the fairy house wasn't exactly *inside* the woods, it was close enough that a little girl might be tempted to walk in more deeply and then end up getting lost. So, no. "We'll look later."

"Okay, 'bye!" And she was gone like a tiny pink hurricane.

Joy glanced out the window and watched her daughter bullet across the lawn to the workshop and then slip inside the doors. Smiling to herself, she thought she'd give a lot to see Sam's reaction to his visitor.

"Hi, Sam! Mommy said I could come play with you!"

She didn't catch him completely by surprise. Thankfully, Sam had spotted the girl running across the yard and had had time to toss a heavy beige tarp over his latest project. Although why he'd started on it was beyond him. A whim that had come on him two days ago, he'd thrown himself into it late last night when he'd left Joy in the great room.

Guilt had pushed him away from her, and it was guilt that had kept him working half the night. Memories crowded his brain, but it was thoughts of Joy herself that kept him on edge. That kiss. The heavy sigh of her breath as she molded herself to him. The eager response and matching need that had thrown him harder than he'd expected.

Shaking his head, he grumbled, "Don't have time to play." He turned to his workbench to find *something* to do.

"I can help you like I did with the fairy house. I want to see if there are fairies there but Mommy said I couldn't go by myself. Do you want to go with me? Cuz we can be busy outside, too, can't we?" She walked farther into the room and, as if she had radar, moved straight to the tarp draped across his project. "What's this?"

"Mine," he said and winced at the sharpness of his tone. But the girl, just like her mother, was impossible to deflate. She simply turned that bright smile of hers on him and said, "It's a secret, right? I like secrets. I can tell you one. It's about Lizzie's mommy going to have another baby. She thinks Lizzie doesn't know but Lizzie heard her mommy tell her daddy that she passed the test."

Too much information coming too quickly. He'd already learned about the wonderful Lizzie and her puppy. And this latest news blast might come under the heading of TMI.

"I wanted a sister, too," Holly said and walked right up to his workbench, climbing onto the stool she'd used the last time she was there. "But Mommy says I have to have a puppy instead and that's all right cuz babies cry a lot and a puppy doesn't…"

"Why don't we go check the fairy house?" Sam said, interrupting the flow before his head exploded. Getting her out of the shop seemed the best way to keep her from asking about the tarp again. It wasn't as if he *wanted* to go look for fairies in the freezing-cold woods.

"Oh, boy!" She squirmed off the stool, then grabbed his hand with her much smaller one.

Just for a second, Sam felt a sharp tug at the edges of his heart, and it was painful. Holly was older than Eli had been, he told himself, and she was a girl—so completely different children. But he couldn't help wondering what Eli would have been like at Holly's age. Or as he would be now at almost nine. But Eli would always be three years old. Just finding himself. Just becoming more of a boy than a baby and never a chance to be more.

"Let's go, Sam!" Holly pulled on his hand and leaned forward as if she could drag him behind her if she just tried hard enough.

He folded his fingers around hers and let her lead him from the shop into the cold. And he listened to her talk, heard again about puppies and fairies and princesses, and told himself that maybe this was his punishment. Being lulled into affection for a child who wasn't his. A child who would disappear from his life in a few short weeks.

And he wasn't completely stupid, he told himself. He could see through Joy's machinations. She wanted to wake him up, she'd said. To drag him back into the land of the living, and clearly, she was allowing her daughter to be part of that program.

"There it is!" Holly's excitement ratcheted up another level, and Sam thought the girl's voice hit a pitch that only dogs should have been able to hear. But her absolute pleasure in the smallest things was hard to ignore, damn it.

She let go of his hand and ran the last few steps to the fairy house on her own. Bending down, she inspected every window and even opened the tiny door to look inside. And Sam was drawn to the girl's absolute faith that she would see *something*. Even disappointment didn't jar the thrill in her eyes. "I don't see them," she said, turning her head to look at him.

"Maybe they're out having a picnic," he said, surprising himself by playing into the game. "Or shopping."

"Like Mommy and me are gonna do," Holly said, jumping up and down as if she simply couldn't hold back the excitement any more. "We're gonna get a Christmas tree today."

He felt a hitch in the center of his chest, but he didn't say anything.

"We're getting a little one this time to put in our room cuz you don't like Christmas. How come you don't like Christmas, Sam?"

"I…it's complicated." He hunched deeper into his black leather jacket and stuffed both hands into the pockets.

"Compulcated?"

"Complicated," he corrected, wondering how the hell he'd gotten into this conversation with a five-year-old. "Why?"

"Because it's about a lot of things all at once," he said, hoping to God she'd leave it there. He should have known better.

Her tiny brow furrowed as she thought about it. Finally, though, she shrugged and said, "Okay. Do you think fairies go buy Christmas trees? Will there be lights in their little house? Can I see 'em?"

So grateful to have left the Christmas thing behind,

he said, "Maybe if you look really hard one night you'll see some."

"I can look *really* hard, see?" Her eyes squinted and her mouth puckered up, showing him just how strong her looking power was.

"That's pretty hard." The wind gave a great gust and about knocked Holly right off her feet. He reached out, steadied her, then said, "You should go on back to the house with your mom."

"But we're not done looking." She grabbed his hand again, and this time, it was more comforting than unsettling. Pulling on him, she wandered over to one side of the fairy house, where the pine needles lay thick as carpet on the ground. "Could we make another fairy house and put it right here, by this big tree? That's like a Christmas tree, right? Maybe the fairies would put lights on it, too."

He was scrambling now. He'd never meant to get so involved. Not with the child. Not with her mother. But Holly's sweetness and Joy's...*everything*...kept sucking him in. Now he was making fairy houses and secret projects and freezing his ass off looking for invisible creatures.

"Sure," he said, in an attempt to get the girl moving toward the house. "We can build another one. In a day or two. Maybe."

"Okay, tomorrow we can do it and put it by the tree and the fairies will have a Christmas house to be all nice and warm. Can we put blankets and stuff in there, too?"

Tomorrow. Just like her mother, Holly heard only what she wanted to hear and completely disregarded everything else. He glanced at the house and somehow wasn't surprised to see Joy in the kitchen window, watching them. Across the yard, their gazes met and heat lit up the line of tension linking them.

All he could think of was the taste of her. The feel of her. The gnawing realization that he was going to have her. There was no mistaking the pulse-pounding sensations linking them. No pretending that it wasn't there. Guilt still chewing at him, he knew that even that wouldn't be enough to keep him from her.

And when she lifted one hand and laid it palm flat on the window glass, it was as if she was touching him. Feeling what he was feeling and acknowledging that she, too, knew the inevitable was headed right at them.

The trunk was filled with grocery bags, the backseat held a Charlie Brown Christmas tree on one side and Holly on the other, and now, Joy was at her house for the boxes of decorations they would need.

"Our house is tiny, huh, Mommy?"

After Sam's house, *anything* would look tiny, but in this case especially. "Sure is, baby," she said, "but it's ours."

She noted Buddy Hall's shop van in the driveway and hurriedly got Holly out of the car and hustling toward the house. Funny, she'd never really noticed before that they didn't have many trees on their street, Joy thought. But spending the last week or so at Sam's house—surrounded by the woods and a view of the lake—she couldn't help thinking that her street looked a little bare. But it wasn't Sam's house that intrigued her. It was the man himself. Instantly, she thought of the look he'd given her just that morning. Even from across the wide yard, she'd felt the power of that stare, and her blood had buzzed in reaction. Even now, her stomach jumped with nerves and expectation. She and Sam weren't finished. Not by a long shot. There was more coming. She just wasn't sure what or when. But she couldn't wait.

"Stay with me, sweetie," Joy said as they walked into the house together.

"Okay. Can I have a baby sister?"

Joy stopped dead on the threshold and looked down at her. "What? Where did that come from?"

"Lizzie's getting a new sister. It's a secret but she is and I want one, too."

Deb was pregnant? Why hadn't she told? And how the heck did Holly know before Joy did? Shaking her head, she told herself they were all excellent questions that would have to be answered later. For now, she wanted to check on the progress of the house repairs.

"Buddy?" she called out.

"Back here." The deep voice came from the kitchen, so Joy kept a grip on Holly and headed that way.

Along the way, her mind kept up a constant comparison between her own tiny rental and the splendor of Sam's place. The hallway alone was a fraction of the length of his. The living room was so small that if four people were in there at the same time, they'd be in sin. The kitchen, she thought sadly, walking into the room, looked about as big as the island in Sam's kitchen. Its sad cabinets needed paint and really just needed to be torn down and replaced, but since she was just a renter, it wasn't up to her. And the house might be small and a little on the shabby side, but it was her home. The one she'd made for her and Holly, so there was affection along with the exasperation.

"How's it going, Buddy?" she asked.

"Not bad." He stood up, all five feet four inches of him, with his barrel chest and broader stomach. A gray fringe of hair haloed his head, and his bright blue eyes sparkled with good humor. "Just sent Buddy Junior down to the hardware store. Thought while I was here we could fix the hinges on some of these cabinets. Some of 'em hang so crooked they're making me dizzy."

Delighted, Joy said, "Thank you, Buddy. That's going the extra mile."

"Not a problem." He pushed up the sleeves of his flannel shirt, took a step back and looked at the gaping hole where a light switch used to be. "Got the wiring all replaced and brought up to code out in the living room, but I'm checking the rest, as well. You've got some fraying in here and a hot wire somebody left uncapped in the smaller bedroom—"

Holly's bedroom, Joy thought and felt a pang of worry. God, if the fire had started in her daughter's room in the middle of the night, maybe they wouldn't have noticed in time. Maybe smoke inhalation would have knocked them out and kept them out until—

"No worries," Buddy said, looking right at her. "No point in thinking about what-ifs, either," he added as if he could look at her and read her thoughts. And he probably could. "By the time this job's done I guarantee all the wiring. You and the little one there will be safe as houses."

"What's a safe house?" Holly asked.

Buddy winked at her. "This one, soon's I'm done."

"Thank you, Buddy. I really appreciate it." But maybe, Joy told herself, it was time to find a new house for her and her daughter. Something newer. Safer. Still, that was a thought for later on, so she put it aside for now.

"I know you do and we're getting it done as fast as we can." He gave his own work a long look. "The way it's looking, you could be back home before Christmas."

Back home. Away from Sam. Away from what she was beginning to feel for him. Probably best, she told herself, though right at the moment, she didn't quite believe it. As irritating as the man could be, he was so much more. And that more was drawing her in.

"Appreciate that, too," Joy said. "We're just here to pick up some Christmas decorations, then we'll get out of your hair."

He grinned and scrubbed one hand across the top of his bald head. "You'd have quite the time getting *in* my hair. You two doing all right up the mountain?"

"Yes." Everyone in town was curious about Sam, she thought. Didn't he see that if he spent more time talking to people they'd be less inclined to talk about him and wonder? "It's been great. Sam helped Holly build a fairy house."

"Is that right?"

"It's pretty and in the woods and I'm going to bring some of my dolls to put in it to keep the fairies company and Sam's gonna help me make another one, too. He's really nice. Just crabby sometimes."

"Out of the mouths of babes," Joy murmured with a smile. "Well, we've got to run. Trees to decorate, cookies to bake."

"You go ahead then," Buddy said, already turning back to his task. Then over his shoulder he called out, "You be sure to tell Sam Henry my wife, Cora, loves that rocking chair he made. She bought it at Crafty and now I can't hardly get her out of it."

Joy smiled. "I'll tell him."

Then with Holly rummaging through her toys, Joy bundled up everything Christmas. A few minutes later, they were back in the car, and she was thinking about the crabby man who made her want things she shouldn't.

Of course, she had to stop by Deb's first, because hello, *news*. "Why didn't you tell me you're pregnant?"

Deb's eyes went wide and when her jaw dropped she popped a mini apple pie into it. "How did you know?"

"Lizzie told Holly, Holly told me."

"Lizzie—" Deb sighed and shook her head. "You think your kids don't notice what's going on. Boy, I'm going to have to get better at the secret thing."

"Why a secret?" Joy picked up a tiny brownie and told herself the calories didn't count since it was so small. Drawing it out into two bites, she waited.

"You know we lost one a couple of years ago," Deb said, keeping her voice low as there were customers in the main room, separated from them only by the swinging door between the kitchen and the store's front.

"Yeah." Joy reached out and gave her friend a sympathetic pat on the arm.

"Well, this time we didn't want to tell anyone until we're at least three months. You know?" She sighed again and gave a rueful smile. "But now that Lizzie's spreading the word…"

"Bag open, cat out," Joy said, grinning. "This is fabulous. I'm happy for you."

"Thanks. Me, too."

"Of course, now Holly wants a baby, too."

Deb gave her a sly look. "You could do something about that, you know."

"Right. Because I'm such a great single mom I should do it again."

"You are and it wouldn't kill you," Deb told her, "but I was thinking more along the lines of gorgeous hermit slash painter slash craftsman."

"Yeah, I don't think so." Of course, she immediately thought of that kiss and the tension that had been coiled in her middle all day. Briefly, her brain skipped to hazy images of her and Sam and Holly living in that big beautiful house together. With a couple more babies running around and a life filled with hot kisses, warm laughter and lots of love.

But fantasies weren't real life, and she'd learned long ago to concentrate on what was real. Otherwise, building dreams on boggy ground could crush your heart. Yes, she cared about Sam. But he'd made it clear he wasn't interested beyond stoking whatever blaze was burning between them. And yet, she thought, brain still racing, he was so good with Holly. And Joy's little girl was blossoming, having a man like Sam pay attention to her. Spend time with her.

Okay, her mind warned sternly, *dial it back now, Joy. No point in setting yourself up for that crush.*

"You say no, but your eyes are saying yum." Deb filled a tray with apple pies no bigger than silver dollars, laying them all out on paper doilies that made them look like loosely wrapped presents.

"Yum is easy—it's what comes after that's hard."

"Since when are you afraid of hard work?"

"I'm not, but—" Not the same thing, she told herself, as working to make a living, to build a life. This was bringing a man out of the shadows, and what if once he was out he didn't want her anyway? No, that way lay pain and misery, and why should she set herself up for that?

"You're alone, he's alone, match made in heaven."

"Alone isn't a good enough reason for anyone, Deb." She stopped, snatched another brownie and asked, "When did this get to be about me instead of you?"

"Since I hate seeing my best friend—a completely wonderful human being—all by herself."

"I'm not alone. I have Holly."

"And I love her, too, but it's not the same and you know it."

Slumping, Joy leaned one hip against the counter and nibbled at her second brownie. "No, it's not. And okay, fine—I'm...intrigued by Sam."

"Intrigued is good. Sex is better."

Sadly, she admitted, "I wouldn't know."

"Yeah, that would be my point."

"It's not that easy," Joy said wistfully. Then she glanced out the window at the house across the yard where Holly and Lizzie were probably driving Sean Casey insane about now. "I mean, he's—and I'm—"

"Something happened."

Her gaze snapped to Deb's. "Just a kiss."

"Yay. And?"

"And," Joy admitted, "then he got a little more involved and completely melted my underwear."

"Wow." Deb gave a sigh and fluttered one hand over her heart.

"Yeah. We were arguing and we were both furious

and he kissed me and—" she slapped her hands together "—boom."

"Oh, boom is good."

"It's great, but it doesn't solve anything."

"Honey," Deb asked with a shake of her head, "who cares?"

Joy laughed. Honestly, Deb was really good for her. "Okay, I'm heading back to the house. Even when it's this cold outside, I shouldn't be leaving the groceries in the car this long."

"Fine, but I'm going to want to hear more about this 'boom.'"

"Yeah," Joy said, "me, too. So are the girls still on for the sleepover?"

"Are you kidding? Lizzie's been planning this for days. Popcorn, princess movies and s'mores cooked over the fireplace."

Ordinarily, Holly would be too young for a sleepover, but Joy knew Deb was as crazy protective as she was. "Okay, then I'll bring her to your house Saturday afternoon."

"Don't forget to pray for me," Deb said with a smile. "Two five-year-olds for a night filled with squeals…"

"You bet."

"And take that box of brownies with you. Sweeten up your hermit and maybe there'll be more 'boom.'"

"I don't know about that, but I will definitely take the brownies." When she left the warm kitchen, she paused on the back porch and tipped her face up to the gray sky. As she stood there, snow drifted lazily down and kissed her heated cheeks with ice.

Maybe it would be enough to cool her off, she told herself, crossing the yard to Deb's house to collect Holly and head home. But even as she thought it, Joy realized that nothing was going to cool her off as long as her mind was filled with thoughts of Sam.

Eight

Once it started snowing, it just kept coming. As if an invisible hand had pulled a zipper on the gray, threatening clouds, they spilled down heavy white flakes for days. The woods looked magical, and every day, Holly insisted on checking the fairy houses—there were now two—to see if she could catch a glimpse of the tiny people living in them. Every day there was disappointment, but her faith never wavered.

Sam had to admire that even as his once-cold heart warmed with affection for the girl. She was getting to him every bit as much as her mother was. In different ways, of course, but the result was the same. He was opening up, and damned if it wasn't painful as all hell. Every time that ice around his heart cracked a little more, and with it came the pain that reminded him why the ice had been there in the first place.

He was on dangerous ground, and there didn't seem to be a way to back off. Coming out of the shadows could blind a man if he wasn't careful. And that was one thing Sam definitely was.

Once upon a time, things had been different. *He* had been different. He'd gone through life thinking nothing could go wrong. Though at the time, everywhere he turned, things went his way so he couldn't really be blamed for figuring it would always be like that.

His talent had pushed him higher in the art world than he'd ever believed possible, but it was his own ego that had convinced him to believe every accolade given. He'd thought of himself as blessed. As *chosen* for greatness. And looking back now, he could almost laugh at the deluded man he'd been.

Almost. Because when he'd finally had his ass handed to him, it had knocked the world out from under his feet. Feeling bulletproof only made recovering from a crash that much harder. And he couldn't even really say he'd recovered. He'd just marched on, getting by, getting through. What happened to his family wasn't something you ever got *over*. The most you could do was keep putting one foot in front of the other and hope that eventually you got somewhere.

Of course, he'd gotten *here*. To this mountain with the beautiful home he shared with a housekeeper he paid to be there. To solitude that sometimes felt like a noose around his neck. To cutting ties to his family because he couldn't bear their grief as well as his own.

He gulped down a swallow of hot coffee and relished the burn. He stared out the shop window at the relentless snow and listened to the otherworldly quiet that those millions of falling flakes brought. In the quiet, his mind turned to the last few days. To Joy. The tension between them was strung as tight as barbed wire and felt just as lethal. Every night at dinner, he sat at the table with her and her daughter and pretended his insides weren't churning. Every night, he avoided meeting up with Joy in the great room by locking himself in the shop to work on what was under that tarp. And finally, he lay awake in his bed wishing to hell she was lying next to him.

He was a man torn by too many things. Too twisted around on the road he'd been walking for so long to know which way to head next. So he stayed put. In the shop. Alone.

Across the yard the kitchen light sliced into the dimness of the gray morning when Holly jerked the door open and stepped outside. He watched her and wasn't disappointed by her shriek of excitement. The little girl turned back to the house, shouted something to her mother and waited, bouncing on her toes until Joy joined her at the door. Holly pointed across the yard toward the trees and, with a wide grin on her face, raced down the steps and across the snow-covered ground.

Her pink jacket and pink boots were like hope in the gray, and Sam smiled to himself, wondering when he'd fallen for the kid. When putting up with her had become caring for her. When he'd loosened up enough to make a tiny dream come true.

Sam was already outside when Holly raced toward him in a wild flurry of exhilaration. He smiled at the shine in her eyes, at the grin that lit up her little face like a sunbeam. Then she threw herself at him, hugging his legs, throwing her head back to look up at him.

"Sam! Sam! Did you see?" Her words tumbled over

each other in the rush to share her news. She grabbed his hand and tugged, her pink gloves warm against his fingers. "Come on! Come on! You have to see! They came! They came! I knew they would. I knew it and now they're here!"

Snow fell all around them, dusting Holly's jacket hood and swirling around Joy as she waited, her gaze fixed on his. And suddenly, all he could see were those blue eyes of hers, filled with emotion. A long, fraught moment passed between them before Holly's insistence shattered it. "Look, Sam. Look!"

She tugged him down on the ground beside her, then threw her arms around his neck and held on tight. Practically vibrating with excitement, Holly gave him a loud, smacking kiss on the cheek, then pulled back and looked at him with wonder in her eyes. "They came, Sam. They're living in our houses!"

Still reeling from that freely given hug and burst of affection, Sam stood up on unsteady legs. Smiling down at the little girl as she crawled around the front of the houses, peering into windows that shone with tiny Christmas lights, he felt another chunk of ice drop away from his heart. In the gray of the day, those bright specks of blue, green, red and yellow glittered like magic. Which was, he told himself, what Holly saw as she searched in vain to catch a glimpse of the fairies themselves.

He glanced at Joy again and she was smiling, a soft, knowing curve of her mouth that gleamed in her eyes, as well. There was something else in her gaze, too— beyond warmth, even beyond heat, and he wondered about it while Holly spun long, intricate stories about the fairies who lived in the tiny houses in the woods.

* * *

"You didn't have to do this," Joy said for the tenth time in a half hour.

"I'm gonna have popcorn with Lizzie and watch the princess movie," Holly called out from the backseat.

"Good for you," Sam said with a quick glance into the rearview mirror. Holly was looking out the side window, watching the snow and making her plans. He looked briefly to Joy. "How else were you going to get into town?"

"I could have called Deb, asked her or Sean to come and pick up Holly."

"Right, or we could do it the easy way and have me drive you both in." Sam kept his gaze on the road. The snow was falling, not really heavy yet, but determined. It was already piling up on the side of the road, and he didn't even want to think about Joy and Holly, alone in a car, maneuvering through the storm that would probably get worse. A few minutes later, he pulled up outside the Casey house and was completely stunned when, sprung from her car seat, Holly leaned over and kissed his cheek. "'Bye, Sam!"

It was the second time he'd been on the receiving end of a simple, cheerfully given slice of affection that day, and again, Sam was touched more deeply than he wanted to admit. Shaken, he watched Joy walk Holly to her friend's house and waited until she came back, alone, and slid into the car beside him.

"She hardly paused long enough to say goodbye to me." Joy laughed a little. "She's been excited by the sleepover for days, but now the fairy houses are the big story." She clicked her seat belt into place, then turned to face him. "She was telling Lizzie all about the lights in the woods and promising that you and she will make Lizzie a fairy house, too."

"Great," he said, shaking his head as he backed out of the driveway. He wasn't sure how he'd been sucked into the middle of Joy's and Holly's lives, but here he was, and he had to admit—though he didn't like to— that he was *enjoying* it. Honestly, it worried him a little just how much he enjoyed it.

He liked hearing them in his house. Liked Holly popping in and out of the workshop, sharing dinner with them at the big dining room table. He even actually liked building magical houses for invisible beings. "More fairies."

"It's your own fault," she said, reaching out to lay one hand on his arm. "What you did was—it meant a lot. To Holly. To *me*."

The warmth of her touch seeped down into his bones and quickly spread throughout his body. Something else he liked. That jolt of heat when Joy was near. The constant ache of need that seemed to always be with him these days. He hadn't wanted a woman like this in years. He swallowed hard against the demand clawing at him and turned for the center of town and the road back to the house.

"We're not in a hurry, are we?" she asked.

Sam stopped at a red light and looked at her warily. "Why?"

"Because, it's early, but we could stay in town for a while. Have dinner at the steak house…"

She gave him a smile designed to bring a man to his knees. And it was working.

"You want to go out to dinner?" he asked.

"Well," she said, shrugging. "It's early, but that won't kill us."

He frowned and threw a glance out the windshield at the swirls of white drifting down from a leaden sky. "Still snowing. We should get up the mountain while we still can."

She laughed and God, he loved the sound of it— even if it was directed at him and his lame attempt to get out of town.

"It's not a blizzard, Sam. An hour won't hurt either of us."

"Easy for you to say," Sam muttered darkly. "You *like* talking to people." The sound of her laughter filled the truck and eased his irritation as he headed toward the restaurant.

Everybody in town had to be in the steak house, and Joy thought it was a good thing. She knew a lot of people in Franklin and she made sure to introduce Sam to most of them. Sure, it didn't make for a relaxing dinner—she could actually *see* him tightening up— but it felt good to watch people greet him. To tell him how much they loved the woodworking he did. And the more uncomfortable he got with the praise, the more Joy relished it.

He'd been too long in his comfort zone of solitude. He'd made himself an island, and swimming to the mainland would be exhausting. But it would so be worth the trip.

"I've never owned anything as beautiful as that bowl you made," Elinor Cummings gushed, laying one hand on Sam's shoulder in benediction. She was in her fifties, with graying black hair that had been ruthlessly sprayed into submission.

"Thanks." He shot Joy a look that promised payback in the very near future. She wasn't worried. Like an injured animal, Sam would snarl and growl at anyone who came too close. But he wouldn't bite.

"I love what you did with the bowl. The rough outside, looks as though you just picked it up off the forest floor—" Elinor continued.

"I did," Sam said, clearly hoping to cut her off, but pasting a polite, if strained, smile on his face.

"—and the inside looks like a jewel," she continued, undeterred from lavishing him with praise. "All of those lovely colors in the grain of that wood, all so polished, and it just gleams in the light." She planted one hand against her chest and gave a sigh. "It's simply lovely. Two sides of life," she mused, "that's what it says to me, two sides, the hard and the good, the sad and the glad. It's lovely. Just lovely."

"All right now, Ellie," her husband said, with an understanding wink for Sam and Joy, "let's let the man eat. Good to meet you, Sam."

Sam nodded, then reached for the beer in front of him and took a long pull. The Cummingses had been just the last in a long stream of people who'd stopped by their table to greet Joy and meet Sam. Every damn one of them had given him a look that said *Ah, the hermit. That's what he looks like!*

And then had come the speculative glances, as they wondered whether Sam and Joy were a couple, and that irritated him, as well. This was what happened when you met people. They started poking their noses into your life and pretty soon, that life was open season to anyone with a sense of curiosity. As the last of the strangers went back to their own tables, he glared at Joy.

"You're enjoying this, aren't you?"

In the light of the candle at their table, her eyes sparkled as she grinned. "I could try to deny it, but why bother? Yes, I am. It's good to see you actually forced to talk to people. And Elinor clearly loves your work. Isn't it nice to hear compliments?"

"It's a bowl." He sighed. "Nothing deep or meaningful to the design. Just a bowl. People always want to analyze, interpret what the artist meant. Sometimes a bowl is just a bowl."

She laughed and shook her head. "You can't fool me. I've seen your stuff in Crafty. Nothing about what you make is 'just' anything. People love your work, and if you gave them half a chance, they'd like you, too."

"And I want that because…"

"Because it's better than being a recluse." Joy leaned forward, bracing her elbows on the table. "Honestly, Sam, you can't stay on the mountain by yourself forever."

He hated admitting even to himself that she was right. Hell, he'd talked more, listened more, in the last couple of weeks than he had in years. His house wasn't empty. Wasn't filled with the careful quiet he normally knew. Kaye generally left him to his own devices, so he was essentially alone, even when his housekeeper was there. Joy and Holly had pushed their way into the center of his life and had shown him just how barren it had been.

But when they left, his life would slide back onto its original course and the silence would seem even deeper. And God, he didn't like the thought of that.

* * *

Sam frowned. "Why are we really here?"

"To eat that amazing steak, for one," Joy said, sipping at her wine. Interesting, she thought, how his facial expressions gave hints to what he was thinking. And even more interesting how fast a smile from him could dissolve into the more familiar scowl. She'd have given a lot in that moment to know exactly what was running through his mind.

"And for another?"

"To show you how nice the people of Franklin are. To prove to you that you can meet people without turning into a pillar of salt..." She sat back, sipped at her wine again and kept her voice lighter than she felt. "Admit it. You had a good time."

"The steak was good," he said grudgingly, but she saw a flash of a smile that appeared and disappeared in a heartbeat.

"And the company."

His gaze fixed on hers. "You already know I like the company."

"I do," she said and felt a swirl of nerves flutter into life in the pit of her belly. Why was it this man who could make her feel things she'd never felt before? Life would have been so much easier if she'd found some nice, uncomplicated guy to fall for. But then she wouldn't be able to look into those golden-brown eyes of his, would she? "But you had a good time talking to other people, too. It just makes you uncomfortable hearing compliments."

"Think you know me, don't you?"

"Yep," she said, smiling at him in spite of the spark of irritation in his eyes. Just as Holly had once said, *he's not mean, he's just crabby.* He didn't fool her anymore. Even when he was angry, it didn't last. Even when she ambushed him with knowledge of his past, he didn't cling to the fury that had erupted inside him. Even when he didn't want to spend time with a child, he went out of his way to make her dreams come true.

Joy's heart ached with all she was feeling, and she wondered if he could see it in her eyes.

The room was crowded. The log walls were smoke-stained from years of exposure to the wood fireplace that even now boasted a roaring blaze. People sat at round tables and a few leather booths along one wall while the wall facing Main Street was floor-to-ceiling windows, displaying the winter scene unfolding outside. Tonight, the music pumping through the speakers overhead was classical, something weepy with strings and piano. And sitting across the table from her, looking like he'd rather be anywhere else but there, was the man who held her heart.

Stupid? Maybe. But there was no going back for Joy now. She'd been stumbling over him a little every day, of course. His kindness to Holly. His company in the dead of night when the house sat quiet around them. His kiss. The way his eyes flared with heat and more whenever he looked at her. His reluctant participation in the "family" dinners in the dining room. All of those things had been drawing her in, making her fall.

But today, she'd simply taken the final plunge.

He must have gone into town on his own and bought those silly little fairy lights. Then he'd sneaked out into the freezing cold late at night when he wouldn't be seen. And he'd decorated those tiny houses because her little girl had believed. He'd given Holly that. Magic.

Sam had sparked her imagination, protected her dreams and her fantasies. Joy had watched her baby girl throw herself into the arms of the man she trusted, loved, and through a sheen of tears had seen Sam hold Holly as tenderly as if she'd been made of glass. And in that one incredible moment, Joy told herself, he'd completely won her heart. Whether he wanted it or not was a different question.

She, Joy thought, was toast.

He could pretend to be aloof, crabby, disinterested all he wanted now, and she wouldn't believe it. He'd given her daughter a gift beyond price and she would always love him for that.

"What?" he asked, frowning a little harder. "What is it?"

She shook her head. "Nothing."

The frown came back instantly. "Makes a man nervous when a woman gets that thoughtful look in her eyes."

"Nervous is good, though I doubt," she said quietly, "that you ever have to worry about nerves."

"You might be surprised," he murmured, then said more firmly, "Let's go before the storm settles in and we're stuck down here."

Right then, Joy couldn't think of anywhere she'd rather be than back in that amazing house, alone with Sam. She looked him dead in the eye and said softly, "Good idea."

The ride up the mountain seemed to take forever, or maybe it was simply because Joy felt so on edge it was as if her skin was one size too tight. Every inch of her buzzed with anticipation because she knew what she wanted and knew she was done waiting. The tension between them had been building for days now, and tonight, she wanted to finally release it. To revel in being with a man she loved—even if she couldn't tell him how she felt.

At the house, they left the car in the garage and walked through the connecting door into the mudroom, where they hung their jackets on hooks before heading into the kitchen. Joy hit a switch on the wall, and the soft lights above the table blinked into life. Most of the room was still dark, and that was just as she wanted it. When she turned to Sam, she went up on her toes, cupped his face in her palms and kissed him, putting everything she was feeling into it.

Her heartbeat jumped into a frantic rhythm, her stomach swirled with excitement and the ache that had been building inside her for days began to pulse. It took only a second for Sam to react. To have his arms come around her. He lifted her off her feet, and she wrapped herself around him like a ribbon around a present.

As if he'd only been awaiting her signal, he took her with a desperation that told Joy he wanted her as much as she wanted him. She *felt* the hunger pumping off him in thick waves and gave herself up to it, letting it feed her own until a raging storm overtook them both. His mouth covered hers, his tongue demanding entry. She gave way and sighed in growing need as he groaned and kissed her harder, deeper.

His hands, those talented, strong hands, dropped to her bottom. He turned her around so fast her stomach did a wild spin, then he slammed her up against the back door. Joy hardly felt it. She'd never experienced anything like what swept over her in those few frantic moments. Every inch of her body was alive with sensations. Her skin was buzzing, her blood boiling, and her mind was a tangled, hazy mass of thoughts that pretty much went, *yes, harder, now, be inside me.*

Her fingers scraped through his hair, held his head to hers. Every breath came strangled, harsh, and she didn't care. All she wanted, all she needed, was the taste of him filling her. The feel of his hands holding her. Then, when she became light-headed, she thought, okay, maybe air, too.

She broke the kiss, letting her head drop back as she gasped for breath. Staring up at the dimly lit ceiling, she concentrated solely on the feel of Sam's mouth at her throat, latching on to the pulse point at the base of her neck. He tasted, he nibbled, he licked, and she sighed heavily.

"Oh, boy. That feels really..." She gasped again. *"Good."*

With his mouth against her throat, he smiled. "You taste good, too."

"Thanks." She chuckled and the sound bubbled up into the room. "Always good to hear."

"I've wanted my hands on you for days." He lifted his head and waited for her to look at him. His eyes were alight with a fire that seemed to be sweeping both of them along in an inferno. "I tried to keep my distance, but it's been killing me."

"Me, too," she said, holding him a little tighter. "I've been dreaming about you."

One corner of his mouth lifted. "Yeah? Well, time to wake up." He let her slide down the length of his body until she was on her feet again. "Let's go."

"Where?"

"Upstairs, where the beds are." He started pulling

her. "After waiting this long, we're not doing this on the kitchen floor."

Right about then, Joy thought, the floor looked pretty good. Or the granite island. Or just the stupid wall she'd been up against a second ago. Especially since her knees felt like rubber and she wasn't sure she'd make it all the way up those stairs. Then she realized they didn't have to.

"Yeah, but my bed's quicker." She gave a tug, too, then grinned when he looked at her in admiration.

"Good thinking. I do like a smart woman." He scooped her up again, this time cradling her in his arms, and headed for Kaye's suite.

"Well, I always wanted to be swept off my feet." Really, her poor, foolish heart was stuttering at being carried off to bed. The romance of it tugged at everything inside her. He stepped into the darkened suite, and she hit the light switch for the living area as she passed it.

Instantly, the tiny, misshapen Christmas tree burst into electric life. Softly glowing lights burned steadily all around the room, but it was the silly tree that had center stage.

"What the—" He stopped, his grip on her tightening, and let his gaze sweep around the room. So Joy looked, too, admiring all she and Holly had done to their temporary home. Sam hadn't wanted the holidays leaking out into the main house, so they'd gone overboard here, in their corner of it. Christmas lights lined the doorways and were draped across the walls like garland. The tiny tree stood on a table and was practically bowed under the weight of the ornaments, popped corn and strings of lights adorning it.

After a long minute or two, he shook his head. "That tree is sad."

"It is not," she argued, spearing it with a critical eye. "It's loved." She looked past the tree in the window to the night outside and the fairy lights just visible through the swirls of snow, and her heart dissolved all over again. Cupping his cheek in her palm, she turned his face to hers. "You lit up Holly's world today with those strings of lights."

He scowled but there wasn't much punch to it. "I hated seeing her check for signs every day and not getting any. But she never stopped believing."

Her heart actually filled up and spilled over into her chest. How could she *not* love a man who'd given life to her baby's imagination?

"I put 'em on a timer," Sam said, "so they'll go off and on at different times and Holly will have something to watch for."

Shaking her head, she looked into his eyes and whispered, "I don't have the words for what I'm feeling right now."

"Then we're lucky. No words required."

He kissed her again and Joy surrendered to the fire. She forgot about everything else but the taste of him, the feel of him. She wanted to stroke her hands all over his leanly muscled body, feel the warm slide of flesh to flesh. Lifting her face, she nibbled at his throat and smiled when she heard him groan tightly.

She hardly noticed when he carried her through the main room and dropped her onto her bed. *Wild*, was all she could think. Wild for him, for his touch, for his taste. She'd been alone for so long, having this man, *the* man with her, was almost more than she could stand.

He felt the same, because in a few short seconds, they were both naked, clothes flying around the room as they tore at them until there was nothing separating them. The quilt on the bed felt cool beneath her, but he was there, sliding on top of her, to bring the heat.

"Been wanting to peel you out of those sweaters you wear for days now," he murmured, trailing kisses up from her belly to just below her breasts.

"Been wanting you to do it," she assured him and ran the flat of her hands over his shoulders in long, sensuous strokes.

His hands moved over her, following every line, every curve. She gasped when he dipped his head to take first one hard nipple then the other into his mouth. Damp heat fractured something inside her as his teeth, tongue, lips teased at her sensitive skin. She was writhing mindlessly, chasing the need, when he dipped one hand to her center and cupped her heat completely.

Joy's mind simply splintered from the myriad sensations slamming into her system all at once. She hadn't felt this way in…ever. He shifted, kissing her mouth, tangling his tongue with hers as those oh-so-talented fingers dipped inside her heat. She lifted her hips into his touch and held his head to hers as they kissed, as they took and gave and then did it all again. Their breath mingled, their hearts pounded in a wild tandem that raced faster and faster as they tasted, explored, discovered.

It was like being caught in a hurricane. There was no safe place to hide, even if she'd wanted to. And she didn't. She wanted the storm, more than she'd ever wanted anything in her life. Demand, need, hands reaching, mouths seeking. Hushed words flew back and forth between them, whispers, breathless sighs. Heat ratcheted up in the tiny bedroom as outside, the snow fell, draping the world in icy white.

Sam's hand at her core drove her higher, faster. A small ripple of release caught her and had Joy calling his name as she shivered, shuddered in response. But she'd barely recovered from that tiny explosion before he pushed her again. His fingers danced over her body, inside and out, caressing, stroking until she thought she'd lose what was left of her mind if he didn't get inside her. Now.

Whimpering, Joy didn't care. All she could think of was the release she wanted more than her next breath. "Be inside me," she told him, voice breaking on every word as air struggled in and out of her lungs.

"Now," he agreed in a strained whisper.

Shadows filled the room, light from the snow, reflections of the lights in the living area. He took her mouth again in a frenzied kiss that stole her breath and gave her his. She arched into him as he moved over her, parting her thighs and sliding into her with one long thrust.

Joy gasped, her head tipping back into the pillow, her hips lifting to welcome him, to take him deeper. His hands held her hips, his fingers digging into her skin as he drove into her again and again. She locked her legs around his hips, pulling him tighter to her, rocking with him, following the frenzied rhythm he set.

The storm claimed them. Hunger roared up into the room and overtook them both. There was nothing in the world but that need and the race to completion. Their bodies moved together, skin to skin, breath to breath. They raced to the edge of the cliff together, and together they took the leap, locked in each other's arms.

* * *

"I think I'm blind."

Sam pushed off her and rolled to one side. "Open your eyes."

"Oh. Right." She looked at him and Sam felt the solid punch of her gaze slam into him. His body was still humming, his blood still pounding in his ears. He'd just had the most intense experience of his life and he wanted her again. Now.

He stroked one hand down her body, following the curve of breast to belly to hip. She shivered and he smiled. He couldn't touch her enough. The feel of her was addictive. How could his craving for her be as sharp now as it had been before? He should be relaxed. Instead, he felt more fired up. The need building inside him was sharper now because he *knew* what he'd been missing. Knew what it was to be inside her, to feel her wrapped around him, holding him tight. To look into her eyes and watch passion burst like fireworks on the Fourth.

It felt as if cold, iron bands were tightening around his chest. Danger. He knew it. He knew that feeling anything for Joy was a one-way trip to disaster, pain and misery. Yet it seemed that he didn't have any choice about that.

"Well." She blew out a breath and gave him a smile that had his body going rock hard again. "That was amazing. But I'm suddenly so thirsty I could drink a gallon of water."

"I'll get some," he told her, "as soon as I'm sure my legs will hold me."

"Isn't that a nice thing to say? There's no hurry," she said, turning into him, snuggling close. She buried her face in the curve of his neck and gave a sigh. "Here's good."

"Here's great." He rolled onto his back, pulling her over with him until she lay sprawled across his chest. Her blond curls tumbled around her face and her eyes sparkled in the dim light. "You caught me by surprise with that kiss."

She folded her arms on his chest and grinned down at him. "Well, then, you have an excellent reaction time."

"Not complaining." He hadn't been prepared for that kiss, and it had pushed him right over the edge of the control he'd been clinging to for days. Wincing a little, he thought he should have taken his time with her. To slowly drive them both to the breaking point. Instead, he'd been hit by an unstoppable force and hadn't been able to withstand it. They'd rushed together so quickly he hadn't—Sam went completely still as reality came crashing down on him, obliterating the buzz of satisfaction as if it had never been.

"What is it? Sam?"

He looked up into her eyes and called himself every kind of name he could think of. How could he have been so stupid? So careless? It was too late now, he told himself grimly. Too late to do anything but worry. "Joy, the downside to things happening by surprise is you're not prepared for it."

She smiled. "I'd say you were plenty prepared."

He rolled again, flopping her over onto the mattress and leaning over her, staring her in the eyes. "I'm trying to tell you that I hope to hell you're on birth control because I wasn't suited up."

Nine

Sam watched her as, for a second or two, she just stared at him as if she were trying to make sense of a foreign language. And since he was staring into those clear blue eyes of hers, he *saw* the shift of emotions when what he'd said finally sunk in.

And even then, the uppermost thought in his mind was her scent and how it clung to her skin and seeped into his bones. Every breath he drew pulled her inside him, until summer flowers filled every corner of his heart, his soul.

What the hell was wrong with him? *Focus.* He'd led them both into a risky situation, and he had to keep his mind on what could, potentially, be facing them. It had been a long time since he'd been with anyone, sure. But it was Joy herself who had blown all thought, all reason, right out of his head with that one surprise kiss in the kitchen. After that, all he'd been able to think about was getting her naked. To finally have her under him, over him. He'd lost control for the first time in his life, and even though the consequences could be steep, he couldn't really regret any of it.

"Oh. Well." Joy lifted one hand and pushed his hair back from his face. Her touch sent a fresh new jolt of need blasting through him, and he had to grit his teeth in the effort to hold on to what was left of the tattered threads of his control.

"Are you," he asked, voice tight, "on birth control?"

"No."

One word. One simple word that hit the pit of his stomach like a ball of ice. "Okay. Look. This is my fault, Joy. I shouldn't have…"

"Fault? If you're looking to place blame here, you're on your own," she said, sliding her fingers through his hair. "This isn't on you alone, so don't look like you're about to be blindfolded and stood up against a wall in front of a firing squad."

He frowned and wondered when he'd become so easy to read.

"You weren't alone in this room, Sam," she said. "This is on me as much as you. We got…carried away—"

He snorted. "Yeah, you could say that."

"—and we didn't think. We weren't prepared," she finished as if he hadn't interrupted her.

He laughed shortly but there was no humor behind it. This had to be the damnedest after-sex conversation he'd ever had. He should have known that Joy wouldn't react as he would have expected her to. No recriminations, no gnashing of teeth, just simple acceptance for what couldn't be changed.

Still. "That's the thing," he said with a shake of his

head. "I thought I was. Prepared, I mean. When I went into town to get those damn fairy lights, I also bought condoms."

She drew her head back and grinned down at him. "You're kidding. Really?"

"Yes, really. They're upstairs. In my room."

She laughed and shook her head. "That's perfect. Well, in your defense, you did try to get me upstairs…"

"True." But they probably wouldn't have made it, as hot as they'd both been. Most likely, they'd have stopped and had at each other right there on the stairs anyway.

"And I love that you bought condoms," she said, planting a soft kiss on his mouth. "I love that you wanted me as much as I wanted you."

"No question about that," he admitted, though the rest of this situation was settling in like rain clouds over an outdoor party.

"But you realize that now everyone in Franklin knows you bought them."

"What?"

"Oh, yes," she said, nodding sagely. "By now, word has spread all over town and everyone is speculating about just what's going on up here."

"Perfect." Small-town life, he told himself, knowing she was right. He hadn't thought about it. Hadn't considered that by buying condoms at the local pharmacy he was also feeding fuel to the gossip. It had been so long since he'd been part of a community that he hadn't given it a thought, but now he remembered the speculative gleam in the cashier's eye. The smile on the face of the customer behind him in line. "Damn."

"We're the talk of the town," Joy assured him, still smiling. "I've always wanted to be gossiped about."

All of that aside for the moment, Sam couldn't understand how she could be so damned amused by any of this. All he could feel was the bright flash of panic hovering on the edges of his mind. By being careless, he might have created a child. He'd lost a child already. Lost his son. How could he make another and not have his heart ripped out of his chest?

"Forget what people are saying, Joy," he said, and his tone, if nothing else, erased her smile. "Look, whatever happens—"

"You can get that unnerved look off your face," she said softly. "I'm a big girl, Sam. I can take care of myself. You don't owe me anything, and I don't need you to worry about me or what might happen."

"I'll decide what I owe, Joy," he told her. It didn't matter what she said, Sam told himself. He would worry anyway. He laid one hand on her belly and let it lay there, imagining what might already be happening deep within her.

"Sam." She cupped his face in her hands and waited until he looked into her eyes. "Stop thinking. Can we just enjoy what we shared? Leave it at that?"

His heartbeat thundered in his chest. Just her touch was enough to push him into forgetting everything but her. Everything but this moment. He wanted her even more than he had before and didn't know how that was possible. She was staring up at him with those wide blue eyes of hers, and Sam thought he could lose himself in those depths. Maybe she was right. At least for now, for this moment, maybe it was better if they stopped thinking, worrying, wondering. Because these moments were all they had. All they would ever have.

He wasn't going to risk loss again. He wouldn't put

his soul up as a hostage to fate, by falling in love, having another family that the gods could snatch from him. A future for them was out of the question. But they had tonight, didn't they?

"Come with me," he said, rolling off the bed and taking her hand to pull her up with him.

"What? Why? Where?"

"My room. Where the condoms live." He kept pulling her after him and she half ran to keep up. "We can stop and get water—or wine—on the way up."

"Wine. Condoms." She tugged him to a stop, then plastered herself against him until he felt every single inch of her body pressed along his. Then she stepped back. "Now, that kind of thinking is a good thing. I like your plan. Just let me get my robe."

Amazing woman. She could be wild and uninhibited in bed but quailed about walking naked through an empty house.

"You don't need a robe. We're the only ones here. There are no neighbors for five miles in any direction, so no one can look in the windows."

"It's cold so I still want it," she said, lifting one hand to cup his cheek.

For a second, everything stopped for Sam. He just stared at her. In the soft light, her skin looked like fine porcelain. Her hair was a tumbled mass of gold and her eyes were as clear and blue as the lake. Her seductively sly smile curved a mouth that was made to be kissed. If he were still an artist, Sam thought, he'd want to paint her like this. Just as she was now.

That knowing half smile on her face, one arm lifted toward him, with the soft glow of Christmas lights behind her. She looked, he thought, like a pagan goddess, a woman born to be touched, adored, and that's how he would paint her. If he still painted, which he didn't. And why didn't he?

Because he'd lost the woman he'd once loved. A woman who had looked at him as Joy did now. A woman who had given him a son and then taken him with her when she left.

Pain grabbed his heart and squeezed.

Instantly, she reacted. "Sam? What is it?"

"I want you," he said, moving in on her, backing her into the wall, looking down into her eyes.

"I know, I feel the same way."

He nodded, swallowed hard, then forced the words out because they had to be said. Even if she pulled away from him right now, they had to be said. "But if you're thinking there's a future here for us, don't. I'm not that guy. Not anymore."

"Sam—" Her hands slid up and down his arms, and he was grateful for the heat she kindled inside him. "I didn't ask you for anything."

"I don't want to hurt you, Joy." Yet he knew he would. She was the kind of woman who would spin dreams for herself, her daughter. She would think about futures. As a mother, she had to. As a former father, he couldn't. Not again. Just the thought of it sharpened the pain in his heart. If he was smart, he'd end this with Joy right now.

But apparently, he had no sense at all.

She gave him another smile and went up on her toes to kiss him gently. "I told you. You don't have to worry about me, Sam. I know what I'm doing."

He wished that were true. But there would be time

enough later for regrets, for second-guessing decisions made in the night. For now, there was Joy.

A few days later, Joy was upstairs, looking out Sam's bedroom window at the workshop below. Holly was out there with Sam right now, probably working on more fairy houses. Since the first two were now filled with fairy families, Holly was determined to put up a housing development at the foot of the woods.

Her smile was wistful as she turned away and looked at the big bed with the forest green comforter and mountain of pillows. She hadn't been with Sam up here since that first night. He came to her now, in Kaye's room, where they made love with quiet sighs and soft whispers so they wouldn't wake Holly in the next room. And after hours wrapped together, Sam left her bed early in the morning so the little girl wouldn't guess what was happening.

It felt secret and sad and wonderful all at the same time. Joy was in love and couldn't tell him because she knew he didn't want to hear it. She might be pregnant and knew he wouldn't want to hear that, either. Every morning when he left her, she felt him go just a bit further away. And one day soon, she knew, he wouldn't come back. He was distancing himself from her, holding back emotionally so that when she left at the end of the month he wouldn't miss her.

Why couldn't he see that he didn't *have* to miss her? It was almost impossible to believe she'd known Sam for less than three weeks. He was so embedded in her heart, in her life, she felt as if she'd known him forever. As if they'd been meant to meet, to find each other. To be together. If only Sam could see that as clearly as Joy did.

The house phone rang and she answered without looking at the caller ID. "Henry residence."

"Joy? Oh, it's so nice to finally talk to you!" A female voice, happy.

"Thanks," she said, carrying the phone back to the window so she could look outside. "Who is this?"

"God, how stupid of me," the woman said with a delighted laugh. "I'm Catherine Henry, Sam's mother."

Whoa. A wave of embarrassment swept over her. Joy was standing in Sam's bedroom, beside the bed where they'd had sex, and talking to his mother. Could this be any more awkward? "Hello. Um, Sam's out in the workshop."

"Oh, I know," she said and Joy could almost see her waving one hand to dismiss that information. "I just talked to him and your adorable daughter, Holly."

"You did?" Confused, she stared down at the workshop and watched as Sam and Holly walked out through the snow covering the ground. Sam was carrying the latest fairy house and Holly, no surprise, was chattering a mile a minute. Joy's heart ached with pleasure and sorrow.

"Holly tells me that she and Sam are making houses for fairies and that my son isn't as crabby as he used to be."

"Oh, for—" Joy closed her eyes briefly. "I'm so sorry—"

"Don't be silly. He *is* crabby," Catherine told her. "But he certainly seemed less so around your little girl."

"He's wonderful with her."

There was a pause and then a sniffle as if the woman was fighting tears. "I'm so glad. I've hoped for a long time to see my son wake up again. Find happiness again. It sounds to me like he is."

"Oh," Joy spoke up quickly, shaking her head as if Sam's mother could see her denial, "Mrs. Henry—"

"Catherine."

"Fine. Catherine, please don't make more of this than there is. Sam doesn't want—"

"Maybe not," she interrupted. "But he needs. So much. He's a good man, Joy. He's just been lost."

"I know," Joy answered on a sigh, resting her hand on the ice-cold windowpane as she watched the man she loved and her daughter kneeling together in the snow. "But what if he doesn't want to be found?"

Another long pause and Catherine said, "Kaye's told me so much about you, Joy. She thinks very highly of you, and just speaking to your daughter tells me that you're a wonderful mother."

"I hope so," she said, her gaze fixed on Sam.

"Look, I don't know how you feel, but if you don't mind my saying, I can hear a lot in your voice when you speak of Sam."

"Catherine—" If she couldn't tell Sam how she felt she certainly couldn't tell his *mother*.

"You don't have to say anything, dear. Just please. Do me a favor and don't give up on him."

"I don't want to." Joy could admit that much. "I... care about him."

"I'm so glad." The next pause was a short one. "After the holidays I'm going to come and visit Sam. I hope we can meet then."

"I'd like that," Joy said and meant it. She just hoped that she would still be seeing Sam by then.

When the phone call ended a moment later, she hung

up the phone and walked back to the window to watch the two people in the world she loved most.

"Will more fairies move in and put up some more lights like the other ones did?" Holly asked, kneeling in the snow to peek through the windows of the tiny houses.

"We'll have to wait and see, I guess," Sam told her, setting the new house down on a flat rock slightly above the others.

"I bet they do because now they have friends here and—"

Sam smiled to himself as the little girl took off on another long, rambling monologue. He was going to miss spending time with Holly. As much as he'd fought against it in the beginning, the little girl had wormed her way into his heart—just like her mother had. In his own defense, Sam figured there weren't many people who could have ignored a five-year-old with as much charm as this one. Even the cold didn't diminish her energy level. If anything, he thought, it pumped her up. Her little cheeks were rosy, her eyes, so much like her mother's, sparkled.

"Do fairies have Christmas trees?"

"What?"

"Like Mommy and me got a tiny little tree because you don't like Christmas, but maybe if you had a great big tree you'd like Christmas more, Sam."

He slid a glance at her. He'd caught on to Holly's maneuvers. She was giving him that sly smile that he guessed females were born knowing how to deliver.

"You want a big Christmas tree," he said.

"I like our little one, but I like big ones, too, and

we could make it really pretty with candy canes and we could make popcorn and put it on, too, and I think you'd like it."

"I probably would," he admitted. Hell, just because he was against Christmas didn't mean a five-year-old had to put up with a sad little tree tucked away in her room. "Why don't you go get your mom and we'll cut down a tree."

Her eyes went wide. "Cut it down ourselves? In the woods?"

"You bet. You can help." As long as he had his hands over hers on the hatchet, showing her how to do it without risking her safety. Around them, the pines rustled in the wind and sounded like sighs. The sky was heavy and gray and looked ready to spill another foot or two of snow any minute. "You can pick out the tree—as long as it's not a giant," he added with a smile.

She studied him thoughtfully for so long, he had to wonder what she was thinking. Nothing could have prepared him, though, for what she finally said. "You're a good daddy."

He sat back on his heels to look at her, stunned into silence. Snow was seeping into the legs of his jeans, but he paid no attention. "What?"

"You're a good daddy," she said again and moved up to lay one hand on his cheek. "You help me with stuff and you show me things and I know you used to have a little boy but he had to go to heaven with his mommy and that's what makes you crabby."

Air caught in his chest. Couldn't exhale or inhale. All he could do was watch the child watching him.

How did she know about Eli? Had her mother told her? Or had she simply overheard other adults talking about him? Kids, he knew, picked up on more than the grown-ups around them ever noticed. As Holly watched him, she looked so serious. So solemn, his heart broke a little.

"But if you want," she went on, her perpetually high-pitched, fast-paced voice softening, "I could be your little girl and you could be *my* daddy and then you wouldn't be crabby or lonely anymore."

His heart stopped. He felt it take one hard beat and then clutch. Her eyes were filled with a mixture of sadness and hope, and that steady gaze scorched him. This little girl was offering all the love a five-year-old held and hoping he'd take it. But how could he? How could he love a child again and risk losing that child? But wasn't he going to lose her anyway? Because of his own fears and the nightmares that had never really left him?

Sam had been so careful, for years, to stay isolated, to protect his heart, to keep his distance from the world at large. And now there was a tiny girl who had pierced through his defenses, showing him just how vulnerable he really was.

She was still looking at him, still waiting, trusting that he would want her. Love her.

He did. He already loved her, and that wasn't something he could admit. Not to himself. Not to the child who needed him. Sam had never thought of himself as a coward, but damned if he didn't feel like one now. How could he give her what she needed when the very thought of loving and losing could bring him to his knees?

He stood up, grabbed her and pulled her in for a tight hug, and her little arms went around his neck and clung as if her life depended on it. There at the edge of the woods with fairy magic shining in the gray, he was humbled by a little girl, shattered by the love freely offered.

"Do you want to be my daddy, Sam?" she whispered.

How to get out of this without hurting her? Without ripping his own heart out of his chest? Setting her down again, he crouched in front of her and met those serious blue eyes. "I'm proud you would ask me, Holly," he said, knowing just how special that request had been. "But this is pretty important, so I think you should talk to your mom about this first, okay?"

Not a no, not a yes. He didn't want to hurt her, but he couldn't give her what she wanted, either. Joy knew her daughter best. She would know how to let her down without crushing that very tender heart. And Joy knew—because he'd told her—that there was no future for them. What surprised him, though, was how much he wished things were different—that he could have told that little girl he would be her daddy and take care of her and love her. But he couldn't do it. Wouldn't do it.

"Okay, Sam." Holly grinned and her eyes lit up. "I'll go ask her right now, okay? And then we can show her the new fairy house and then we can get our big tree and maybe have hot chocolate and—" She took off at a dead run, still talking, still planning.

He turned to look at the house and saw Joy in the bedroom window, watching them. Would he always see her there, he wondered? Would he walk through his empty house and catch the faint scent of summer flowers? Would he sit in the great room at night and wait for her to come in and sit beside him? Smile at him? Would he spend the rest of his life reaching across the bed for her?

A few weeks ago, his life was insular, quiet, filled with the shadows of memories and the ghosts he carried with him everywhere. Now there would be *more* ghosts. The only difference being, he would have *chosen* to lose Joy and Holly.

That thought settled in, and he didn't like it. Still looking up at Joy, Sam asked himself if maybe he was wrong to pass up this opportunity. Maybe it was time to step out of the shadows. To take a chance. To risk it all.

A scream ripped his thoughts apart and in an instant, everything changed. Again.

Five stitches, three hot chocolates and one Christmas tree later, they were in the great room, watching the lights on the big pine in the front window shine. They'd used the strings of lights Joy had hung on the walls in their room, and now the beautiful pine was dazzling. There were popcorn chains and candy canes they'd bought in town as decorations. And there was an exhausted but happy little girl, asleep on the couch, a smile still curving her lips.

Joy brushed Holly's hair back from her forehead and kissed the neat row of stitches. It had been a harrowing, scary ride down the mountain to the clinic in town. But Sam had been a rock. Steady, confident, he'd already had Holly in his arms heading for his truck by the time Joy had come downstairs at a dead run.

Hearing her baby scream, watching her fall and then seeing the bright splotch of blood on the snow had shaken Joy right down to the bone. But Holly was crying and reaching for her, so she swallowed her own fear to try to ease Holly's. The girl had hit her head on a rock under the snow when she fell. A freak accident, but seeing the neat row of stitches reminded Joy how fragile her child was. How easily hurt. Physically. Emotionally.

Sam stood by the tree. "You want me to carry her to bed?"

"Sure. Thanks."

He nodded and stalked across the room as if every step was vibrating with repressed energy. But when he scooped Holly into his arms, he was gentle. Careful. She followed after him and neither of them spoke again until Holly was tucked in with her favorite stuffed dog and they were safely out in the great room again.

Sam walked to the fireplace, stared down into the flames as if looking for answers to questions he hadn't asked, and shoved both hands into his pockets. Joy walked over to join him, hooked her arm through his and wasn't really surprised when he moved away. Hurt, yes. But not surprised.

She'd known this was coming. Maybe Holly being hurt had sped up the process, but Joy had been expecting him to pull away. To push her aside. He had been honest from the beginning, telling her that they had no future. That he didn't want forever because, she knew, he didn't trust in promises.

He cared for her. He cared for Holly, but she knew he didn't want to and wouldn't want to hear how much she loved him, so she kept it to herself. Private pain she could live with. She didn't think she could bear him throwing her love back in her face and dismissing it.

"Sam…"

"Scared me," he admitted in a voice so low she almost missed the words beneath the hiss and snap of the fire.

"I know," Joy said softly. "Me, too. But Holly's fine, Sam. The doctor said she wouldn't even have a scar."

"Yeah, and I'm glad of that." He shook his head and looked at her, firelight and shadow dancing over his features, glittering in his eyes. "But I can't do this again, Joy."

"Do what?" Heart aching, she took a step toward him, then stopped when he took one back.

"You know damn well what," he ground out. Then he took a deep breath and blew it out. "The thing is, just before Holly got hurt, I was thinking that maybe I could. Maybe it was time to try again." He looked at her. "With you."

Hope rose inside her and then crashed again when he continued.

"Then that little girl screamed, and I knew I was kidding myself." Shaking his head slowly, he took another deep breath. "I lost my family once, Joy. I won't risk that kind of pain again. You and Holly have to go."

"If we go," she reminded him, "you *still* lose us."

He just stared at her. He didn't have an answer to that, and they both knew it.

"Yeah, I know. But you'll be safe out there and I won't have to wonder and worry every time you leave the damn house."

"So you'll never think of us," she mused aloud. "Never wonder what we're doing, if we're safe, if we're happy."

"I didn't say that," he pointed out. "But I can block that out."

"Yeah, you're good at blocking out."

"It's a gift." The smile that touched his mouth was wry, unhappy and gone in an instant.

"So just like that?" she asked, her voice low, throbbing with banked emotions that were nearly choking her. "We leave and what? You go back to being alone in this spectacular cage?" She lifted both hands to encompass the lovely room and said, "Because no matter how beautiful it is, it's still a *cage*, Sam."

"And it's my business." His voice was clipped, cold, as if he'd already detached from the situation. From *her*.

Well, she wasn't going to make it that easy on him.

"It's not just your business, Sam. It's mine. It's Holly's. She told me she asked you to be her daddy. Did that mean nothing to you?"

"It meant *everything*," he said, his voice a growl of pain and anger. "It's not easy to turn away from you. From her."

"Then don't do it."

"I have to."

Fury churned in the pit of her stomach and slid together with a layer of misery that made Joy feel sick to her soul. "How could I be in love with a man so stubborn he refuses to see what's right in front of him?"

He jolted. "Who said anything about love?"

"I did," she snapped. She wasn't going to walk away from him never saying how she felt. If he was going to throw her away like Mike had, like every foster parent she'd ever known had, then he would do it knowing the full truth. "I love you."

"Well," he advised, "*stop*."

She choked out a laugh that actually scraped at her throat. Amazing. As hurt as she was, she could still be amused by the idiot man who was willing to toss aside what most people never found. "Great. Good idea. I'll get right on that."

He grabbed her upper arms and drew her up until

they were eye to eye. "Damn it, Joy, I told you up front that I'm not that guy. That there was no future for us."

"Yes, I guess I'm a lousy listener." She pulled away from him, cleared her throat and blinked back a sheen of tears because she *refused* to cry in front of him. "It must be your immense load of charm that dragged me in. That warm, welcoming smile."

He scowled at her.

"No, it was the way that you grudgingly bent to having us here. It was your gentleness with Holly, your sense of humor, your kiss, your touch, the way you look at me sometimes as if you don't know quite what to do with me." She smiled sadly. "I fell in love and there's no way out for me now. You're it, Sam."

He scrubbed one hand across his face as if he could wipe away her words, her feelings.

"You don't have to love me, Sam." That about killed her to say, but it was truth.

"I didn't want to hurt you, Joy."

"I believe you. But when you *care*, you hurt. That's life. But if you don't love me, try to love someone else." Oh God, the thought of that tore what was left of her heart into tiny, confetti-sized pieces. "But stop hiding out here in this palace of shadows and live your life."

"I like my life."

"No you don't," she countered, voice thick with those unshed tears. "Because you don't have one. What you have is sacrifice."

He pushed both hands through his hair then let them fall to his sides. "What the hell are you talking about?"

She took a breath, steadying herself, lowering her voice, *willing* him to hear her. "You've locked yourself away, Sam. All to punish yourself for surviving. What happened to your family was terrible, I can't even imagine the pain you lived through. But you're still alive, Sam. Staying closed down and shut off won't alter what happened. It won't bring them back."

His features went tight, cold, his eyes shuttered as they had been so often when she first met him.

"You think I don't know that?" He paced off a few steps, then whirled around and came right back. His eyes glittered with banked fury and pain. "Nothing will bring them back. Nothing can change why they died, either."

"What?" Confused, worried, she waited.

"You know why I had to drive you into town for Holly's sleepover?"

"Of course I do." She shook her head, frowning. "My car wouldn't start."

"Because I took the damn distributor cap off."

That made no sense at all. "What? Why?"

Now he scrubbed his hands over his face and gave a bitter sigh. "Because, I couldn't let you drive down the mountain in the snow."

"Sam…"

Firelight danced around the room but looked haunting as it shadowed his face, highlighting the grief carved into his features, like a mask in stone. As she watched him, she saw his eyes blur, focus on images in his mind rather than the woman who stood just opposite him.

"I was caught up in a painting," he said. "It was a commission. A big one and I wanted to keep at it while I was on a roll." He turned from her, set both hands on the fireplace mantel and stared down into the crackling flames. "There was a family reunion that weekend and Dani was furious that I didn't want to go. So I told her to take Eli and go ahead. That I'd meet her at the re-union as soon as I was finished." He swiveled his head to look at Joy. "She was on the interstate and a front tire blew. Dani lost control of the car and slammed into an oncoming semi. Both she and Eli died instantly."

Joy's heart ripped open, and the pain she felt for him nearly brought her to her knees. But she kept quiet, wanting him to finish and knowing he needed to get it all said.

"If I'd been driving it might have been different, but I'll never know, will I?" He pushed away from the mantel and glared at her, daring her to argue with him. "I chose my work over my family and I lost them. You once asked me why I don't paint anymore, and there's your reason. I chose my work over what should have been more important. So I don't paint. I don't go out. I don't—"

"Live," she finished for him. "You don't *live*, Sam. Do you really think that's what Dani would want for you? To spend the next fifty years locked away from everything and everyone? Is that how she wanted to live?"

"Of course not," he snapped.

"Then what's the point of the self-flagellation?" Joy demanded, walking toward him, ignoring the instinctive step back he took. "If you'd been in that car, you might have died, too."

"You don't know that."

"You don't, either. That's the point."

Outside, the wind moaned as it slid beneath the eaves. But tonight, it sounded louder, like a desperate keening, as if even the house was weeping for what was ending.

Trying again, Joy said, "My little girl loves you. I love you. Can you really let that go so easily?"

His gaze snapped to hers. "I told you that earlier today, I actually thought that maybe I could risk it. Maybe there was a chance. And then Holly was hurt and my heart stopped."

"Kids get hurt, Sam," she said, still trying, though she could see in his eyes that the fight was over. His decision was made whether she agreed or not. "We lose people we shouldn't. But life keeps going. *We* keep going. The world doesn't stop, Sam, and it shouldn't."

"Maybe not," he said softly. "But it's going to keep going without me."

Ten

Joy spent the next few days taking care of business. She buried the pain beneath layers of carefully constructed indifference and focused on what she had to do. In between taking care of her clients, she made meals for Sam and froze them. Whatever else happened after she left this house, he wouldn't starve.

If she had her way, she wouldn't leave. She'd stay right here and keep hammering at his hard head until she got through. And maybe, one day, she'd succeed. But then again, maybe not. So she couldn't take the chance. It was one thing to risk her own heart, but she wouldn't risk Holly's. Her daughter was already crazy about Sam. The longer they stayed here in this house, the deeper those feelings would go. And before long, Sam would break her baby's heart. He might not mean to, but it was inevitable.

Because he refused to love them back. Sooner or

later, Holly would feel that and it would crush her. Joy wouldn't let that happen.

She would miss this place, though, she told herself as she packed up Holly's things. Glancing out the bedroom window, she watched her little girl and Sam placing yet another fairy house in the woods. And she had to give the man points for kindness.

She and Sam hadn't really spoken since that last night when everything had been laid out between them. They'd sidestepped each other when they could, and when they couldn't they'd both pretended that everything was fine. No point in upsetting Holly, after all. And despite—or maybe because of how strained things were between her and Sam—he hadn't changed toward Holly. That alone made her love him more and made it harder to leave. But tomorrow morning, she and Holly would wake up back in their own house in Franklin.

"Thank God Buddy finished the work early," she muttered, folding up the last of Holly's shirts and laying them in the suitcase.

Walking into the kitchen of her dreams, Joy sighed a little, then took out a pad of paper and a pen. Her heart felt heavy, the knot of emotion still stuck at the base of her throat, and every breath seemed like an event. She hated leaving. Hated walking away from Sam. But she didn't have a choice any longer. Sitting on a stool at the granite counter, she made a list for Sam of the food she had stocked for him. There was enough food in the freezer now to see him through to when Kaye returned.

Would he miss her? she wondered. Would he sit in that dining room alone and remember being there with her and Holly? Would he sit in the great room at night and wish Joy was there beside him? Or would he wipe it all out of his mind? Would she become a story never talked about like his late wife? Was Joy now just another reason to block out life and build the barricades around his heart that much higher?

She'd hoped to pull Sam out of the shadows—now she might have had a hand in pushing him deeper into the darkness. Sighing a little, she got up, stirred the pot of beef stew, then checked the bread in the oven.

When she looked out the window again, she saw the fairy lights had blinked on and Holly was kneeling beside Sam in the snow. She couldn't hear what was being said, but her heart broke a little anyway when her daughter laid her little hand on Sam's shoulder. Leaving was going to be hard. Tearing Holly away was going to be a nightmare. But she had to do it. For everyone's sake.

Two hours later, Holly put on her stubborn face.

"But I don't wanna go," Holly shouted and pulled away from her mother to run down the hall to the great room. "Sam! Sam! Mommy says we're leaving and I don't want to go cuz we're building a fairy house and I have to help you put it in the woods so the fairies can come and—"

Joy walked into the main room behind her daughter and watched as Holly threw herself into Sam's lap. He looked at Joy over the child's head even as he gave the little girl a hug.

"Tell her we have to stay, Sam, cuz I'm your helper now and you need me."

"I do," he said, and his voice sounded rough, scratchy. "But your mom needs you, too, so if she says it's time to go, you're going to have to."

She tipped her head back, looking at him with rivers of tears in her eyes. "But I don't want to."

"I know. I don't want you to, either." He gave her what looked to Joy like a wistful smile, then tugged on one of her pigtails. "Why don't I finish up the fairy house and then bring it to you so you can give it to Lizzie."

She shook her head so hard, her pigtails whipped back and forth across her eyes. "It's not the same, Sam. Can't I stay?"

"Come on, Holly," Joy spoke up quickly because her own emotions were taking over. Tears were close, and watching her daughter's heart break was breaking her own. "We really have to go."

Holly threw her a furious look, brows locked down, eyes narrowed. "You're being mean."

"I'm your mom," Joy said tightly, keeping her own tears at bay. "That's my job. Now come on."

"I love you, Sam," Holly whispered loud enough for her voice to carry. Then she gave him a smacking kiss on the cheek and crawled off his lap. Chin on her chest, she walked toward Joy with slow, dragging steps, as if she was pulling each foot out of mud along the way.

Joy saw the stricken look on Sam's face and thought, *Good. Now you know what you've given up. What you're allowing yourself to lose.*

Head bowed, shoulders slumped, Holly couldn't have been more clear in her desolation. Well, Joy knew just how she felt. Taking the little girl's hand, she gave it a squeeze and said, "Let's go home, sweetie."

They headed out the front door, and Joy didn't look back. She couldn't. For the first time in days, the sun was out, and the only clouds in the sky were big and white and looked as soft and fluffy as Santa's beard. The pines were covered in snow, and the bare branches of the aspens and birches looked like they'd been decorated with lace as the snow lay on every tiny twig. It was magical. Beautiful.

And Joy took no pleasure in any of it.

Holly hopped into her car seat and buckled herself in while Joy did a quick check of everything stuffed into the car. Their tiny tree was in the backseat and their suitcases in the trunk. Holly sat there glowering at the world in general, and Joy sighed because she knew her darling daughter was going to make her life a living hell for the next few days at least.

"That's it then," Joy said, forcing a smile as she turned to look at Sam. He wore that black leather jacket, and his jeans were faded and stacked on the toes of his battered work boots. His hair was too long, his white long-sleeved shirt was open at the neck, and his brown eyes pinned her with an intensity that stole her breath.

"Drive safely."

"That's all you've got?" she asked, tipping her head to one side to study him.

"What is there left to say?" he countered. "Didn't we get it all said a few days ago?"

"Not nearly, but you still don't understand that, do you?" He stood on his drive with the well-lit splendor of his house behind him. In the front window, the Christmas tree they'd decorated together shone in a fiery blaze of color, and behind her, she knew, there were fairy lights shining at the edge of the woods.

She looked up at him, then moved in closer. He didn't move, just locked his gaze with hers as she approached. When she was close enough, she cupped his cheeks in her palms and said softly, "We would have been good for you, Sam. I would have been. You and I could have been happy together. We could have built something that most people only dream about." She went up on her toes, kissed his grim, unyielding mouth, then looked at him again. "I want you to remember something. When you lost your family there was nothing you could do about it. *This* time, it's your choice. You're losing and you're letting it happen."

His mouth tightened, his eyes flashed, but he didn't speak, and Joy knew it was over.

"I'm sorry for you," she said, "that you're allowing your own pain to swallow your life."

Before he could tell her to mind her own business, she turned and walked to the car. With Holly loudly complaining, she fired up the engine, put it in gear and drove away from Sam Henry and all the might-have-beens that would drive her crazy for the rest of her life.

For the next few days, Sam settled back into what his life was like pre-Joy and Holly. He worked on his secret project—that didn't really need to be a secret anymore, because he always finished what he started. He called his mother to check in because he should—but when she asked about Joy and Holly, he evaded, not wanting to talk about them any more than he wanted to think about them.

He tried to put the two females out of his mind, but how could he when he sensed Joy in every damn corner of his house?

In Kaye's suite, Joy's scent still lingered in the air. But the rooms were empty now. No toys, no stuffed dog. Joy's silky red robe wasn't hanging on the back of the door, and that pitiful excuse for a Christmas tree was gone as if it had never been there at all.

Every night, he sat in the great room in front of the fire and looked at the tree in the window. That it was there amazed him. Thinking about the night he and Joy and Holly had decorated it depressed him. For so many years, he'd avoided all mention of Christmas because he hadn't wanted to remember.

Now, though, he *did* want to. He relived every moment of the time Joy and Holly had been a part of his life. But mostly, he recalled the afternoon they had *left* him. He remembered Holly waving goodbye out the rear window of her mother's car. He remembered the look in Joy's eyes when she kissed him and told him that he was making a mistake by letting her go. And he particularly remembered Joy's laugh, her smile, the taste of her mouth and the feel of her arms around him when he was inside her.

Her image remained uppermost in his mind as if she'd been carved there. He couldn't shake it and didn't really want to. Remembering was all he had. The house was too damn quiet. Hell, he spent every day and most of the night out in the workshop just to avoid the suffocating silence. But it was no better out there because a part of him kept waiting for Holly to rush in, do one of her amazing monologues and climb up on the stool beside him.

When he was working, he found himself looking at the house, half expecting to see Joy in one of the windows, smiling at him. And every time he didn't, another piece of him died. He'd thought that he could go back to his old life once they were gone. Slide back into the shadows, become again the man fate had made him. But that hadn't happened and now, he realized, it never could.

He wasn't the same man because of Joy. Because she had brought him back to life. Awakened him after too many years spent in a self-made prison.

"So what the hell are you going to do about it?" he muttered, hating the way his voice echoed in the vast room. He picked up his beer, took a long drink and glared at the glittering Christmas tree. The night they'd decorated it flooded his mind.

Holly laughing, a fresh row of stitches on her forehead to remind him just how fear for her had brought him to his knees. Joy standing back and telling him where lights were missing. The three of them eating more candy canes than they hung and finally, Holly falling asleep, not knowing that he was going to screw everything up.

He pushed up out of the chair, walked to the tree and looked beyond it, to the lights in the fairy houses outside. There were pieces of both of them all over this place, he thought. There was no escaping the memories this time, even if he wanted to.

Turning, he looked around the room and felt the solitude press in on him. The immense room felt claustrophobic. Joy should be here with him, drinking wine and eating "winter" cookies. Holly should be calling for a drink of water and trying to stay up a little later.

"Instead," he muttered, like the hermit he was, "you're alone with your memories."

Joy was right, he told himself. Fate had cheated him once, stealing away those he loved best. But he'd done it to himself this time. He'd taken his second chance and thrown it away because he was too afraid to grab on and never let go. He thought about all he'd lost—all he was about to lose—and had to ask himself if pain was really all he had. Was that what he'd become? A man devoted to keeping his misery alive and well no matter the cost?

He put his beer down, stalked out of the room and headed for the workshop. "Damned if it is."

Christmas morning dawned with a soft snow falling, turning the world outside the tiny house in Franklin into a postcard.

The small, bent-over tree stood on a table in the living room, and even the multiple strings of lights it boasted couldn't make it a quarter as majestic as the tree they'd left behind in Sam's great room. But this one, Joy assured herself, was *theirs*. Hers and Holly's. And that made it perfect. They didn't need the big tree. Or the lovely house. Or Sam. They had each other and that was enough.

It just didn't *feel* like enough anymore. Giving herself a mental kick for even thinking those words, Joy pushed thoughts of Sam out of her mind. No small task since the last four or five days had been a study in loneliness. Holly was sad, Joy was miserable, and even the approach of Christmas hadn't been enough to lift the pall that hung over them both.

Deb had tried to cheer her, telling her that everything happened for a reason, but really? When the reason was a stubborn, foolish man too blind to see what he was giving up, what comfort was there?

Ignoring the cold hard stone settled around her heart, Joy forced a smile and asked, "Do you want to go outside, sweetie? Try out your new sled?"

Holly sat amid a sea of torn wrapping paper, its festive colors and bold ribbons making it look as though the presents had exploded rather than been opened. Her blond hair was loose, and her pink princess nightgown was tucked up around her knees as she sat cross-legged in the middle of the rubble.

She turned big blue eyes on Joy and said, "No, Mommy, I don't want to right now."

"Really?" Joy was trying to make Christmas good for her daughter, but the little girl missed Sam as much as Joy did, so it was an uphill battle. But they had to get used to being without him, didn't they? He'd made his choice. He'd let them go, and she hadn't heard a word from him since.

Apparently Sam Henry had found a way to go on, and so would she and Holly. "Well, how about we watch your favorite princess movie and drink some hot chocolate?"

"Okay…" The lack of enthusiasm in that word told Joy that Holly was only agreeing to please her mother.

God, she was a terrible person. *She's* the one who had allowed Holly to get too close to Sam in the hopes of reaching him. She had seen her daughter falling in love and hadn't done enough to stop it. She'd been too caught up in the sweetness of Holly choosing her own father to prepare either of them for the time when it all came crashing down on them.

Still, she had to try to reach her baby girl. Ease the pain, help her to enjoy Christmas morning.

"Are you upset because Santa couldn't bring you the puppy you wanted? Santa left you the note," Joy said, mentally thanking Sam for at least coming up with that brilliant idea. "He'll bring you a puppy as soon as he's old enough."

"It's okay. I can play with Lizzie's puppy." Holly got up, walked to her mother and crawled into her lap. Leaning her head against Joy's chest, she sighed heavily. "I want to go see Sam."

Joy's heart gave one hard lurch as everything in her yearned for the same thing. "Oh, honey, I don't think that's a good idea."

"Sure it is." Holly turned in her lap, looked up into her eyes and said softly, "He misses me, Mommy. It's Christmas and he's all by himself and lonely and probably crabby some more cuz we're not there to make him smile and help him with the fairy houses. He *needs* us. And we belong with Sam. It's Christmas and we should be there."

Her baby girl looked so calm, so serious, so *sure* of everything. The last few days hadn't been easy. They'd slipped back into their old life, but it wasn't the same. Nothing was the same anymore. They were a family as they'd always been, but now it felt as if someone was missing.

She'd left Sam to protect Holly. But keeping her away from the man she considered her father wasn't helping her either. It was a fine line to walk, Joy knew. She smoothed Holly's hair back from her face and realized her baby girl was right.

Sam had let them leave, but it was Joy who had packed up and walked out. Neither of them had fought for what they wanted, so maybe it was time to make a stand. Time to let him know that he could try to toss them aside all he wanted—but they weren't going to go.

"You're right, baby, he *does* need us. And we need him." Giving Holly a quick, hard kiss, she grinned and said, "Let's get dressed."

* * *

Sam heard the car pull into the drive, looked out the window and felt his heart jump to life. How was *that* for timing? He'd just been getting into his coat to drive into Franklin and bring his girls home. He felt like Ebenezer Scrooge when he woke up on Christmas morning and realized he hadn't missed it. Hadn't lost his last chance at happiness.

He hit the front door at a dead run and made it to the car before Joy had turned off the engine. Snow was falling, he was freezing, but he didn't give a good damn. Suddenly everything in his world had righted itself. And this time, he was going to grab hold of what was most important and never let it go again.

"Sam! Sam! Hi, Sam!" Holly's voice, hitting that high note, sounded like the sweetest song to him.

"Hi, Holly!" he called back, and while the little girl got herself out of her seat belt, he threw open the driver's door and pulled Joy out. "Hi," he said, letting his gaze sweep over her features before focusing back on the eyes that had haunted him from the first moment they met.

"Hi, Sam. Merry Christmas." She cupped his cheek in her palm, and her touch melted away the last of the ice encasing his heart.

"I missed you, damn it," he muttered and bent to kiss her. That first taste of her settled everything inside him, brought the world back into focus and let him know that he was alive. And grateful.

"We're back!" Holly raced around the car, threw herself at Sam's legs and held on.

Breaking the kiss, he grinned down at the little girl and then reached down to pick her up. Holding her tight, he looked into bright eyes and then spun her in circles until she squealed in delight. "You're back. Merry Christmas, Holly."

She hugged his neck tightly and kissed his cheek with all the ferocity of a five-year-old's love. "Merry Christmas!"

"Come on, you two. It's cold out here." He carried Holly and followed behind Joy as she walked into the house and then turned for the great room. "I've got a couple surprises for you two."

"For Christmas?" Holly gave him a squeeze, then as she saw what was waiting for her, breathed, "Oh my goodness!" That quick gasp was followed by another squeal, this one higher than the one before. She squirmed to get out of Sam's arms, then raced across the room to the oversize fairy castle dollhouse sitting in front of the tree.

Beside him, Sam heard Joy give a soft sigh. When he looked at her, there were tears in her eyes and a beautiful smile on her amazing mouth. His heart gave another hard lurch, and he welcomed it. For the last few days, he'd felt dead inside. Coming back to life was much better.

"You made that for her."

He looked to where the girl he already considered his daughter was exploring the castle he'd built for her. It was red, with turrets and towers, tiny flags flying from the points of those towers. Glass windows opened and closed, and wide double doors swung open. The back of the castle was open for small fingers to explore and redecorate and dream.

"Yeah," he said. "Holly needed a fairy house she could actually play with. I'm thinking this summer we might need to build a tree house, too."

"This summer?" Joy's words were soft, the question hanging in the air between them.

"I've got plans," he said. "And so much to tell you. Ask you."

Her eyes went soft and dreamy and as he watched, they filled with a sheen of tears he really hoped she wouldn't let fall.

"I can't believe you made that for Holly," Joy said, smiling at her daughter's excitement. "She loves it."

"I can't believe you're here," Sam confessed, turning her in his arms so he could hold her, touch her, look into her eyes. Sliding his hands up her arms, over her shoulders to her face, his palms cradled her as his thumbs stroked gently over her soft, smooth skin. "I was coming to you."

"You were?" Wonder, hope lit her eyes, and Sam knew he hadn't blown it entirely. He hadn't let this last best chance at love slip past him.

"You arrived just as I was headed to the garage. I was going to bring you back here to give you your presents. Here. In our home."

Her breath caught and she lifted one hand to her mouth. "*Our* home?"

"If you'll stay," he said. "Stay with me. Love me. Marry me."

"Oh, Sam…"

"Don't answer yet," he said, grinning now as he took her hand and pulled her over to the brightly lit Christmas tree. "Just wait. There's more." Then to the little girl, he said, "There's another present for you, Holly. I think Santa stopped off here last night."

"He *did*?" Holly's eyes went wide as saucers as her smile danced in her eyes. "What did he bring?"

"Open it and find out," he said and pointed to a big white box with a red ribbon.

"How come it has holes in the top?" Holly asked.

"You'll see."

Joy already guessed it. She squeezed Sam's hand as they watched Holly carefully lift off the lid of the box and peer inside. "Oh my goodness!"

The little girl looked up at Sam. "He's for me?"

"She is. It's a girl."

Holly laughed in delight then reached into the box and lifted out a golden retriever puppy. Its fur was white and soft, and Holly buried her face against that softness, whispering and laughing as the puppy eagerly licked her face. "Elsa. I'm gonna name her Elsa," Holly proclaimed and laid out on the floor so her new best friend could jump all over her in wild abandon.

"I can't believe you did that," Joy said, shaking her head and smiling through her tears. "Where did you find a white puppy? I looked everywhere."

Sam shrugged and gave her a half smile. "My sister knew a breeder and, well… I chartered a jet and flew out to Boston to pick her up two days ago."

"Boston." Joy blinked at him. "You flew to Boston to pick up a Christmas puppy so my little girl wouldn't be disappointed."

"*Our* little girl," he corrected. "I love her, Joy. Like she's my own. And if you'll let me, I'll adopt her."

"Oh my God…" Joy bit down hard on her bottom lip and gave up the battle to stem her tears. They coursed down her cheeks in silvery rivers that only made her smile shine more brightly.

"Is that a yes?"

"Yes, of course it's a yes," Joy managed to say when

she threw her arms around him and held on. "She already considers you her father. So do I."

Sam held Joy tight, buried his face in the curve of her neck and said, "I love you. Both of you. So much. I won't ever let you go, Joy. I want you to marry me. Give me Holly. And give us both more children. Help me make a family so strong nothing can ever tear it down."

"You filled my heart, Sam." She pulled back, looked up at him and said, "All of this. What you've done. It's the most amazing moment of my life. My personal crabby hermit has become my hero."

His mouth quirked at the corner. "Still not done," he said and drew her to the other side of the tree.

"You've already given me everything, Sam. What's left?" She was laughing and crying and the combined sounds were like music to him.

The big house felt full of love and promise, and Sam knew that it would never be empty again. There would be so much light and love in the house, shadows would be banished. He had his memories of lost love, and those would never fade, but he wouldn't be ruled by them anymore, either.

When Kaye finally came home from her annual vacation, she was going to find a changed man and a household that was filled with the kind of happiness Sam had thought he'd never find again.

"What is it, Sam?" Joy asked when he pulled her to a stop in front of a draped easel.

"A promise," he said and pulled the sheet from the painting he'd only just finished the night before, to show her what he dreamed. What he wanted. For both of them.

"Oh, Sam." Her heart was in her voice. He heard it and smiled.

* * *

Joy stared at the painting, unable to tear her eyes from it. He'd painted this room, with the giant, lit-up tree, with stacks of presents at its feet, and the hint of fairy lights from the tiny houses in the woods shining through the glass behind it.

On the floor, he'd painted Holly, the puppy climbing all over her as the little girl laughed. He'd painted him and Joy, arms around each other, watching the magic unfold together. And he'd painted Joy pregnant.

There was love and celebration in every stroke of paint. The light was warm and soft and seemed to make the painting glow with everything she was feeling. She took it all in and felt the wonder of it all settle in the center of her heart. He'd painted her a promise.

"I did it all yesterday," he said, snaking both arms around her middle as they stared at his creation. "I've never had a painting come so quickly. And I know it's because this is what's meant to be. You, me, Holly."

"I love it," Joy said softly, turning her face up just enough to meet his kiss. "But we don't know if I'm pregnant."

"If you're not now," he promised, both eyebrows lifting into high arches, "you will be soon. I want lots of kids with you, Joy. I want to live again—risks and all—and I can only do that if you love me."

She turned around in his arms, glanced at her daughter, still giggling with puppy delight, then smiled up at Sam. "I love you so much, Sam. I always will. I want to make that family with you. Have lots of kids. Watch Holly and the others we'll make together grow up with a father who loves them."

"We can do that. Hell," he said, "we can do anything together."

She took a long, deep breath and grinned up at him. "And if you ask me to marry you right this minute, this will be the best Christmas ever."

He dipped into his pocket, pulled out a sapphire and diamond ring and slid it onto her finger while she watched, stunned. Though she'd been hoping for a real proposal, she hadn't expected a ring. Especially one this beautiful.

"It wasn't just a puppy I got in Boston," he said. "Though I will admit my sister helped me pick out this ring."

"Your family knows?"

"Absolutely," he said, bending to kiss her, then kiss the ring on her finger as if sealing it onto her hand. "My mother's thrilled to have a granddaughter and can't wait to meet you both in person. And be prepared, they'll all be descending after the holidays to do just that."

"It'll be fun," she said. "Oh, Sam, I love *you*."

"That's the only present I'm ever going to need," Sam said and kissed her hard and long and deep.

She'd come here this morning believing she would have to fight with Sam to make him admit how much he loved her. The fact that he had been on his way to get her and Holly filled her heart. He wanted her. He loved them both. And he was willing to finally leave the past behind and build a future with her. It really was the best Christmas she'd ever known.

"Hey!" Holly tugged at both of them as the puppy jumped at her feet. "You're kissing! Like mommies and daddies do!"

Joy looked at her little girl as Sam lifted her up to

eye level. "Would you like that, baby girl? Would you like Sam to be your daddy and for all of us to live here forever?"

"For really?"

"For really," Sam said. "I'd like to be your daddy, Holly. And this summer, you and I are going to build you a fairy tree house. How does that sound?"

She gave him a wide, happy grin. "You'll be good at it, Sam. I can tell and I love you lots."

"I love you back, Holly. Always will." He kissed her forehead.

"Can I call you Daddy now?"

"I'd really like that," he said and Joy saw the raw emotion glittering in his eyes.

Their little girl clapped and grinned hugely before throwing her arms around both their necks. "This is the bestest Christmas ever. I got just what I wanted. A puppy. A fairy house. And my own daddy."

Sam looked into Joy's eyes and she felt his love, his pleasure in the moment, and she knew that none of them would ever be lonely again.

"Merry Christmas, Sam."

"Merry Christmas, Joy."

And in the lights of the tree, he sealed their new life with a kiss that had Holly applauding and sent the new puppy barking.

Everything, Joy thought, was *perfect*.

* * * * *

MY FAIR
BILLIONAIRE

ELIZABETH BEVARLY

For David and Eli.
Thanks for always having my back.
I love you guys. OXY.

One

T. S. Eliot was right, Ava Brenner thought as she quickened her stride down Michigan Avenue and ducked beneath the awning of a storefront. April really was the cruelest month. Yesterday, the skies above Chicago had been blue and clear, and temperatures hovered in the high fifties. Today, gray clouds pelted the city with freezing rain. She tugged her scarf from the collar of her trench coat and over her head, knotting it beneath her chin. The weather would probably ruin the emerald silk, but she was on her way to meet a prospective vendor and would rather replace an injured scarf than have the perfect auburn chignon at her nape get wet and ragged.

Image was everything. Bottom line. That was a lesson life hammered home when Ava was still in high school. April wasn't the only thing that was cruel—teenage girls could be downright brutal. Especially the rich, vain, snotty ones at posh private schools who wore the latest designer fashions and belittled the need-based-scholarship students who made do with discount-store markdowns.

Ava pushed the thought away. A decade and a half lay between her and graduation. She was the owner of her own business now, a boutique called Talk of the Town that rented haute couture fashions to women who wanted only the best for those special occasions in life. Even if the shop was operating on a shoestring and wishful thinking, it was starting to show a profit. At least she looked the part of successful businesswoman. No one had to know she was her own best customer.

She whipped the scarf from her head and tucked it into the pocket of her trench coat as she entered an elegant eatery. Beneath, she wore a charcoal-gray Armani jacket and trousers, paired with a sage-colored shell she knew enhanced her green eyes. The outfit had arrived at Talk of the Town just this week, and she'd wanted to test-drive it for comfort and wearability.

As she approached the host stand, her cell phone twittered. It was the vendor she was supposed to be meeting, asking to postpone their appointment for an evening later in the week. So Ava would be on her own for dinner tonight. As usual. Still, she hadn't taken herself out in a long time, and she had been working extra hard this month. She'd earned a bit of a treat.

Basilio, the restaurant's owner, greeted her by name with a warm smile. Every time she saw him, Ava was reminded of her father. Basilio had the same dark eyes, close-cropped salt-and-pepper hair and neatly trimmed mustache. But she was reasonably certain that, unlike her father, Basilio had never done time in a federal prison.

Without even checking the seating chart, he led Ava to her favorite table by the window, where she could watch the passersby as she ate. As she lifted her menu, however, her attention was yanked away by a ruckus in the bar. When she glanced up, she saw Dennis, her favorite bartender, being berated by a customer, a tall man with broad shoulders and coal-black hair. He was evidently offended by Dennis's suggestion that he'd had too much to drink, a condition that was frankly obvious.

"I'm fine," the man insisted. Although his words weren't slurred, his voice was much louder than necessary. "And I want another Macallan. Neat."

Dennis remained calm as he replied, "I don't think—"

"That's right," the man interrupted him. "You don't think. You serve drinks. Now serve me another Macallan. Neat."

"But, Mr.—"

"*Now,*" the man barked.

Ava's pulse leaped at the angrily uttered word. She'd worked her way through college at three jobs, one of which had been as a waitress. She'd dealt with her share of patrons who became bullies after drinking too much. Thankfully, Basilio and her waiter, Marcus, were on the spot quickly to attend to the situation.

Dennis shook his head at the others' approach, holding up a hand for them to wait. In gentling tones, he said, "Mr. Moss, maybe it would be better if you had a cup of coffee instead."

Heat splashed into Ava's belly at hearing the name. Moss. She had gone to school—long ago, in a galaxy far away—with a Moss. Peyton Moss. He had been a grade ahead of her at the tony Emerson Academy.

But this couldn't be him, she told herself. Peyton Moss had sworn to everyone at Emerson that he was leaving Chicago the moment he graduated and never coming back. And he'd kept that promise. Ava had returned to Chicago only a few months after earning her business degree and had run into a handful of her former classmates—more was the pity—none of whom had mentioned Peyton's return.

She looked at the man again. Peyton had been Emerson's star hockey player, due not just to his prowess, but also his size. His hair had been shoulder-length, inky silk, and his voice, even then, had been dark and rich. By now, it could have easily deepened to the velvety baritone of the man at the bar.

When he turned to look at Marcus, Ava bit back a gasp. Although the hair was shorter and the profile harsher, it was indeed Peyton. She'd know that face anywhere. Even after sixteen years.

Without thinking, she jumped up and hurried to place herself between Peyton and the others. With all the calm she could muster, she said, "Gentlemen. Maybe what we need here is an unbiased intermediary to sort everything out."

Peyton would laugh himself silly about that if he recognized her. Ava had been anything but *unbiased* toward him in high school. But he'd been plenty biased toward her, too. That was what happened when two people moved in such disparate social circles in an environment where the lines of society were stark, immutable and absolute. When upper class met lower class in a place like Emerson, the sparks that flew could immolate an entire socioeconomic stratum.

"Ms. Brenner, I don't think that's a good idea," Basilio said. "Men in his condition can be unpredictable, and he's three times your size."

"My condition is fine," Peyton snapped. "Or it would

be. If this establishment honored the requests of its paying customers."

"Just let me speak to him," Ava said, dropping her voice.

Basilio shook his head. "Marcus and I can handle this."

"But I know him. He and I went to school together. He'll listen to me. We're…we were…" Somehow she pushed the word out of her mouth. "Friends."

It was another word that would have made Peyton laugh. The two of them had been many things at Emerson—unwilling study partners, aggressive sparring partners and for one strange, intoxicating night, exuberant lovers—but never, ever, friends.

"I'm sorry, Ms. Brenner," Basilio said, "but I can't let you—"

Before he could stop her, Ava spun around and made her way to the bar. "Peyton," she said when she came to a halt in front of him.

Instead of looking at Ava, he continued to study Dennis. "What?"

"This has gone far enough. You need to be reasonable."

He opened his mouth, but halted when his gaze connected with hers. She'd forgotten what beautiful eyes he had. They were the color and clarity of good cognac, fringed by sooty lashes.

"I know you," he said, suddenly more lucid. His tone was confident, but his expression held doubt. "Don't I?"

"You and I went to school together," she said, deliberately vague. "A long time ago."

He seemed surprised by the connection. "I don't remember you from Stanford."

Stanford? she echoed to herself. Last she'd heard he

was headed to a university in New England with a double major in hat tricks and cross-checking and a minor in something vaguely scholastic in case he injured himself. How had he ended up on the West Coast?

"Not Stanford," she said.

"Then where?"

Reluctantly, she told him, "The Emerson Academy here in Chicago."

His surprise multiplied. "You went to Emerson?"

Well, he didn't need to sound so shocked. Did she still look that much like a street urchin?

"Yes," she said evenly. "I went to Emerson."

He narrowed his eyes as he studied her more closely. "I don't remember you from there, either."

Something sharp pricked her chest at the comment. She should be happy he didn't remember her. She wished she could forget the girl she'd been at Emerson. She wished she could forget Peyton, as well. But so often over the past sixteen years, he and the other members of his social circle had crept into her brain, conjuring memories and feelings she wished she could bury forever.

Without warning, he lifted a hand to cradle her chin and jaw. Something hot and electric shot through her at the contact, but he didn't seem to notice. He simply turned her face gently one way, then the other, looking at her from all angles. Finally, he dropped his hand back to the bar. He shook his head, opened his mouth to speak, then—

Then his expression went slack. "Oh, my God. Ava Brenner."

She expelled an irritated sigh. Damn. She didn't want anyone to remember her the way she'd been at Emerson, especially the kids like Peyton. Especially Peyton, period. In spite of that, a curl of pleasure wound through her when she realized he'd made a space for her, however small, in his memory.

Resigned, she replied, "Yes. It's me."

"Well, I'll be damned," he said, his tone belying nothing of what he might be thinking.

He collapsed onto a barstool, gazing at her with those piercing golden eyes. A rush of conflicting emotions washed over her that she hadn't felt for a very long time—pride and shame, arrogance and insecurity, blame and guilt. And in the middle of it all, an absolute uncertainty about Peyton, about herself, about the two of them together. Then as well as now.

Oh, yes. She definitely felt as if she was back in high school. And she didn't like it now any better than she had then.

When it became clear that Peyton wasn't going to cause any more trouble, Dennis snatched the empty cocktail glass from the bar and replaced it with a coffee mug. Basilio released a slow breath and threw Ava a grateful smile. Marcus went back to check on his diners. Ava told herself to return to her table, that she'd done her good deed for the day and should just leave well enough alone. But Peyton was still staring at her, and something in his expression made her pause. Something that sent another tumble of memories somersaulting through her brain. Different memories from the others that had plagued her tonight, but memories that were every bit as unpleasant and unwanted.

Because it had been Ava, not Peyton, who had led the ruling social class at the posh, private Emerson Academy. It had been Ava, not Peyton, who had been rich, vain and snotty. It had been Ava, not Peyton, who had worn the latest designer fashions and belittled the need-based-scholarship students who made do with discount-store markdowns. At least until the summer before her senior year, when her family had lost everything, and she'd suddenly found herself walking in their discount-store markdowns herself. Then she'd been the one who was penniless, unwanted and bullied.

Peyton didn't say a word as Ava studied him, pondering all the things that had changed in the decade and a half since she'd seen him. A few threads of silver had woven their way into his dark hair, and the lower half of his face was shadowed by a day's growth of beard. She couldn't remember him shaving in high school. But perhaps he had, even if that morning when she'd woken up beside him in her bedroom, he—

She tried to stop the memories before they could form, but they came anyway. How it had all played out when the two of them were forced to work together on a semester-long project for World Civ, one of the classes that combined seniors and juniors. Money really did change everything—at least at Emerson, it had. School rules had dictated that those whose families had lots of money must belittle those whose families had none, and that those who had nothing must resent those who had everything. In spite of that, there had always been... something...between Ava and Peyton. Something hot and heavy that burned up the air in any room the two of them shared. Some strange, combustible reaction due to...something. Something weird. Something volatile. Something neither of them had ever been able to identify or understand.

Or, ultimately, resist.

It had culminated one night at her house when the two of them had been working late on that class project and had ended up... Well, it hadn't exactly been making love, since whatever they'd felt for each other then had had nothing to do with love. But it hadn't been sex, either. There had been more to it than the mingling of two bodies. It had just fallen short of the mingling of two souls.

The morning after, Peyton had jumped out of bed on one side, and Ava had leaped out on the other. They had hurled both accusations and excuses, neither listening to the other. The only thing they'd agreed on was that they'd made a colossal mistake that was never to be mentioned again. Peyton had dressed and fled through her bedroom window, not wanting to be discovered, and Ava had locked it tight behind him. Monday morning, they turned in their assignment and went back to being enemies, and Ava had held her breath for the remainder of the year. Only after Peyton graduated and took off for college had she been able to breathe again.

For all of three weeks. Until her entire life came crashing down around her, pitching her to the bottom rung of the social ladder among the very people she had treated so callously before. People whom she quickly learned had deserved none of the treatment she had spent years dishing out.

She turned to Basilio. "I need a favor. Could I ask one of your waiters to run back to my shop for my car so I can drive Mr. Moss home? I'll stay here and have coffee with him until then."

Basilio looked at her as if she'd lost every marble she possessed.

"It's only a fifteen-minute walk," she told him. "Ten if whoever you send hurries."

"But, Ms. Brenner, he's not—"

"—himself," Ava quickly interjected. "Yes, I know, which is why he deserves a pass tonight."

"Are you sure that's a good idea?"

No, she wasn't. This Peyton was a stranger to her in so many ways. Not that the Peyton she used to know had exactly been an open book. He might not have thought much of her kind when they were in high school, and maybe he hadn't been much of a gentleman, but he hadn't been dangerous, either. Well, not in the usual sense of the word. Whatever had made him behave badly tonight, he'd calmed down once he recognized a familiar face.

Besides, she owed him. She owed him more than she could ever make up for. But at least, by doing this, she might make some small start.

"My keys are in my purse at my table," she told Basilio, "and my car is parked behind the shop. Just send someone down there to get it, and I'll take him home. Please," she added.

Basilio looked as if he wanted to object again, but instead said, "Fine. I'll send Marcus. I just hope you know what you're doing."

Yes, well, that, Ava thought, made two of them.

Peyton Moss awoke the way he hadn't awoken in a very long time—hungover. Really hungover. When he opened his eyes, he had no idea where he was or what time it was or what he'd been doing in the hours before wherever and whatever time he was in.

He lay still in bed for a minute—he was at least in a bed, wasn't he?—and tried to figure out how he'd arrived in his current position. Hmm. Evidently, his current position was on his stomach atop a crush of sheets, his face shoved into a pillow. So that would be a big yep on the bed thing. The question now was, *whose* bed?

Especially since, whoever the owner was, she wasn't currently in it with him.

But he concluded the owner of the bed must be a she. Not only did the sheets smell way too good to belong to a man, but the wallpaper, he discovered when he rolled over, was covered with roses, and a chandelier above him dripped ropes of crystal beads. He drove his gaze around the room and saw more evidence of gender bias in an ultrafeminine dresser and armoire, shoved into a corner by the room's only window, which was covered by billows of lace.

So he'd gone home with a strange woman last night. Nothing new about that, except that going home with strangers was something he'd been more likely to do in his youth. Not that thirty-four was old, dammit, but it was an age when a man was expected to start settling down and figuring out what he wanted. Not that Peyton hadn't done that, too, but… Okay, so maybe he hadn't settled down that much. And maybe he hadn't quite figured out everything he wanted. He'd settled some and figured out the bulk of it. Hell, that was why he'd come back to a city he'd sworn he would never set foot in again.

Chicago. God. The last time he was here, he'd been eighteen years old and wild as a rabid badger. He'd left his graduation ceremony and gone straight to the bus station, stopping only long enough to cram his cap and gown into the first garbage can he could find. He hadn't even gone home to say goodbye. Hell, no one at home had given a damn what he did. No one in Chicago had.

He draped an arm over his eyes and expelled a weary sigh. Yeah, nothing like a little adolescent melodrama to start the day off right.

He jackknifed to a sitting position and slung his legs

over the bed. His jacket and tie were hanging over the back of a chair and his shoes were on the floor near his feet. His rumpled shirt and trousers were all fastened, as was his belt. Obviously, nothing untoward had happened the night before, so, with any luck, there wouldn't be any awkward moments once he found out who his hostess was.

Carefully, he made his way to the door and headed into a bathroom on his right, turning on the water to fill the sink. After splashing a few handfuls onto his face, he felt a little better. He still looked like hell, he noted when he caught his reflection in the mirror. But he felt a little better.

The mirror opened to reveal a slim cabinet behind it, and he was grateful to see a bottle of mouthwash. At least that took care of the dead-animal taste in his mouth. He found a comb, too, and dragged that through his hair, then did his best to smooth the wrinkles from his shirt.

Leaving the bathroom, he detected the aroma of coffee and followed it to a kitchen that was roughly the size of an electron. The light above the stove was on, allowing him to find his way around. The only wall decoration was a calendar with scenes of Italy, but the fridge door was crowded with stuff—a notice about an upcoming Italian film festival at the Patio Theater, some pictures of women's clothing cut out of a magazine and a postcard reminding whoever lived here of an appointment with her gynecologist.

The coffeemaker must have been on a timer, because there was no evidence of anyone stirring but him. Glancing down at his watch, he saw that it was just after five, which helped explain why no one was stirring. Except that the coffeemaker timer must have been set for now, so whoever lived here was normally up at this ungodly hour.

He crossed the kitchen in a single stride and exited on the other side, finding himself in a living room that was barely as big as the bedroom. Enough light from the street filtered through the closed curtains for him to make out a lamp on the other side of the room, and he was about to move toward it when a sound to his right stopped him. It was the sound a woman made upon stirring when she was not ready to stir, a soft sough of breath tempered by a fretful whimper. Through the semidarkness, he could just make out the figure of a woman lying on the couch.

Peyton had found himself in a lot of untenable positions over the years—many of which had included women—but he had no idea what to do in a situation like this. He didn't know where he was, had no idea how he'd gotten here and was clueless about the identity of the woman under whose roof he had passed the night. For all he knew, she could be married. Hell, for all he knew, she could be a knife-wielding maniac. Then his hostess made that quiet sound of semiconsciousness again, and he decided she couldn't be the last. Knife-wielding maniacs couldn't sound that delectable. Still, if she was sleeping out here and he'd spent the night in her bedroom, he had nothing to feel guilty about, right? Except for tossing her out of her bed when he should have been the one sleeping on the couch. And except for passing out on her in the first place.

What the hell had happened last night? He mentally retraced his steps from the moment he set foot back on his native soil. Although he'd left Chicago via Greyhound bus more than fifteen years ago, his return had been aboard a private jet. His private jet. He might have been a street dog in his youth, but in adulthood… Ah, who was he kidding? In adulthood, he was still a street dog. That was the reason he was back here.

Anyway, after landing, he'd headed straight to the Hotel Intercontinental on Michigan Avenue. That much Peyton remembered with crystal clarity, because the Hotel Intercontinental was the sort of place that A) he never would have had the nerve to enter when he was a kid, and B) would have tossed him out on his ass if he *had* tried to enter when he was a kid. Funny how they'd had no problem accepting his platinum card yesterday.

He further remembered walking into his suite and tossing his bag onto the massive bed, then going to the window and pushing aside the curtains. He recalled looking out on Michigan Avenue, at the gleaming high-rises and upscale department stores that had always seemed off-limits to him when he lived here. This whole neighborhood had seemed off-limits to him when he was a kid. In spite of that, he'd come to this part of town five days a week, nine months a year, because the Emerson Academy for College Preparatory Learning sat in the middle of it. For those other two days of the week and three months of the year, though, Peyton had always had to stay with his own kind in the rough South Side neighborhood where he'd grown up.

Yesterday, looking out that window, he had been brutally reminded of how his teenage life in this part of town had been juxtaposed to the life—if he could even call it that—that he'd led in his not-even-marginal neighborhood. As much as he'd hated Emerson, it had always felt good to escape his home life for eight hours a day. Yesterday, looking out at the conspicuous consumption of Michigan Avenue, Peyton had, ironically, been transported back to his old neighborhood instead.

He'd been able to smell the grease and gasoline of the garage he and his old man had lived above—and where he'd worked to save money for college when he wasn't at school. He'd heard the police sirens that pelted the crumbling urban landscape, had seen the roving packs of gangs that considered his block fair game. He'd felt the grime on his skin and tasted the soot that belched from the factory smokestacks. And then…

Then had come memories of Emerson, where he'd won a spot on the school hockey team—along with a full scholarship—thanks to his above-average grades and his ruthlessness on the rink. God, he'd hated that school, teeming as it had been with blue-blooded trust-fund babies who were way too rich for his system. But he'd loved how clean and bright the place was, and how it smelled like floor wax and Calvin Klein perfume. He'd liked the quiet during classes and how orderly everything ran. He'd liked being able to eat one decent meal a day. He'd liked feeling safe, if only for a little while.

Not that he would have admitted any of that back then. Not that he would admit it to anyone now. But he'd been smart enough to know that an education from a place like Emerson would look a hell of a lot better on a college application than the decaying public school he would have attended otherwise. He'd stomached the rich kids—barely—by finding the handful of other students like himself. The wretched refuse. The other scholarship kids who were smart but poor and determined to end up in a better place than their parents. There had been maybe ten of them in a school where they were outnumbered a hundred to one. Peyton hadn't given a damn about those hundreds. Except for one, who had gotten under his skin and stayed there.

Ava Brenner. The Golden Girl of the Gold Coast. Her daddy was so rich and so powerful, and she was so snotty and so beautiful, she'd ruled that school. Not a day had passed at Emerson that didn't revolve around Ava and her circle of friends—all handpicked by the princess herself, and all on eggshells knowing they could be exiled at her slightest whim. Not a day had passed that Peyton hadn't had to watch her strolling down the hall, flipping that sweep of red-gold hair around as if it was spun copper…and looking at him as if he were something disgusting stuck to the bottom of her shoe. And not a day had passed when he hadn't wanted her. Badly. Even knowing she was spoiled and shallow and vain.

He opened his eyes. Yeah, he remembered now that he had been thinking about Ava yesterday. In fact, that was what had made him beat a hasty retreat to the hotel bar. He remembered that, too. And he remembered tossing back three single malts on an empty stomach in rapid succession. He remembered being politely asked to leave the hotel bar and, surprisingly, complying. He remembered lurching out onto Michigan Avenue and looking for the first place he could find to get another drink, then being steady enough on his feet to convince the bartender to fix him a couple more. Then…

He tried harder to remember what had happened after that. But all he could recall was a husky—sexy— voice, and the soft scent of gardenias, and a pair of beautiful sea-green eyes, all of which had seemed oddly familiar somehow.

That brought his gaze back to the woman sleeping on the couch. In the semidarkness, he could see that she lay on her side, facing the room, one hand curled in front of her face. The blanket with which she had covered herself was drooping, part of it pooled on the floor. For some reason, he was compelled to move to the couch and pick it up, to drape it across her sleeping form. As he bent over her, he inhaled the faint scent of gardenias again, as if it had followed him out of his memories.

And just like that, he was pummeled by another one.

Ava Brenner. Again. She was the one who had smelled of gardenias. Peyton remembered the night the two of them had— Well, the night they'd had to finish a school project together at her house. In her room. When her parents were out of town. At one point, she'd gone downstairs to fix them something to eat, and he'd taken advantage of her absence to shamelessly prowl around her room, opening her closet and dresser drawers, snooping for anything he could discover about her. When he came across her underwear drawer, he actually stole a pair of her panties. Pale yellow silk. God help him, he still had them. As he'd stuffed them into his back pocket that night, his gaze lit on a bottle of perfume on her dresser. Night Gardenia, it was called. That was the only way he knew that what she smelled like was gardenias. He'd never smelled—or even seen— one before that night.

As he draped the cover over the sleeping woman, his gaze fell to her face, and his gut clenched tight. He told himself he was imagining things. He was just so overcome with memories of Ava that he was imprinting her face onto that of a stranger. The odds of him running into the last person he wanted to see in Chicago—within hours of his arrival—were too ridiculous to compute. There were two and a half million people in this city. No way could fate be that cruel. No way would he be thrown back into the path of—

Before the thought even formed in his head, though,

Peyton knew. It was her. Ava Brenner. Golden Girl of the Gold Coast. Absolute ruler of the Emerson Academy for College Preparatory Learning. A recurring character in the most feverish dreams he'd ever had as a teenage boy.

And someone he'd hoped he would never, ever see again.

Two

"Ava?"

As if he'd uttered an incantation to free a fairy-tale princess from an evil spell, her eyes fluttered open. He tried one last time to convince himself he was only imagining her. But even in the semidarkness, he could see that it was Ava. And that she was more beautiful than he remembered.

"Peyton?" she said as she pushed herself up from the sofa.

He stumbled backward and into a chair on the other side of the room. Oh, God. Her voice. The way she said his name. It was the same way she'd said it that morning in her bedroom, when he'd opened his eyes to realize the frenetic dream he'd had about the two of them having sex hadn't been a dream at all. The panic that welled up in him now was identical to the feeling he had then, an explosion of fear and uncertainty and insecurity. He *hated* that feeling. He hadn't felt it since…

Ah, hell. He hadn't felt it since that morning in Ava's bedroom.

Don't panic, he told himself. He wasn't an eighteen-year-old kid whose only value lay in his ruthlessness on the rink. He wasn't living in poverty with a drunk for a father after his mother had deserted them both. He sure as hell wasn't the refuse of the Emerson Academy who wasn't worthy of Ava Brenner.

"Um, hi? I guess?" she said as she sat up, pulling up her covers as if she were cloaking herself in some kind of protective device. She was obviously just as anxious about seeing him as he was about seeing her.

As much as Peyton told himself to reply with a breezy, unconcerned greeting, all he could manage was another quiet "Ava."

She pulled one hand out of her cocoon to switch on a lamp by the sofa. He squinted at the sudden brightness but didn't glance away. Her eyes seemed larger than he remembered, and the hard angles of her cheekbones had mellowed to slender curves. Her hair was shorter, darker than in high school, but still danced around her shoulders unfettered. And her mouth—that mouth that had inspired teenage boys to commit mayhem—was... Hell. It still inspired mayhem. Only now that Peyton was a man, *mayhem* took on a whole new meaning.

"You want coffee?" she asked. "It should be ready. I set the coffeemaker for the usual time, thinking I would wake up when I normally do, but I don't think it's been sitting too long. If memory serves, you like it strong, anyway."

If memory serves, he echoed to himself. She had brewed a pot of coffee for them at her house that night, in preparation for the all-nighter they knew lay ahead. He had told her he liked it strong. She remembered.

Even though the two of them had barely spoken to each other after that night. Did that mean something? Did he want it to?

"Coffee sounds good," he said. "But I can get it. You take yours with cream and sugar, if *I* recall correctly."

Okay, okay. So Ava wasn't the only one who could remember that night in detail. That didn't mean anything.

She pulled the covers more snugly around herself. "Thanks."

Peyton hurried to the kitchen, grateful for the opportunity to collect himself. Ava Brenner. Damn. It was as if he'd turned on some kind of homing device the minute he got into town in order to locate her. Or maybe she had turned on one to locate him. Nah. No way would she be looking for him after all this time. She'd made her feelings for him crystal clear back at Emerson. They'd only shone with an even starker clarity after that night at her parents' house. And no way would he be looking for her, either. It was nothing but a vicious twist of fate or a vengeful God or bad karma that had brought them together again.

By the time he carried their coffee back to the living room, she had swept her hair atop her head into a lopsided knot that, amazingly, made her look even more beautiful. The covers had fallen enough to reveal a pair of flannel pajamas, decorated with multicolored polka dots. Never in a million years would he have envisioned Ava Brenner in flannel polka dots. Weirdly, though, they suited her.

She mumbled her thanks as he handed her her coffee—and he told himself he did *not* linger long enough to skim his fingers over hers to see if she felt as soft as he remembered, even if he did notice she felt softer than he remembered. He briefly entertained the idea of sitting down beside her on the couch but thankfully came to his senses and returned to the chair.

When he trusted himself not to screw up the question, he asked, "Wanna tell me how I ended up spending the night with you again?"

He winced inwardly. He really hadn't wanted to make any reference to that night in high school. But her head snapped up at the question. Obviously, she'd picked up on the allusion, too.

"You don't remember?" she asked.

There was an interesting ambiguity to the question. She could have been asking about last night or that night sixteen years ago. Of course she must have meant last night. Still, there was an interesting ambiguity.

He shook his head. As much as it embarrassed him to admit it, he told her, "No. I don't remember much of anything after arriving at some restaurant on Michigan Avenue."

Except, of course, for fleeting recollections of green eyes, soft touches and the faint aroma of gardenias. But she didn't have to know that.

"So you do remember what happened before that?" she asked.

"Yeah." Not that he was going to tell her any of that, either.

She waited for him to elaborate. He elaborated by lifting one eyebrow and saying nothing.

She sighed and tried again. "When did you get back in town?"

"Yesterday."

"You came in from San Francisco?"

The question surprised him. "How did you know?"

"When I offered to take you home last night, you told

me I was going to have a long drive. Then you told me you live in an area called Sea Cliff in San Francisco. Sounds like a nice neighborhood."

That was an understatement. Sea Cliff was one of San Francisco's most expensive and exclusive communities, filled with lush properties and massive estates. His two closest neighbors were a globally known publishing magnate and a retired '60s rock and roll icon.

"It's not bad," he said evasively.

"So what took you to the West Coast?"

"Work." Before she could ask more, he turned the tables. "Still living in the Gold Coast?"

For some reason, she stiffened at the question. "No. My folks sold that house around the time I graduated from high school."

"Guess they figured those seven thousand square feet would be too much for two people instead of three. Not including the servants, of course."

She dropped her gaze to her coffee. "Only two of our staff lived on site."

"Well, then. I stand corrected." He looked around the tiny living room, recalled the tiny kitchen and tiny bedroom. "So what's this place?"

"It's..." She glanced up, hesitated, then looked down into her coffee again. "I own the shop downstairs. A boutique. Women's designer fashions."

He nodded. "Ah. So this apartment came with the place, huh?"

"Something like that."

"Easier to bring me here than to someplace where you might have to explain my presence, huh?"

For the first time, it occurred to him that Ava might be married. Hell, why wouldn't she be? She'd had every guy at Emerson panting after her. His gaze fell to the hands wrapped around her coffee mug. No rings. Any-where. Another interesting tidbit. She'd always worn jewelry in high school. Diamond earrings, ruby and sapphire rings—they were her parents' birthstones, he'd once heard her tell a friend—and an emerald necklace that set off her eyes beautifully.

Before he had a chance to decide whether her ring-less state meant she wasn't married or she just removed her jewelry at night, she said, "Well, you're not exactly an easy person to explain, are you, Peyton?"

He decided not to speculate on the remark and in-stead asked about her status point-blank. "Husband wouldn't approve?"

Down went her gaze again. "I'm not married."

"But you still have someone waiting for you at home that you'd have to explain me to, is that it?"

The fact that she didn't respond bothered Peyton a lot more than it should have. He told himself to move along, to just get the condensed version of last night's events and call a cab. He told himself there was nothing about Ava he wanted to know, nothing she could say that would affect his life now. He told himself to remember how bad things were between them in high school for years, not how good things were that one night.

He told himself all those things. But, as was so often the case, he didn't listen to a single word he said.

Ava did her best to reassure herself that she wasn't lying to Peyton. Lies of omission weren't really lies, were they? And what was she supposed to do? No way had she wanted him to see the postage stamp-size apart-ment she called home. She was supposed to be a massive success by now. She was supposed to have a posh ad-dress in the Gold Coast, a closet full of designer clothes and drawers full of designer jewelry. Well, okay, she did have those last two. But they belonged to the shop, not her. She could barely afford to rent them herself.

People believed what they wanted to believe, anyway. Even sitting in her crappy apartment, Peyton assumed she was the same dazzling—if vain, shallow and snotty—Gold Coast heiress who'd had everyone wrapped around her finger in high school. He thought she still lived in a place like the massive Georgian townhouse on Division Street where she grew up, and she still drove a car like the cream-colored Mercedes convertible she'd received for her sixteenth birthday.

He obviously hadn't heard how the Brenners of the Gold Coast had been reduced to a state of poverty and hardship that rivaled the one he'd escaped on the South Side. He didn't know her father was still doing time in a federal prison for tax evasion, embezzlement and a string of other charges, because he'd had to support a drug-and-call-girl habit. He didn't know her mother had passed away in a mental hospital after too many years of trying to cope with the anguish and ostracism brought on by her husband's betrayal. He didn't know how, before that, Colette Brenner had left Ava's father and taken her to Milwaukee to finish high school, or that Ava had done so in a school much like Emerson—except that *she* had been the poor scholarship student looked down on by the ruling class of rich kids, the same way she had looked down on Peyton and his crowd at Emerson.

Sometimes karma was a really mean schoolgirl.

But that was all the more reason she didn't want Peyton to know the truth now. She'd barely made a dent in her karmic debt. Spending her senior year of high school walking in the shoes of the students she'd treated so shabbily for years—being treated so shabbily herself—she had learned a major life lesson. It was only one reason she'd opened Talk of the Town: so that women who hadn't had the same advantages in life that she'd taken for granted could have the chance to walk in the designer shoes of high society, if only for a little while.

It was something she was sure Peyton would understand—if it came from anyone but Ava. If he found out what she'd gone through her senior year of high school, he'd mock her mercilessly. Not that she didn't deserve it. But a person liked to have a little warning before she found herself in a situation like that. A person needed a little time to put on her protective armor. Especially a person who knew what a formidable force Peyton Moss could be.

"There's no one waiting for me at home," she said softly in response to his question.

Or anywhere else, for that matter. No one in her former circle of friends had wanted anything to do with her once she started living below the poverty line, and she'd stepped on too many toes outside that circle for anyone there to ever want to speak to her. Peyton would be no exception.

When she looked up again, he was studying her with a scrutiny that made her uncomfortable. But all he said was, "So what did happen last night?"

"You were in Basilio's when I got there. I heard shouting in the bar and saw Dennis—he's the bartender," she added parenthetically, "talking to you. He suggested, um, that you might want a cup of coffee instead of another drink."

Instead of asking about the conversation, Peyton asked, "You know the bartender by name?"

"Sure. And Basilio, the owner, and Marcus, the

waiter who helped me get you to the car. I eat at that restaurant a lot." It was the only one in the neighborhood she could afford when it came to entertaining potential clients and vendors. Not that she would admit that to Peyton.

He nodded. "Of course you eat there a lot. Why cook for yourself when you can pay someone else do it?"

Ava ignored the comment. Peyton really was going to believe whatever he wanted about her. It didn't occur to him that sixteen years could mature a person and make her less shallow and more compassionate. Sixteen years evidently hadn't matured him, if he was still so ready to think the worst of her.

"Anyway," she continued, "you took exception to Dennis's suggestion that you'd had too much to drink— and you *had* had too much to drink, Peyton—and you got a little…belligerent."

"Belligerent?" he snapped. "I never get belligerent."

Somehow Ava refrained from comment.

He seemed to realize what she was thinking, because he amended, "Anymore. It's been a long time since I was belligerent with anyone."

Yeah, probably about sixteen years. Once he graduated from Emerson, all the targets of his belligerence— especially Ava Brenner—would have been out of his life.

"Basilio was going to throw you out, but I…I mean, when I realized you were someone I knew…I…" She expelled a restless sound. "I told him you and I are… That we were—" Somehow, she managed not to choke on the words. "Old friends. And I offered to drive you home."

"And he let you?" Peyton asked. "He let you leave with some belligerent guy he didn't know from Adam?

Wow. I guess he really didn't want to offend the regular cash cow."

Bristling, Ava told him, "He let me because you calmed down a lot after you recognized me. By the time Marcus and I got you into the car, you were actually being kind of nice. I know—hard to believe."

There. Take *that,* Mr. Belligerent Cow-Caller.

"But once you were in the car," she hurried on before he could comment, "you passed out. I didn't have any choice but to bring you here. I roused you enough to get you into the apartment, but while I was setting up the coffee, you found your way to the bedroom and went out like a light again. I thought maybe you'd sleep it off in a few hours, but... Well. That didn't happen."

"I've been working a lot the last few weeks," he said shortly, "on a demanding project. I haven't gotten much sleep."

"You were also blotto," she reminded him. Mostly because the cow comment still stung.

In spite of that, she wondered what kind of work he did and how he'd spent his life since they graduated. How long had he been in San Francisco? Was he married? Did he have children? Even as Ava told herself it didn't matter, she was helpless not to glance at his left hand. No ring. No indentation or tan line to suggest one had ever been there. Not that that was any definer of status. Even if he wasn't married, that didn't mean there wasn't a woman who was important in his life.

Not that Ava cared about any of that. She didn't. Really. All she cared about was getting him out of her hair. Getting him out of her apartment. Getting him out of her life.

In spite of that, she heard herself ask, "So why *are* you back in Chicago?"

He hesitated, as if he were trying to figure out how to reply. Finally, he said, "I'm here because my board of directors made me come."

Board of directors? she thought incredulously. *He* had a board of directors? "Board of directors?" she asked. "*You* have a board of directors?"

The question sounded even worse coming out of her mouth than it had sitting in her head, where it had sounded pretty bad.

Before she had a chance to apologize, Peyton told her—with a glare that could have boiled an ice cube, "Yeah, Ava. I have a board of directors. They're part of the multimillion-dollar corporation of which I am chief shareholder, not to mention CEO. A company that's named after me. On account of, in case I didn't mention it, I own it."

Ava grew more astonished with every word he spoke. But her surprise wasn't from the discovery that he was an enormous success—she'd always known Peyton could do or be whatever he wanted. She just hadn't pegged him for becoming the corporate type. On the contrary, he'd always scorned the corporate world. He'd scorned anyone who strove to make lots of money. He'd despised people like the ones in Ava's social circle. And now he was one of them?

This time, however, she kept her astonishment to herself.

At least, she thought she did, until he added, "You don't have to look so shocked. I did have one or two redeeming qualities back in high school, not the least of which was a work ethic."

"Peyton, I didn't mean—"

"The hell you didn't." Before she could continue, he added, "In fact, Moss Holdings Incorporated is close to becoming a *billion*-dollar corporation. The only thing standing between me and those extra zeroes after my net worth is a little company in Mississippi called Montgomery and Sons. Except that it's not owned by Montgomery or his sons anymore. They all died more than a century ago. It's now owned by the Montgomery sons' granddaughters. Who are both in their eighties."

Ava had no idea what to say. Not that he seemed to expect a response from her, because he suddenly became agitated and rose from the chair to pace the room.

He sounded agitated, too, when he continued, "Helen and Dorothy Montgomery. They're sweet little old Southern ladies who wear hats and white gloves to corporate meetings and send holiday baskets to everyone every year filled with preserves and socks they make themselves. They're kind of legendary in the business and financial communities."

He stopped pacing, looking at something near the front door that Ava couldn't see. At something he probably couldn't see, either, since whatever it was must have existed far away from the apartment.

"Yeah, everybody loves the Montgomery sisters," he muttered. "They're so sweet and little and old and Southern. So I'm going to look like a bully and a jerk when I go after their company with my usual…how did the *Financial Times* put it?" He hesitated, feigning thought. "Oh, yeah. Now I remember. With my usual 'coldhearted, mind-numbing ruthlessness.' And no one will ever want to do business with me again."

Now he looked at Ava. Actually, he glared at Ava, as if all of this—whatever *this* was—was her fault. "Not that there are many in the business and financial communities who like me much now. But at least they do business with me. If they know what's good for them."

Even though she wasn't sure she was meant to be a part of this conversation, she asked, "Then why are you going after the Montgomerys' company? With ruthlessness or otherwise?"

Peyton sat down again, still looking agitated. "Because that's what Moss Holdings does. It's what *I* do. I go after failing companies and acquire them for a fraction of what they're worth, then make them profitable again. Mostly by shedding what's unnecessary, like people and benefits. Then I sell those companies to someone else for a huge profit. Or else I dismantle them and sell off their parts to the highest bidder for a pile of cash. Either way, I'm not the kind of guy people like to see coming. Because it means the end of jobs, traditions and a way of life."

In other words, she translated, what he did led to the dissolution of careers and income, plunging people into the sort of environment he'd had to claw his way out of when he was a teenager.

"Then why do you do it?" she asked.

His answer was swift and to the point. "Because it makes me huge profits and piles of cash."

She would have asked him why making money was so important that he would destroy jobs and alienate people, but she already knew the answer. People who grew up poor and underprivileged often made making money their highest priority. Many thought if they just had enough money, it would make everything in their life all right and expurgate feelings of want and need. Some were driven enough to become tremendous successes—at making money, anyway. As far as making everything in their life right and expurgating feelings of want and need, well…that was a bit trickier.

Funnily, it was often people like Ava, who had grown

up with money and been afforded every privilege, who realized how wrong such a belief was. Money didn't make everything all right, and it didn't expurgate feelings of anything. Sure, it could ease a lot of life's problems. But it didn't change who a person was at her core. It didn't magically chase away bad feelings or alleviate stresses. It didn't make other people respect or admire or love you. At least not for the right reasons. And it didn't bring with it the promise of…well, anything.

"And jeez, why am I even telling you all this?" Peyton said with exasperation.

Although she was pretty sure he didn't expect an answer for that, either, Ava told him, "I don't know. Maybe because you need to vent? Although why would you need to vent about a business deal, seeing as you make them all the time? Unless there's something about this particular business deal that's making you feel like… how did you put it? A bully and a jerk."

"Anyway," he said, ignoring the analysis, "for the sake of good PR and potential future projects, my board of directors thought it would be better to not go after the Montgomery sisters the way I usually go after a company—by yanking it out from under its unsuspecting owners. They think I should try to—" he made a restless gesture "—to…finesse it out from under them with my charm and geniality."

Somehow, the words *finesse* and *Peyton Moss* just didn't fit, never mind the charm and geniality stuff. Ava did manage to keep her mouth shut this time. But he seemed to need to talk about what had brought him back here, and for some reason, she hesitated to stop him.

"The BoD think it will be easier to fend off lawsuits and union problems if I can charm the company away from the Montgomerys instead of grabbing it from them. So they sent me back here to, and I quote, 'ex-orcise your street demons, Peyton, and learn to be a gentleman.' They've even set me up with some Henry Higgins type who's supposed to whip me into shape. Then, when I'm all nice and polished, they'll let me come back to San Francisco and go after Montgomery and Sons. But *nicely,*" he added wryly. "That way, my tarnished reputation will stay only tarnished and not firebombed into oblivion."

Now he looked at Ava as if he were actually awaiting a reply. Not that she had one to give him. Although she was finally beginning to understand what had brought him back to Chicago—kind of—she wasn't sure what he expected her to say. Certainly Peyton Moss hadn't been bred to be a gentleman. That didn't mean he wasn't capable of becoming one. Eventually. Under the right tutelage. Which even Ava was having a hard time try-ing to imagine.

When she said nothing, he added quietly, "But you wanna hear the real kicker?"

She did, actually—more than she probably should admit.

"The real kicker is that they think I should pick up a wife while I'm here. They've even set me up with one of those millionaire matchmakers who's supposed to in-troduce me to—" he took a deep breath and released it slowly, as if he were about to reveal something of great importance "—the right kind of woman."

Ava's first reaction was an odd sort of relief that he wasn't already in a committed relationship. Her second reaction was an even odder disappointment that that was about to change. There was just something about the thought of Peyton being introduced to the "right kind of woman"—meaning, presumably, the kind of woman she herself was supposed to have grown up to be—that did something funny to her insides.

He added, "They think the Montgomery sisters might look more favorably at their family business being appropriated by another family than they would having it go to a coldhearted single guy like me." He smiled grimly. "So to finally answer your question, Ava, I'm back in Chicago to erase all evidence of my embarrassing, low-life past and learn to be a gentleman in polite society. And I'm supposed to find a nice society girl who will give me an added aura of respectability."

Ava couldn't quite keep the flatness from her voice when she replied, "Well, then. I hope you, in that society, with that nice society girl, will be very happy."

"Aw, whatsamatter, Ava?" he asked in the same cool tone. "Can't stand the fact that you and I are now social and financial equals?"

"Peyton, that's not—"

"Yeah, there goes the neighborhood."

"Peyton, I didn't mean—"

"Once you start letting in the riffraff, the whole place goes to hell, doesn't it?"

Ava stopped trying to explain or apologize, since he clearly wasn't going to let her do either. What was funny—or would have been, had it not been so biting—was that they actually weren't social and financial equals. Ava was so far below him on both ladders, she wouldn't even be hit by the loose change spilling out of his pockets.

"So what about you?" he asked.

The change of subject jarred her. "What about me?"

"What are you doing now? I remember you wanted to go to Wellesley. You were going to major in art or something."

She couldn't believe he remembered her top college choice. She'd almost forgotten it herself. She hadn't allowed herself to think about things like that once the family fortune evaporated. Although Ava had been smart, she'd been a lazy student. Why worry about grades when she had parents with enough money and connections to ensure admission into any school she wanted? The only reason she'd been accepted at her tony private school in Milwaukee was that she'd tested so high on its entry exam.

How was she supposed to tell Peyton she'd ended up studying business at a community college? Not that she hadn't received a fine education, but it was a far cry from the hallowed halls of academia for which she'd originally aimed.

"English," she said evasively. "I wanted to major in English."

He nodded. "Right. So where'd you end up going?"

"Wisconsin," she said, being deliberately vague. Let him think she was talking about the university, not the state.

He arched his brows in surprise. "University of Wisconsin? Interesting choice."

"The University of Wisconsin has an excellent English department," she said. Which was true. She just hadn't been a part of it herself. Nor had she lied to Peyton, she assured herself. She never said she went to University of Wisconsin. He'd just assumed, the same way he'd made lots of other assumptions about her. Why correct him? He'd be out of her life in a matter of minutes.

"And now you own a clothing store," he said. "Good to see you putting that English degree to good use. Then again, it's not like you actually work there, is it? Now that I think about it, I guess English is a good major for an heiress. Seeing as you don't have to earn a living like the rest of us working stiffs."

Ava bit her tongue instead of defending herself. She still had a tiny spark of pride that prohibited her from telling him the truth about her situation. Okay, there was that, and also the fear that he would gloat relentlessly once he found out how she'd gone from riches to rags.

"Have you finished your coffee?" she asked. It was the most polite way she knew how to say *beat it*.

He looked down into his mug. "Yeah. I'm finished."

But he made no move to leave. Ava studied him again, considering everything she had learned. He'd achieved all his success in barely a decade's time. She'd been out of school almost as long as he, but she was still struggling to make ends meet. And she would consider herself ambitious. Yet he'd gone so much further in the same length of time. That went beyond ambitious. That was…

Well, that was Peyton.

Still, she never would have guessed his stratospheric status had he not told her. When she'd removed his jacket and shoes last night, she had noted their manufacturers—it was inescapable in her line of work. Both could have been purchased in any department store. His hair was shorter than it had been in high school, but he didn't look as if he'd paid a fortune for the cut, the way most men in his position would. He might be worth almost a billion dollars now—and don't think that realization didn't stop her heart a little—but he didn't seem to be living any differently than any other man.

But then, Peyton wasn't the kind of guy to put on airs, either.

When he stood, he hesitated, as if he wanted to say

something. But he went to the kitchen without a word. She heard him rinse his cup and set it in the drainer, then move back to her bedroom. When he emerged, he was wearing his shoes and jacket, but his necktie hung loose from his collar. He looked like a man who'd had too much to drink the night before and slept in a bed other than his own. But even that couldn't detract from his appeal.

And there was the hell of it. Peyton did still appeal. He appealed to something deep inside Ava that had lain dormant for too long, something she wasn't sure would ever be able to resist him. Thankfully, that part of her wasn't the dominant part. She *could* resist Peyton Moss. Provided he left now and never came back.

For a moment, they only gazed at each other in silence. There were so many things Ava wanted to say, so many things she wanted him to know. About what had happened to her family that long-ago summer and how her senior year had changed her. About the life she led now. But she couldn't find the words. Everything came out sounding self-pitying or defensive or weak. She couldn't tolerate the idea of Peyton thinking she was any of those things.

Finally—thankfully—he ended the silence. "Thanks, Ava, for…for making sure I didn't spend last night in an alley somewhere."

"I'm sure you would have done the same for me."

He neither agreed nor disagreed. He only made his way to the front door, opened it and stepped over the threshold. She thought for a moment that he was going to leave without saying goodbye, the way he had sixteen years ago. But as he started to pull the door closed, he turned and looked at her.

"It was…interesting…seeing you again."

Yes, it had certainly been that.

"Goodbye, Peyton," she said. "I'm glad you're—"
What? she asked herself. Finally, because she knew
too long a hesitation would make her look insincere,
she finished, "Doing well. I'm glad you're doing well."

"Yeah, doing well," he muttered. "I'm sure as hell
that."

The comment was curious. He sounded kind of sarcastic, but why would he think otherwise? He had everything he'd striven to achieve. Before she could say
another word, however, the door closed with a soft click.
And then, as he had been sixteen years ago, Peyton
was gone.

And he hadn't said goodbye.

Three

It wasn't often that Ava heard a man's voice in Talk of the Town. So when it became clear that the rich baritone coming from beyond her office door didn't belong to anyone delivering mail or freight, her concentration was pulled from next month's employee schedule to the sales floor instead. Particularly when she recognized the man's voice as Peyton's.

No sooner did recognition dawn, however, than Lucy, one of her full-time salesclerks, poked her dark head through the office door. "There's a man out here looking for you, Ava," she said, adjusting her little black glasses. "A Mr. Moss? He seemed surprised when I told him you were here." She lowered her voice as she added, "He was kind of fishing for your phone number. Which of course I would never give out." She smiled and lowered her voice to a stage whisper. "You might want to come out and talk to him. He's pretty yummy."

Ava sighed inwardly. Clearly, Peyton hadn't lost his ability to go from zero to sixty on the charm scale in two seconds flat.

What was he doing here? Five days had passed since their exchange in her apartment, not one of which had ended without her thinking about all the things she wished she'd said to him. She'd always promised herself—and karma—that if she ever ran into any of her former classmates from Emerson whom she had mistreated as a teenager, she would apologize and do whatever it took to make amends. It figured that when fate finally threw one of her former victims into her path, it would start with the biggie.

So why hadn't she tried to make amends on Saturday? Why hadn't she apologized? Why had she instead let him think she was still the same vain, shallow, snotty girl she'd been in high school?

Okay, here was a second chance to put things to right, she told herself. Even if she wasn't sure how to make up for her past behavior, the least she could do was apologize.

"Actually, Lucy, why don't you show him into the office instead?"

Lucy's surprise was obvious. Ava never let anyone but employees see the working parts of the boutique. The public areas of the store were plush and opulent, furnished with gilded Louis Quatorze tables and velvet upholstered chairs, baroque chandeliers and Aubusson carpets—reproductions, of course, but all designed to promote the same air of sumptuousness the designer clothes afforded her clients. The back rooms were functional and basic. Her office was small and cluttered, the computer and printer the only things that could be called state-of-the-art. The floor was concrete, the walls were cinder block, the ceiling was foam board and nothing was pretty.

Lucy's head disappeared from the door, but her voice trailed behind her. "You can go back to the office. It's right through there."

Ava swiped a hand over the form-fitting jaguar-print dress she had donned that morning—something new from Yves Saint Laurent she'd wanted to test for comfort and wearability. She had just tucked a stray strand of auburn back into her French twist when Peyton appeared in the doorway, dwarfing the already tiny space.

He looked even better than he had the last time she saw him. His hair was deliciously wind tossed, and his whiskey-colored eyes were clearer. He'd substituted the rumpled suit of Saturday morning with faded jeans and a weathered leather jacket that hung open over a baggy chocolate-brown sweater. Battered hiking boots replaced the businesslike loafers.

He looked more like he had in high school. At least, the times in high school when she'd run into him outside of Emerson. Even in his school uniform, though, Peyton had managed to look different from the other boys. His shirttail had always hung out, his shoes had always been scuffed, his necktie had never been snug. Back then, she'd thought he was just a big slob. But now she suspected he'd deliberately cultivated his look to differentiate himself from the other kids at Emerson. Nowadays, she didn't blame him.

He said nothing at first, only gazed at her the way he had on Saturday, as if he couldn't quite believe she was real. Gradually he relaxed, and even went so far as to lean against the doorjamb and shove his hands into the pockets of his jeans. Somehow, though, Ava sensed he was striving for a nonchalance he didn't really feel.

"Hi," he finally said.

"Hi yourself."

She tried to be as detached as he was, but she felt the same way she had Saturday—as if she were in high school again. As if she needed to shoulder the mantle of rich bitch ice princess to protect herself from the barbs she knew would be forthcoming. She was horrified by the thought—horrified that the girl she used to be might still be lurking somewhere inside her. She never wanted to be that person again. She never *would* be that person again. In spite of that, something about Peyton made the haughty teenager bubble up inside her.

Silence descended for an awkward moment. Then Peyton said, "You surprised me, being here. I came into the shop to see if anyone working knew where I could find you. I didn't expect you to actually be here."

Because he didn't think she actually *worked* here, Ava recalled, battling the defensiveness again. She told herself not to let his comment get to her and reminded herself to make amends. The best way to do that was to be the person she was now, not the person she used to be.

"I'm here more often than you might think," she said—sidestepping the truth again.

Then again, one couldn't exactly hurry the appeasement of karma. It was one thing to make amends for past behaviors. It was another to spill her guts to Peyton about everything that happened to her family and admit how she'd ended up in the same position he'd been in in high school, and now she was really, really sorry for how she had behaved all those years. That wasn't really necessary, was it? To go into all that detail? A woman was entitled to some secrets. And Ava wasn't sure she could bear Peyton's smug satisfaction after he learned about it. Or, worse, if he displayed the same kind of fake pity so many of her former so-called friends did.

Oh, Ava, they would say whenever she ran into them. *Has your poor father gotten out of prison yet? No? Darling, how do you stand the humiliation? We must meet for lunch sometime, get you out of that dreary store where you have to work your fingers to the bone. I'll call you.*

No calls ever came, of course. Not that Ava wanted them to. And their comments didn't bother her, because she didn't care about those people anymore. But coming from Peyton... For some reason, she suspected such comments would bother her a lot.

So she stalled. "We're supposed to be receiving a couple of evening gowns from Givenchy today, and I wanted to look them over before they went out on the floor." All of which was true, she hastened to reassure herself. She just didn't mention that she would have also been at the store if they were expecting a shipment of bubble wrap. She put in more hours at Talk of the Town than her two full-timers did combined.

"Then I guess I was lucky I came in today," he said, looking a little anxious. Sounding a little anxious.

"What made you come in?" she asked. "I thought you were going to be all booked up with Henry Higginses and millionaire matchmakers while you were in town."

He grinned halfheartedly and shifted his weight from one foot to the other. Both actions were probably intended to make him look comfortable, but neither really did.

"Yeah... Well... Actually..." He took a breath, released it slowly and tried again. "Actually, that's kind of why I'm here."

He gestured toward the only other chair in the office and asked, "Mind if I sit down?"

"Of course not," she replied. Even though she did kind of mind, because doing that would bring him closer, and then she would be the one trying to look comfortable when she felt anything but.

He folded himself into the other chair and continued to look uneasy. She waited for him to say something, but he only looked around the office, his gaze falling first on the Year in Fashion calendar on the wall—for April, it was Pierre Cardin—then on the fat issues of *Vogue, Elle* and *Marie Claire* that lined the top shelf of her desk, then lower, on the stack of catalogs sitting next to the employee schedule she'd been working on, and then—

Oh, dear. The employee schedule, which had her name and hours prominently at the top. Hastily, she scooped up the catalogs and laid them atop the schedule, tossing her pencil onto both.

He finally returned his gaze to her face. "The Henry Higgins didn't work out."

"What happened?"

His gaze skittered away again. "He told me I had to stop swearing and clean up my language."

Ava bit her lip to keep from smiling, since, to Peyton, this was clearly an insurmountable problem. "Well, if you're going to be dealing with two sweet little old ladies from Mississippi who are in their eighties and wear hats and white gloves, that's probably good advice."

"Yeah, but the Montgomery sisters are like five states away. They can't hear me swearing in Chicago."

"But if it's a habit, now is a good time to start breaking it, since—"

"Dammit, Ava, I can stop swearing anytime I want to."

"Oh, really?" she said mildly.

"Hell, yes."

"I see."

"And you should have seen the suits he tried to put me into," Peyton added.

"Well, suits are part and parcel for businesspeople," Ava pointed out, "especially those in your position. You were wearing a suit at Basilio's the other night. What's the sudden problem with suits?"

"The problem wasn't suits. It was the suits this guy wanted to put me into."

She waited for him to explain, and when he didn't, asked, "Could you be a little more specific?"

He frowned. "One was purple. Oh, excuse me," he quickly corrected himself. "I mean *eggplant*. The other was the same color green the guys on the team used to spew after getting bodychecked too hard."

Ava thought for a minute, then said, "Loden, I think, is the color you're looking for."

"Yeah. That's it."

"Those are both very fashionable colors," she said. "Especially for younger guys like you. Sounds to me like Henry knew his stuff."

Peyton shook his head. "Suits should never be anything except gray, brown or black. Not slate, not espresso, not ebony," he added in a voice that indicated he'd already had this conversation with Henry Higgins. "Gray. Brown. Black. Maybe, in certain situations, navy blue. Not midnight," he said when she opened her mouth to comment. "Navy blue. They sure as hell shouldn't be purple or puke-green."

Ava closed her mouth.

"And don't get me started on the etiquette lessons the guy said I had to take," Peyton continued. "Or all that crap about comportment. Whatever the hell that is. He even tried to tell me what I can and can't eat in a restaurant."

"Peyton, all of those things are important when it comes to dealing with people in professional situations. Especially when you're conducting business with people who do it old school, the way it sounds like the Montgomery sisters do."

He frowned. "Ava, I didn't get where I am today by studying etiquette books or comporting myself—whatever the hell that is. I did it by knowing what I want and going after it."

"And that's obviously worked in the past," she agreed. "But you admitted yourself that you'll have to operate differently with the Montgomerys. That means using a new rule book."

"I like my rule book just fine."

"Then do your takeover your way."

Why was he here? she asked herself again. This was an odd conversation to be having with him. Still, they were getting along. Kind of. Maybe she should just go with the flow.

He growled something unintelligible under his breath, but if she had to wager a guess, she'd bet it was more of that profanity he was supposed to be keeping under wraps.

His voice gentled some. "All I'm saying is that this guy doesn't know me from Adam, and he has no idea what's going to work for me and what isn't. I need to work with someone who can, you know, smooth my rough edges without sawing them off."

Okay, she was starting to understand. He wanted to see if she could recommend another stylist for him. Since she owned a shop like Talk of the Town, he figured she had connections in the business that might help him out.

"There are several stylists in Chicago who are very good," she said. "Some of them bring their clients to me." She reached for a binder filled with business cards she'd collected over the years. "Just give me a minute to find someone whose personality jibes with yours."

Ha. As if. There wasn't a human being alive whose personality jibed with Peyton's. Peyton was too larger-than-life. The best she could hope for was to find someone who wasn't easily intimidated. Hmm...maybe that guy who worked with the Bears before their last Super Bowl appearance. He'd had to have a couple of teeth replaced, but still...

Peyton placed his hand over hers before she had a chance to open the binder. She tried to ignore the ruffle of butterflies in her midsection. Ha. As if.

His voice seemed to come from a very great distance when he spoke again. "No, Ava, you don't understand. Anyone you recommend is going to be in the same boat as Henry Higgins. They won't know me. They won't have any idea what to do with me."

She said nothing for a moment, only gazed at his hand covering hers, noting how it was twice the size of her own, how much rougher and darker, how his nails were blunt and square alongside her smooth, taupe-lacquered ovals. Their hands were so different from each other. So why did they fit together so well? Why did his touch feel so...right?

Reluctantly, she pulled her hand from beneath his and moved it to her lap. "Then why are you..."

The moment her gaze connected with his again, she began to understand. Surely, he wasn't suggesting...

There was no way he… It was ludicrous to even think… He couldn't want *her* to be his stylist.

Could he?

She was his lifelong nemesis. He'd said so himself. Not to her face, but to a friend of his. She'd overhead the two of them talking as they came out of the boys' restroom near her locker at Emerson. The seniors had been studying *Romeo and Juliet,* and she'd heard him say that the Montagues and Capulets had nothing on the Mosses and Brenners. He'd told his friend that he and Ava would be enemies forever. Then he'd ordered a plague on her house.

Very carefully, she asked, "Peyton, why exactly are you here?"

He leaned forward in the chair, hooking his hands together between his legs. His gaze never leaving hers, he said, "Exactly? I'm here because I didn't know where else to go. There aren't many people left in this city who remember me—"

Oh, she sincerely doubted that.

"And there are even fewer I care about seeing."

That she could definitely believe.

"And I'm not supposed to go back to San Francisco until I'm, um—" he made a restless gesture with his hand, as if he were literally groping for the right word "—until I'm fit for the right kind of society."

When Ava said nothing in response—because she honestly had no idea what to say—he expelled a restless breath and leaned back in the chair again.

Finally, point-blank, he said, "Ava, I want you to be my Henrietta Higgins."

Peyton told himself he shouldn't be surprised by Ava's deer-in-the-headlights reaction. He'd had a similar one when the idea popped into his head as he was escaping Henry Higgins's office the previous afternoon. But there was no way he could have kept working with that guy, and something told him anyone else was going to be just as bad or worse.

How was someone going to turn him from a sow's ear into a silk purse if they didn't even know how he'd become a sow's ear in the first place? He'd never be a silk purse anyway. He needed to work with someone who understood that the best they could hope for would be to turn him into something in between. Like a... hmm...like maybe a cotton pigskin. Yeah, that's it. Like a denim football. He could do that. He could go from a sow's ear to a denim football. But he was still going to need help getting there. And it was going to have to be from someone who not only knew how to look and act in society, but who knew him and his limitations.

And who knew his limitations better than Ava? Who understood society better than Ava? Maybe she didn't like him. Maybe he didn't like her. But he knew her. And she knew him. That was more than he could say for all the Henry Higginses in the world. He and Ava had worked together once, in spite of their differences— they'd actually pulled off an A-minus on that World Civ project in high school. So why couldn't they work together as adults? Hell, adults should be even better at putting aside their differences, right? Peyton worked with people he didn't like all the time.

The tension between him and Ava on Saturday morning had probably just been a result of their shock at seeing each other again. Probably. Hey, they were being civil to each other now, weren't they? Or at least they had been. Before he dropped the Henrietta Higgins bombshell and Ava went all catatonic on him.

"So what do you say, Ava?" he asked in an effort to get the conversation rolling again. "Think you could help me out here?"

"I, ah…" she nonanswered.

"I mean, this sort of thing is right up your alley, right? Even if you didn't own a store that deals with, you know, fashion and stuff." *Fashion and stuff?* Could he sound more like an adolescent? "You know all about how people are supposed to dress and act in social situations."

"Yes, but…"

"And you know me well enough to not to dress me in purple."

"Well, that's certainly true, but…"

"And you'd talk to me the right way. Like you wouldn't say—" He adopted what he thought was a damned good impression of the man who had tried to dress him in purple. "'Mr. Moss, would you be ever so kind as to cease usage of the vulgar sort of language we decided earlier might be a detriment to your reception by the ladies whom you are doing your best to impress.' You'd just say, 'Peyton, the Montgomerys are going to wash your mouth out with soap if you don't stop dropping the F-bomb.' And just like that, I'd know what the hell you were talking about, and I'd do it right away."

This time, Ava only arched an eyebrow in what could have been amusement or censure…or something else he probably didn't want to identify.

"Okay, so maybe I wouldn't do it right away," he qualified. "But at least I would know what you were talking about, and we could come to some sort of compromise."

The eyebrow lowered, but the edge of her mouth twitched a little. Even though he wasn't sure whether it was twitching up or down, Peyton decided to be optimistic. At least she hadn't thrown anything at him.

"I just mean," he said, "that you…that I…that we…" He blew out an irritated breath, sat up straighter, and looked her straight in the eye. "Look, Ava, I know we were never the best of friends…" *Even if we were—for one night, anyway—lovers,* he couldn't help thinking. Hoping she wasn't thinking that, too. Figuring she probably was. Not sure how he felt about any of it. "But I obviously need help with this new and improved me, and I'm not going to get it from some total stranger. I don't know anyone here who could help me except you. Because you're the only one here who knows me."

"I *did* know you," she corrected him. "When we were in high school. Neither of us is the person we were then."

There was something in her voice that made Peyton hesitate. Although it was true that in a lot of ways he wasn't the person he'd been in high school, Ava obviously still was. Maybe the adult wasn't quite as snotty, vain or superficial as the girl had been, but she could still put a guy in his place. She was still classy. She was still beautiful. She was still out of his league. Hell, she hadn't changed at all.

"So will you do it?" he asked, deliberately not giving her time to think it over.

She thought it over anyway. Dammit. Her gaze never left his, but he could almost hear the crackling of her brain synapses as she connected all the dots and came to her conclusions. He was relieved when she finally smiled.

Until she asked, "How much does the position pay?"

His mouth fell open. "Pay?"

She nodded. "Pay. Surely you were paying your previous stylist."

"Well, yeah, but that was his job."

She shrugged. "And your point would be?"

He didn't know what his point was. He'd just figured Ava would help him out. He hadn't planned on her being mercenary about it.

Wow. She really hadn't changed since high school.

"Fine," he said coolly. "I'll pay you what I was paying him." He named the figure, one that was way too high to pay anyone for telling people how to dress and talk and eat.

Ava shook her head. "No, you'll have to do better than that."

"What?"

"Peyton, if you want to make use of my expertise in this matter, then I expect to be compensated accordingly."

Of course she did. Ava Brenner never did anything unless she was compensated.

"Fine," he said again. "How much do you charge for your expertise?"

She thought for another minute, then quoted a figure fifty percent higher than what he had offered.

"You're nuts," he told her. "You could build the Taj Mahal for that."

She said nothing.

He offered her 10 percent more.

She said nothing.

He offered her 25 percent more.

She tilted her head to one side.

He offered her 40 percent more.

"All right," she said with a satisfied smile.

"Great," he muttered.

"Well, I didn't want to be unreasonable."

This time Peyton was the one who said nothing. But he suddenly realized it wasn't because he was irritated with their lopsided bargaining—as if Ava was any kind of bargain. It was because it felt kind of good to be sparring with her again. He remembered now how, despite the antagonism of their exchanges in high school, he'd always come away from them feeling weirdly energized and satisfied. Although he still sparred with plenty of people these days, none ever left him feeling the way he'd felt taking on Ava.

"But Peyton, you'll have to do things my way," she said, pulling him out of his musing.

Peyton hated it when people told him they had to do things any way other than his own. He waited for the resentment and hostility that normally came along with such demands to coil inside him. Instead, he felt strangely elated.

"All right," he conceded. "We'll do this your way."

She grinned. He told himself it was smugly. But damned if she didn't look kind of happy to have taken on the task, too.

Four

Scarcely an hour after Ava agreed to be Peyton's makeover artist, she sat across from him at a table in a State Street restaurant. He'd asked her if they could get started right away, since he was eager to get on with his corporate takeover and had already lost a week to his previous stylist. And since—Hey, Ava, would ya look at that?—it was coming up on noon anyway, lunch sounded like a really good idea. After ensuring that one of her morning clerks would be able to pull an afternoon shift, too, Ava had agreed.

As surprised as she'd been by his request to help him out, she was even more surprised to realize she was happy to be doing it. Though not because he was paying her, since the figure she'd quoted him would barely cover the cost of the two additional salesclerks she'd need at Talk of the Town to cover for her. The strange happiness, she was certain, stemmed from the fact that she would finally be able to make amends for the way she had treated him in high school. It was that, and nothing more, that caused the funny buzz of delight that hummed inside her.

Anyway, what difference did it make? The point was that she would be helping Peyton become a gentleman, thereby ensuring he added to his already enormous financial empire. The point was that she would be performing enough good deeds over the next week or so to counter a lot of the mean things she'd said and done to him in high school. And the point was that, by helping him this way, she wouldn't have to bare her soul about the specifics of her current lifestyle. Specifically, she wouldn't have to tell him how she didn't have any style in her life, save what she was surrounded by at work every day.

What would telling Peyton about what happened to her family sixteen years ago accomplish? It wouldn't change anything. Why shouldn't she just do this nice thing for him and make some small amends for her past? No harm, no foul. They could complete the mission, job well done, then he could be on his way back to the West Coast none the wiser.

Yeah. That's the ticket.

She sighed inwardly as she looked at Peyton. Not because of how handsome he was sitting there looking at the menu—though he was certainly handsome sitting there looking at the menu—but because he was slumped forward with one elbow on the table, his chin settled in his hand. He had also preceded her to the table and seated himself without a second thought for her, then snatched up the menu as if it he hadn't eaten in a week. Combined, the actions gave her some small inkling of what his previous Henry Higgins had been up against.

"Peyton," she said quietly.

His gaze never left the menu. "Yeah?"

She said nothing until he looked up at her. She hoped he would realize she was setting an example for him to follow when she straightened in her chair and plucked the menu delicately from the table, laying her other hand in her lap.

He changed his posture not at all. "What is it?"

She threw her shoulders back and sat up even straighter.

"What?" he repeated, more irritably this time.

Fine. If he was going to behave like a child, she'd treat him like a child. "Sit up straight."

He looked confused. "Say what?"

"Sit up straight."

He narrowed his eyes and opened his mouth as if he were going to object, but she arched one eyebrow meaningfully and he closed his mouth again. To his credit, he also straightened in his chair and leaned against its back. She could tell he wasn't happy about completing the action. But he did complete it.

"Take your elbow off the table," she further instructed.

He frowned at her, but did as she said.

Satisfied she had his attention—maybe a little more than she wanted—she continued with her lesson. "Also, when you're in a restaurant with a woman and the host is taking you to your table, you should always invite her to walk ahead of you and follow her so that—"

"But how will she know where she's going if she's walking ahead of me?" he interrupted.

Ava maintained her calm, teacherly persona. "This may come as a surprise to you, Peyton, but women can generally follow a restaurant host to a table every bit as

well as a man can. Furthermore," she hurried on when
he opened his mouth to object again, "when the two of
you arrive at the table, if the host doesn't direct her to
a chair and pull it out for her, then you need to do that."

"But I thought you women hated it when men pull
out a chair for you, or open the door for you, or do anything else for you."

"Some women would prefer to do those things themselves, true, but not all women. Society has moved past
a time when that kind of thing was viewed as sexist,
and now it's simply a matter of common—"

"Since when?" he barked. Interrupting her. Again.
"The last time I opened a door for a woman, she about
cleaned my clock for it."

Ava managed to maintain her composure. "And when
was that?"

He thought for a minute. "Actually, I think it was
you who did that. I was on my way out of chemistry
and you were on your way in."

Ava remembered the episode well. "The reason I
wanted to clean your clock wasn't because you held the
door open for me. It was because you and Tom Sellinger
made woofing sounds as I walked through it."

Instead of looking chagrined, Peyton grinned. "Oh,
yeah. I forgot that part."

"*Anyway*," she continued, "these days it's a matter of
common courtesy to open a door for someone—male
or female—and to pull out a woman's chair for her. But
you're right that some women prefer to do that themselves. You'll know a woman who does by the way she
chooses a chair when she arrives at the table and immediately pulls it out for herself. That's a good indication that you don't have to do it for her."

"Gotcha," he said. Still grinning. Damn him.

"But from what you've told me about the Misses Montgomery," Ava said, "they'll expect you to extend the courtesy to them."

"Yeah, okay," he muttered. "I guess you have a point."

"Don't mutter," she said.

He narrowed his eyes at her again. But his voice was much clearer when he said, "Fine. The next time I'm in a restaurant with a woman, I'll let her go first and watch for clues. Anything else?"

"Oh, yes," Ava assured him enthusiastically. "We've only just begun. Once you sit down, let her open her menu first." When he started to ask another question that would doubtless be more about when women had changed their minds about this sort of thing—as if women had ever stopped having the prerogative to change their minds about whatever they damned well pleased—she continued, "And when you're looking at your menu, it's nice to make conversation over the choices. Don't just sit there staring at it until you make a decision. Ask your companion what she thinks looks good, too. If you're in a restaurant where you've eaten before, you might even make suggestions about dishes you like."

He considered her for another moment, then asked, "You're not going to make me order for you, are you? I hate that."

"*I* won't make you order for *me*," she said. "But some women like for men to do that."

"Well, how the hell will I know if they want me to or not?"

Ava cleared her throat discreetly. He looked at her as if he had no idea why. She stood her silent ground. He replayed what he had just said, then rolled his eyes.

"Fine. How…will I know?" he enunciated clearly, pausing over the spot where the profanity had been.

"You'll know because she'll tell you what she's planning to have, and when your waiter approaches, you'll look at her, and she'll look back at you and not say anything. If she looks at the waiter and says she'll start with the crab bisque and then moves on to the salad course, you'll know she's going to order for herself."

"So what do you think the Montgomerys will do?"

"I have no idea."

"Dammit, Ava, I—"

She arched her eyebrow again. He growled his discontent.

"I hate this," he finally hissed. "I hate having to act like someone I'm not."

Ava disagreed that he was being forced to act like someone he wasn't, since she was confident that somewhere deep inside he did have the potential to be a gentleman. In spite of that, she told him, "I know you do. And after your takeover of the Montgomerys' company is finished, if you want to go back to your reprobate ways, no one will stop you. Until then, if you want your takeover to be successful, you're going to have to do what I tell you."

He blew out an exasperated sound and grumbled another ripe obscenity. So Ava snapped her menu shut and stood, collecting her purse from the back of her chair as she went.

"Hey!" he said as he rose, too, following her. "Where the hell do you think you're going? You said you would help me out."

She never broke stride. "Not if you won't even try. I have better things to do with my afternoon than sit here watching you sulk and listening to you swear."

"Yeah, I guess you could get a crapload of shopping done this afternoon, couldn't you?" he replied. "Then you could hit that restaurant where you know everyone's name. Some guy there will pull out your chair for you and do all the ordering. And I bet he never swears."

She halted and spun around to face him. "You know, Peyton, I'm not sure you *are* fit for polite society. Go ahead and bulldoze your way over two nice old ladies. You were always much better at that than you were asking for something politely."

Why had she thought this could work? Just because the two of them had managed to be civil to each other for ten minutes in her office? Yeah, right. Ten minutes was about the longest the two of them had ever been able to be in each other's presence before the bombs began to drop.

Well, except for that night at her parents' house, she remembered. Then again, that had been pretty explosive, too...

"Excuse me," she said as civilly as she could before turning her back on him again and making her way toward the exit.

She took two steps before he caught her by the arm and spun her around. She was tempted to take advantage of the momentum to slam her purse into his shoulder, but one of them had to be a grown-up. And she was barely managing to do that herself.

She steeled herself for another round of combat, but he only said softly, sincerely, "I'm sorry."

She relaxed. Some. "I forgive you."

"Will you come back to the table? Please?"

She knew the apology hadn't come easily for him. His use of the word *please* had probably been even harder. He was trying. Maybe the two of them would always be like fire and ice, but he was making an effort. It would be small of her not to give it—not to give him—another chance.

"Okay," she said. "But, Peyton…" She deliberately left the statement unfinished. She'd made clear her terms already.

"I know," he said. "I understand. And I promise I'll do what you tell me to do. I promise to be what you want me to be."

Well, Ava doubted that. Certainly Peyton would be able to do and say the things she told him to do and say. But be what she wanted him to be? That was never going to happen. He would never be forgiving of the way she had treated him in high school. He would never be able to see her as anything other than the queen bee she'd been then. He would never be her friend. Not that she blamed him for any of those things. The best she could hope for was that he would, after this, have better memories of her to replace the ugly ones. If nothing else, maybe, in the future, when—if—he thought of her, it would be with a little less acrimony.

And, hey, that wasn't terrible, right?

"Let's start over," she said.

He nodded. "Okay."

She was talking about the afternoon, of course. But she couldn't help thinking how nice it would be if they could turn back the clock a couple of decades and start over there, too.

The last time Peyton was in a tailor's shop—in fact, the only time Peyton was in a tailor's shop—it had been a cut-rate establishment in his old neighborhood that had catered to low-budget weddings and proms. Which was why he'd been there in the first place, to rent a tux for Emerson's prom. The place had been nothing like the mahogany-paneled, Persian-carpeted wonder in which he now stood. He always bought his clothes off the rack and wore whatever he yanked out of the closet. If the occasion was formal, there was the tux he'd bought at a warehouse sale not long after he graduated from college. His girlfriend at the time had dragged him there, and she'd deemed it a vintage De la Renta—whatever the hell that was—that would remain timeless forever. It had cost him forty bucks, which he'd figured was a pretty good deal for timelessness.

Ava, evidently, had other ideas. All it had taken was one look at the dozen articles of clothing he'd brought with him, and she'd concluded his entire wardrobe needed revamping. Sure, she'd been tactful enough to use phrases like *a little out-of-date* and *not the best fitting* and *lower tier.* The end result was the same. She'd hated everything he brought with him. And when he'd told her about the vintage De la Renta back in San Francisco and how he'd worn it as recently as a month ago, she'd looked as though she wanted to lose her breakfast.

Now she stood beside him in front of the tailor's mirror, and Peyton studied her reflection instead of his own—all three panels of it. He still couldn't get over how beautiful she was. The clingy leopard-print dress she'd worn the day before had been replaced by more casual attire today, a pair of baggy tan trousers and a creamy sweater made of some soft fuzzy stuff that didn't cling at all. She'd left her hair down but still had it pulled back in a clip at her nape. He wondered what it took—besides going to bed—to make her wear it loose, the way it had been Saturday morning. Then again, as reasons went for a woman wearing her hair loose, going to bed was a pretty good one.

"Show him something formal in Givenchy," she said, speaking to the tailor. "And bring him some suits from Hugo Boss. Darks. Maybe something with a small pinstripe. Nothing too reckless."

The tailor was old enough to be Peyton's grandfather, but at least his suit wasn't purple. On the contrary, it was a sedate dark gray that was, even to Peyton's untrained eye, impeccably cut. He had a tape measure around his neck, little black glasses perched on his nose and a tuft of white hair encircling his head from one ear to the other. His name was the very no-nonsense Mr. Endicott.

"Excellent choices, Miss Brenner," Mr. Endicott said before scurrying off to find whatever it was she had asked him to bring.

Ava turned her attention to Peyton, studying his reflection as he was hers. She smiled reassuringly. "Hugo Boss is a favorite of men in your position," she said. "He's like the perfect designer for high-powered executives. At least, the ones who don't want to wear eggplant, loden or espresso."

Peyton started to correct her about the high-powered-executive thing, then remembered that he was, in fact, a high-powered executive. Funny, but he hadn't felt like one since coming back to Chicago.

"I promise he won't bring you anything in purple or puke-green," she clarified when he didn't reply. "He's one of the most conservative tailors in Chicago."

Peyton nodded, but still said nothing. A weird development, since he'd never been at a loss for words around Ava before. He'd said a lot of things to her when they were in high school that he shouldn't have. Even if she'd been vain, snotty and shallow, she hadn't deserved some of the treatment she'd received from him. There were a couple of times in particular that he maybe, possibly, perhaps should apologize for...

"It's not that your other clothes are bad," she added, evidently mistaking his silence as irritation. "Like I said, they just need a little, um, updating."

She was trying hard not to say anything that might create tension between them. And the two of them had gotten along surprisingly well all morning. They'd been stilted and formal and in no way comfortable with each other, but they'd gotten along.

"Look, Ava, I'm not going to jump down your throat for telling me I'm not fashionable," he said. "I know I'm not. I'm doing this because I'm about to enter a sphere of the business world I've never moved in before, one that has expectations I'll have to abide by." He shrugged. "But I have to learn what they are. That's why you're here. I won't bite your head off if you tell me what I'm doing wrong."

She arched that eyebrow at him again, the way she had the day before at the restaurant, when he'd bitten her head off for telling him what he was doing wrong.

"Anymore," he amended. "I won't bite your head off anymore."

The eyebrow went back down, and she smiled. It wasn't a big smile, but it was a start. If nothing else, it told him she was willing to keep reminding him, as long as he was willing to remember he'd reminded her to do it.

The tailor returned with a trio of suits and a single tuxedo, and Peyton blew out a silent breath of relief that none of them could be called anything but *dark*. The man then helped Peyton out of his leather jacket and gestured for him to shed the dark blue sweater beneath it. When he stood in his white V-neck T-shirt and jeans, the tailor helped him on with the first suit jacket, made some murmuring sounds, whipped the tape measure from around his neck, and began to measure Peyton's arms, shoulders and back.

"Now the trousers," the man said.

Peyton looked at Ava in the mirror.

"I think it's okay if you go in the fitting room for that," she said diplomatically.

Right. Fitting room. He knew that. At least, he knew that *now*.

When he returned some minutes later wearing what he had to admit was a faultless charcoal pinstripe over a crisp white dress shirt the tailor had also found for him, Ava had her back to him, inspecting two neckties she had picked up in his absence.

"So...what do you think?" he asked.

As he approached her, he tried to look more comfortable than he felt. Though his discomfort wasn't due to the fact that he was wearing a garment with a price tag higher than that of any of the cars he'd owned in his youth. It was because he was worried Ava still wouldn't approve of him, even dressed in the exorbitant plumage of her tribe.

His fear was compounded when she spun around smiling, only to have her smile immediately fall. Dammit. She still didn't like him. No, he corrected himself—she didn't like what he was wearing. Big difference. He didn't care if she didn't like him. He didn't. He only needed for her to approve of his appearance. Which she obviously didn't.

"Wow," she said.

Oh. Okay. So maybe she did approve.

"You look..." She drew in a soft breath and expelled it. "Wow."

Something hot and fizzy zipped through his midsection at her reaction. It was a familiar sensation, but one he hadn't felt for a long time. More than fifteen years, in fact. It was the same sensation he'd felt one time when Ava looked at him from across their shared classroom at Emerson. For a split second, she hadn't registered that it was Peyton she was looking at, and her smile had been dreamy and wistful. In that minuscule stretch of time, she had looked at him as if he were something worth looking at, and it had made him feel as if nothing in his life would ever go wrong again.

Somehow, right now, he had that feeling again.

"So you like it?" he asked.

"Very much," she said. Dreamily. Wistfully. And heat whipped through his belly again. She finally seemed to remember where she was and what she was supposed to be doing, because she looked down at the lengths of silk in her hand. He couldn't help thinking she sounded a little flustered when she said, "But you, ah, you need a tie."

She took a few steps toward him, stopped for some reason, then completed a few more that brought her within touching distance. Instead of closing the gap, though, she held up the two neckties, one in each hand.

"I hope you don't mind," she said, "but I'm of the opinion that the necktie is where a man truly shows his personality. The suit can be as conservative as they come, but the tie can be a little more playful and interesting." She hesitated. "Provided that fits the character of the man."

He wanted to ask if she actually thought he was playful, never mind interesting, but said nothing. Mostly because he had noted two spots of pink coloring her cheeks and had become fascinated by them. Was she blushing, or was the heat in the store just set too high? Then he realized it was actually kind of cool in there. Which meant she must be—

"If you don't like these, I can look for something different," she told him, taking another step that still didn't bring her as close as he would have liked. "But these two made me think of you."

Peyton forced himself to look at the ties. One was splashed with amorphous shapes in a half dozen colors, and the other looked like a watercolor rendition of a tropical rain forest. He was surprised to discover he liked them. The colors were bold without being obnoxious, and the patterns were masculine without being aggressive. The fact that Ava said they reminded her of him made him feel strangely flattered.

"I'll just look for something different then," she said when he didn't reply, once again misinterpreting his silence as disapproval. "There were some nice striped ones you might like better." She started to turn away.

"No, Ava, wait."

In one stride, he covered the distance between them and curled his fingers around her arm, spinning her gently around to face him. Her eyes were wide with surprise, her mouth slightly open. And God help him, all he wanted was to keep tugging her forward until he could cover her mouth with his and wreak havoc on them both.

"I, uh, I like them," he said, shoving aside his errant thoughts.

Once again, he forced himself to look at the ties. But all he saw was the elegant fingers holding them, her nails perfect ovals of red. That night at her parents' house, her nails had been perfect ovals of pink. He'd thought the color then was so much more innocent-looking than Ava was. Until the two of them finally came together, and he realized she wasn't as experienced as he thought, that he was the first guy to—

"Let's try that one," he said, not sure which tie he was talking about.

"Which one?"

"The one on the right," he managed.

"My right or your right?"

He stifled the frustrated obscenity hovering at the back of his throat. "Yours."

She held up the tie with the unstructured forms and smiled. "That was my favorite, too."

Great.

Before he realized what she was planning, she stepped forward and looped the tie around his neck, turning up the collar of his shirt to thread it underneath. He was assailed by a soft, floral scent that did nothing to dispel the sixteen-year-old memories still dancing in his head, and the flutter of her fingers as she wrapped the length of silk around itself jacked his pulse rate higher. In an effort to keep his sanity, he closed his eyes and began to list in alphabetical order all the microbreweries he had visited on his travels. Thankfully, by the time he came to Zywiec in Poland, she was pulling the knot snug at his throat.

"There," she said, sounding a little breathless herself. "That should, ah, do it."

He did his best to ignore the last two words and the fact that she had stumbled over them. She couldn't be thinking about the same thing he was.

"Thanks," he muttered, the word sounding in no way grateful.

"You're welcome," she muttered back, the sentiment sounding in no way generous.

When he opened his eyes, he saw Ava glaring at him. Worse, he knew he was glaring at her, too. Before either of them could say anything that might make the situation worse, he went back to the mirror. Mr. Endicott took that as his cue to start with the measuring and adjusting again. He made a few notations on a pad of paper, struck a few marks on the garment with a piece of chalk, stuck a few pins into other places and told Peyton to go try on the next suit.

When he returned in that one, Ava was near the mirror draping a few more neckties onto a wooden valet. Upon his approach, she hurriedly finished, then strode to nearly the other side of the room. Jeez, it was as though anytime the two of them spent more than an hour in each other's presence, a switch flipped somewhere that sent a disharmony ray shooting over them. What the hell was up with that?

This time Peyton tied his own damned tie—though not with the expertise Ava had—then turned for her approval. Only to see her still riffling through some neckties on a table that she'd probably already riffled through.

He cleared his throat to get her attention.

She continued her necktie hunt.

He turned back to the tailor. "This one is fine, too."

Out came the tape measure and chalk again. The ritual was performed twice more—including Peyton's futile efforts to win Ava's attention—until even the tuxedo was fitted. Only when he was stepping down from the platform in that extraformal monkey suit did Ava look up at him again. Only this time, she didn't look away. This time, her gaze swept him from the top of his head to the tips of his shoes and back.

He held his breath, waiting to see if she would smile.

She didn't. Instead she said, "I, um, I think that will do nicely." Before Peyton had a chance to say thanks, she added, "But you need a haircut."

All Peyton could think was, *Two steps forward, one step back.* What the hell. He'd take it.

"I'm guessing that's somewhere on our to-do list?" he asked.

She nodded. "This afternoon. I made an appointment for you at my salon. They're fabulous."

"Your *salon?*" he echoed distastefully. "What's wrong with a barbershop?"

"Nothing. If you're a dockworker."

"Ava, I've never set foot in a salon. A record I plan to keep."

"But it's unisex," she said, as if that made everything okay.

"I don't care if it's forbidden sex. Find me a good barber."

She opened her mouth to argue, but his unwillingness to bend on the matter must have shown in his expression. So she closed her mouth and said nothing. Not that that meant she would find him a barber. But at least they could bicker about it after they left the tailor's.

And why was he kind of looking forward to that?

When it became obvious that neither of them was going to say more, Peyton made his way back to Endicott, who led him back to the fitting room.

"Don't worry, Mr. Moss," the tailor said. "You're doing fine."

Peyton looked up at that. "What?"

"Miss Brenner," Endicott said as he continued to walk, speaking over his shoulder. "She likes the suits. She likes the tuxedo even more."

"How can you tell?"

The tailor simply grinned. "Don't worry," he repeated. "She likes you, too."

Peyton opened his mouth to reply, but no words emerged. Which was just as well, because Mr. Endicott continued walking, throwing up a hand to gesture him forward.

"Come along, Mr. Moss. I still need to pin those trousers."

Sure thing, Peyton thought. Just as soon as he pinned some thoughts back into his brain.

Five

After addressing Peyton's wardrobe and hair, ah, challenges, Ava turned his attention to the appreciation of life's finer things—art, music, theater. At least, that was where she was planning to turn his attention the morning after their sartorial adventures. No sooner did she rap lightly on the door of his hotel suite, however, than did she discover her plans were about to go awry.

"Sorry," he said by way of a greeting. "But we have to cancel this morning. I'm supposed to meet with the matchmaker. I forgot all about it yesterday when you and I made plans for this morning."

Ava told herself the reason for the sudden knot her stomach was because she was peeved at his last-minute canceling of their date. Ah, she meant *plans*. And she was peeved because they were *plans* she'd given herself the day off from work for when she might have saved herself some money instead of paying Lucy overtime.

It had nothing to do with the fact that Peyton would be spending the morning with another woman.

Not that the other woman was, you know, *another woman,* since for her to be that, Ava would have to be the primary woman in his life, and of course that wasn't the case. Besides, the other woman he was seeing today was only a matchmaker. A matchmaker who would be setting him up with, well, *other women.* Women he would be seeing socially. Confidentially. Romantically.

The knot squeezed tighter. Because she was peeved, Ava reminded herself. Peeved that he was messing up their *plans.*

"Oh. Okay," she said, sounding troubled and unhappy, and in no way peeved.

"I'm really sorry," he apologized again. "When I checked my voice mail last night, there was a message from Caroline—she's the matchmaker—reminding me. By then it was too late to call you, and you didn't answer your phone this morning."

He must have called while she was in the shower. "Well, you don't want to miss a meeting with her. I'm sure you and she have a lot to go over before you can launch your quest for Ms. Right."

"Actually, I've already met with her once. We're meeting today because she's rounded up some possible matches, and she wants me to look at their photos and go over their stats before she makes the actual introductions. Maybe we could just push things back to this afternoon?"

"Sure. No problem."

So what if Peyton was meeting with his matchmaker? Ava asked herself. He was supposed to be doing that. Finding an appropriate woman was half the reason he was back in Chicago, and Ava didn't even have to work with him on that part. She only had to make sure he was presentable to any woman he did meet.

She leaped on that realization. "But you know, Peyton, I'm not sure you're ready to meet any prospective dates just yet. We still have a lot of work to do to get you ready for that."

"How much more do we have to do?"

He'd actually come a long way in four days, Ava had to admit. And not just because of his stylish new wardrobe and excellent new haircut—which he had finally agreed to get at her salon, but not after much haggling. Haggling that, in hindsight, hadn't been all that unpleasant, especially when he seemed to be enjoying it as much as she did.

At any rate, his faded jeans and bulky sweater of the day before had made way for expensive dark-wash denim and a more fitted sweater in what she knew was espresso, but which she'd conceded to Peyton—after more surprisingly enjoyable haggling—was actually brown. His shorter hair had showcased the few threads of silver amid the black, something that gave him a definite executive aura—not to mention an added bit of sexiness. Ava's charcoal skirt and claret cashmere sweater set—both by Chanel—should have seemed dressy, but he made denim and cotton aristocratic to the point where she felt like the palace gardener. He was the kind of client that would make a matchmaker drool—never mind the effect he would have on his prospective matches. It was amazing what a little polish would do for a guy.

Then again, it wasn't always the clothes that made the man. What made Peyton Peyton was what was beneath the clothes. And that was something even teaching him about the finer things in life wouldn't change.

Yes, he needed to learn to become a gentleman if he wanted to impress the sisters Montgomery and acquire their company. But there was too much roughneck in him to ever let the gentleman take over for very long.

It was a realization that should have made Ava even more peeved, since it suggested that everything she was doing to help him was pointless. Instead, it comforted her.

Remembering he'd asked her a question that needed a response, she said, "Well, I was kind of hoping to cover the arts this week. And we still need to fine-tune your restaurant etiquette. And we should—" She halted. There was no reason to make him think there was still tons more to do, since there really wasn't. For some reason, though, she found herself wishing there was still tons more to do. "Not a lot," she said. "There's not a lot."

Instead of looking pleased about that, he looked kind of, well, peeved.

"I should go," she told him. "What time do you think you'll be finished?"

"I don't know. Maybe I could call you when we're done?"

She nodded and started to turn away.

"Unless…"

She turned to face him. "Unless what?"

He looked a little uncomfortable. "Unless maybe…" He shoved his hands into the pockets of his jeans, a restless gesture. "Unless maybe you want to come with me?"

It was an odd request. For one thing, Caroline the matchmaker would be curious—not to mention possibly peeved—if Peyton showed up with a woman. A woman who, by the way, Caroline had had no part in setting him up with, so she wouldn't be collecting a finder's fee. For another thing, why would Peyton want Ava with him when he considered a potentially life-changing decision?

As if he'd heard her unspoken question, he hurried on, "I mean, you might be able to give me some advice or something. I've never worked with a matchmaker before."

Oh, and she had? Jeez, she hadn't even had a date in more than a year. She was the last person who should be giving advice about matters of the heart. Not that Peyton needed to know any of that, but still.

"Please, Ava?" he asked, sounding as if he genuinely wanted her to come along. "You know what kind of woman I need to find. One who's just like—"

You. That was what he had been about to say. That was the word his lips had been about to form, the one hanging in the air between them, the one exiting his head and entering her own. Ava knew it as surely as she knew her own name.

After an almost imperceptible pause, he finished, "—Jackie Kennedy. I need to find a woman like Jackie Kennedy."

Oh, sure. As if there were *any* women in the world like Jackie Kennedy. How Peyton could have jumped from thinking about Ava to thinking about her was a mystery.

"Okay, I'll come with you," she said. She had no idea when she had made the decision to do so. And she was even more uncertain about why. What was really odd, though, was how, suddenly, somehow, she didn't feel quite as peeved as she had before.

The office of Attachments, Inc. had surprised Peyton on his first visit. He'd thought a matchmaker's office would be full of hearts and flowers, furnished with overblown Victorian furniture in a million different colors, with sappy chamber music playing over it all. Instead, the place was much like his own office in San Francisco, twenty stories above the city, with wide windows that offered panoramic views of Lake Michigan and Navy Pier, furnished in contemporary sleekness and soothing earth tones. The music was jazz, and the only plants were potted bamboo.

Caroline, too, had come as a surprise that first time. He'd expected a gingham-clad grandmother with a graying bun and glasses perched on her nose, but the woman who greeted him and Ava was a far cry from that. Yes, her hair was silver, but it hung loose and was stylishly cut, and her glasses were shoved atop her head. In place of gingham, she was wrapped in a snug, sapphire-colored dress and wearing mile-high heels that click-click-clicked on the tile floor as she approached them.

"Mr. Moss," she gushed when she came to a stop in front of him and extended her hand the way any high-powered business CEO would. "It is so nice to see you again." Her gushing ebbed considerably, however—in fact, the temperature seemed to drop fifty degrees—when she turned to Ava and said, "Now who are you?"

Before Ava had a chance to answer, Peyton replied, "She's my, ah, my assistant. Ava Brenner."

Caroline gave Ava a quick once-over and, evidently satisfied with his answer, immediately dismissed her. She turned to Peyton again. "Well, then. If you'd like to come back to my office, we can get down to business."

Confident the two of them would follow, she spun on her mile-high heels and click-click-clicked in the direction from which she'd come. Peyton turned to Ava and started to shrug, but stopped when he saw her expression. She looked kind of…peeved. Although that wasn't a word in his normal vocabulary, he couldn't think of any other adjective to describe her. She was looking at him as if he'd just insulted her. He backtracked the last few seconds in his brain, then remembered he'd introduced her as his assistant. Okay, so maybe that suggested she was his subordinate, but he was paying her to help him out, so that sort of made her an employee, and that kind of made her a subordinate. And what was the big deal anyway? Some of his best friends were subordinates.

Anyway, they didn't have time for another argument. So he only gestured after the hastily departing Caroline and asked, "Are you coming?"

"Do I have a choice?" she replied crisply.

He did shrug this time, hoping the gesture looked more sincere than it felt. "You could wait out here if you want."

For a moment, he thought she would take him up on that, and a weird panic rose in his belly. She wouldn't. He needed her to help him with this. He had no idea what kind of woman would be acceptable to his board of directors. Other than that she had to have all the qualities Ava had.

Caroline called back to them, and although Ava tensed even more, she turned in the direction of the matchmaker and began to march forward. Relief—and a strange kind of happiness—washed over Peyton as he followed. Because he needed her, he told himself. Or rather, he needed her *help*. That was why he was glad she hadn't stayed in the waiting room. It had nothing to do with how he just felt better having her at his side. The reason he felt better having her at his side was because, you know, she was helping him. Which he needed. Her help, he meant. Not her at his side.

Ah, hell. He was just happy—he meant *relieved*—that she was with him.

Caroline's office was a better reflection of her trade. The walls were painted the color of good red wine, and a wide Persian rug spanned a floor that had magically become hardwood. Her desk was actually kind of Victorian-looking, but it was tempered by the sleek city skyline in the windows behind her. On one wall hung certificates for various accomplishments, along with two degrees in psychology from Northwestern. Her bookshelf was populated less by books than by artifacts from world travels, but the books present were all about relationships and sexuality.

Instead of deploying her strategy from behind her desk, Caroline scooped up a small stack of manila folders atop it, invited Peyton and Ava to seat themselves on an overstuffed sofa on the opposite wall, then sat down in a matching chair beside it.

"May I call you Peyton?" she asked with a warm smile.

"Sure," he told her.

He waited for her to smile warmly at Ava and ask if she could call her by her first name, too, but Caroline instead began to sift through the folders until she homed in on one in particular.

Still smiling her warm smile—which Peyton would have sworn was genuine until she dismissed Ava so readily—she said, "I inputted your vital statistics, your likes and dislikes, and what you're looking for in a match into the computer, and I found four women I think you'll like very much. This one in particular," she added as she opened the top folder, "is quite a catch.

Very old-money Chicago, born and raised here, Art Institute graduate, active volunteer in the local arts community, a curator for a small gallery on State Street, contributing reviewer for the *Tribune,* member of the Daughters of the American Revolution.... Oh, the list just goes on and on. She has every quality you're looking for."

Caroline handed the open folder to Peyton, who took it automatically. It contained a few sheets of printed information with a four-by-six head shot attached. It was to the latter that his gaze was naturally drawn. The woman was—well, there was no other word for it—breathtakingly beautiful. Okay, okay, that was two words, but that just went to show how amazingly gorgeous and incredibly dazzling she was. Women who looked like her just demanded adverbs to go along with the adjectives. Her hair was dark auburn and pooled around her bare shoulders; her eyes were huge, green and thickly lashed. He didn't kid himself that the photo wasn't retouched or that she would look the same had she not been so artfully made up with the kind of cosmetic wizardry that made a woman look as though she wasn't wearing makeup at all. She was still... Wow. Breathtakingly beautiful, amazingly gorgeous and incredibly dazzling.

"Wow," he said, speaking his thoughts aloud. Well, part of them, anyway. There were some that were best left in his head.

"Indeed," said Caroline with a satisfied smile. "Her name is—"

"Vicki," Ava finished, at the same time Caroline was saying, "Victoria."

The women exchanged looks, then spoke as one again. But, again, they each said something different.

"Victoria Haverty," said the matchmaker.

"Vicki Nielsson," said Ava.

The two women continued to stare at each other, but it was Caroline alone who spoke this time. "Do you know Ms. Haverty?"

Ava nodded. "Oh, yes. We debuted together. But Haverty is her maiden name. She's Vicki Nielsson now."

Caroline's eyes fairly bugged out of her head. "She's *married?*"

"I'm afraid so," Ava told her. "And living in Reykjavik with her husband, Dagbjart, last I heard. Which was about two weeks ago."

"But she gave me an address here in Chicago," Caroline objected, as if that would negate everything Ava had said.

"On Astor Street?" Ava asked.

Caroline went to her desk and tapped a few keys on a laptop sitting atop it. It was then that Peyton realized all the information on his pages was nonidentifying statistics such as age, education, occupation and interests. "Yes," the matchmaker said without looking up.

"That's her parents' place," Ava replied. "She does come home to visit fairly often."

The matchmaker looked at Ava incredulously. "But why would she apply with a Chicago matchmaker if she's happily married and living in…um, where is Reykjavik?"

"Iceland," Peyton and Ava said in unison.

The matchmaker looked even more confused. "Why would she apply with Attachments if she's married and living in Iceland?"

When Peyton looked at Ava, she seemed to be trying very hard not to grin. A smug grin, too, if he wasn't mistaken. He knew that because she wasn't doing a very good job fighting it.

"Well," she began smugly, "maybe Vicki's not as happily married as ol' Dagbjart would like to think. And ol' Dagbjart is, well, ol'," she added. "He was seventy-six when Vicki married him. He must be pushing ninety by now. The Havertys have always been known for marrying into families even wealthier than they are, but clearly Vicki underestimated that Scandinavian life expectancy. Did you know men in Iceland live longer than men in any other country?"

The matchmaker said nothing in response to that. Neither did Peyton, for that matter. What could he say? Other than, *Hey, Caroline, way to go on the background checks.*

The matchmaker finally seemed to remember she was with a client who was paying her a crapload of money to find him a mate—a mate who wasn't already married, by the way—and returned to the sofa to snatch the folder out of Peyton's hands and replace it with another. "An honest mistake," she said. "I'm sure you'll like this one even better."

He opened that folder to find another sheet of vital statistics affixed to another four-by-six glossy, this time of a woman who wasn't quite as breathtaking, amazing or incredible as the first, but who was still beautiful, gorgeous and dazzling. She, too, had auburn hair, a few shades lighter than the first, and eyes so clear a blue, they could have only been enhanced with Photoshop. Still, even without retouching, the woman was stunning.

"This young woman," Caroline said, "is the absolute cream of Chicago society. One of her ancestors helped found the Chicago Mercantile Exchange and her father is on the Chicago Board of Trade. Her mother's family are the Lauderdales, who own the Lauderdale department store chain, among other things. She herself has two college degrees, one in business and one in fashion design. Her name is…"

The matchmaker hesitated, glancing over at Ava.

As if taking the cue, Ava looked at Peyton and said, "Roxy Mittendorf. Roxanne," she corrected herself when Caroline looked as if she would take exception. "But she went by Roxy when we were kids."

Now Ava was the one to hesitate, as if she were weighing whether or not to say more. Finally, the weight fell, and she added, "At least until after that college spring break trip, when she came home with the clap. Then people started calling her Doxy. I'm not sure if that's because they thought she was, you know, a doxy, or because her doctor prescribed doxycycline to treat it." She brightened. "But I guess that's really neither here nor there, is it? I mean, it's not like she still has the clap. At least, I don't think that's one that flares up again, is it?"

She traded glances with both Peyton and Caroline, and when neither of them commented, she evidently felt it necessary to add, "Well, *I* never called her Doxy. I didn't even find out about the clap thing until after graduation."

Peyton closed the file folder and handed it back to Caroline without comment. Caroline fished for the third in her lap and exchanged it for the second one. When he opened this one he found—taa-daa!—another red-headed beauty, this one with eyes a lighter blue that might actually occur in nature. Interesting that the matchmaker was three for three with regard to red hair.

When he glanced back at Caroline, she seemed to sense his thoughts, because she said, "Well, you did indicate you had a preference for redheads. And also green eyes, but except for that first, all my other candidates for you have blue eyes. Still, not so very different, right?"

For some reason—Peyton couldn't imagine why—they both looked over at Ava. Ava with her dark red hair and green, green eyes.

"What?" she asked innocently.

"Nothing," Peyton said, grateful she hadn't made the connection.

Had he actually stated on his application that he had a preference for green-eyed redheads? He honestly couldn't remember. Then again, he'd been on the jet heading to Chicago at the time, surrounded by a ton of work he'd wanted to finish before his arrival. He'd only been half paying attention to how he was answering the questions. He thought about several of the women he had dated in the past and was surprised to realize that most of them had been redheads. Odd. He liked all women. He didn't care if their hair was blond, brown, red or purple, or what color eyes they had, or what their ethnic, educational or economic origins were. If they were smart, funny and beautiful, if they made him feel good when he was with them, that was all he cared about. So why had he dated so many redheads? Especially when redheads were such a minority?

Instead of looking where he wanted to look just then, he turned his attention to his third prospective date. Before Caroline had a chance to say a word, he held up the photo to show Ava. "Do you know her?"

Ava looked almost guilty. "I do, actually. But you know her, too. She went to Emerson with us. She was in my grade."

Peyton looked at the photo again. The woman was

in no way familiar. Which was weird, because a girl that pretty he would have remembered. "Are you sure? I don't remember her at all."

"Well, you should," Ava said. "You two played hockey together for three years."

He shook his head. "That's not possible. There weren't any girls on the Emerson hockey team."

"No, there weren't."

Understanding dawned on him then. Dawned like a good, solid blow to the back of the head. He looked at the photo again, shortening the hair and blunting the features a bit. "Oh, my God," he finally said. "Is that Nick Boorman?"

"Nicolette," Ava corrected him. "She goes by Nicolette now."

Peyton closed the folder and handed it back to Caroline. "Not that there's anything wrong with that," he said. "But it would just be kind of, um…"

"Awkward," Ava whispered helpfully.

"Yeah."

Caroline took the folder from him and tucked it under the other two candidates that were a no-go. But she was looking at Ava when she did it. "Who *are* you?" she asked.

Ava shrugged. "I'm just Mr. Moss's *assistant*."

Caroline didn't look anywhere near convinced. She lifted the last of her folders defiantly. She spoke not to Peyton this time, but to Ava. "*This* candidate has only lived in Chicago for four years. She's originally from Miami. Do you have any friends or family in Miami, Ms. Brenner? Any connection to that city at all?"

Ava shook her head. "No, I don't."

Caroline opened the folder and showed the photo

to Ava before allowing Peyton to look at it. "Do you know this woman?"

Ava shook her head again. "I haven't had the pleasure of meeting her. Yet," she added, seemingly pointedly.

"Good," Caroline said. She turned to Peyton and finally allowed him to view the file. "This is Francesca Stratton. She started off as a software developer but is now the CEO of her own company. Her father is a neurosurgeon in Coral Gables, and her mother is a circuit court judge for the state of Florida. Their lineage in that state goes back six generations. *And* she's a distant cousin to King Juan Carlos of Spain."

Now Caroline looked at Ava, as if daring her to come up with something that might challenge the woman's pedigree. When Ava only smiled benignly, the matchmaker continued, "Peyton, I think you and she would be perfect for each other."

He tried not to think about how Caroline had considered the three candidates ahead of Francesca more perfect, and instead took the file to look over the rest of the woman's particulars. He liked that she had built her own company, the way he had, and her knowledge of computers and software design could definitely come in handy with regard to his own work. She was outdoorsy—she cited a love of scuba diving, rock climbing and horseback riding. She preferred nonfiction over fiction, rock and roll over any other music, eating out over eating in. And she was a fan of both the Florida Panthers and Chicago Blackhawks. There wasn't a single thing in her vitals to dissuade him from agreeing with Caroline. She really did seem perfect for him.

So why wasn't he more excited about the prospect of meeting her?

A movement to his left caught his eye, and he found

Ava trying to read the file from where she sat. Instead of making her work for it, he handed it to her.

"What do you think?" he asked as she turned to the final page.

"Ivy League–educated, accomplished pianist, member of the United States Dressage Federation, one of Chicago's One Hundred Women Making a Difference. What's not to love?"

Funny, but she didn't sound as though she loved Francesca.

"So on the Jackie Kennedy scale," he said, "where do you think she'd fall?"

Ava closed the file and returned it to the matchmaker. "Well, if Jackie Kennedy were a young woman today, I think she'd be a lot like Francesca Stratton."

"So…maybe eight?"

With what sounded like much resignation and little satisfaction, she said, "Ten."

That was exactly what Peyton wanted to hear. So why was he disappointed hearing it?

In spite of his reaction, he turned to Caroline and said, "Sounds like we have a winner. When can you set something up?"

The matchmaker looked both relieved and happy. "Let me contact Francesca to see what works for her, and I'll get back to you. What evenings work best for you?"

"Just about any evening is fi—" Peyton started to say. But the delicate clearing of a throat to his left him kept him from finishing.

He looked over at Ava, who was shaking her head.

"What?" he asked.

"You said you didn't think you were ready to meet any of your prospective dates just yet," she reminded him.

"No, you said that."

"And you agreed. We still have several lessons we need to go over."

He said nothing. He had agreed. And really, he didn't mind that much putting off the meeting. Odd, since he really did want to get out of Chicago and back to San Francisco. Maybe he hadn't felt as antsy over the past few days as he had when he'd first arrived, but he did need to get back to the West Coast soon. So he and Ava needed to wrap things up pronto.

"How long do you think we'll need to get me through them?" he asked. And for some really bizarro reason, he found himself hoping she would tell him it would be weeks and weeks and weeks.

Instead, she told him, "Another week, at least."

"So maybe by the weekend after this one?"

She looked as if she wanted to say, *No, it will be weeks and weeks and weeks.* Instead, she replied, "Um, sure. If we work hard, and if you follow the rules," she added meaningfully, "then we can probably get you where you need to be by then."

Following the rules. Not his favorite thing to do. Still, if it would get him a date with a modern-day Jackie Kennedy...

He turned to Caroline again. "How about next Friday or Saturday if she's available?"

Caroline jotted the dates down on the top of the file folder. "I'm reasonably certain that one of those days will be fine. I'll let you know which one after I've spoken to Francesca."

Great, he thought without much enthusiasm. "Great!" he said with much enthusiasm.

He stood, with Ava quickly following suit, thanked Caroline for all her work, and they both started to make their way to the door. They halted, however, when the matchmaker called Ava's name.

"Ms. Brenner," she said tentatively, "you, ah…you wouldn't happen to be looking for a job, would you? Something part-time that wouldn't interfere with your work as Peyton's assistant? You'd be an enormous asset to us here at Attachments, Inc."

Looking a little startled, Ava replied, "Um, no. But thank you."

Peyton told Caroline, "The reason Ava knew all those women is because she moves in the same social circles they do. Her family is loaded. She doesn't have to work." Unable to help himself, he added, "Never mind that she's bleeding me dry for being my *assistant* at the moment."

Caroline suddenly looked way more interested in Ava than she had when Ava was just a prospective part-timer. Funny, though, how Ava suddenly looked kind of panicky.

"I see," the matchmaker said. "Well then, maybe *I* could help *you*. Introduce you to a nice man who has the same set of values you have?"

In other words, Peyton translated, a nice man who had the same *value* that Ava had. *Cha-ching*. For some reason, he suddenly felt kind of panicky, too.

"What do you say, Ava?" the matchmaker added. And it wasn't lost on Peyton that she had switched to the first-name basis she evidently only used with her clients, not to mention the almost genuinely warm smile. "Would you like to fill out an application while you're here?"

Ava smiled back, but somehow looked even more alarmed. "Thank you, Caroline, but I'm really not in the market right now."

Her response made Peyton wonder again if she was seriously involved with someone, and if that was why she wasn't currently in the market. During the week the two of them had spent together, she had never said anything that made him think there was a significant other in her life, and she seemed to have plenty of time on her hands if she was able to work with him every day. Call him crazy, but he didn't think a guy who had a woman like Ava waiting for him at home—hell, who had *Ava* waiting for him at home—would be too happy about her spending so much time with another guy. If Peyton had Ava waiting at home for him, he'd sure as hell never—

But he didn't have Ava waiting at home for him, he reminded himself. And he didn't want her waiting at home for him. So what was the point of even thinking about it?

"Well, if you change your mind..." Caroline said, leaving the statement incomplete but her intention stated.

"You'll be the first person I call," Ava promised.

Peyton did his best not to wish he could be the first person she'd call. Even though he kind of did.

Dammit, what was wrong with him? He'd just been paired up with a modern-day Jackie Kennedy. He should be over the moon. He was just distracted, that was all—too much going on. The takeover of Montgomery and Sons, massive self-improvement, the hunt for the right woman, the ghost of high school past...it was no wonder his brain was scrambled.

"Are we finished here?" he asked, more irritably than he intended.

Both Caroline and Ava seemed to notice that, too. But it was Ava who replied, "You tell me."

"Yes," he snapped.

Without awaiting a reply, he made his way to the door. Let the women draw whatever conclusion they wanted from his behavior. As far as he was concerned, any lessons Ava might have in store for the rest of the day were canceled. He had work to do. Work that didn't include anything or anyone with more than one X chromosome.

Six

Ava and Peyton sat on a bench at the Chicago Institute of Art studying Edward Hopper's *Nighthawks,* neither saying a word. She had instructed him to spend five minutes in silence taking in the details of several paintings that morning, but none of them had captured his attention the way this one had. It almost seemed as if he wanted to walk right into the painting and join the people sitting at the café bar for a cup of late-night coffee.

As he studied the painting, Ava studied him. He was wearing a different pair of dark-wash jeans today, with another fitted sweater—this one the color of good cognac that set off his amber eyes beautifully. She'd opted for a pair of tobacco-colored trousers and a dark green tailored shirt. She couldn't help thinking that, fashion-wise, they complemented each other perfectly. But that was about the only compatibility the two of them were enjoying today.

He'd barely spoken to her after they left the match-maker's office yesterday, barring one angry outburst that had left her flummoxed. After saying they were finished for the day, he'd offered to have his driver drop her at her house on the way back to his hotel, wherever her house was, since she hadn't told him her address, and why was that, anyway, did she still think he wasn't fit to enter the premises the way she had when they were kids, since he'd had to climb out the window when he left her house that one time he was there, not use the front door like a normal—meaning blue-blooded, filthy-rich—person would?

Ava had been stunned to momentary silence. Until then, they'd seemed to have an unspoken agreement that they would never, under any circumstances, spe-cifically mention that night. Then she'd gathered her-self enough to snap back that he could have used the front door if he'd wanted to, but he'd chosen to go out the window because he'd been too ashamed to be seen with her, reeking of old money as she was, which was at least better than reeking of gasoline and gutter scum.

What followed might have been an explosion of re-sentment and frustration that had been steeping for six-teen years. Instead, both had been too horrified by what they'd said to each other, by what they knew they could never take back, that neither had said another word. Nei-ther had apologized, either. They'd just looked out their respective windows until they reached Talk of the Town. Ava had hopped out of the car with a hastily uttered in-struction for Peyton to meet her at the Art Institute this morning and slammed the door before he could object.

Neither had mentioned the exchange today. Their conversation had focused exclusively on art commen-tary, but it had been civil. In spite of that, a stagnant uneasiness surrounded them, and neither seemed to know what to do to ease it.

She glanced at her watch and saw that the five minutes she'd asked Peyton to give to the painting had become eight. Instead of telling him time was up, she turned her attention to the painting, too. It was one she had responded to immediately the first time she'd seen it, during an Emerson Academy field trip when she was in ninth grade. The people in the painting had always looked to her as if they were displaced and at loose ends, as though they were just biding their time in the diner while they waited for something—anything—to change.

The painting still spoke to her that way. Except that now the people looked lonely, too.

"I like how the light is brightest on the guy behind the counter," Peyton said suddenly, stirring Ava from her thoughts. "It makes him look like some kind of...I don't know...spiritual figure or something. He's the guy providing the sustenance, but maybe that sustenance is more than coffee and pie, you know?"

Ava turned to look at him, surprised at the pithiness of the comment.

Before she could say anything, and still looking at the picture, he added, "What's also interesting is that the only real color on the people is with the woman, and both times, it's warm colors. The red on her dress, and the orange in her hair. Although maybe I only notice that because I've always been partial to redheads."

He'd said the same thing at the matchmaker's, she recalled. Or, at least, Caroline had said that was what he'd stated on his questionnaire. Just as he had yesterday after the comment, he turned to look at Ava...then at Ava's hair. Warmth oozed through her belly, because he looked at her now the way he had that night at her parents' house. The two of them had been sitting on the floor in her bedroom, bleary-eyed from their studies, when Ava had cupped the back of her neck, complaining of an incessant ache. Peyton had uncharacteristically taken pity on her and moved her hand to place his there, rubbing gently to ease the knot. One minute, the two of them had been overtaxed and stressed by their homework, and the next...

"I mean..." he sputtered. "That is...it's just...uh..."

"That's so interesting, what you said about the light and the guy behind the counter," she interrupted, pretending she didn't understand why he suddenly seemed edgy. Pretending she didn't feel edgy herself. "I've never thought about that before."

Instead of turning his attention back to the painting, Peyton continued to look at Ava. Oh, God, that was all she needed. If they followed the pattern from sixteen years ago, the two of them were going to end up horizontal on the bench, fully entwined and half-naked. That was how it had been that night at her parents' house. The first time, anyway—they'd been on each other so fast, so fiercely, that they'd only managed to undo any buttons and zippers that were in their way. The second time had been much more leisurely, much more thorough. Where the first time had been a physical act intended to release pressure, the second time had been much more...

"In fact," Ava hurried on, looking back at the painting herself, "it's the sort of interpretation that might lead to a discussion that could go on for hours."

Her heart was racing, and heat was seeping into her chest and face. So she made herself do what she'd done in high school whenever she started reacting that way to Peyton. She channeled her inner Gold Coast ice princess—who she was dismayed to find still lurked beneath the surface—and forced herself to be distant, methodical…and not a little bitchy. She was Peyton's teacher, not his…not someone who should be experiencing odd, decades-old feelings she never should have felt in the first place. She'd never be able to compete with a modern-day Jackie Kennedy anyway. She was the last sort of woman Peyton wanted or needed to accomplish his goals.

"Which is exactly why," she said frostily, "I don't want you saying things like that."

Sensing his annoyance at her crisp tone, she pressed on. She didn't dwell on how she was behaving exactly the way she had sworn not to—treating him the way she had in high school—but she was starting to feel way too many things she shouldn't be feeling, and she didn't know what else to do.

"What I really want for you to take away from this exercise," she told him coolly, "is something less insightful. That shouldn't be too difficult, should it?"

"*Less* insightful?" he echoed. "I thought the whole point of this museum thing was to teach me how to say something about art that wouldn't make me sound like an idiot."

She nodded. "Which is why I've focused on the works I have today. These are artists and paintings that are familiar to everyone. For your purposes, you only need to master some passing art commentary. Not deep, pithy insight."

"Then tell me, oh great art guru," he said sarcastically, "what do I need to know about this one?"

Looking at the painting, again—since it was better than looking at the angry expression on Peyton's face—Ava said, "You should say how interesting it is that the themes in *Nighthawks* are similar to Hopper's *Sunlight in a Cafeteria,* but that the perspective of time is reversed."

"But I haven't seen *Sunlight in a Cafeteria,*" he pointed out. "Not to mention I don't know what the fu— Uh…what you're talking about."

"No one else you'll be talking to has seen it, either," she assured him. "And you don't have to understand it. The minute you offer some indication that you know more about art than your companion, they'll change the subject." She smiled her cool, disaffected smile and told him, "I think you're good to go with the major players in American art. Tomorrow, we'll take on the Impressionists. Then, if we have time, the Dutch masters."

Peyton groaned. "Oh, come on, Ava. How often is this stuff really going to come up in conversation?"

"More often than you think. And we still have to cover books and music, too."

He eyed her flatly. "There's no way I need to know all this stuff before my date with Francesca. I don't need to know it for moving in business circles, either. I think you're just stalling."

Ava gaped at him. "That's ridiculous. Why would I want to spend more time with you than I have to?"

"Got me," he shot back. "God knows it's not like you need the money I'm sure you'll charge me for overtime. I think I've got all this…stuff…covered. Let's move on."

Well, at least he was abiding by the no-profanity rule, she thought. She decided not to comment on the other part of his charge. "Music," she reiterated instead. "Books."

He expelled an exasperated breath. "Fine. I've been

a huge Charles Dickens fan since high school. How's that?"

She couldn't quite hide her surprise. "You read Charles Dickens for fun?"

He clamped his jaw tight. "Yeah." More icily, he added, "And Camus and Hemingway, too. Guess that comes as a shock to you, doesn't it? That gasoline-reeking gutter scum like me could have understood anything other than the sports stats in the *Sun-Times*."

"Peyton, that wasn't what I was think—"

"The hell it wasn't."

So much for the profanity rule. Not that Ava called him on it, since she was kind of responsible for its being broken. She started to deny her charge, then stopped. "Okay, maybe that was kind of what I was thinking. But you didn't exactly show your brainy side in school. Still, I'm sorry. I shouldn't have assumed that. Especially in light of what you've accomplished since then."

He seemed surprised—and a little confused—by her apology. He didn't let her off the hook, though. "And in light of what I accomplished then, too," he added. "Which was something you never bothered to discover for yourself."

Now it was Ava's turn to be surprised. He still sounded hurt by something that had happened—or, rather, hadn't happened—half a lifetime ago. Nevertheless, she told him, "I wasn't the only one who didn't bother to get to know my classmates. I was more than I appeared to be in high school, too, Peyton, but did you ever notice or care?"

He uttered an incredulous sound. "Right. More than just a beautiful shell filled with nothing but self-interest? I don't think so."

"You don't *think* so?" she echoed. "Present tense?

You still think I'm just a—" She halted herself, thinking it would be best to skirt the whole *beautiful* thing. "I'm just a shell filled with nothing but self-interest?"

He said nothing, only continued to look at her the way the teenage Peyton had.

"You think the reason I'm helping you out like this is all for *myself?*" she asked. "You don't think maybe I'm doing it because it's a nice thing for me to do for an old…for a former classmate?"

Now he barked in disbelief. "You're doing it because I'm paying you a bucket of money. If that isn't self-interest, I don't know what is."

There was no way she could set him straight without revealing the reality of her situation. Of course, she *could* do that. She could tell him about how she had walked in his figurative shoes her senior year. She could tell him how she understood now the battles between pride and shame, and desire and need, and how each day had been filled with wondering how she was going to survive into the next one. She could tell him how she'd listened to her mother crying in the next room every night, and how she had forbidden herself to do the same, because nothing could come from that. She could tell him how she'd stood in the yard of the Milhouse Prewitt School every morning and steeled herself before going in, only to be worn to a nub by day's end by the relentless bullying.

Just do it, Ava. Be honest with him. Maybe then karma really will smile upon you.

But on the heels of that thought came another: *Or maybe Peyton will laugh and say the same things you heard every day at Prewitt, about looking like you live in a box under a bridge, and stealing extra fruit from the lunch line—don't think we haven't seen you do it,*

Ava—and not being fit to clean the houses of your class-mates because no one wants their house smelling the way you smell, and maybe you don't live in box under a bridge, after all, maybe you live in a Dumpster.

She opened her mouth, honestly not sure what would come out. And she heard herself say, "Right. I forgot. Money and social standing are more important to me than anything." Conjuring her before-the-fall high school self again, she cocked her head to one side and smiled an icy smile. In a voice that could freeze fire, she said, "But that's because they *are* more important than anything, aren't they, Peyton? That's something you've learned, too, isn't it? That's what you want more than anything now. Guess that makes us two of a kind."

His mouth dropped open, as if it had never occurred to him how much he resembled the people for whom he'd had so much contempt in high school. The two of them really had switched places. In more than just a so-cial context. In a philosophical one, as well. She under-stood better than ever now that what defined a person was their character, not what kind of car was parked in their garage or what kind of clothes hung in their closet. She was poor in an economic sense, but she was rich in other ways—certainly richer than the integrity-starved girl she'd been in high school.

Peyton, on the other hand, had money to burn, but was running short on integrity, if what he'd told her about his business methods were any indication. He'd thrust plenty of families into the sort of life he'd clawed his way out of. And he was currently trying to take a family business away from the last remaining members of that family, to plunder and dismember it. He'd be put-ting even more people out of work and more families on the dole. And he was going to do it under the manufactured guise of being a decent, mannerly individual. Really, which one of them had the most to feel guilty about these days?

"I think we've both had enough for today," she said decisively.

"We finally get to escape the museum?" he asked with feigned hopefulness, still looking plenty irritated by her last remark.

"Yes, we've had enough of that, too. Since it looks like you have the literary angle covered, tomorrow we can tackle music."

He looked as if he were going to protest, then the fight seemed to go out of him. "Okay. Fine. Whatever. What time should I pick you up?"

She shook her head, as she did every time he asked that question—and he'd asked it every day. She said the same thing she always said in response. "I'll meet you."

Before he could object—something else he did every day—she gave him the address of a jazz record store on East Illinois and told him to be there when they opened.

"And then I bet we get to have lunch at another pretentious restaurant," he said, sounding as weary as she felt. "Hey, I know. I'll even wear one of my new suits this time."

She knew he meant for the comment to be sarcastic. So she only echoed his ennui back. "Okay. Fine. Whatever."

Ennui. Right. As if the tension and fatigue they were feeling could be ascribed to a lack of interest. Then again, maybe for Peyton, it was. He'd made no secret about his reluctance to be My Fair Gentlemanned to within an inch of his life. He really didn't give a damn about any of this and was only doing it to further his business. Ava wished she could share his disinterest.

The reason for her impatience and irritation this week had nothing to do with not caring.

And it had everything to do with caring too much.

Seven

Peyton gazed at Ava from across the smallest table he'd ever been forced to sit at and did his best to ignore the ruffled lavender tablecloth and flowered china tea set atop it. He tried even harder to ignore the cascade of lace curtains to his right and the elaborately scrolled ironwork tea caddy to his left. And it would be best not to get him started on the little triangular sandwiches with the crusts cut off or the mountain of frothy pastries.

Tea. She was actually making him *take tea* with her. In a tea shop. Full of women in hats and gloves. Hell, even Ava was wearing a hat and gloves. A little white hat with one of those netted veil things that fell over her eyes, and white gloves that went halfway up her arm with a bazillion buttons. Her white dress had even more buttons than her gloves did.

She hadn't been wearing the hat or gloves when she'd

walked into the record store earlier, so he hadn't realized what was in store for him. She'd pulled them out of her oversize purse as the two of them rode to the damned *tea* shop—except she hadn't said they were going to a *tea* shop. She'd said they were going to a late lunch.

Still, the appearance of a hat and gloves should have been his first clue that "lunch" was going to be even worse than something he'd put on a damned suit for. Something that would, in Ava's words, aid in his edification. He just wished he could believe this was for his edification instead of being some kind of punishment for his behavior at the museum yesterday.

He also wished he could think Ava looked ridiculous in her dainty alabaster frock and habiliments. Which was the kind of language to use for a getup like that, even if those were words he had always—before this week, anyway—manfully avoided. Hell, she looked as if she was an escapee from an overbudgeted period film set during the First World War. Unfortunately, there was something about the getup that was also… Well… Dammit. Unbelievably hot.

Which was just what he needed. To be turned on by Ava, the last woman on the planet who should be turning him on. He'd been so sure he could remain unaffected by her while they were undertaking this self-improvement thing. After all, they hadn't gotten along at all that first morning at her apartment. Instead, with every passing day, he'd just become more bewitched by her.

Just as he had in high school.

It was only physical, he told himself. The same way it had only been physical in high school. There was just some kind of weird chemistry between them. Her pheromones talking to his pheromones or something. Talking, hell. More like screaming at the top of their lungs. People didn't have to like each other to be sexually attracted to each other. They just had to have loud, obnoxious pheromones.

Tea, he reminded himself distastefully. *Focus on the fact that she's making you sit in a tearoom drinking—gak—tea and eating the kind of stuff that no self-respecting possessor of a Y chromosome should ingest.* God knew what this was going to do to his testosterone levels.

"Now then," she said in a voice that was every bit as prissy as her outfit. "Taking tea. This will probably be your biggest challenge yet."

Oh, Peyton didn't doubt that for a minute. What he did doubt was that many people actually *took tea*—he just couldn't think that phrase in anything but a snotty tone of voice…tone of mind…whatever—in this country. Not any people with a Y chromosome, anyway.

"A lot of people think the art of tea has fallen by the wayside over the years," she continued, obviously reading his mind. Or maybe his distasteful expression. "But it's actually been rising in popularity. Hence your need to be familiar with it."

"Ava," he said, mustering as much patience as he could, "I think I can safely say that no matter how high in society I go, I will never, ever, ask anyone to—" he could barely get the words out of his mouth "—*take tea* with me."

She smiled a benign smile. "I bet the sisters Montgomery would be charmed by a man who asked them to tea. And I bet not one of your competitors would think to do it."

She was right. Dammit. Two sweet old Southern ladies would find this place enchanting. Crap. *Enchanting.* There was another word he normally avoided manfully. Where the hell had his testosterone gotten off to?

He blew out an exasperated breath. "Fine. Just don't expect me to wear white gloves."

"I suppose we could allow that small concession," she agreed. "Now then. As Henry James wrote in *The Portrait of a Lady,* 'There are few hours in life more agreeable than the hour dedicated to the ceremony known as afternoon tea.'"

Oh, good. At least this wouldn't last more than an hour.

"And I, for one," she continued, "couldn't agree more."

Peyton did his best to look as if he gave a crap. "Yeah, well, ol' Henry obviously never spent an afternoon sharing a case of Anchor Steam with his friends while the Blackhawks trounced the Canucks."

Ava smiled thinly. "No doubt."

She launched into a monologue about the history of afternoon tea—all three centuries of it—then moved on to the etiquette of afternoon tea, then on to the menu selection of afternoon tea. She talked about the differences between cream tea, light tea and full tea— thankfully, they were having full tea, since Peyton was getting hungrier with every word she spoke—then she pointed to the selections on the caddy beside them, categorizing them as savories, scones and pastries, even though they looked to him like sandwiches, biscuits and dessert. By the time she wrapped up her dissertation, his stomach was grumbling so forcefully even his Y chromosome was thinking the little flowery cakes looked good.

Unfortunately, as he reached for one, Ava smacked his hand as if he were a toddler.

"Don't reach," she said. "Ask for them to be passed."

"But they're sitting right there."

"They're closer to me than they are to you."

"Oh, sure, by an inch and a half."

"Nonetheless, whoever is closer should pass to the person who is farther away."

Okay, she was definitely going out of her way to be ornery, deliberately to get a rise out of him. Well, he'd show her. He'd kill her with kindness. He'd be as courteous as he knew how to be. And thanks to her lessons, he'd learned how to be pretty damned courteous.

Sitting up straighter in his tiny chair, he channeled the inner Victorian he didn't even know he possessed and said, "If you please, Miss Brenner, and if it wouldn't trouble you overly, would you pass the…" What had she called them? "The savories?"

She eyed him suspiciously, clearly doubting his sincerity. But what was she going to do? He'd been a perfect effing gentleman. He'd even thought the word *effing,* instead of what he really wanted to think, which was…uh, never mind.

Still looking at him as if she expected him to start a food fight, she asked, "May I suggest the cucumber sandwiches or the crab puffs?"

He unclenched his jaw long enough to reply, "You may."

"Which would you prefer?"

"The cucumber sandwiches," he said. Mostly because he didn't think he could say *crab puffs* with a straight face. Not that *cucumber sandwiches* was exactly easy. "If you please."

Before retrieving the plate, she began to unbutton

her gloves. Evidently good manners precluded wearing such garments whilst one was taking tea.

Dammit, he thought when he played that back in his head. There was no way he was going to last an hour in this place.

When she finally had her gloves off—a good fortnight after initiating their unbuttoning—she reached for the plate of sandwiches and passed it the three inches necessary to place it on the table between them. Then she poured them each a cup of tea from the pot, adding three sugar cubes—jeez, they had flowers on them, too—to her own. Peyton eschewed them—since no one taking tea would ever *blow off* something; they would always *eschew* it—and lifted the cup to his mouth. At Ava's discreetly cleared throat, he looked up, and she tilted her head toward the cup he was holding. Holding by its bowl having grabbed the entire thing in his big paw, because he'd been afraid he'd break off the handle if he tried to pick it up that way. Gah. After a moment of juggling, he managed the proper manipulation of the cup, holding it by its handle, if just barely. Only then did Ava nod her head to let him know he was allowed to continue.

Man, had she actually had to grow up this way? Had her mother sat her down, day after day, and made her memorize all the stuff she was making him memorize? Had she been forced to dress a certain way and unfold her napkin just so, and talk about only approved subjects with other people, the way she was teaching him to do? Or did that just come naturally to people who were born with the bluest blood in the highest income bracket? Was good taste and polite behavior encoded on her DNA the way green eyes and red hair were? Did refinement run in her veins? And if so, did that mean

Peyton's DNA was encoded with garbage-strewn streets and fighting dirty and that transmission fluid flowed through his veins?

It hit him again, even harder, how far apart the two of them were. How far apart they'd been since birth. How far apart they'd be until they died. Even with his income rivaling hers now, even mastering all these lessons that would grant him access to her world, he'd never, ever be her social equal. Because he'd never, ever be as comfortable with this stuff as she was. It would never be second nature to him the way it was to her. He would hate it in her world. All the rules and customs would suffocate him. It would kill everything that made him who he was, the same way taking Ava *out* of her world would doubtless suffocate her and kill everything that made her her.

And why did it bug him so much to realize that? He wasn't a kid anymore. He didn't care what world she lived in or that he'd never be granted citizenship there. Truth be told, now that he was a monster success, he kind of reveled in his mean-streets background. Even as a teenager, he'd taken a perverse sort of pride in where he came from, because where he came from hadn't destroyed his spirit the way it had so many others in the neighborhood. So why had it been such a sticking point with him in high school, the vast socioeconomic chasm between him and Ava? Why was it still a sticking point now, when that chasm had shrunk to a crack? Why did it bother him so much that his and Ava's worlds would never meet? What difference did her presence in the scheme of things—or lack thereof—make anyway?

His cup was nearly to his mouth when an answer to that question exploded in his head. It bothered him, he suddenly knew, because the thing that had sparked his

success, the thing that had made him escape his neighborhood and muscle his way into a top-tier college, the
thing that had kept him from giving up the hundreds
of times he wanted to give up, the thing that had made
him seize the business world with both fists and driven
him to make money, and then more money, and then
more money still…the thing that had done all that was…

Hell. It wasn't a thing at all. It was a person. It was
Ava.

Down went the teacup, landing on the table with a
thump that sent some of its contents spilling onto his
hand. Peyton scarcely felt the burn. He looked at Ava,
who was studying a plate of cakes and cookies, trying
to decide which one she wanted. She was oblivious to
both his spilled tea and tumultuous thoughts, but she
had flipped back the veil from her face, leaving her features in clear profile.

She really hadn't changed since high school. Not just
her looks, but the rest of her, too. She was as beautiful
now as she'd been then, as elegant, as refined. And, he
couldn't help thinking further, as off-limits. When all
was said and done, the Ava of adulthood was no different from the Ava of adolescence. And neither was he.
He was still—and would always be—the basest kind
of interloper in her world.

As if to hammer home their differences, she finally
decided on a frilly little pastry cup filled with berries
and whipped cream and transferred it to her plate with
a pair of dainty little silver tongs. Then she went for one
of the prissy little flowered cakes. Then a couple of the
lacy little cookies. All the fragile little things Peyton
would have been afraid of touching because he would
probably crush them. He was way better suited to a big,
bloody hunk of beef beside a mountain of stiff mashed

potatoes, with a sweaty longneck bottle of beer to wash it all down. The nectar of the working-class male.

When Ava finally looked up to see how he was faring, her brows knitted downward in confusion. He glanced at the plate of sandwiches sitting between them. Although they were heartier than the pastries, those, too, looked just as off-limits as everything else, so small and delicate and pretty were they. He tried to focus on them anyway, pretending to be indecisive about which one he wanted. But his thoughts were still wrapped up in his epiphany. *God. Ava.* It had been Ava all along.

He wasn't trying to master the art of fine living because he wanted to take over another company and add another zero to his bottom line. Not really. Sure, taking over Montgomery and Sons was the impetus, but he wouldn't be trying to do that if it weren't for Ava. He wouldn't have done anything over the past sixteen years if it weren't for Ava. He'd still be in the old neighborhood, working in the garage with his old man. He'd be spending his days under the chassis of a car, then going home at night to an apartment a few blocks away to watch the Hawks, Bulls or Cubs while consuming a carryout value meal and popping open a cold one.

And, hell, he might have even been happy doing that. Provided he'd never met Ava.

But from the moment he'd laid eyes on her in high school, something had pushed him to rise above his lot in life. Not even pushed him. *Driven* him. Yeah, that was a better word. Because after Ava had walked into his life, nothing else had mattered. Nothing except bringing himself up to standards she might approve of. So that maybe, someday, she *would* approve of him. And so that maybe, someday, the two of them...

He didn't allow himself to finish the thought. He

was afraid of what else he might discover about himself. Bad enough he understood what had brought him this far. But he did understand now. Too well. What he didn't understand was why. Why had Ava had that effect on him when nothing else had? Why would he have been satisfied with the blue-collar life for which he had always assumed he was destined until he met her? What was it about her that had taken up residence deep inside him? Why had she been the catalyst for him to escape the mean streets when the mean streets themselves hadn't been enough to do that?

"Is something wrong?" she asked, pulling him out of his musings.

"No," he answered quickly. "Just trying to decide what I want."

Which was true, he realized. He just didn't want anything that was on the plate of sandwiches.

"The petit fours here are delicious," she told him.

He'd just bet they were. If he knew what the hell a petit four was.

"Though you'd probably prefer something a little more substantial."

Oh, no doubt.

"Maybe one of the curried-egg sandwiches? They're not the kind of thing you get every day."

And naturally Peyton didn't want the kind of thing he could get every day. Hell, that was the whole problem.

"Or if you want something sweeter…"

He definitely wanted something sweeter.

"…you might try one of the ginger cakes."

Except not that.

Oh, man, this thing with Ava wasn't turning out the way he'd planned *at all*. She was supposed to be schooling him in the basics of social climbing, not advanced soul-searching. And what man wanted to discover the workings of his inner psyche for the first time in a frickin' tearoom?

"Aaahhh…" he began, stringing the word over several time zones in an effort to stall. Finally, he finished, "Yeah. Gimme one of those curried-egg sandwiches. They sound absolutely…" The word was out of his mouth before he could stop it, so overcome by his surroundings, and so weakened by his musings, had he become. "Scrumptious."

Okay, that did it. With that terrible word, he could feel what little was left of his testosterone oozing out of every pore. A man could only take so much tea and remain, well, manly. And a man could only take so much self-discovery and remain sane. If Peyton didn't get out of this place soon…if he didn't get away from Ava soon…if he didn't get someplace, anyplace, far away from here—far away from *her*—ASAP, someplace where he could look inside himself and figure out what the hell was going on in his brain…

Bottom line, he just had to get outta here. Now.

"Look, Ava, do you mind if we cut this short?" he asked. "I just remembered a conference call I'm supposed to be in on in—" He looked at his watch and pretended to be shocked at the time. "Wow. Thirty minutes. I really need to get back to my hotel."

She looked genuinely crushed. "But the tea…"

"Can we get a doggie bag?"

Judging by the way her expression changed, he might as well have just asked her if he could jump up onto the table, whip off his pants and introduce everyone to Mr. Happy.

"No," she said through gritted teeth. "One does not

ask for a doggie bag for one's afternoon tea. Especially not in a place like this."

"Well, I don't know why the hell not," he snapped.

Oh, yeah. There it was. With even that mild profanity, he sucked some of his retreating testosterone back in. Now if he could just figure out how to reclaim the rest of it...

He glanced around until he saw a waiter—or whatever passed for a waiter in this place, since they were all dressed like maître d's—and waved the guy down in the most obnoxious way he knew how.

"Hey, you! Garson!" he shouted, deliberately mispronouncing the French word for *waiter*. "Could we get a doggie bag over here?"

Everyone in the room turned to stare at him—and Ava—in frank horror. That, Peyton had to admit, helped a lot with his masculine recovery. Okay, so he was acting like a jerk, and doing it at Ava's expense. Sometimes, in case of emergency, a man had to break the glass on his incivility. No, on his crudeness, he corrected himself. His grossness. His bad effin' manners. Those were way better words for what he was tapping into. And wow, did it feel good.

He braved a glance at Ava and saw that she had propped her elbows on the table and dropped her head into her hands.

"Yo, Ava," he said. "Take your elbows off the table. That is so impolite. Everyone is staring at us. Jeez, I can't take you anywhere." He looked back at the waiter, who hadn't budged from the spot where he had been about to serve a couple of elderly matrons from a pile of flowered cakes. "What, am I not speakin' English here?" he yelled. Funny, but he seemed to have suddenly developed a Bronx accent. "Yeah, you in the penguin suit. Could we get a doggie bag for our—" he gestured toward the tea caddy and the plates on the table "—for all this stuff? I mean, at these prices, I don't want it to go to waste. Know what I'm sayin'?"

"Peyton, what are you doing?" Ava asked from behind her hands. "Are you trying to get us thrown out of here?"

Wasn't that obvious? Was he really not speakin' English here?

"Garson!" he shouted again. "Hey, we don't got all day."

Ava groaned softly from behind her hands, then said something about how she would never be able to take tea here again. It was all Peyton could do not to reply, *You're welcome.*

Instead, he continued to channel his inner bad-mannered adolescent—who he wasn't all that surprised to discover lurked just beneath his surface. "The service in this place sucks, Ava. Next time, we should hit Five Guys instead. At least they give you your food in a bag. I don't think this guy's going to bring us one."

He figured he'd said enough now to make her snap up her head and blast him for being such a jerk—as politely as she could, naturally, since they were in a public place. Instead, when she dropped her hands, she just looked tired. Really, really tired. And she didn't say a word. She only stood, gathered her purse and gloves, turned her back, and walked away with all the elegance of a czarina.

Peyton was stunned. She wasn't going to say something combative in response? She wasn't going to call him uncouth? She wasn't going to tell him how it was men like him who gave his entire gender a bad name?

She wasn't going to glare daggers or spit fire? She was just going to walk away without even trying?

When he realized that yep, that was exactly what she was going to do, he bolted after her. He was nearly to the exit when he realized they hadn't paid their bill, so ran back to the table long enough to drop a handful of twenties on top of it. He didn't wait for change. Hell, their server deserved a 100-percent tip for the way he had just behaved.

When he vaulted out of the tearoom onto the street, he found himself drowning in a river of people making the Friday-afternoon jump start from work to weekend. He looked left, then right, but had no idea which way Ava had gone. Remembering her outfit, he searched for a splash of white amid the sullen colors of business suits, driving his gaze in every direction. Finally, he spotted her, in the middle of a crosswalk at the end of the block, buttoning up those damned white gloves, as if she were Queen Elizabeth on her way to address the royal guard.

He hurtled after her, but by the time he made it to the curb, she was on the other side of the street and the light was changing. Not that that deterred him. As he sprinted into the crosswalk against the light, half a dozen drivers honked their displeasure, and he was nearly clipped by more than one bumper. Even when he made it safely to the other side of the street, he kept running, trying to catch up to the wisp of white that was Ava.

Every time he thought he was within arm's reach, someone or something blocked him from touching her, and for every step he took forward, she seemed to take two. Panic welled in him that he would never reach her, until she turned a corner onto a side street that was much less crowded. Still, he had to lengthen his stride to catch up with her, and still, for a moment, it seemed he never would. Finally, he drew near enough to grasp her upper arm and spin her around to face him. She immediately jerked out of his hold, swinging her handbag as she came. Peyton let her go, dodging her bag easily, then lifted both hands in surrender.

"Ava, I'm sorry," he said breathlessly. "But... Stop. Just stop a minute. Please."

For a moment, they stood there on the sidewalk looking at each other, each out of breath, each poised for... something. Peyton had no idea what. Ava should have looked ridiculous in her turn-of-the-century garb, brandishing her handbag in her little white gloves, her netted hat dipping to one side. Instead, she seemed ferocious enough to snap him in two. A passerby jostled him from behind, sending him forward a step, until he was nearly toe to toe with her. She took a step in retreat, never altering her pose.

"Leave me alone," she said without preamble.

"No," he replied just as succinctly.

"Leave me alone, Peyton," she repeated adamantly. "I'm going home."

"No."

He wasn't sure whether he uttered the word in response to her first sentence or the second, but really, it didn't matter. He wasn't going to leave her alone, and he didn't want her to go home. Despite his conviction only moments ago that he needed to be by himself to sort out his thoughts, isolation was suddenly the last thing he wanted. Not that he was sure what the *first* thing was that he wanted, but... Well, okay, maybe he did kind of know what the first thing was that he wanted. He just wasn't sure he knew what to do with it if he got it. Well, okay, maybe he did kind of know that, too, but...

"You said we still have a lot of work to do before I can go out with Francesca," he reminded her, shoving his thoughts to the back of his brain and hoping they stayed there. "That's only a week away."

She relaxed her stance, dropping her purse to her side. It struck him again that she looked tired. He couldn't remember ever seeing her looking like that before. Not since reacquainting himself with her in Chicago. Not when they were kids. It was...unsettling.

Then he remembered that yes, he had seen her that tired once. That night at her parents' house when they'd been up so late studying. It had unsettled him then, too. Enough that he'd wanted to do something to make her less weary. Enough that he'd placed his hands on her shoulders to rub away the knots in her tense muscles. But the moment he'd touched her—

He pushed that thought to the back of his brain, too. He *really* didn't need to be thinking about that right now.

"You should have thought about your date with Francesca before you humiliated us the tearoom," she said.

"Yeah, about that," he began. Not that he had any idea what to say about that, but *about that* seemed like a good start.

Ava spared him, however. "Peyton, we could work for a year, and it wouldn't make any difference. You'll just keep sabotaging us."

He couldn't help noting her use of the word *us*. She hadn't said he was sabotaging himself. She hadn't said he was sabotaging her efforts. She'd said he was sabotaging the two of them. He wondered if she noticed, too, how she'd lumped the two of them together, or if she even realized she'd said it. Even if she did, what did it mean, if anything?

"I only sabotaged us today," he told her. "And only because you were going out of your way to make things harder than they had to be."

Even though that was true, it wasn't why he'd behaved the way he had. He'd done that because he'd needed to get out of that place as fast as he could. The problem now was convincing Ava that he still wanted to move forward after deliberately taking so many giant steps backward.

And the problem was that, suddenly, his wanting to continue with this ridiculous makeover had less to do with winning over the Montgomery sisters in Mississippi…and more to do with winning over Ava right here in Chicago.

Eight

Ava trudged up the stairs to her apartment with Peyton two steps behind, silently willing him to twist his ankle. Not enough to do any permanent damage. Just enough to make him have to sit down and rub it for a few minutes so she could escape him.

In spite of her demands to leave her alone, he had followed her for three blocks, neither of them saying a word. She'd thought he would give up when they reached the door behind the shop that opened onto the stairwell leading up to her apartment. But he'd stuck his foot in it before she had a chance to slam it in his face. At this point, she was too tired to argue with him. If he wanted to follow her all the way up so she could slam her apartment door in his face, then that was his prerogative.

But he was too fast for her there, as well, shoving the toe of his new Gucci loafer between door and jamb before she had a chance to make the two connect. She leaned harder on the door, trying to put enough force into it that he would have to remove his foot or risk having his toes crushed. But his shoe held firm. Damn the excellence of Italian design anyway.

"Ava, let me in," he said, curling his fingers around the door and pushing back.

"Go. Away," she told him. Again.

"Just talk to me for a few minutes. Please?"

She sighed wearily and eased up on the door. Peyton shouldered it harder, gaining enough ground to win access to the apartment. But he halted halfway in, clearly surprised by his success. His face was scant inches from Ava's, and his fingertips on the door skimmed hers. Even though she was still wearing her white gloves, she could feel the warmth of his hand against hers. He was close enough for her to see how the amber of his irises was circled by a thin line of gold. Close enough for her to see a small scar on his chin that hadn't been there in high school. Close enough for her to smell the faint scent of something cool and spicy that clung to him. Close enough for her to feel his heat mingling with her own.

Close enough for her to wish he would move closer still.

Which was why she sprang away from the door and hurried toward the kitchen. Tea, she told herself. That was what she needed. A nice, calming cup of tea. She'd hardly had a chance to taste hers in the shop. She had a particularly soothing chamomile that would be perfect. Anything to take her thoughts off wanting to be close to Peyton. *No!* she quickly corrected herself. Anything to take her thoughts off her lousy afternoon.

Without wasting a moment to remove her gloves or

hat—barely even taking the time to shove the netting of the latter back from her face—she snatched the kettle from the stove, filled it with water and returned it to the burner as she spun the knob to turn it on. Then she busied herself with retrieving the tea canister from the cupboard and searching a drawer for the strainer. She felt Peyton's gaze on her the entire time, so knew he had followed as far as the kitchen, but she pretended not to notice. Instead, after readying the tea and cup, she began sorting through other utensils in the drawer, trying to look as if she were searching for something else that was very important—like her peace of mind, since that had completely fled.

"Ava," he finally said when it became clear she wouldn't continue the conversation.

"What?" she asked, still focused on the contents of the drawer.

"Will you please talk to me?"

"Are we not talking?" she asked, not looking up. "It sounds to me as if we're talking. If we're not talking, then what are we doing?"

"I don't know what you're doing, but I'm trying to get you to look at me so I can explain why I did what I did earlier."

He wasn't going to leave until they'd hashed this out. So she halted her phony search and slammed the drawer shut, turning to face him fully. "You were trying to get us thrown out of there on purpose," she said.

"You're right. I was," he admitted, surprising her.

He stood in the entry to the kitchen, filling it, making the tiny space feel microscopic. During their walk, he had wrestled his necktie free of his collar and unbuttoned his jacket and the top buttons of his shirt, but he still looked uncomfortable in the garments. Truth be told, he hadn't looked comfortable this week in any of his new clothes. He'd always looked as if he wanted to shed the skin of the animal she was trying to change him into. He looked that way now, too.

But he'd asked her to change him, she reminded herself. There was no reason for her to feel this sneaking guilt. She was trying to help him. She *was*. He was the one who had wrecked their afternoon today with his boorish behavior. He even admitted it.

"Why did you do it?" she asked. "We were having such a nice time."

"No, *you* were having a nice time, Ava. *I* was turning into Mary fu—uh… Mary friggin' Poppins."

"But Peyton, if you want to get along in—" somehow, she managed to get the words out "—my world, then you need to know how to—"

"I don't need to know how to *take tea*," he interrupted her, fairly spitting the last two words. "Admit it, Ava. The only reason you took me to that place was to get even with me for something. For being less than a gentleman—what you consider a gentleman, anyway—at the Art Institute yesterday. Or maybe for something else this week. God knows you're as hard to read now as you were in high school."

Ignoring his suggestion that she'd made him go to the tearoom as a punishment—since, okay, maybe possibly perhaps there was an element of truth in that—and ignoring, too, his charge that she was hard to read since he'd never bothered to see past the superficial—she latched on to his other comment instead. "What *I* consider a gentleman?" she said indignantly. "News flash, Peyton—what I'm teaching you to be is what any woman in her right mind would want a man to be."

He grinned at that. An arrogant grin very like the

ones to which he'd treated her in high school. "Oh, yeah? Funny, but a lot of women who knew me before this week liked me just fine the way I was. *A lot* of women, Ava," he reiterated with much emphasis. "Just *fine*."

She smiled back with what she hoped was the same sort of arrogance. "Note that I said, 'any woman in her *right* mind.' I doubt you've known too many of those, considering the social circle—or whatever it was—you grew up in."

She wanted to slap herself for the comment. Not just because it was so snotty, but because it wasn't true. Right-minded people weren't defined by their social circles. There were plenty of people in Chicago's upper crust who were crass and insufferable, and there were plenty of people living in poverty who were the picture of dignity and decency. But that was the effect Peyton had on her—he made her want to make him feel as small as he made her feel. The same way he had in high school.

He continued to smile, but his eyes went flinty. "Yeah, but these days, I move in the same kind of circle you grew up in. And hell, Ava, at least I *earned* my money. That's more than you can say for yourself. Your daddy gave you everything you ever had. And even Daddy didn't work for what he had. He got it from his old man. Who got it from his old man. Who got it from his old man. Hell, Ava, how long has it been since anyone in your family actually *worked* for all the nice things they own?"

Something in her chest pinched tight at that. Not just because what he said about her father was true—although Jennings Brenner III earned pennies these days working in the prison kitchen, he'd inherited his wealth the same way countless Brenners before him had. But also because Ava still hated the reminder of the way her family used to be, and the way they'd treated people like Peyton. She hated the reminder of the way *she* used to be, and the way *she'd* treated people like Peyton. He was right about her money, too—about the money she'd had back in high school, anyway. It hadn't been hers. She hadn't earned any of it. At least Peyton had had a job after school and paid his own way in the world. In that regard, he'd been richer back then than she. She'd *really* had no right to treat him the way she had when they were kids.

The kettle began to boil, and, grateful for the distraction, she spun around to pour the hot water carefully into her cup. For long moments, she said nothing, just focused on brewing her tea. Peyton's agitation at her silence was almost palpable. He took a few steps into the kitchen, pausing right beside her. Close enough that she could again feel his heat and inhale the savory scent of him. Close enough that she again wanted him to move closer still.

"So that's it?" he asked.

Still fixing her attention on her cup, she replied, "So what's it?"

"You're not going to say anything else?"

"What else am I supposed to say?"

"I don't know. Something about how my money is new money, so it's not worthy of comparison to yours, being as old and moldy as it is, or something like that."

The teenage Ava would have said exactly that. Only she would have delivered the comment in a way that made it sound even worse than Peyton did. Today's Ava wanted no part of it. What today's Ava did want, however...

Well. That was probably best not thought about. Not while Peyton was standing so close, looking and smelling as good as he did.

She sidestepped his question by replying, "Why would I say something like that when you've already said it?"

"Because I didn't mean it."

"Fine. You didn't mean it."

Instead of placating him, her agreement only seemed to irritate him more. "Why aren't you arguing with me?"

"Why do you want me to argue?"

"Stop answering my questions with a question."

"Am I doing that?"

"Dammit, Ava, I—"

She spoke automatically, as she had all week, when she said, "Watch your language."

He hesitated a moment, then said, "No."

That, finally, made her look up. "What?"

He smiled again, but this time it was less arrogant than it was challenging. "I said, 'No,'" he repeated. "I'm not going to watch my language. I'm sick of watching my language."

To prove his point, he followed that announcement with a string of profanity that made Ava wince. Then he fairly rocked back on his heels, as if waiting for her to retaliate. No, as if he was looking forward to her retaliation. As if he would relish it.

So, in retaliation, Ava went back to her tea. She dunked the strainer a few more times, removed it from the brew and set it aside. Then she lifted the cup to her lips and blew softly to cool it. When she braved a glimpse at Peyton, she could see that his annoyance had steeped into anger. She replaced her tea on the counter without tasting it. But she continued to gaze into its pale yellow depths when she spoke.

"No more arguing, Peyton. I'm tired of it, and it gets us nowhere."

He said nothing in response, only stood with his body rigid, glaring at her. Then, gradually, he relented. She could almost feel the fight go out of him, too, as if he were just as tired of the antagonism as she was.

"If I apologize for my behavior this afternoon," he asked, "will you come back to work for me?"

She told herself to say no and assure him that he'd learned enough to manage the rest of the way by himself. But for some reason, she said nothing.

"You said we still have a lot of work to do," he reminded her.

She told herself to admit she'd only said that because she hadn't wanted to end their time together. But for some reason, she said nothing.

"I mean, what if Caroline sets up a date for me and Francesca that involves seafood? I don't know how to eat a lobster that doesn't include slamming it on a picnic table a half dozen times."

She told herself to tell him he should just ask the matchmaker not to send them to Catch Thirty-Five.

"Or what if she makes us go to a wine bar? You and I have barely covered wine, and that's something you rich people always end up talking about at some point."

She told herself to tell him he should just ask the matchmaker not to send them to Avec.

"Or, my God, dancing. I don't know how to do any of that Arthur Murray stuff. I can't even do that 'Gangnam Style' horse thing."

Although that made her smile, Ava told herself to

tell him he should just ask the matchmaker not to send them to Neo.

She told herself to tell him all those things. Then she heard herself say, "All right. I'll teach you about seafood, wine and dancing between now and the end of next week."

"And some other stuff, too," he interjected.

She looked up at that and immediately wished she hadn't. Within the passage of a few moments, he'd somehow become even more attractive than he was before. He looked...gentler. More personable. More approachable. Like the sort of man any woman in her right mind would want...

"What other stuff?" she asked, quelling the thought before it fully formed.

He seemed at a loss for a minute, then said, "I'll make a list."

"Okay," she agreed reluctantly. It was only for another week. Surely she could be around him for one more week without losing her heart. *Mind,* she quickly corrected herself. Without losing her mind.

"Do you promise?" he asked, sounding uncertain.

It was an odd request. Why did he want her to promise? It was as if they were back to being adolescents. Why didn't he trust her to follow through? She'd done her part this week to teach him all the things he'd asked her to help him with. It was only when he'd thrown those lessons out the window and turned into a boor that she'd walked away.

"Yes, I promise."

"You promise to help me with everything I need help with?"

"Yes. I promise. But in return, you have to promise you'll stop challenging me every step of the way."

He grinned at that, but there was nothing arrogant or challenging in the gesture this time. In fact, this time, when Peyton smiled, he looked quite charming. "Oh, come on. You love it when I challenge you."

Oh, sure. About as much as she had loved it in high school.

"Promise me," she insisted.

He lifted his right hand, palm out, as if taking a pledge. "I promise."

"This day's a wash, though," she told him. "It's too late to get started on anything new."

"I'm sorry for the way I behaved at the tearoom," he said, surprising her again.

"And I'm sorry I made you go to a tearoom," she conceded.

The remark reminded her she was still wearing her hat and gloves, and she lifted her hands to inspect the latter. She'd seen them in a vintage clothing store when she was still in college and hadn't been able to resist them. What had possessed her to buy white gloves with more buttons than a lunar module? Oh, right. To match the white dress with more buttons than Cape Canaveral that she'd bought at a different vintage clothing store. She began the task of unfastening each of the pearly little buttons on her left glove.

"No, don't," Peyton said abruptly.

When she looked at him, she saw that his gaze was fixed on her two gloved hands. "Why not?"

Now his gaze flew to her face, and she couldn't help thinking he looked guilty about something. "Uh...it's just...um...I mean...ah..." He swallowed hard. "They just look really nice on you."

His cheeks were tinged with the faintest bit of pink, she noted with astonishment. Was he actually blushing?

Was that possible? Surely it was due to the bad lighting in the kitchen. Even so, something in his eyes made heat spark in her belly, spreading quickly outward, warming parts of her that really shouldn't be warming at the moment.

"Thank you," she said, the words coming out a little unevenly.

When she started to unbutton her glove once more, Peyton lifted a hand halfway to hers, looking as if he wanted to object again. She halted, eyeing him in silent question, and he dropped his hand with clear reluctance. *How odd,* she thought. She went back to the task, but couldn't help noticing how he still pinned his gaze to her hands, and how a muscle in his jaw twitched as his cheeks grew ruddier. Where she normally had no trouble removing the garments, for some reason, suddenly, her hands didn't want to cooperate. When the second button took longer to free than the first, and the third took even longer than the second, Peyton started to lift a hand toward hers again, closer this time, as if he wanted to help. And this time, he didn't drop it.

The more his scrutiny intensified, the more awkward Ava felt, slowing her progress even more. At this rate, he and Francesca would be sending their firstborn off to college before she finished with her first glove. Finally, she surrendered, dropping her right hand to her side and extending the left toward him.

"Could you help me out?" she asked, the question coming out softly and uncertainly.

It seemed to take a moment for her question to sink in, as Peyton was still fixed so intently on her gloved hand. Even when he moved his gaze from her hand to her face, he still looked acutely distracted.

"What?" he asked, sounding distracted, too.

"My glove," she said. "The buttons. I'm having trouble getting them undone. Do you mind?"

Color seeped into his cheeks again. "Uh, no. No, of course I don't mind. I'll be glad to do…ah, *undo*… you…I mean *them*. Help you. Undo them. Of course. No problem."

He moved both of his hands to her left one, but he hesitated before making contact. Instinctively, Ava took a step forward, as if doing so would help him close the hairbreadth of space that hovered between their hands. But all that did was diminish to a hairbreadth the space between their bodies, bringing them close enough that she more keenly felt his heat and more fully enjoyed his scent.

Close enough that, this time, Peyton did move closer, completely erasing any space left between them.

As his torso bumped hers, something at Ava's core caught fire. When he closed his hands over her glove, capturing the fourth button between his thumb and forefinger, that fire exploded, sending rockets of heat through her entire body. It was such an exquisitely tender touch, coming so unexpectedly from a man like him, so unlike anything she'd felt before.

Then she remembered that that wasn't true. Years ago, surrounded by girlish accoutrements in the bedroom of a Gold Coast mansion, she'd felt a touch that was just as tender, just as exquisite. That night, when Peyton had curled the fingers of one hand gingerly over her shoulder and skimmed the others along her nape, the gesture had been so tentative, so gentle, it was as if he were touching a girl for the first time. Which was ridiculous, because everyone at Emerson knew he was already hugely experienced, even at seventeen. With a carefulness no teenage boy should have been able to manage, he had begun to soothe her tense muscles.

The soothing, however, had quickly escalated. His touch did more to agitate than to placate, stirring feelings in Ava she'd spent months—years, even—trying to deny. Each stroke of his fingers over her flesh had made her crave more, until her thoughts became a jumble of desire and want and need. Peyton had been no more immune to the touching than she had. Within moments, what had started as an effort to calm erupted into a demand to incite. They'd been on each other like animals, scarcely breaking apart long enough to breathe.

But they'd been kids, she reminded herself, trying to ignore the heat building in her belly—and elsewhere. They'd been at the mercy of uncontrollable adolescent hormones. They were adults now, and could contain themselves. Yes, she was still physically attracted to Peyton. She suspected he was still physically attracted to her. But they were mature enough and experienced enough to recognize the pointlessness of such an attraction when there was nothing else between them to make it last. Sex was only sex without emotion to enrich it. And she was beyond wanting to have sex with someone when there was no future in it for either of them.

Now the caress of his fingers on her hand began to sway her thinking in that regard. Maybe, just this once, sex without a future wouldn't be such a bad thing...

Then Ava realized Peyton wasn't unbuttoning her glove. He was, in fact, rebuttoning it.

"Peyton, what are you doing?" she asked, surprised by how breathless she sounded. Surprised by how breathless she was. "I need you to help me get my gloves *off*."

He sounded a little breathless himself when he replied, "Oh, I think I like them better on."

"But—"

She wasn't able to complete her objection—she wasn't even able to complete a thought—because he dipped his head to press his mouth against hers. A little gasp of surprise escaped her, and he took advantage of her open mouth to taste her more deeply. With one hand still tangled in her gloved fingers, he pulled her close with the other, opening his hand at the small of her back to hold her in place. Not that Ava necessarily wanted to go anywhere. Not just yet. This was starting to get interesting...

Instinctively, she kissed him back, curving her free hand over his shoulder, tilting her head to facilitate the embrace. When she did, her hat bumped his forehead and tipped to one side. She released his shoulder to pull out the trio of hairpins keeping it in place, but Peyton captured that hand, too, pulling both away from her body.

"Don't," he said softly.

"But it's in the way."

He shook his head. "No. It's perfect where it is."

They were both breathing hard, their gazes locked, neither seeming to know what to do. The whole thing made no sense. Moments ago, they were arguing, and she was telling him to leave her alone. Yes, they'd ultimately arrived at an uneasy truce, but this went beyond every treaty they'd ever studied in World Civ.

Finally, she asked, "Peyton, what are we doing?"

He said nothing for a moment, only continued to hold her hands at her sides and study her face. Then he said, "Something that's been coming for a long time, I think."

"It can't have been that long. You've only been back in Chicago for two weeks."

"Oh, this started long before I came back to Chicago."

That was true. It had probably started her freshman year at Emerson, the first time she'd laid eyes on the bad boy of the sophomore class. The bad boy of every class. Even before she knew what it was to want someone, she'd wanted Peyton. She just hadn't understood how deeply that kind of wanting could run. Now—

Now she understood all too well. And now she wanted it—wanted him—even more.

Nevertheless, she resisted. "It's not a good idea."

"Why not?"

"Because there's no point in it."

"There was no point in it sixteen years ago, either, but that didn't stop us then."

"That's exactly my point."

He smiled at that. "But we were so good together, Ava."

"That one night we were."

He lifted one shoulder and let it drop. "Most people don't get one night like that their entire lives."

Implicit in his statement was that if they let things continue the way they had started, she and Peyton could have not just one but two nights like that. But was it enough? And wanting him more now, would it be even harder to let him go this time?

She didn't have a chance to form an answer to either question, because Peyton lowered his head and kissed her again. He was more careful this time, tilting to avoid her hat, brushing his lips gently over hers once, twice, three times, four. With every stroke of his mouth, Ava's heart raced more wildly, her temperature shot higher, and her thoughts melted away. The next thing she knew, she was framing Peyton's face in her gloved hands and kissing him back with all the tenderness he was showing her.

But just as before, that deliberation quickly escalated. She pushed her hands through his hair to cup one over his nape and the other along his throat. Then both hands were skimming under his lapels to push his jacket from his shoulders. He shrugged the garment off, then moved his hands to the top of her dress, unfastening the first of its many buttons. She wanted to undo the ones on his shirt, but her gloves hindered her once more. She pulled her mouth away from his to attempt their removal again, only to have him stop her.

"I want them off so I can touch you," she said.

"And I want them on," he told her. He grinned in a way that was downright salacious. "At least the first time. And the little hat, too."

Her pulse quickened at the prospect of a second—and perhaps even a third—time. Just as there had been that night when they were teenagers, even if the third time had been thanks to Peyton's gentle touches, because she'd been too tender to accommodate him again. Touching was good. She liked touching. It had been so long since she'd enjoyed such intimacies with anyone. In a way, she supposed she hadn't truly enjoyed them since that night with Peyton—at least not as much as she had with him. When a woman's first time was with someone like him, it left other guys at a disadvantage.

Then the second part of his statement came clear, and she couldn't help but smile back. "Just how long have you been thinking about this?"

"All afternoon."

"But I'm having trouble unbuttoning anything with them on," she told him. She hesitated to add that that was mostly because his touch made her tremble all over.

"Oh, that's okay," he assured her. "I can unbutton anything you—or I—want."

He dropped his fingers to the second button on her dress and deftly slipped it free, then moved on to the third. And the fourth. And the fifth. As he went, he moved his body slowly forward, gently urging her toward the kitchen door. Then into the hallway. Then to her bedroom door. Then into her bedroom. He reached her hem just as they arrived at her bed and, with the release of the final button, he spread her dress open. Beneath it, she wore a white lace demicup bra and matching panties. He hooked his thumbs into the waistband of the latter and eased them down over her hips, then gently pushed her down to a sitting position on the bed.

Ava started to scoot backward to make room for him, too, but he gripped her thighs and halted her.

"Don't get ahead of yourself," he murmured.

He started pulling down her panties again, over her thighs and knees, kneeling to push them along her calves and over her ankles. Instead of rising again, however, he moved between her legs, pushing her thighs apart. When Ava threaded her white-gloved hands through his hair, he gripped one of her wrists to place a kiss at the center of her palm. She closed her eyes, feeling the kiss through the fabric, through her skin, down to her very core. Then she felt his mouth on her naked thigh, and she gasped, her eyes flying open. Instinctively, she tried to close her legs, but he caught one in each hand and opened her wider. Then he moved his mouth higher, and higher, and higher still, until he was tasting her in the most intimate way he could.

Pleasure pooled in her belly as he darted his tongue against her, rippling outward to send ribbons of deliciousness echoing through her. Over and over, he savored her, relished her, aroused her. Little by little, those ribbons began to coil tight. Closer and closer they drew, until she didn't think she would be able to tolerate the chaos surging through her. Then, just when she thought she would shatter, those coils sprang free and she fell back onto the bed, arms spread wide, surrendering as one wave after another engulfed her.

Delirious, panting for breath, she somehow managed to lift her head enough to see Peyton stand. As he moved his hands to the buttons of his shirt, his grin was smug and satisfied. As much as she had enjoyed the last—how long had she been lying here? Moments? Months? An eternity?—she enjoyed watching him undress even more. He did it methodically, intently, his eyes never leaving hers, casting his shirt to the floor and then reaching for the waistband of his trousers.

He might have been a workaholic, but he clearly also took time to work out. His torso was roped with muscle and sinew, and his shoulders and biceps bunched and flexed as he jerked his belt free and lowered his zipper. Beneath, he wore a pair of silk boxers Ava had been in no way instrumental in encouraging him to buy. So either he cared more about undergarments than he did about what he wore over them, or else he wanted to impress someone. She remembered he would be meeting soon with a woman who'd been handpicked for him. And she pushed the thought away. He was with her now. That was all that mattered. For now.

When he stepped out of his boxers, he was full and ready for her. Ava caught her breath at the sight of him, so confident, so commanding, so very, very male. He lay alongside her and draped an arm over her waist, then lowered his head to hers, pushed back the netting on her hat, and kissed her deeply. She curled her fingers around his neck and pulled him closer, vying momentarily for possession of the kiss before giving herself over to him completely. He covered her breast with one hand, kneading gently. Then he followed the lace of her bra until he found the front closure, unsnapping it easily. After that, his bare hand was on her bare flesh, warm and insistent, his skin exquisitely rough.

He moved his mouth from hers, dragging kisses over her cheek, across her forehead, along her jaw. Then lower still, along her neck and collarbone, between her breasts. Then on her breast, tracing the tip of his tongue along the lower curve before opening wide over the sensitive peak. As he drew her into his mouth, he flattened his tongue against her nipple, tasting her there as intimately as he had everywhere else. Those little coils began to tighten inside her again, eliciting a groan of need.

Peyton seemed to understand, because he levered himself above her and returned his mouth to hers. As he kissed her, he entered her, long and hard and deep. Ava sighed at the feeling of completion that came over her. Never had she felt fuller or more whole. She opened her legs wider to accommodate him and he gave her a moment to adjust. Then he withdrew and bucked his hips forward again. Ava cried out at the second thrust, so perfect was the joining of their bodies. When Peyton braced himself on his forearms, she wrapped her legs around his waist and he propelled himself forward again. She lifted her hips to meet him, and together they set a rhythm that started off leisurely before building to a forceful crescendo.

They came together, both crying out at the fierceness of their release. Peyton rolled onto his back, bringing

Ava with him so that she was the one on top, gazing down at him. His breathing was as rapid and ragged as her own, his skin as slick and hot with perspiration. But he smiled as he looked at her, moving a hand to the back of her head to unpin her hat and free her hair until it tumbled around them both.

He was so beautiful. So intoxicating. Such a generous, powerful lover. She'd been thinking she would be able to handle him better as an adult. She'd thought her hormones had calmed down to the point where she would be in control of herself this time. She'd thought she would be immune to the adolescent repercussions of her first time with Peyton.

Wrong. She had been so wrong. He was more potent now than he had ever been, and she was even more susceptible to him. Her control had evaporated the moment he covered her mouth with his. The repercussions this time would be nothing short of cataclysmic. Because where she had responded to Peyton before as a girl who knew nothing of love and little of the workings of her own body, now she responded to him as a woman who understood those things too well. But it wasn't the physical consequences she might worry about in a situation like this—he had slipped on a condom before entering her. It was her heart. A part of her that was considerably more fragile.

And a part that was far more prone to breaking.

Nine

The second time Peyton awoke in Ava's bedroom, he was just as disoriented as he'd been the first time. Only this time it wasn't due to overindulgence in alcohol. This time, it was due to overindulgence in Ava.

Like that first time, he lay facedown, but today he was under the sheet instead of on top of it. And today he was sharing Ava's pillow, because his, he vaguely recalled, had been thrust under her hips during a particularly passionate moment, only to be cast blindly aside when he turned her over. Her face was barely an inch from his, and her eyes were closed in slumber, one of them obscured by a wayward strand of dark auburn. She was lying on her side, the sheet down around her waist, her arm folded over her naked breasts, her hands burrowed under the pillow. She looked tumbled and voluptuous and sexy as hell, and he swelled to life, just looking at her.

Probably shouldn't bother her with that again, though. Yet. A body did need some kind of refueling before it undertook those kinds of gymnastics a second—third? Fourth? They all got so jumbled together—time.

As carefully as he could, he climbed out of bed, halting before going anywhere to make sure he hadn't woken her up. Coffee. He needed coffee. She doubtless would, too, once she was conscious. He located his boxers and trousers and pulled both on, shrugged into his shirt without buttoning it, then made his way to the kitchen. He still couldn't get over the smallness of this place and wondered again where Ava's main residence was. Wondered again, too, why she was so determined that he not find out where it was. Maybe she would take him home with her, to her real home, now that the two of them had—

He halted the thought right there. There was no reason for him to think today would be any different from yesterday, especially considering the history the two of them shared. The last time he and Ava had spontaneously combusted like that, not a single thing had changed from the day before to the day after. They'd both gone right back to their own worlds and returned to their full-blown antagonism. Nothing had been different. Except that they'd both known just how explosive—and how amazing—things could be between them. Physically, anyway.

Which, now that he thought about it, might have been why they had both been so determined to return to business as usual. It had scared the crap out of him when he was a teenager, the way he and Ava came together that night. Not just because he hadn't understood why it had happened or how it could have been so unbelievably good, but because of how much he'd wanted it to happen again. That had probably scared him most of all. Somehow he'd known he would never have enough of Ava. And talk about forbidden fruit. He'd had to work even harder after that night to make sure he stayed at arm's length.

It hadn't made any sense. He'd still disliked her, even after the two of them made love…ah, he meant had sex. Hadn't he? He'd still thought she was vain, shallow and snotty. Hadn't he? And she'd made clear she still didn't like him, either. Hadn't she? So why had he, every day during the rest of his senior year, fantasized about being with her again? Sometimes he'd even fantasized about being with her in ways that had nothing to do with sex— taking in a midnight showing of *The Rocky Horror Picture Show* at the Patio Theater or sledding in Dan Ryan Woods. Hell, he'd even entertained a brief, lunatic idea about inviting her to the Emerson senior prom.

Sex, he told himself now, just as he'd told himself then. He'd been consumed by thoughts of Ava after that night because he associated her with sex after that night. He hadn't been a virgin then, but he hadn't seen nearly as much action as his reputation at Emerson had made others believe. Adolescent boys in the throes of testosterone overload weren't exactly picky when it came to sex with a willing participant. They didn't have to like the person they hooked up with. They only had to like the physical equipment that person had. Hell, even grown men weren't all that discriminating.

In high school, with Ava, it had just been one of those weird chemical reactions between two people who had nothing in common otherwise. Who would never have anything in common otherwise. Great sex. Bad rapport. There was no reason to think last night had changed that. Yeah, the two of them got along better these days than they had in high school—usually. But that was only because they'd matured and developed skills for dealing with people they didn't want to deal with. Sure, they could burn up the sheets in a sexual arena. But in polite society? Probably still best to stay at arm's length.

Yeah. That had to be why they'd ended up in bed together last night. So it made sense to conclude that today's morning after wouldn't be any different from their morning after sixteen years ago. Except that he and Ava probably wouldn't yell at each other the way they had then, and he was reasonably certain he wouldn't have to climb out the bedroom window to avoid being seen. He was likewise certain that Ava would agree.

A sound behind him made him spin around, and he saw her standing in the doorway looking like a femme fatale from a fabulous '40s film. She was wrapped in a robe made of some flimsy, silky-looking fabric covered with big red flowers, and her hair spilled over her forehead and danced around her shoulders.

"You're still here," she said, sounding surprised.

"Where else would I be?"

She lifted one shoulder and let it drop, a gesture that made the neck of the robe open wider, revealing a deep V of creamy skin. It was with no small effort that Peyton drew his gaze back up to her face.

"I don't know," she said. "When I woke up and you weren't there, I just thought…"

When she didn't finish, he said, "You thought I climbed out your bedroom window and down the rainspout, and that you'd see me at school on Monday?"

He had meant to make her smile. Instead, her brows knitted downward. "Kind of."

In other words, Ava was thinking last night was a repeat of the one sixteen years ago, too. That, once again, nothing had changed between the two of them. That this morning it was indeed back to business as usual. Otherwise, she wouldn't look as somber as she did. Otherwise, the room would have been filled with warmth and relief instead of tension and anxiety. Otherwise, they would both be happy.

"Coffee?" he asked, to change the subject. Then he remembered he hadn't fixed any yet. "I mean, I was going to make coffee, but I don't know where it is."

"In the cabinet to your right."

He opened it and discovered not just coffee, but an assortment of other groceries, as well. He remembered from his previous visit how well stocked the bathroom was, too. Just how often did Ava use this place, anyway?

Neither of them said a word as he went about the motions of setting up the coffeemaker and switching it on. With each passing moment, the silence grew more awkward.

"So," Peyton said, "what's on the agenda for today? It's Saturday. That should leave things wide open."

For a moment, Ava didn't reply. But she looked as if she were thinking very hard about something. "Actually, I'm thinking maybe it's time to make a dry run," she finally said.

The comment confused him. Wasn't that what they'd done last night? And look how it had turned out. All awkward and uncertain this morning. "What do you mean?" he asked, just to be sure.

She hesitated again before speaking. "I mean maybe it's time we launched you into society to see how things go."

He felt strangely panicked. "But you said we still had a lot of stuff to go over."

"No, you said that."

"Oh, yeah. But that's because there is."

Once again she hesitated. "Maybe. But that's another reason to go ahead and wade into the waters of society. To see where there might still be trouble spots that need improvement. Who knows? You might feel right at home and won't need any more instruction."

He doubted that. As much as he'd learned in the last couple of weeks, he wasn't sure he would ever feel comfortable in Ava's world, even if they spent the next ten years studying for it. And why did she sound kind of hopeful about him not needing any more instruction? It was almost as though she wanted to get rid of him.

Oh, right. After last night, she probably did. But then, he wanted to get rid of her, too, right? So why was he digging in?

"What did you have in mind?" he asked.

"There's a fund-raiser for La Rabida Children's Hospital at the Palmer House tonight. It will be perfect. Everyone who's anyone will be there. It's invitation only, but I'm sure if news got around that Peyton Moss, almost billionaire, was in town, you could finagle one."

"Why can't I just be your guest?" No sooner did he ask the question than did it occur to him that she might already be taking someone else. His panic multiplied.

Her gaze skittered away from his. "Because I wasn't invited."

His mouth dropped open at that. Ava Brenner hadn't been invited to an event where everyone who was anyone would be making an appearance?

"Why not?" he asked.

She said nothing for a moment, only pulled the sides of her robe closed and cinched the belt tight. She continued to avoid his gaze when she replied. "I, um…I had kind of a falling-out with the woman who organized it.

Since then, I tend not to show up on any guest list she's associated with." Before he could ask for more details, she hurried on, "But a word in the right ear will put you on the guest list with no problem."

Wow. It took a brave soul—or someone with a death wish—to exclude the queen bee of Chicago's most ruthless rich-kid high school from a major social event. Whoever organized this thing must have come to Chicago recently and didn't realize what kind of danger she was courting, ignoring Ava.

"Then who's going to put that word into the right ear?" he asked.

"A friend of mine who's attending owes me a favor. I'll have her contact the coordinator this morning. You should get a call by this afternoon."

Of course. No doubt Ava had lots of friends attending this thing who owed her favors that could get done at a moment's notice. Favors to pay her back for not walking all over them at Emerson and grinding them into dust.

"But..."

"But what?" she asked. "Either you're ready or you're not. If we can find that out tonight, all the better."

Right. Because if he was ready, then the two of them could part ways sooner rather than later. And that would be for the best. He knew it. Ava knew it. They didn't belong together now any more than they had sixteen years ago.

"Will you come, too?" he asked.

"I told you. I wasn't invited."

"But—"

"You'll be fine going solo."

"But—"

"You can report back to me tomorrow."

"But—"

"But *what?*"

This time, it was Peyton's turn to hesitate. "Couldn't you come with me as my guest or something?"

He'd thought she would jump at the chance. Wouldn't it be the perfect opportunity to stick it to whoever had kept her off the guest list, showing up anyway? Invited, nonetheless, even if by default? She could swoop in with all that imperiousness that was second nature to her and be the center of everything, the same way she'd been in high school. Peyton even found himself kind of looking forward to seeing the old Ava in action.

But she didn't look or sound anything like the old Ava when she replied, "I don't think it's a good idea."

"Then I'm not going."

She drove her gaze back to his, and for an infinitesimal moment, he did indeed see a hint of the old Ava. The flash of her eyes, the ramrod posture and the haughty set to her mouth. But as quickly as she surfaced, the old Ava disappeared.

"Fine," she said wearily. "I'll go. But only as an observer, Peyton. You'll be on your own when it comes to mingling."

"Mingling?" he repeated distastefully. That sounded about as much fun as *taking tea.*

"And anything else that comes up."

He wanted to argue, but backed down. For now. It was enough that he'd convinced her to come with him to this thing. Okay, to *come,* even if it wasn't technically *with him.* They could work on that part later. What was weird was that Peyton discovered he actually did kind of want to work on that part. He wanted to work on that part very much. Which was totally different from how he'd felt on that morning after sixteen years ago. In a word, *hmm...*

So now that he had the *who,* the *when* and the *what,* all he had to do was figure out the *why.* And, most confounding of all, the *how.*

Ava studied her reflection in the mirror of a fitting room at Talk of the Town, feeling the way her clients must. Mostly, she was wondering if she would be able to fool others into thinking this was her dress, not a rental, and that she was rich and glamorous and refined like everyone else at the party, not some poser who was struggling to make payments on the business loan that had bumped her up—barely—to middle class.

That was why most women came to Talk of the Town. To look wealthier and more important than they really were. Sometimes they wanted to impress a potential employer. Sometimes it was for a school reunion where they wanted to show friends and acquaintances—and prom queens and bullies—that they were flourishing. Others simply wanted to move in a level of society they'd never moved in before, even if for one night, to see what it was like.

Fantasies. That was really what they rented at Talk of the Town. And a fantasy was what Ava was trying to create for herself tonight. Because only in a fantasy would she be welcomed in the society where she had once held dominion. And only in a fantasy would she and Peyton walk comfortably in that world together. Sixteen years ago, that would have been because no one moving in her circle wanted to include him at the party. Today, Peyton was welcome, but she wasn't.

Before Peyton's return to Chicago, Ava hadn't given a fig about moving in that world again. But since his arrival two weeks ago—and making love with him last night—she'd begun to feel differently. Not about wanting to rule society again. But about at least being welcome there. Because that was Peyton's world now. And she wanted to be where he was.

Over the past two weeks, she'd begun to feel differently about him. Or maybe she was just finally being honest with herself about how she'd always felt about him, even in high school. She'd remembered so many things about him that she'd forgotten over the years—things she had consciously ignored back then, but which had crept into her subconscious anyway. Things that, for that one night at her parents' house, had allowed her to let down her guard and feel for him the way she truly felt and respond to him the way she truly wanted to respond.

She'd remembered how his smile hooked up more on one side than the other, making him look roguish and irreverent. She'd remembered how once, in the library, he had been so engrossed in his reading that she'd enjoyed five full minutes of just watching him. She'd remembered how he'd always championed the other scholarship kids at Emerson and acted as their protector when the members of her crowd were so cruel. And she'd remembered seeing him stash his lunch under his shirt one day to carry it out to a starving stray dog behind the gym.

They were all acts that had revealed his true character. Acts that made her realize he was none of the things she and her friends had said about him and everything any normal girl would love in a boy. But Ava had chosen to ignore them. That way she wouldn't have to acknowledge how she really felt about him, for fear that she would be banished from the only world she knew, the only world in which she belonged.

Even with the passage of years and the massive reversal in his fortune, Peyton was still that same guy. He still grinned like a rabble-rouser and could still hone his concentration to the exclusion of everything else. He still rooted for the underdog, and he couldn't pass a busker on the street without tossing half the contents of his wallet into the performer's cup. He hadn't changed a bit. Not really. And neither had the feelings she had buried so deep inside her teenage self.

She expelled a soft sound of both surprise and defeat. Sixteen years ago, she and Peyton couldn't have maintained a relationship because their social circles had prohibited it—his as much as hers. No one in his crowd would have accepted her any more than her crowd would have accepted him. And neither of them had had the skill set or maturity to sustain a liaison in secret. Eventually it would have ended, and it would have ended badly. They would have burned hot and fast for a while, but they would have burned out. And they would have burned each other. And that would have stayed with them forever. Now...

Now it was the same, only reversed. Peyton's success had launched him to a place where he wanted and needed the "right" kind of woman for a wife—the kind of woman who would boost his image and raise his status even more. Someone with cachet, who had entrée into every facet of society. Someone whose pedigree and lineage was spotless. He certainly didn't want a woman whose father was a felon and whose mother had succumbed to mental illness, a woman who could barely pay her own way in the world. He'd fought hard to claw his way to the level of success he had—he'd said so himself. He wasn't going to jeopardize that for someone like her. Not when the only thing she had to offer him was a physical release, no matter how explosive.

Maybe there was emotion, even love, on her part, but on Peyton's? Never. There hadn't been when they were teenagers—he hadn't been able to get out of her bedroom fast enough, and his antagonism toward her for the rest of the school year had been worse than ever—and not now, either. This morning he'd said nothing about last night, had only wondered what today's lesson would be, as if their making love hadn't changed anything. Because it *hadn't* changed anything. At least, not for him.

Nerves tumbled through her midsection as she surveyed herself in the mirror one last time. On the upside, the fund-raiser tonight was one of the biggest ones held in Chicago, so there was an excellent chance she and Peyton wouldn't run into anyone from the Emerson Academy. On the downside, the fund-raiser tonight was one of the biggest ones held in Chicago, so there was an excellent chance she and Peyton would run into everyone from the Emerson Academy.

Maybe if she wore a pair of those gorgeous, gemstone-encrusted Chanel sunglasses…

She immediately pushed the idea away. Not only was it déclassé to wear sunglasses to a society function—unless it involved a racetrack or polo match—she couldn't afford to add any more accessories. As it was, the form-fitting gold Marchesa gown, along with the blue velvet Escada pumps, clutch and shawl, and the Bulgari sapphire necklace, were going to set her back enough that she would have to exist on macaroni and cheese until July. Still, she thought as she turned to view the plunging back of the dress and the perfect French twist she'd managed for her hair, she looked pretty smashing if she did say so herself.

When she stepped out of the fitting room to find

Lucy waiting for her, Ava could tell by her look of approval that she agreed.

"You know, I didn't think the blue shoes and clutch were going to work," the salesclerk said, "but with that necklace, it all comes together beautifully. I guess that's why you're the big boss."

Well, you could take the girl out of society, but you couldn't take society out of the girl. Not that some of her former friends hadn't tried.

The thought made her stomach roil. She really, really, really hoped she didn't see anyone she knew tonight.

"I have to go," she said. "Thank you again for working so many hours this week. I'll make it up to you."

"You already have," Lucy told her with a grin. "You've made it up to me time and time and a half again."

Ava grinned back. "Don't spend it frivolously."

Not the way Ava had spent so frivolously with this outfit. She wished she'd had the foresight to charge Peyton for expenses.

"Have fun tonight!" Lucy called as Ava made her way to the door. "Don't do anything I wouldn't do!"

Not to worry, Ava assured her friend silently. She'd already done that. By falling in love with a man who would never, ever love her back.

Ten

Peyton paced in front of the Palmer House Hilton, checking his watch for the tenth time and tugging the black tie of his new tuxedo. Ava had been right about the phone call. That morning, she'd called someone named Violet, who said she would call someone named Catherine, and before he'd even left Ava's apartment, his phone had rung with a call from that same Catherine, who had turned out to be someone from Ava's social circle at Emerson—and someone who had treated him even worse than Ava had—gushing about how much she would love it if he would come to their "little soiree." She'd also made him promise to seek her out as soon as he arrived so the two of them could catch up on old times.

As if he wanted to catch up with anyone from Emerson who wasn't Ava. Jeez.

Where the hell was she? She should have been here

seven and a half minutes ago. He scanned the line of
taxis and luxury cars that snaked halfway down Mon-
roe Street. As if his thoughts made it happen, the door
of a yellow cab three cars back opened and Ava climbed
out. And not just any Ava. But a breathtaking twenty-
four-carat-gold Ava.

Holy crap, she looked— He stopped himself. Not just
because he couldn't think of an adjective good enough
to do her credit, but because there would be no *holy
crap* tonight. Tonight he was supposed to be a gentleman. Tonight, he would be a—he tried not to gag—society buck. Guys like that didn't say *Holy crap*. Guys
like that didn't even say *Guys like that*. They said… He
racked his brain, trying to remember some of the stuff
Ava had taught him to say, since even saying stuff like
stuff was off-limits when it came to presenting a dignified, articulate image.

Aw, screw it. He could think whatever words he
wanted, as long as he didn't say them out loud. And
what he thought when he saw Ava gliding toward him,
covered in gold and sapphire-blue, was…was…

Huh. Even allowing himself to use his usual vocabulary, he still couldn't think of anything. Except maybe
about what she was wearing *under* all the gold and
sapphires.

Crap.

Okay, so the past couple of weeks had been the best
of times and the worst of times. The best of times because he'd been around Ava, and he now knew how to
do things that increased his social value to women like
her. But the worst of times because, even with his increased social value, Ava still didn't want him. Not the
way he wanted her.

Well, okay, she *wanted* him. At least, last night she

had. She had definitely wanted him the way he wanted her last night. She just didn't want him today. Not the way he wanted her. And it was a different kind of wanting he felt today—a way more important kind of wanting—than it had been last night. Which was weird, because last night he'd wanted her in a way that was pretty damned important. What was even worse—in fact, what was the worst part of all—was that she was more firmly entrenched in his head now than ever, and he had no idea how to deal with it. And she wasn't just in his head. She was in other body parts, too. And not just the ones that liked to have sex.

She'd changed since high school. A lot. Yeah, there had been times when she'd tried to shroud herself in the same ice-princess disguise she'd worn in high school, but Peyton had seen past the facade. She was warmer now, more accessible. More fun to be around. Even when the two of them sparred with each other, there was something enjoyable about it.

But then, he'd kind of enjoyed sparring with her in high school, too. Really, now that he thought about it, he realized Ava couldn't have been *that* cold and distant back then. Not all the time. There must have been something about her that attracted him—something only his subconscious had been able to see. Otherwise he wouldn't have been attracted. Since coming back to Chicago, his conscious had started to pick up on it, too. Ava wasn't vain, shallow or snotty. Had she been vain, she wouldn't have thought about anyone but herself, and she never would have helped him out with his self-improvement, even if he was paying her. Why shouldn't he pay her? He was going to pay someone else for their expertise, and hers was even more expert because she'd grown up in the environment he was trying to penetrate. Uh…he meant *enter*. Uh…he meant *join*. Yeah, join.

She wasn't shallow, either, because she knew a lot of stuff about a lot of stuff. Had she been shallow, he could have tallied her interests on one hand. She'd introduced him to things he'd never thought about before, a lot of which wasn't even related to social climbing. And she wasn't snotty, because she'd shared that knowledge with him, knowing he would use it for social climbing, not caring that his new money would mix with old. Not once had she criticized him for being nouveau riche. Only Peyton had done that.

Yep, he definitely knew now what he liked about Ava. And, at the moment, it was all wrapped in gold and walking right toward him.

"What are you doing out here?" she asked by way of a greeting when she came to a halt before him.

"I'm waiting for you."

"You were supposed to leave my name at the door as your plus-one and go in without me to start mingling. We're not together, remember?"

How could he forget? She'd made clear this morning that last night hadn't changed anything between them. "But I don't know anyone in there. How am I supposed to mingle when I don't know anyone?"

"Peyton, that's the whole point of mingling."

But mingling sucked. It sucked as much as having to tame his profanity. It sucked as much as having to pay ten times what he normally did for a haircut. It sucked as much as not being able to wear ten-year-old blue jeans that were finally broken in the way he liked.

Why did he want to join a class of people who had to do so many things that sucked? Oh, yeah. To increase his social standing. Which would increase his business standing. Which would allow him to take over a company that would increase his monetary standing. That was the most important thing, wasn't it? Making money? Increasing his value? At least, that had been the most important thing before he landed back in Chicago. Somehow, over the past couple of weeks, that had fallen a few slots on his most important stuff in the world list.

Huh. Imagine that.

"Just promise me you won't slip out of view," he told Ava.

"I promise. Now get in there and be the status-seeking, name-dropping, social-climbing parvenu I've come to know and lo— Uh...I've come to know."

Peyton's stomach clenched at the way she first stumbled over the word *love,* then discarded it so easily. Instead, he focused on another word. "Parvenu? What the hell is that? That's not one of those upper-crusty words you taught me. See? I told you we still have a lot to do."

"Just give them my name and get in there," she told him, pointing toward the door. "I'll count to twenty and follow." As he started to move away, she hissed under her breath, "And no swearing!"

Peyton forced himself to move forward, ignoring the flutter of nerves in his belly. He had nothing to be nervous about. He'd been entering fancy, expensive places like this for years and had stopped feeling self-conscious in them a long time ago. Even so, it surprised him when a doorman stepped up to open the door for him, welcoming him to the Palmer House Hilton, punctuating the greeting with a respectful *sir.* Because in spite of all that Peyton had achieved since the last time he was in Chicago, tonight he felt like an eighteen-year-old kid who had never left. A kid from the wrong side of town who was trying to sneak into a place he shouldn't be. A place he wasn't welcome. A place he didn't belong.

The feeling was only amplified once he was inside the hotel. The Palmer House was an unassuming enough building on the outside, but inside it looked like a Byzantine cathedral, complete with ornamental columns, gilt arches and a lavishly painted ceiling. The place was packed with people who were dressed as finely as he, the men in black tie and the women in gowns as richly colored as precious gems. Catherine Bellamy, he remembered. That was the name of his former classmate who had asked him to look for her. Except that now her name was Catherine Ellington, because she married Chandler Ellington, who'd been on the Emerson hockey team with Peyton, and who was the biggest...

He tried to think of a word for Chandler that would be socially acceptable but couldn't come up with a single one. That was how badly the guy had always treated Peyton in high school. Suffice it to say Chandler had been a real expletive deleted in high school. So had Catherine. So they were perfect for each other. Anyway, he was pretty sure he'd recognize them if he saw them.

He followed the well-heeled crowd, figuring they were all destined for the same place, and found himself in the grand ballroom, which was every bit as sumptuous—and intimidating—as the lobby. Chandeliers of roped crystal hung from the ceiling above a room that could have been imported from the Palace of Versailles. A gilt-edged mezzanine surrounded it, with people on both levels clutching flutes of champagne and cut-crystal glasses of cocktails. A waiter passed with a tray carrying both, and Peyton automatically went for one of the latter, something brown he concluded would be whiskey of some kind, a spirit he loved in all its forms.

He took a couple of fortifying sips, but they did nothing to dispel his restlessness. So he scanned the crowd for a flash of gold that was splashed with sapphire. He found it immediately. Found her immediately. Ava had just entered the ballroom and was reaching for a glass of champagne herself. He waited until he caught her eye, then lifted his glass in salute. She smiled furtively and did likewise, subtly enough so that only he would see the gesture.

It was enough. Ava had his back. Taking a deep breath, Peyton turned and ventured into the crowd.

Ava managed to make it through the first hour of the fund-raiser without incident, mostly by tucking herself between a couple of potted topiaries on the mezzanine. That way, she could keep an eye on the crowd below and still snatch the occasional glass of champagne or canapé from a passing server. Even if Peyton moved from one place to another, it was easy to keep an eye on him.

It quickly became evident, however, that he didn't need an eye on him. He was a natural. From the moment he flowed into the sea of people, he looked as if he'd been one of them since birth. She kept waiting for him to make a misstep—to untie his tie or ask a waiter for a longneck beer—but he never did. Even now, he was cradling a drink with all the sophistication of James Bond and smiling at a silver-Givenchy-clad Catherine Bellamy as if she were the most fascinating woman he'd ever had the pleasure to meet.

He'd located her within moments of his arrival— or rather, Catherine had located him—and had yet to escape her. Catherine was clearly taking great delight in escorting him through the crowd, reacquainting him with dozens of their former schoolmates. Peyton had greeted each of them with one of his toe-curling smiles, never once hinting at how appallingly they had all treated him in high school.

If he could manage that, there was no way he needed further instruction in etiquette from Ava. After tonight, she could send him on his merry way without her. Off to be the toast of whatever society he might happen to find himself in. Off to his multimillion-dollar estate that was half a continent away. Off to meet the "right" kind of woman his matchmaker had found for him. Off to live his successful life with his blue-blooded wife and his perfectly pedigreed children. Off to launch his business into the stratosphere and line his pockets with even more money. That was the life he wanted. That was the life he had fought so hard, for so long, to achieve. That was the life he wouldn't sacrifice anything for. He was the master of his own destiny now. And that destiny didn't include—

"Ava Brenner. Oh, my God."

It was amazing, Ava thought, how quickly the brain could process information it hadn't accessed in years. She recognized the voice before she turned around, even though she hadn't heard it since high school. Deedee Hale. Of the Hinsdale Hales. At her side was Chelsea Thomerson, another former classmate. Both looked fabulous, of course, blonde Deedee in her signature red—this one a lush Zac Posen—and brunette Chelsea in a clingy strapless black Lagerfeld.

"What on *earth* are you doing here?" Deedee asked. She never could utter a complete sentence without emphasizing at least one word. "Not that I'm not *incredibly* happy to see you, of course. I'm just so *surprised*."

"What a beautiful dress," Chelsea added. "I don't think I've ever seen a knockoff that looked more genuine."

"Hello, Deedee. Chelsea," Ava said. As politely as she could, she added, "It's not a knockoff. It's from Marchesa's new spring collection." And because she couldn't quite help herself, she also added, even more politely, "You just haven't seen it anywhere else yet. I have the only one in Chicago."

"Ooooh," Chelsea said. "You carry it in that little shop of yours."

"I do," Ava said with almost convincing cheeriness.

"How *is* that little project going, by the way?" Deedee asked. "Are we *still* pulling ourselves up by our little bootstraps, hmm?"

"Actually," Ava said, "tonight, we're pulling ourselves up by our little Escadas."

"Ooooh," Deedee said. "You carry *those* in your little shop, too."

"Yes, indeed."

"Have you *seen* Catherine?" Deedee asked. "I'm guessing she was *very* surprised to find you here."

"I haven't, actually," Ava said. "There are just so many people, and I haven't had a chance to—"

Before she could finish, Deedee and Chelsea were on her like a pack of rabid debutantes. As if they'd choreographed their movements before coming, each positioned herself on one side of Ava and looped an arm through hers.

"But you *must* see Catherine," Deedee said. "She's been so adamant about speaking to *everyone* on the guest list."

Translation, Ava thought, *Catherine will want to know there's a party crasher among us.*

"And since you so rarely attend these things," Chelsea added, "I'm sure Catherine will especially want to see you."

Translation, Ava thought, *You don't belong here, and when Catherine sees you, she's gonna kick your butt from here to Saks Fifth Avenue.*

Ava opened her mouth to say something that might allow her to escape, but to no avail. The women chatted nonstop as they steered her to the stairs and down to the ballroom, barely stopping for breath. Short of breaking free like a panicked Thoroughbred and galloping for the exit, there was little Ava could do but go along for the ride.

The two women located Catherine—and, by extension, Peyton—in no time, and herded Ava in that direction. Peyton looked up about the same time Catherine did, and Ava wasn't sure which of them looked more surprised. Catherine recovered first, however, straightening to a noble posture, plastering a regal smile on her face and lifting an aristocratic hand to brush back a majestic lock of black hair. Honestly, Ava thought, it was a wonder she hadn't donned a tiara for the event. Her gaze skittered from Chelsea to Deedee then back to Ava.

"Well, my goodness," she said flatly. "Ava Brenner, as I live and breathe. It's been years. Where have you been keeping yourself?"

Ava knew better than to reply, because Catherine always answered her own questions. But unlike Deedee and Chelsea, who at least pretended to be polite—kind of—Catherine, having ascended to the queen bee throne the moment Ava was forced to abdicate, saw no reason to pull punches. Especially when she was dealing with peasants.

Sure enough, Catherine barely paused for breath.

"Oh, wait. I know. Visiting your father in the state pen and your mother in the loony bin, and running your little shop for posers. It's amazing you have any time left for barging into events to which you were in no way invited."

Ava had had enough run-ins with her former friends by now that nothing Catherine could say would surprise or rattle her. Or hurt her feelings, for that matter. No, only having Peyton hear what Catherine said could do that. That could hurt quite a lot, actually.

She'd also endured enough encounters with ex-acquaintances to have learned that the best way to deal with them was to look them in the eye and never flinch. Which was good, since doing that meant Ava didn't have to look at Peyton. Imagining his reaction to what Catherine had just revealed was bad enough.

"Actually, Catherine, my father is in a federal correctional institution," she said with all the courtesy she could muster. She lowered her voice to the sort of stage whisper she would have used at parties like this in the past when gossiping about those who weren't quite up to snuff. "Federal institutions are *much* more exclusive than state ones, you know. They don't admit all the posers and wannabes."

Her reply had the hoped-for effect. Catherine was momentarily stunned into silence. Score one for the party crasher. Yay.

Sobering and returning to her normal voice, Ava added, "And my mother passed away three years ago. But it's so kind of you to ask about her, Catherine. I hope your mother is doing well. She and my mother were always such good friends."

Until Ava's father was revealed to be such a cad. Then Mrs. Bellamy had led the charge to have Ava's mother blacklisted everywhere from the Chicago Kennel Club to Kappa Kappa Gamma.

Catherine looked flummoxed by Ava's graciousness. Anyone else might have, if not apologized, at least backed off. But not a queen bee like Catherine. Once again, she recovered her sovereignty quickly.

"And your father?" she asked. "Will he be coming up for parole any time in the near future?"

"Four years," Ava said with equanimity. "Do give my regards to your father as well, won't you?"

Even though Ava had had little regard for Mr. Bellamy since he'd cornered her at Catherine's sweet sixteen party and invited her to his study for a cocktail and God knew what else.

Catherine narrowed her eyes in irritation that Ava was neither rising to the bait nor whittling down to a nub. Really, being polite and matter-of-fact was the perfect antidote to someone so poisonous. It drove Catherine mad when people she was trying to hammer down remained pleasantly upright instead.

"And it sounds like your little shop is just flourishing," she continued tartly. "Why, Sophie Bensinger and I were talking just the other day about how many crass little interlopers we've been seeing at *our* functions lately. Like tonight, for instance," she added pointedly. "All of them dressed in clothes they couldn't possibly afford, so they had to be rented from your pretentious little shop." She scanned Ava up and down. "I had no idea you were one of your own customers. And it *is* nice of you to clothe the needy, Ava, but honestly, couldn't you do it somewhere else?"

"What, and miss running into all my old friends?" Ava replied without missing a beat.

Now Catherine turned to Peyton. Knowing there was

no way to avoid it, Ava did, too. She told herself she was ready for anything when it came to his reaction—confused, angry, smug, even stung. But she wasn't ready for a complete absence of reaction. His expression was utterly blank, as if he were meeting her for the first time and had no idea who she was. She could no more tell what he thought of everything he'd just heard than she could turn back time and start the evening over.

Where Catherine's voice had been acid when she spoke to Ava, it oozed sweetness now. "Peyton, I'm sure you remember Ava Brenner from Emerson." After a telling little chuckle, she added, "I mean, who could forget Ava? She ruled that school with an iron fist. None of us escaped her tyranny. Well, not until her father was arrested for stealing millions from the hedge funds he was supposed to be managing, not to mention the IRS, so that he could pay for his cocaine and his whores. He even gave Ava's mother syphilis, can you imagine? And herpes! Of course they took everything from him to pay his debts, right down to the Tiffany watch Ava's grandmother gave her for her debut, one that had been in the family for generations. After that, Ava had to leave Chicago and go… Well. She went to live with others of her kind. In Milwaukee. You know the kind of people I'm talking about, Peyton, of course."

As if Catherine feared he might not realize she was talking about the very sort of people he'd grown up among—but whom he'd had the good taste and cunningness to rise above—she shivered for effect. And so well had Ava taught him manners, Peyton hesitated only a microsecond before smiling. But his smile never reached his eyes. Then again, neither did Catherine's. Or Chelsea's. Or Deedee's. Wow. Ava really had taught him well.

"Of course I remember Ava," he said as he extended his hand. "It's good to see you again."

Ava tugged her arm free of Chelsea's and placed her hand in his, trying to ignore how even that small touch made her stomach flip-flop. How even that small touch made her remember so many others and made her wish for so many things she knew she would never have. Before she could even get out a hello, Catherine chimed in again.

"Of course you remember Ava," she echoed Peyton's words. "How could you forget someone who treated you as atrociously as she treated you? And have I told you, Peyton, how very much I admire your many accomplishments since you graduated?"

Still looking at Ava, still holding her hand, still making her stomach flip-flop, he replied, "Yes, you have, Catherine. Several times, in fact."

"Well, you have had so many accomplishments," she gushed. "All of them so admirable. All of us at Emerson are so proud of you. Of course, we all saw your potential when you were a student there. We all knew you would rise above your, ah, meager beginnings and become an enormous success." She looked at Ava. "Well, except for Ava. But then, look how she turned out. A criminal father and an unstable mother, and not a dime to her name." She waved a hand negligently. "But there are so many nicer things to talk about. I'm sure she was on her way out. If not, we can find someone who will show her the way."

For one taut, immeasurable moment, Ava thought—hoped—Peyton would come to her rescue and tell Catherine she was here as his guest. She even hoped he would ignore every lesson she'd taught him about manners and tell all of them that furthermore, they could all go do something to themselves that no gentleman would ever tell anyone to do. But she really had taught him well. Because all he did was release her hand and take a step backward, then lift his drink to his mouth for an idle sip.

A small breath of disappointment escaped her. Well, what had she expected? Not only was he behaving exactly the way he was supposed to—the way she had taught him to—but it wasn't as though Ava didn't deserve his dismissal. Back in high school, she would have done the same thing to him. She'd said herself that karma was a really mean schoolgirl. After all, it took one to know one.

Very softly, she said, "I can find my own way out, thank you, Catherine." She turned to Peyton. "It really was nice to see you again, Peyton. Congratulations on your many admirable accomplishments."

She was following her own lesson book, turning to make a polite exit, when she thought, *What the hell?* They weren't in high school anymore. She didn't have to stay on her side of the social line the way she had at Emerson. Nor did she have to silently suffer the barbs of bullies as she had at the Prewitt School. She wasn't part of either society anymore. She was her own woman.

And this society had tossed her out on her keister sixteen years ago. She didn't have to rely on them to further her business or her fortune. On the contrary, any success she saw would be because of people who were like her. People who hoped for something better but were doing their best with what they had in the meantime. People who didn't think they were better than everyone else while behaving worse. Normal people. Real people. People who didn't care about social lines or what might happen when they crossed them. care about social lines or crossing them.

She turned back to the group, willing Peyton to meet her gaze. When he did, she told him, "It isn't true, what Catherine said, Peyton. I knew you were better than all of us at Emerson. You still are. I wouldn't have made love with you in high school if I hadn't known that. And I wouldn't have...I wouldn't have fallen in love with you now if I hadn't known on some level, always, that you were the best there was. That you *are* the best there is."

Catherine had been sipping her champagne when Ava said the part about making love with him, and she must have choked on a gasp she wasn't able to avoid. Because that was when Cristal went spewing all over Chelsea and Deedee, not to mention down the front of Catherine's Givenchy.

"You *slept* with him in high school?" she sputtered. *"Him?"*

That final word dripped with so much contempt and so much revulsion, there was no way to mistake Catherine's meaning. That Ava had sunk to the basest, scummiest level of humanity there was by consorting with someone of Peyton's filthy lower class. That even today, in spite of his *many admirable accomplishments,* he would never be fit for "polite" society like theirs.

Peyton, of course, noticed it, too. As did Catherine, finally. Probably because of the scathing look he shot her.

Immediately, she tried to mask her blunder. "I mean...I'm just so surprised to discover the two of you had a...ah, liaison...in high school. You were both so different from each other."

"It surprised me, too," Ava said, still looking at Peyton. Still unable to tell how he was reacting to what

ELIZABETH BEVARLY 175

he'd just heard. "That he would lower his standards so much to get involved with a member of our crowd. It's no wonder he didn't want anyone to know about it."

Finally, he reacted. But not with confusion, anger or smugness. Judging by his reaction, he was first startled, then incredulous, then...something that kind of looked like happiness? The flip-flopping in Ava's belly turned into flutters of hopeful little butterflies.

"*I* didn't want anyone to know?" he said. "But you were the one who—"

He halted, looking at the others, who all appeared to be more than a little interested in what he might say next. Gentleman that he was, he closed his mouth and said nothing more about that night in front of them. Nothing else Ava might say was any of their business, either. She'd said what she needed to say for now. What Peyton chose to do with everything he'd learned tonight was up to him—whether he still wanted high society's stamp of approval or whether he wanted anything more to do with her.

If he valued his professional success and the wealth and social standing that came with it more than anything, he would be as courteous as Ava had taught him to be and pretend the last several minutes had never happened. He would watch her leave and continue chatting with his new best friends, even knowing how they truly felt about him. He would collect invitations to more events like this and exchange contact info with like-minded wealthy types. He would field introductions to more members of their tribe, doubtless meeting enough single women that Caroline the matchmaker would no longer be necessary.

In spite of what Catherine had said, and in spite of the way they all felt about him deep down, he was one of them now—provided he didn't screw up. A full-fledged member of the society he'd so eagerly wanted to join. Even if he was nouveau riche instead of moldy old-moneyed, because of his colossal wealth, his membership in this club would never be revoked—provided he didn't screw up. He had his pick of their women and could plant one at his side whenever he wanted, then produce a passel of beautiful, wealthy children to populate schools like Emerson. Except that Peyton's children would enjoy all the benefits he'd been denied in such a place—provided he didn't screw up. Even if Peyton's past was soiled, his present—and future—would be picture-perfect. He was Peyton Moss, gentleman tycoon. No one would ever openly criticize him or treat him like a guttersnipe again.

Provided he didn't screw up.

"If you'll all excuse me," Ava said to the group, "I'll be going. I've been asked to leave."

She had turned and completed two steps when Peyton's voice stopped her.

"The hell you will," he said. Loudly. "You're my—" the profanity he chose for emphasis here really wasn't fit for print "—guest. You're not going anywhere, dammit."

She turned back around and automatically started to call him on his language, then stopped when she saw him smile. Because it was the kind of smile she'd seen from him only twice before. That night at her parents' house sixteen years ago, and last night, in her apartment. A disarming smile that not only rendered Ava defenseless, but stripped him of his armaments, too. A smile that said he didn't give a damn about anything or anybody, as long as he had one moment with her. Only this time, maybe it would last more than a moment.

He started to wrestle his black tie free of its collar, then stopped a passing waiter and asked him what the hell a guy had to do to get a—again with the profane adjective—bottle of beer at this—profane adjective—party. When the waiter assured him he'd be right back with one, Peyton turned not to Ava, but to Catherine.

"You're full of crap, Catherine." Except he chose a different word than *crap*. "I know no one at Emerson, including you, ever thought I would amount to anything. But, hell, I never thought any of you—" now he looked at Ava "—well, except for one of you—would amount to anything, either. It's not my fault I'm the one who turned out to be right. And furthermore..."

At that point, Peyton told them they could all go do something to themselves that no gentleman would ever tell anyone to do. Ava's heart swelled with love.

Catherine sputtered again, but this time managed not to spit on anyone. However, neither Peyton nor Ava stayed around long enough to hear what she had to say. Catherine was a big nobody, after all. Who cared what she had to say?

As they headed for the exit, they passed the server returning with Peyton's longneck bottle of beer, and in one fluid gesture, he snagged both it and a slender flute of champagne for Ava. But when they reached the hotel lobby, they slowed, neither seeming to know what to do next. Ava's heart was racing, both with exhilaration from having stood up to Catherine's bullying and exuberance at having told Peyton how she felt about him. Until she remembered that he hadn't said anything about his feelings for her. Then her heart raced with something else entirely.

Ava looked at Peyton. Peyton looked at Ava.

Then he smiled that disarming—and disarmed—

smile again. "What do you say we blow this joint and find someplace where the people aren't so low-class?"

She released a breath she hadn't been aware of holding. But she still couldn't quite feel relieved. There was still so much she wanted to tell him. So many things she wanted—needed—him to know.

"You were only half-right in there, you know," she said.

He looked puzzled. "What do you mean?"

"What you said about everyone at Emerson. As wrong as Catherine was about you, everything she said about me is true. Every dime my family ever had is gone. My father is a convicted felon and a louse. My mother was a patient in a psychiatric hospital when she died. My car is an eight-year-old compact and my business is struggling. The most stylish clothing I own, I bought at an outlet store. That apartment above the shop? That's been my home for almost eight years, and I'm not going to be able to afford anything nicer anytime soon. I'm not the kind of woman your board of directors wants within fifty feet of you, Peyton."

She knew she was presuming a lot. Peyton hadn't said he wanted her within fifty feet of himself anyway. But he'd just completely sabotaged his entrée into polite society in there. Even if his home base of operation was in San Francisco, word got around fast when notable people behaved badly at high-profile events. He wouldn't have done that if his social standing was more important to him than she was.

He said nothing for a moment, only studied her face as if he were thinking very hard about something. Finally, he lifted his hand to the back of her head and, with one gentle tug, freed her hair from its elegant twist.

"Looks better down," he said. "It makes you look

vain, shallow and snotty when you wear it up. And you're not any of those things. You never were."

"Yeah, I was," she said, smiling. "Well, maybe not shallow. I mean, I did fall in love with you."

There. She'd said it twice. If he didn't take advantage this time, then he wasn't ever going to.

He smiled back. "Okay, maybe you were vain and snotty, but so was I. Maybe that was why we…" He hesitated. "Maybe that was what attracted us to each other. We were so much alike."

She smiled at that, but the giddiness she'd been feeling began to wane. He wasn't going to say it. Because he didn't feel it. Maybe he didn't care about his place in society anymore. Maybe he didn't even care about his image. But he didn't seem to care for her anymore, either. Not the way he once had. Not the way she still did for him.

"Yes, well, we're not alike anymore, are we?" she asked. "You're the prince, and I'm the pauper. You deserve a princess, Peyton. Not someone who'll sully your professional image."

He smiled again, shaking his head. "You've taught me so much over the past couple of weeks. But you haven't learned anything, have you, Ava?"

Something in the way he looked at her made her heart hum happily again. But she ignored it, afraid to hope. She'd forgotten what life was like when everything worked the way it was supposed to. She'd begun to think she would never have a life like that again.

"You tell me," she said. "You went to all the top-tier schools. I could only afford community college."

"See, that's just my point. It doesn't matter where you go to school." He gestured toward the ballroom they'd just left. "Look at all those people whose parents spent a fortune to send them to a tony school like Emerson and what losers they all turned out to be."

"We went to Emerson, too."

"Yeah, but we got an education that had nothing to do with classrooms or the library or homework. The only thing I learned at Emerson that was worth anything… the only thing I learned there that helped me achieve my many admirable accomplishments…" Now he grinned with genuine happiness. "I learned a girl like you could love a guy like me, no matter what—no matter who—I was. You taught me that, Ava. Maybe it took me almost two decades to learn it, but…" He shrugged. "You're the reason for my many admirable accomplishments. You're the reason I went after the gold ring. Hell, you are the gold ring. It doesn't matter what anyone thinks of you or me. Not our old classmates. Not my board of directors. Not anyone I have to do business with. Why would I want a princess when I can have the queen?"

Ava grinned back, feeling her own genuine happiness. "Actually, it does matter what someone thinks of me," she said. "It matters what *you* think."

"No, it doesn't. It only matters what I feel."

"It matters what you think and feel."

He lifted a hand to her hair again, threading it through his fingers. "Okay. Then I think I love you. I think I've always loved you. And I know I always will love you."

Now Ava remembered what life was like when everything worked the way it was supposed to. It was euphoric. It was brilliant. It was sublime. And all it took to make it that way was Peyton.

"We have a lot to talk about," he told her.

She nodded. "Yes. We do."

He tilted his head toward the hotel exit. "No time like the present."

Yeah, the present was pretty profane-adjective good, Ava had to admit. But then, really, their past hadn't been too shabby. And their future? Well, now. That was looking better all the time.

Epilogue

Peyton sat at a table only marginally less tiny than the one in the Chicago tearoom Ava had dragged him to three months ago, watching as she curled her fingers around the little flower-bedecked china teapot. No way was he going to touch that thing, even if it might win him points with the Montgomery sisters, who had joined him and Ava in the favorite tearoom of Oxford, Mississippi. It was one thing to be a gentleman. It was another to spill scalding tea on the little white gloves of his newest business partners.

"Peyton," Miss Helen Montgomery said, "you must have found the only woman worth having north of the Mason-Dixon Line. You'd better keep a close eye on her."

Miss Dorothy Montgomery agreed. "Why, with her manners and fashion sense, she could run the entire Mississippi Junior League."

"Now, Miss Dorothy, Miss Helen," Ava said as she set the teapot back down. "You're going to make me blush."

Wouldn't be the first time, Peyton thought, remembering how radiant Ava's face had been that evening in her apartment when he'd asked her to keep her gloves on while they made love. There had been plenty of evenings—and mornings and afternoons—like that one since then. In fact, now that he thought about it, he couldn't wait to get back to their hotel. She was wearing a pair of those white gloves now, along with a pale gray Jackie Kennedy suit and hat that were driving him nuts.

It was their last day in Mississippi. They'd met that afternoon with the Montgomerys and all the requisite corporate and legal types to fine-tune the deal Peyton had been fine-tuning himself for months. Now all that was left was to draw up the contracts and sign them. Montgomery and Sons would stay Montgomery and Sons, with Helen and Dorothy Montgomery as figureheads, and Peyton planned to keep the company intact. In fact, he was going to invest in it whatever was necessary to make the textile company profitable again, and it would become the flagship for his and Ava's new enterprise. Brenner Moss Incorporated would produce garments for women and men that were American made, from the farm-grown natural fibers to the mills that wove them into fabric to the couturiers who designed the fashions to the workers who pieced them together. Eventually, there would even be Brenner Moss retail outlets. And CEO Ava was chomping at the bit to get it all underway.

Miss Helen moved two sugar cubes to her cup and stirred gently. "Now, remember. You all promised to come back in October for homecoming."

Miss Dorothy nodded. "Helen and I are staunch Ole Miss alumnae. It's a very big deal around here."

"Oh, you bet," Peyton promised. "And you'll both be coming to Chicago for the wedding in September, right?"

"We wouldn't miss it for the world."

For now, Peyton and Ava would be dividing their time between Chicago and San Francisco, but eventually they would merge everything together on the West Coast. She wanted to include Talk of the Town under the Brenner Moss umbrella and open a chain of stores nationwide, but for now had turned the management of the Chicago shop over to her former sales associate, Lucy Mulligan. However, she was grooming Lucy to become her assistant at Brenner Moss once things took off there.

Funny, how Peyton had returned to Chicago for the single-minded purpose of enlarging his business and making money and had ended up enlarging his business and making money...and gaining so much that was way more important—and way more valuable—than any of that.

Who needed high society when everything he'd ever wanted was wherever Ava happened to be?

"By the way," Ava said, darting her attention from one Montgomery to the other, "thank you both so much for the homemade preserves."

"And the socks," Peyton added.

"Well, we know how cold those northern nights can be," Miss Helen said. "We went to Kentucky once. In the fall. It must have gotten down to fifty degrees!"

"In Chicago, it gets down in the teens during the winter," Peyton said. "But I promise it will be nice when you're there in September."

Miss Dorothy shivered, even though here in Mississippi, in July, it was a soggy ninety-five degrees in the shade. "Honestly, how do you people survive up there?"

Peyton and Ava exchanged glances, his dropping momentarily to her white gloves before reconnecting with hers—only to see her eyes spark. "Oh, we find ways to keep the fires going."

Hell, their fires never went out. He could barely remember what his life had been like before reconnecting with Ava. Just days of endless work and nights of endless networking. And yeah, there would still be plenty of that in the future, but he wouldn't be doing it alone, and it wouldn't be endless. It would only be until he and Ava had time to themselves again.

"You two are the perfect power couple, I must say," Miss Dorothy declared. "Intelligent and hardworking and obviously of very good breeding." With a smile, she added, "Why, you remind me of Helen and myself. You were obviously brought up right."

True enough, Peyton thought. They'd just had to wait until they were adults so they could bring each other up right. Still, in a lot of ways, Ava made him feel like a kid again. But the good parts about being a kid. Not the rest of it. The parts with the stolen glances, the secret smiles, the breathless wanting and the nights when everything came together exactly the way it was meant to be. He'd never be too old for any of that.

"When your new business gets going," Miss Helen said, "you two will be the talk of the town."

"That's our plan, Miss Helen," Ava agreed with a grin. But she was looking at Peyton when she said it. "Well, that and living happily ever after, of course."

Peyton grinned, too. Maybe some people thought living well was the best revenge. But he was more of the opinion that living well was the best reward. And it didn't matter where or how he and Ava lived that made it worthwhile. It only mattered that they were together. Talk of the town? Ha. He was happy just being the apple of Ava's eye.

* * * * *

SECOND CHANCE WITH THE CEO

ANNA DePALO

For Colby, Nicholas & Olivia,
for understanding that I write.

One

"Cole Serenghetti," she muttered, "come out, come out, wherever you are."

She knew she sounded like a corny fairy-tale character, but she'd been short on happy endings lately, and the words couldn't hurt, could they?

Then again, there was always *be careful what you wish for...*

As if she'd conjured him, a tall man appeared under a crossbeam at the construction site.

A feeling of dread curled in her stomach. How many times had she started out thinking she could do this and then her courage had flagged? Three? Four?

Still, the students at Pershing School depended on her bringing Cole Serenghetti to heel—her job could hinge on it, as well.

Marisa lifted her hand from the steering wheel and squeezed it to stop a sudden tremor. Then she raised her field glasses.

Features obscured under his yellow hard hat, the man

strode down the dirt path leading to the opening in the chain-link fence surrounding the construction site, which would soon be a four-story medical office complex. Clad in jeans, a plaid shirt and vest and work boots, he could have been just any other construction worker. But he had an air of command…and his physique showed potential for inclusion in a beefcake calendar.

Marisa's heart pounded hard in her chest.

Cole Serenghetti. Former professional hockey player returned to the family fold as CEO of Serenghetti Construction, high school troublemaker and her disastrous teenage crush.

Could the package be worse?

Marisa slunk lower in the driver's seat, letting the binoculars dangle against her chest from their cord. The last thing she needed was for a police officer to come around and ask why she was stalking a rich bad-boy real estate developer.

Blackmail? Pregnant with his child? Planning to steal his Range Rover, parked oh-so-tantalizingly close and unguarded at the curb of the office building under construction?

Would anyone believe that the truth was much more mundane? Everyone knew her as Miss Danieli, sweet-natured teacher at the Pershing School. Ironic if her new secret life as a millionaire stalker came at the cost of her job and reputation when all she was trying to do was help the high school-aged students at her college-preparatory school.

Tossing aside her field glasses, she popped out of her Ford Focus and darted down the street, her open coat flapping around her, as her quarry reached the sidewalk. There were no pedestrians on this side street at four in the afternoon, though it was nearing evening rush in the city of Springfield. She'd seen construction workers earlier, but there were none on the street now.

As she approached, the dank smells of the construction site hit her. It was dirty, and the air was heavy with parti-

cles that she could almost feel, even in the damp cold that
clung to western Massachusetts in March.

She heard her stomach grumble. She'd been too nervous
about this meeting to eat lunch.

"Cole Serenghetti?"

He turned his head while taking off his hard hat.

Marisa slowed her steps as she was jerked back in time
by the sight of the dark, ruffled hair, the hazel eyes and the
chiseled lips. A scar now bisected his left cheek, joining the
small one on his chin that had been there in high school.

Marisa felt her heart squeeze. His newest scar looked as
if it had hurt—*bad*.

But he was still the sexiest man she'd ever crossed.

She tried hard to hold on to her scattered thoughts even
as she drank in the changes in him.

He was bigger and broader than he'd been at eighteen,
and his face had more hard planes. But the charisma of being
a former National Hockey League star—and sex symbol—
turned millionaire developer was the biggest change of all.
And while he sported the new scar, he showed no signs of
the injury that had been serious enough to end his hockey
career. He moved fine.

Even though Pershing was located on the outskirts of
Welsdale, Massachusetts, the town that the Serenghettis
called home, she hadn't been anywhere near Cole since
high school.

She didn't miss the once-over he gave her, and then a
slow smile lit his face.

Relief swept through her. She'd been dreading this reunion ever since high school, but he seemed willing to put
the past behind them.

"Sweetness, even if I wasn't Cole Serenghetti, I'd be saying yes to you." The lazy smile stayed on his face but his
gaze traveled downward again, lingering on the cleavage
revealed by her long-sleeved dress, and then on her legs,
shown off by her favorite wedge-heeled espadrilles.

Oh...crap.

Cole looked up and smiled into her eyes. "You're a welcome ray of sunshine after a muddy construction site."

He didn't even recognize her. Crazy giddiness welled up inside. She'd never forgotten him in the past fifteen years, worrying over her betrayal—and his. And all that time, he'd been sleeping like a baby.

She knew she looked different. Her hair was loose for a change and highlighted, the ends shorter and curling around her shoulders. Her figure was fuller, and her face was no longer hidden behind owlish glasses. But still...she plummeted to Earth like a hang glider that had lost the wind.

She had to get this over with, much as she hated to end the party.

She took a steadying breath. "Marisa Danieli. How are you, Cole?"

The moment hung between them, stretching out.

Then Cole's face closed, his smile dimming.

She curved her lips tentatively. "I'm hoping to hold you to that *yes*."

"Think again."

Ouch. Well, this was more like the script that had been playing in her head. She forced herself to keep up the polite professionalism without, she hoped, tipping into desperation. "It's been a long time."

"Not long enough." He assessed her. "And I'm guessing it's no accident you're here now—" he quirked a brow "—unless you've developed a weird compulsion to prowl construction sites?"

She'd always been bad at door-to-door solicitation jobs, and now, it seemed, was no exception. *Breathe. Breathe.* "The Pershing School needs your help. We're reaching out to our most important alumni."

"We?"

She nodded. "I teach tenth-grade English there."

Cole twisted his lips. "They're still putting their best foot forward."

"Their only foot. I'm the head of fund-raising."

He narrowed his eyes. "Congratulations and good luck."

He stepped around her, and she turned with him.

"If you'll just listen—"

"To your pitch?" He shot her a sideways look. "I'm not as big a sucker for the doe-eyed look as I was fifteen years ago."

She filed away *doe-eyed* for later examination. "Pershing needs a new gym. I'm sure that as a professional hockey player, you can appreciate—"

"*Former* NHL player. Check the yearbook for athletics. You'll come up with other names."

"Yours was at the top of the list." She picked her way over broken sidewalk, trying to keep up with his stride. Her espadrilles had seemed like a good choice for a school day. Now she wished she'd worn something else.

Cole stopped and swung toward her, causing her to nearly run into him. "Still at the top of your list?" He lifted his mouth in a sardonic smile. "I should be flattered."

Marisa felt the heat sting her cheeks. He made it sound as if she was throwing herself at him all over again—and he was rejecting her.

She had an abysmal record with men—wasn't her recent broken engagement further proof?—and her streak had started with Cole in high school. Humiliation burned like fire.

A long time ago she and Cole would have had their heads bent together over a book. She could have shifted in her seat and brushed his leg. In fact, she had brushed his leg, more than once, and he'd touched his lips to hers…

She plunged ahead. "Pershing needs your help. We need a headliner for our fund-raiser in a couple of months to raise money for the new gym."

He looked implacable, except that twin flames danced in

his eyes. "You mean *you* need a headliner. Try your pitch on someone else."

"The fund-raiser would be good for Serenghetti Construction, too," she tried, having rehearsed her bullet points. "It's an excellent opportunity to further community relations."

He turned away again, and she placed a staying hand on his arm.

Immediately, she realized her mistake.

They both looked down at his biceps, and she yanked her hand back.

She'd felt him, strong and vital, his arm flexing. Once, fifteen years ago, she'd run her hands over his arms and moaned his name, and he'd taken her breast in his mouth. *Would she ever stop having a heated response to his every touch, every look and every word?*

She stared into his eyes, which were now hard and indecipherable—as tough as the rocks he blasted for a living.

"You need something from me," he stated flatly.

She nodded, her throat dry, feeling hot despite the weather.

"Too bad I don't forgive or forget a deliberate betrayal easily. Consider it a character flaw that I can't forget the facts."

She flushed. She'd always wondered whether he'd known for certain who'd ratted out his prank to the school administration, earning him a suspension and likely costing Pershing the hockey championship that year. Now it seemed she had her answer.

She'd had her reasons for doing what she'd done, but she doubted they'd have satisfied him—then or now.

"High school was a long time ago, Cole," she said, her voice thin.

"Right, and in the past is where the two of us are going to stay."

His words hurt even though it had been fifteen years. Her chest felt tight, and it was difficult to breathe.

He nodded at the curb. "Yours?"

She hadn't realized it, but they were near her car. "Yes."

He pulled open her door, and she stepped off the curb.

A swimming sensation came over her, and she swayed.

Still, she tried for a dignified exit. A few more steps and she'd put an end to this uncomfortable reunion…

As the edges of her vision faded to black, she had one last thought. *I should have eaten lunch.*

She heard Cole curse and his hard hat hit the ground. He caught her in his arms as she slumped against him.

When she floated to consciousness again, Cole was saying her name.

For a moment she thought she was fantasizing about their sexual encounter in high school…until the smells of the construction site penetrated her brain, and she realized what had happened.

She was cradled against a warm, solid body. Her trench coat was bunched around her like a cocoon.

She opened her eyes, and her gaze connected with Cole's. His golden-green eyes were intense.

She was also up close and personal with the new scar traversing his cheek. It looked painful but not jagged. *Had he taken a skate blade to the face?* She wanted to reach up and trace it.

He frowned. "Are you okay?"

Heat rushed to her cheeks. "Yes, let me down."

"May be a bad idea. Are you sure you can stand?"

Whatever the effects were of his career-ending injury, he seemed to have no problem holding a curvy woman of medium height in his arms. He was all hard muscle and restrained power.

"I'm fine! Really."

Looking as if he still had misgivings, Cole lowered his arm. When her feet hit the ground, he stepped back.

Her humiliation was complete. So total, she couldn't bear to face it right now.

"Just like old times," Cole remarked, his tone tinged with irony.

As if she needed the reminder. She'd fainted during one of their study sessions in high school. It was how she'd first wound up in his arms...

"How long was I out?" she asked, not meeting his eyes.

"Less than a minute." He shoved his hands in his pockets. "Are you all right?"

"Perfectly fine. I haven't been to an emergency room since I was a kid."

"You still have a tendency to faint."

She shook her head, looking anywhere but at him. *Talk about being overwhelmed by seeing him again.* Anticipating and yet dreading this meeting, she'd been too nervous to eat. "No, I haven't fainted in years. The medical term is vasovagal syncope, but my episodes are very infrequent."

Except she had a terrible habit of fainting around him. It was their first meeting in fifteen years, and she'd already managed a replay of high school. She didn't even want to consider what *he* was thinking right now. Probably that she was a consummate schemer with great acting skills.

He suddenly looked bland and aloof. "You couldn't have planned a better Hail Mary pass."

She cringed inwardly. He was suggesting that fainting had allowed her to buy time and get his sympathy. She was too embarrassed to get angry, however. "You play hockey, not football. Hail Mary is football. And why would I want to make a desperate last move with little chance of success?"

He shrugged his shoulders. "Confuse the other side."

"And did I?"

He looked as if he wished he were wearing all the protective gear of a hockey uniform. She was throwing *him* off balance. She was dizzy with momentary power, though her arms and legs still felt rubbery.

"I haven't changed my mind."

She lowered her shoulders and stepped toward her car.

"Are you okay to drive?" he asked, hands still shoved into his pockets.

"Yes. I feel fine now." *Tired, defeated and mortified, but fine.*

"Goodbye, Marisa."

He'd closed the door on her years ago, and now he was doing it again, with a note of finality in his voice.

She pushed aside the unexpectedly forceful emotional pain. As she stepped into her car, she was aware of Cole's brooding gaze on her. And when she pulled away, she glanced in her rearview mirror and saw that he was still watching her from the curb.

She should never have come. And yet, she had to get him to say yes. She hadn't come this far to accept defeat like this.

"You look like a man in need of a punching bag," Jordan Serenghetti remarked, hitting his boxing gloves together. "I'll spring for this round."

"Lucky bastard," Cole responded, moving his head from side to side, loosening up. "You get to work out the kinks by slamming someone on the ice rink."

Jordan still had a high-velocity NHL career with the New England Razors, whereas Cole's own had finished with a career-ending injury.

Still, whenever Jordan was in town, the two of them had a standing appointment in the boxing ring. For Cole, it beat the monotony of working out at the gym. Even as a construction executive, it paid to lead by example and stay in shape.

"Next hockey game isn't for another three days," Jordan responded, approaching with gloves raised. "That's a long time to be holding punches. Anyway, don't you have a babe to work out the kinks with?"

Marisa Danieli was a babe, all right, but Cole would be

damned if he worked out anything with her. Unfortunately, she'd intruded on his thoughts too often since she'd dropped back into his arms last Friday.

Jordan touched a glove to his boxing helmet and then grinned. "Oh yeah, I forgot. Vicki dumped you for the sports agent—what's his name, again?"

"Sal Piazza," Cole said and sidestepped Jordan's first jab.

"Right, Salami Pizza."

Cole grunted. "Vicki didn't dump me. She—"

"Got tired of your inability to commit."

Cole hit Jordan with his right. "She wasn't looking for commitment. It was the perfect fling that way."

"Only because she'd heard of your reputation, so she knew she had to move on."

"As I said, everyone was happy." They danced around the ring, oblivious to the gym noises around them.

Even on a Wednesday evening, Jimmy's Boxing Gym was humming with activity. The facility was kept cold but even the cool air couldn't diminish the smell of sweat and sounds of exertion under the fluorescent lights.

Jordan rolled his neck. "You know, Mom wants you to settle down."

Cole bared his teeth. "She'd also be happy if you quit risking thousands of dollars in orthodontia on the ice rink, but that's not going to happen, either."

"She can pin her hopes on Rick, then," Jordan said, referring to their middle brother, "if anyone knew where he was."

"On a movie set on the Italian Riviera, I've heard."

Their brother was a stuntman, the risk taker among them, which was saying a lot. Their long-suffering mother claimed she'd lived at the emergency room while raising three boys and a girl. It was true they'd all broken bones, at one time or another, but Camilla Serenghetti still wasn't aware of her sons' most hair-raising thrills.

"It figures he's on a paparazzi-riddled set," Jordan grumbled. "No doubt there's at least one hot actress in the picture."

"Mom has Mia to fall back on, even if she is in New York." Their youngest sibling was off pursuing a career as a fashion designer, which meant Cole was the only one based in Welsdale full-time.

"It sucks being the oldest, Cole," Jordan said, as if reading his thoughts, "but you've got to admit you're more suited to run Serenghetti Construction than any of the rest of us."

In the aftermath of Cole's career-ending hockey injury, their father, Serg, had suffered a debilitating stroke. Cole had grasped the reins of Serenghetti Construction eight months ago and never let go.

"It doesn't suck," Cole said. "It just needs to be done."

He took the opportunity to hit Jordan with a surprise right. Damn, it felt good to rid himself of some frustration in the ring. He loved his brother, so it stunk to be even a little envious of Jordan's life. It wasn't just that Jordan was still a star with the Razors, because Cole had had a good run with the team himself. His younger brother also enjoyed a freedom missing from Cole's own life these days.

Their father had always hoped one or more of his sons would carry on the family business. And in the casino of life, Cole had drawn the winning card.

Cole had been familiar with the construction business ever since he'd spent summers working on sites as a teenager. He just hadn't anticipated having his hockey dream cut short and needing to pull his family together at the same time. Business had been tight until recently, and with Serg nearly flat on his back, Cole had been doing some scrambling with the hand he'd been dealt.

With any luck, one way or another, Cole could get on with his life again soon. Even if his future wasn't on the ice, he had his own business and investment opportunities to pursue, particularly in the sports field. Coaching, for one thing, was beckoning…

"So why don't you tell me what's got you in a bad mood?" Jordan asked, as if they weren't in a ring trying to knock each other off their feet.

Cole's mind went to his more immediate problem—if she could even be called that instead of...oh yeah, a wrecking ball in heels. He built things, and she destroyed them—dreams being at the top of her list. *Best remember her evil powers.* "Marisa Danieli stopped by the construction site today."

Jordan looked puzzled.

"High school," Cole elaborated and then watched his brother's frown disappear.

He and his brothers had graduated from different high schools, but Jordan knew of Marisa. After her pivotal role in Cole's suspension during senior year, she had for a time become infamous among the Serenghetti brothers and their crowd.

"Luscious Lola Danieli?" Jordan asked, the side of his mouth turning up.

Cole had never liked the nickname—and that was even before he'd started thinking of Marisa Lola Danieli as the high school Lolita who had led him down the path to destruction. She'd earned the tongue-in-cheek nickname in high school because she'd dressed and acted the opposite of sexy.

He hadn't told anyone about his intimate past with Marisa. His brothers would have had a field day with the story of The Geek and The Jock. As far as anyone knew, she was just the girl who'd scored off him—ratting out his prank to the principal like a hockey player slapping the puck into the goal for the game-winning shot.

For years the moment the principal had let slip that Marisa was the person who'd blabbed about him had been seared into his memory. He'd never pulled another prank again.

Still, he wasn't merely dwelling on what had happened

when they'd been about to graduate. The fact that his hockey career had ended in the past year made it bad timing for Marisa to show up and remind him of how close she'd come to derailing it before it had begun. And as he'd told Jordan, he'd accepted his new role as CEO, but it wasn't without its frustrations. He was still on a big learning curve trying to drive Serenghetti Construction forward.

His brother's punch caught him full on the shoulder, sending him staggering. He brought his mind back to what was happening in the ring.

"Come on. Show me what you've got," Jordan jeered, warming up. "I haven't run into Marisa since you two graduated from Pershing."

"Until today, I could say the same thing," Cole replied.

"So, what? She's come back for round two now that you're on your feet again?"

"Hilarious."

"I was always the funny brother."

"Your sense of fraternal loyalty warms my heart," he mocked.

Jordan held up his hands in a gesture of surrender, nearly coming to a stop. "Hey, I'm not defending what she did. It sucked big-time for you to miss the final game and for Pershing to lose the hockey championship. Everyone avoided her wherever she went in town. But people can change."

Cole hit his brother with his left. "She wants me to headline a fund-raiser so Pershing can build a new gym."

Jordan grunted and then gave a low whistle. "Or maybe not. She's still got guts."

Marisa had changed, but Cole wasn't going to elaborate for his brother. These days there'd be nothing tongue-in-cheek about the nickname Luscious Lola, and that was the damn problem.

Before he'd recognized her, his senses had gone on high alert, and his libido had gleefully raced to catch up. The woman was sex in heels. It should be criminal for a school-teacher to look like her.

The eyeglasses that she used to wear in high school were gone, and her hair was longer and loose—the ends curling in fat, bouncy curls against her shoulders. She was no longer hiding her figure under shapeless sweatshirts, and she'd filled out in all the right places. Everything was fuller, curvier and more womanly. He should know—once he'd run his hands over those breasts and thighs.

Before she'd announced who she was, he'd been thinking the gods of TGIF were smiling down at him at the end of a long workweek. Then he'd gotten a reprieve until she'd literally fallen into his arms—a one-two punch.

In those seconds staring down into her face, he'd been swamped by conflicting emotions: surprise, anger, concern and yeah, lust. More or less par for the course for him where Marisa was concerned. He could still feel the imprint of her soft curves. She sent signals that bypassed the thinking part of his brain and went straight to the place that wanted to mate.

Jordan caught him square on the chest this time. "Come on, come on. You're dazed. Woman on your mind?"

Cole lifted his lips in a humorless smile. "She suggested that participating in the fund-raiser for Pershing might be good PR for Serenghetti Construction."

Jordan paused before dancing back a step. "Marisa is a smart cookie. Can't fault her there."

Cole grumbled. Marisa's suggestion made some sense though he'd rather have his front teeth knocked out than admit it. He'd never liked publicity and couldn't have cared less about his image during his professional hockey days, to the everlasting despair of his agent. And since taking over the reins at Serenghetti Construction, he'd been focused on mastering the ropes to keep the business operating smoothly. Community relations had taken a backseat.

Marisa had a brain, all right—in contrast to many of the

women who'd chased after him in his pro days. She'd literally been a book-hugger in high school. The jocks in the locker room hadn't even been able to rate her because it had been hard to do reconnaissance.

He'd eventually had the chance to discover the answer—she'd been a C-cup bra. But the knowledge had ultimately come at a steep price.

These days he'd bet the house that she had an A-plus body. She was primed to set men on their path to crashing and burning, just like old times.

Except this time, her next victim wouldn't be him.

Two

Squash racquet back of hall closet. I'll pick it up.

Marisa hit the button to turn off her cell phone. The message from Sal had come while she was out. She'd been so shaken by talking to Cole for the first time in fifteen years that she hadn't realized she had a text until after she'd gotten back to her apartment.

Annoyance rose up in her. As far as text messages went, it wasn't rude. But it hadn't come from just anybody. It had come from her former fiancé, who'd broken things off three months ago.

During their brief engagement, she'd been sliding into the role of the good little wife, picking up Sal's dry cleaning and making runs to the supermarket for him. From Sal's perspective, asking her to retrieve his squash racquet from her hall closet was unquestionably fair game. No doubt Sal had an appointment to meet a client at the gym, because even sports agents had to establish their athleticism—though

Sal played squash only once in a blue moon when an invitation was issued.

She contemplated heaving the racquet out the window and onto the lawn, and then asking Sal to come find it.

Before she could overrule her scruples, she heard someone turn the lock in the front door. She frowned, nonplussed. *Hadn't she asked Sal to return his key...?*

She yanked the door open, and her cousin Serafina stumbled inside.

Marisa relaxed. "Oh, it's you."

"Of course it's me," Serafina retorted, straightening. "You gave me a key to the apartment, remember?"

"Right." She'd been so lost in thought, she'd momentarily assumed Sal had come back to retrieve the racquet, letting himself in with an extra copy of the key. *And he was uptight enough to do it. The rat.*

She was glad now she'd kept her condo even when her relationship with Sal had started getting serious enough that they'd contemplated moving in together. She'd bought the small two-bedroom five years ago, and at the time, it had been a major step toward independence and security.

She wondered where Cole called home these days. In all likelihood, a sprawling penthouse loft. She wouldn't be surprised if he lived in one of his own constructions.

One thing was for sure. He was still one of Welsdale's hottest tickets while she... Well, shapely was the most forgiving adjective for her curves. She was still a nobody, even if she had a name at the Pershing School these days.

"What's with you?" Serafina asked, taking off her crossbody handbag and letting it slide to the floor.

"I was thinking of a place to bury Sal's squash racquet," she responded and then waved a hand at the back of the apartment. "It's in the hall closet."

"Nice." Serafina smiled. "But with all the dogs in this complex, someone's bound to sniff out the cadaver real quick."

"He needs it back." She'd been hurt when she'd been dumped. But notwithstanding her irritation at Sal at the moment, these days she simply wanted to move on.

Serafina's lips twitched. "The racquet is an innocent bystander. It's not like you to misdirect anger, especially the vindictive kind."

After a moment Marisa sighed and lowered her shoulders. "You're right. I'll tell him that I'm leaving it on the table in the building foyer downstairs."

Ever since her debacle with Cole in high school, she'd been worried about being thought of as a bitch. She didn't need Cole Serenghetti; she needed a therapist.

"But tell the jerk what he can go do with it!" Serafina added.

She gave her cousin a halfhearted smile. Serafina was a little taller than she was, and her hair was a wavy dirty blond. She'd been spared the curly dark brown locks that were the bane of Marisa's existence. But they both had the amber eyes that were a family trait on their mothers' side, and their facial features bore a resemblance. Anyone looking at them might guess they were related, though they had different last names: Danieli and Perini.

While they were growing up, Marisa had treated Sera as a younger sister. She'd passed along books and toys, and shared advice and clothes. More recently, having had her cousin as a roommate for a few months, until Serafina found a job in her field and an apartment, had been a real lifesaver. Marisa appreciated the company. And with respect to men, her cousin took no prisoners. Marisa figured she could learn a lot there.

"Now for some good news," Serafina announced. "I'm moving out."

"That's great!" Marisa forced herself to sound perky.

"Well, not now, but after my trip to Seattle next week to visit Aunt Filo and Co."

"I didn't mean I'm glad you're leaving, I meant I'm happy

for you." Three weeks ago her cousin had received the news that she'd landed a permanent position. Serafina had also gotten plane tickets to see Aunt Filomena and her cousins before starting her new job.

Serafina laughed. "Oh, Marisa, you're adorable! I know you're happy for me."

"Adorable ceases to exist after age thirty." She was thirty-three, single and holding on to sexy by a fraying thread. *And* she'd recently been dumped by her fiancé.

Of course, Cole had been all sunshine and come-here-honey…until he'd recognized who she was. Then he'd turned dark and stormy.

Serafina searched her face. "What?"

Marisa turned, heading down the hall toward the kitchen. "I asked Cole Serenghetti to do the Pershing Shines Bright fund-raiser for the school."

She hadn't died of mortification when she approached him for a favor after all these years, but she'd come close. She'd fainted in his arms. A hot wave of embarrassment washed over her, stinging her face. *When would the humiliation end?*

Some decadent chocolate cake was in order right now. There should be some left in the fridge. A pity party was always better with dessert.

"And?" Serafina followed behind.

Marisa waved her hand. "It was like I always dreamt it would be. He jumped right on my proposal. Chills and thrills all around."

"Great…?"

"Lovely." She spied the cake container on her old scarred moveable island. "And yummy."

Cole Serenghetti qualified as yummy, too. There were probably women lined up to treat him as dessert. A decade and a half later he was looking better than ever. She'd seen the occasional picture of him in the press during his hockey days, but nothing was like experiencing the man in person.

And tangling with him was just as much a turn-yourself-inside-out experience as it had always been.

"Um, Marisa?"

Marisa set the cake container on the table. "Time for dessert, I think."

The kind in front of her, not the Cole Serenghetti variety, even though he probably thought of her as a man-eater.

Marisa uncovered the chocolate seven-layer cake. She'd been so insecure about her body around Sal—she had too many rounded curves to ever be considered svelte. But now that he was in the past, she felt free to indulge again. Of course, Sal had a new and skinny girlfriend. He'd found the person he was looking for, and she was the size of a runway model.

"So Cole was thrilled to see you?" Serafina probed.

"Ecstatic."

"Now I know you're being sarcastic."

Long after high school Marisa had told Sera about her past with Cole, and how things had heated up between her and the oldest Serenghetti brother during senior year—before they'd gone into a deep freeze. Her cousin knew Marisa had confessed that Cole was responsible for the ultimate school prank, that Cole had been suspended as a result and that Pershing had lost the Independent School League hockey championship soon after.

Getting out two plates and cutlery, Marisa said, "It's not a party unless you join me."

Serafina sat down in one of the kitchen chairs. "I hope this guy is worth five hundred calories. Let me guess, he still blames you for what you did in high school?"

"Bingo."

Marisa relayed snatches of her encounter with Cole, the way she'd been doing in her mind since leaving the construction site earlier. All the while, Cole's words reverberated in her head. *I'm not as big a sucker for the doe-eyed look as I was fifteen years ago.* Oh yes, he still held a grudge. He'd been impossible to sway about the fund-raiser. And yet, damningly, she felt a little frisson of excitement that he had fallen under the spell of her big, brown eyes long ago...

Serafina shook her head. "Men never grow up."

Marisa slid a piece of cake in front of her cousin. "It's complicated."

"Isn't it always? Cut yourself a bigger piece."

"All the cake in the world might not be enough."

"That bad, huh?"

Marisa met her cousin's gaze and nodded. Then she took a bite of cake and got up again. "We need milk and coffee."

A little caffeine would help. She felt so tired in the aftermath of a faint.

She loaded water and coffee grinds into the pot and then plugged the thing into the outlet. She wished she could afford one of those fancy coffeemakers that were popular now, but they weren't in her budget.

Why had she ever agreed to approach Cole Serenghetti? She knew why. She was ambitious enough to want to be assistant principal. It was part of her long climb out of poverty. She credited her academic scholarship to Pershing with helping to turn her life around. And now that she was single and unattached again, she needed something to focus on. Pershing and her teaching job were the thing. *And* she owed it to the kids.

Marisa shook her head. She'd volunteered to be head of fund-raising at Pershing, but she hadn't anticipated that the current principal would be so set on getting Cole Serenghetti for their big event. She should have tried harder to talk Mr. Dobson out of it. But he'd discovered from the school yearbook that Cole and Marisa had been in the same graduating class, so he'd assumed Marisa could make a personal appeal to the hockey star, one former classmate to another. There was no way Marisa was going to explain how her high school romance with Cole had ended disastrously.

"So what are you going to do now?" Serafina asked as Marisa set two coffee mugs on the table.

"I don't know."

"It's not like you to give up so easily."

"You know me well."

"I've known you forever!"

Marisa summoned the determination that had helped her when she'd been the child of a single mother who worked two jobs. "I'll have to give it another try. I can't go back to the board admitting defeat this fast. But I can't lie in wait for Cole again at a construction site, like some crazed stalker."

Serafina wiped her mouth with a napkin. "You may want to give Jimmy's Boxing Gym a go."

"What?"

Serafina gave her an arch look. "It's beefcake central. Also, Cole Serenghetti is known to be a regular."

Marisa's brow puckered. "And you know this, how?"

"The guys down at the Puck & Shoot. The hockey players are regulars." Sera paused and pulled a face. "Jordan Serenghetti stops in from time to time."

Judging from Sera's expression, Marisa concluded her cousin didn't much care for the youngest Serenghetti brother.

"Are you doing more than moonlighting as a waitress there?" Marisa asked with mock severity.

Serafina shrugged. "If you hung out in bars, you wouldn't need the tip." Then she flashed a mischievous grin. "Use it in good health."

Of course Cole Serenghetti would go to a boxing gym. The place was most likely the diametric opposite of the fancy fitness center where Sal played squash. She'd given up her own membership—with guilty relief—when Sal had unsubscribed from their relationship.

She rolled her eyes heavenward. "What do I wear to a boxing gym…?"

"My guess is, the less, the better." Serafina curved her lips. "Everyone will be sweaty and hot, hot, hot…"

One week later…

Cole saw his chance in Jordan's sudden loss of focus and hit him hard, following up with a one-two punch that sent his brother staggering.

Then he paused and wiped his brow while he let Jordan regain his balance, because their purpose was to get some exercise and not to go for a knockout. "I don't want to ruin your pretty face. I'll save that thrill for the guys on the ice."

Jordan grimaced. "Thanks. One of us hasn't had his nose broken yet, and—" he focused over Cole's shoulder "—I need to talk pretty right now."

"What the hell?"

Jordan indicated the doorway with his chin.

When Cole turned around, he cursed.

Marisa was here, and from all the signs, she didn't have any more sense about a boxing gym than she did about showing up at a construction site in heels. She was drawing plenty of attention from the male clientele—and some were going back for a second look. But her gaze settled nowhere as she made her way toward the ring that he and Jordan were using. She looked pure and unaware of her sexuality in a floaty polka-dot dress that skimmed her curves. The heels and bouncy hair were back, too.

She was the perfect picture of an innocent little schoolteacher—except Cole knew better. Still, for all outward appearances, the tableau was Bambi surrounded by wolves.

"Now that," Jordan said from behind him, "is a welcome Wednesday night surprise."

Cole scowled. *Not for him, it wasn't.* He moved toward the ropes, pulling at the lacing of one glove with the other. A staff member for the gym came up to the side of the ring to help him.

"Where are you going?" Jordan called.

"Take a breather!"

"I saw her first," his brother joked, coming up along-side him.

From when they'd hit puberty, the Serenghetti broth-ers had one rule: whoever saw a woman first got to make a move.

Cole leveled his brother with a withering look as the gym assistant pulled off his gloves. "That is Marisa Danieli."

Jordan's eyes widened, and then a slow grin spread across his face. "Wow, she's changed."

"Not as much as you think. Hands off."

"Hey, I'm not the one who needs a warning. Who yanked off his gloves?" Jordan looked over Cole's shoulder and then raised his eyebrows.

Cole turned. Marisa had pulled the ropes apart and was stepping into the ring, one shapely leg after the other.

"This should be good," Jordan murmured.

"Shut up."

Cole pulled off his padded helmet. The front of his sleeveless shirt was damp with perspiration, and his sweat-pants hung low on his hips. It was a far cry from the way he looked in meetings these days—where he often wore a jacket and tie.

He handed off his helmet before turning toward the woman who'd crept into his thoughts too often during the past week. Sweeping aside any need for pleasantries, he demanded, "How did you find me?"

Marisa hesitated, looking as if her bravado was leaving her now that she was facing her opponent in the ring. "A tip at the Puck & Shoot."

Cole figured he shouldn't be surprised she was a patron of the New England Razors' hangout. She could scout for her next victim at a sports bar, and it would be easy pickings.

Marisa took a deep breath, and Cole watched her chest rise and fall.

"Is that how you start the day in school? Correcting your students' manners?"

"Sometimes," she admitted.

Jordan stepped forward. "Don't mind Cole. Mom sent us to Miss Daisy's School for Manners, but only one of us graduated." Jordan flashed the mega-kilowatt grin that had earned him an underwear advertising campaign. "I'm Jordan Serenghetti, Cole's brother. I'd shake your hand but as you can see—" he held up his gloves, his smile turning rueful "—I've been pounding Cole to a pulp."

Marisa blinked, her gaze moving from Jordan to Cole. "He doesn't look the worse for wear."

Cole's muscles tightened and bunched, and then he frowned. He should be used to compliments… Besides, he knew she had an ulterior motive—she still needed him for her fund-raiser.

"We stay away from faces," Jordan added, "but his nose has been broken and mine hasn't."

"Yes," she said, "I see…"

Cole knew what he looked like. Not bad, but not model-handsome like Jordan. He and his brother shared the same dark hair and tall build, but Jordan's eyes were green while his were hazel. And he'd always been more rough-hewn—not that it mattered at the moment.

Jordan flashed another smile at Marisa. "You may remember me from Cole's high school days."

Cole forced himself to remember the expensive orthodontia as the urge hit to rearrange his brother's teeth. He noticed how Jordan didn't reference the high school fiasco in which Marisa had had a starring role.

"Jordan Serenghetti…I know you from the sports news," Marisa said, sidestepping the whole sticky issue of high school.

Cole had had enough.

"You don't take no for an answer," Cole interrupted, and had the pleasure of seeing Marisa flush.

She turned her big doe eyes on him. "I'm hoping you'll reconsider, if you'll just listen to what I have to say."

"If he won't listen, I will," Jordan joked. "In fact, why don't we make an evening of it? Everything goes down better with a little champagne—unless you prefer wine?"

Cole gave his brother a hard stare, but Jordan kept his gaze on Marisa.

"The Pershing School needs a headliner for its Pershing Shines Bright benefit," Marisa said to Jordan.

"I'll do it," Jordan said.

"You didn't graduate from the Pershing School."

"A minor detail. I was a student for a while."

Marisa took a step and swayed, her heels failing to find firm ground in the ring. Cole reached out to steady her, but she grasped one of the ropes for support, and he let his arm fall back to his side.

Careful. Touching Marisa was a bad idea, as he'd been reminded only last week.

"Cole's the better choice because he graduated from Pershing," Marisa said, looking into his eyes. "I know you have some loyalty to your school. You had a few good hockey seasons there."

"And thanks to you, no championship."

She looked abashed and then recovered. "That has to do with me, not Pershing, and anyway, there's a new school principal."

"But you're the messenger."

"A very pretty one," Jordan volunteered.

Cole froze his brother with a look. He and Marisa had known each other in a carnal sense, which should make her off-limits to Jordan. But he wasn't about to let his brother in on those intimate details—which meant he was in a bind about issuing a warning. Jordan was a player who liked women, making Marisa a perfect target for the charm that he never seemed to turn off.

Jordan shrugged his shoulders. "Maybe it wasn't Marisa's fault."

None of them needed him to elaborate.

"It was me at the principal's office," she admitted.

"But you're sorry…?" Jordan prompted, throwing her a lifeline.

"I regret my role, yes," she said, looking pained.

Cole lowered his shoulders. He'd gotten the closest thing to an apology.

Still, Marisa had another motive for showing up today. And while he may have gotten over high school and his suspension a long time ago, forgiving and forgetting *her* treachery was still a long time coming…

Jordan shot him a speaking glance. "And Cole apologizes for being Cole."

Cole scowled. "Like hell."

They hadn't even touched on intimate levels of betrayal that Jordan knew nothing about.

Jordan gestured with his glove. "Okay, I typically leave the mediation talks to the NHL honchos, but let's give this one more try. Cole regrets messing up with his last prank."

"Right," Cole said tightly but then couldn't resist taking a shot at his brother to dislodge the satisfied look on his face. "Jordan, talk show host is not in your future."

His brother produced a wounded look. "Not even sportscaster?"

"Since we're all coming clean," Cole continued pleasantly, looking at Marisa, "why don't you tell me what's in this for you?"

She blinked. "I told you. I want to help the Pershing School get a new gym."

"No, how does this all help you personally?"

Marisa bit her lip. "Well… I hope I'll be considered for assistant principal someday."

"Now we're getting warmer," he said with satisfaction, cocking his head because this was the Marisa he expected—full of guile and hidden motives. "Funny, I had you pegged for the type who'd be walking up the aisle in a white dress by now and then juggling babies and teaching."

Marisa paled, and Cole's hand curled. She looked as if he'd scored a dead hit.

"I was engaged until a few months ago," she said in a low voice.

"Oh yeah? Anyone I know?" Had Marisa entrapped someone else from high school? Unlikely.

"Maybe. He's a sports agent named Sal Piazza."

Beside them, his brother whistled before Cole could react.

"You might know him," Marisa continued, "because he's now dating your last girlfriend. Or at least you were photographed in the stands at a hockey game with her. Vicki Salazar."

Damn.

"Hey, can this be called *entangled by proxy*?" Jordan interjected, his brow furrowing. "Or how about *engaged by one degree of separation*? Is that an oxymoron?"

Cole felt a muscle in his face working. His brother didn't know the half of it. "Put a lid on it, Jordan."

Cole looked around. They were attracting an audience. The speculative ones were wondering whether this was a lovers' spat and Marisa was his girlfriend—and whether they could intercept her as she made her way out of the gym. "This is ridiculous. The ring isn't the place for this conversation. We're a damn spectacle."

Marisa looked startled.

He fastened his hand on her arm against his better judgment. "Come on." He lifted the rope. "After you."

Marisa cast a glance at Jordan.

"He isn't coming," Cole said shortly.

Marisa stepped between the ropes and Cole followed, taking the wooden steps down to the gym floor.

Ignoring curious looks, he steered Marisa toward the back entrance—the one leading to the parking lot. When they reached the rear door, he turned to face her and said, "So you're engaged to Sal Piazza."

"I was." She lifted her chin. "Not anymore."

"Still can't resist the sports guys?"

"I'm a slow learner."

She'd been anything but a slow learner the one time they'd had sex. She'd been the sweetest thing he'd ever tasted.

He cursed silently. He had to stop thinking about her. Even though right now, the sunlight from a nearby window caught in her hair, creating a halo effect, and illuminated the fascinating flecks in her eyes. But what really drew him was the bow of her mouth. Soft, pink and unadorned—just waiting to be kissed, even now, fifteen years later.

She frowned. "Are you okay?"

"Fine. I'm stalked by schoolteachers all the time."

She flushed.

"If you came to get my attention, you've got it." He jerked his head toward the way they had come. "Along with that of most of the guys in there."

"It's not my problem if they have a fetish for overworked and underpaid educators."

He almost burst out laughing. "Your job of recruiting me makes you overworked and underpaid?"

She pursed her lips.

"Your sports agent fiancé didn't give you any pointers about recruiting athletes?" The dig rolled off his tongue, and then he cocked his head. "Funny, you don't strike me as Sal Piazza's type."

"I'm not." She smiled tightly, looking as if she'd be dangerous with a hockey stick right now. "He left me for Vicki."

"He cheated on you?"

"He denied it had gone as far as…sex. But he said he'd met someone else…and he was attracted to her." Marisa looked as if she couldn't believe what she was telling him.

"So Sal Piazza broke up with you to get Vicki in bed." Cole smiled humorlessly. "I should warn the guy that Vicki prefers anything to a bed."

"Don't be crude."

Hell if he could puzzle out Sal. Vicki and Marisa couldn't even be compared. One was a zero-calorie diet cola—you could guzzle twenty and they wouldn't fill you up—and the other a decadent dessert that could kill you.

He was also still wrapping his head around the fact that Sal and Marisa had been engaged. Sal was a sports nut, center-court wannabe. And in high school at least, Marisa couldn't have cared less about sports—her hookup with the captain of the hockey team aside.

On the other hand, from the few times Cole had run into Sal at some sports-related event or another, he'd struck Cole as an affable, conventional kind of guy. Medium build, average looks—bland and colorless. No surprise if Marisa had thought of him as safe and reliable. Not that the relationship with Sal had worked out the way she'd expected.

"When did the breakup happen?" he asked.

"In January."

Cole and Vicki had last seen each other in November.

"Worried that Vicki might have cheated on you with a mere sports agent?" Marisa asked archly.

"No." His involvement with Vicki had been so casual it had barely qualified as a relationship. Still, he couldn't resist getting another reaction out of Marisa. "Even ex-hockey players rank above sports agents in the pecking order."

She got a spark in her eyes. "So, according to you, I've been on a downward trajectory since high school?"

"Only you can speak to that, sweet pea."

He felt some satisfaction at provoking her. She'd been

working hard to maintain a crumbling wall of polite and professional civility between them.

"Your hubris leaves me breathless."

He smiled mirthlessly. "That's the effect that I often have on women, but it's because of my huge—"

"Stop!"

"—reputation. What did you think I was going to say?"

"You're impossible."

"So you give up?" He glanced around them. "Good match. We both got in some nice jabs. I accept your concession."

"The way you accepted my apology?"

He jerked his head toward the interior of the gym. "Is that what it was?"

She nodded. "Take it or leave it."

"And if I leave it?"

She twitched her lips, her eyes flashing. "Time to go for Plan B. Fortunately, Jordan's already given me one. Now all I need to do is convince the school that he'd be a good substitute."

She started to turn away, and Cole reached out and caught hold of her upper arm.

"Stay away from Jordan," he said. "You've already messed up one Serenghetti. Don't go for another."

He'd gotten first dibs on Marisa more than a decade ago. And given their history, first dibs held even now, whether Jordan knew the details or not.

"I'm flattered you think so highly of my evil powers, but Jordan is a big boy who can take care of himself."

"I'm not kidding."

"Neither am I. I'm running out of time to find a headliner for the Pershing fund-raiser."

"Not Jordan."

She pulled out of his grasp. "We'll see. Goodbye, Cole."

Broodingly, Cole watched her exit the gym.

Their meeting hadn't ended the way she'd wanted, but it wasn't the way he'd envisioned it, either.

Damn it.

He had to keep her away from Jordan, and his script didn't include admitting, *I slept with her*.

Three

Cole had to wait a week to corner his brother because Jordan had three away games. But he figured their parents' house was as good a location as any for a showdown. As he exited his Range Rover, he looked up at the storm clouds. *Yup.* The weather fit his mood.

When he didn't spot Jordan's car on his parents' circular drive, he quelled his impatience. His brother would be here soon enough. Jordan had replied to his text and agreed they would both stop by the house this evening to check on how their parents were doing. So Cole would soon have blessed relief from the irritation that had been dogging him for the past week. Marisa and his brother—*over his cold dead body.*

Cole made his way to the front doors. The Serenghetti house was a Mediterranean villa with a red-tile roof and white walls. In warmer months, a lush garden was his mother's pride and joy, keeping both her and a landscaper busy. As Serg's construction business had grown, Cole's parents had traded up to bigger homes. The move to the Mediterranean villa had been completed when Cole was in middle school. Serg had built a house big enough to accommodate the Serenghetti brood as well as the occasional visiting relatives.

Cole's jaw tightened. If Jordan had been contacted by Marisa, then his brother needed to be warned off. His brother had to understand that Marisa couldn't be trusted. She may have changed since high school, but Cole wasn't taking any chances. On the other hand, if Marisa had been bluffing about asking Jordan to be her second choice, so much the better. Either way, Cole was going to make damn sure there wasn't anything going on.

Memories had snuck up on him ever since Marisa had traipsed back into his life. Yeah, he'd taken a lot for granted when he'd been at Pershing—his status as top jock, his popularity with girls and the financial security that allowed him a ride at a private school. Still, there'd been pressure. Pressure to perform. Pressure to *outperform himself*—on and off the ice. He'd set himself up for a fall by trying to outdo his biggest game, his latest prank, his most recent sexual experience…

Back in high school, Marisa had been outside his inner circle but had seemingly been able to look in without judging. At least that was what he'd thought. And then she'd betrayed him.

Sure, he hadn't liked it one bit when Jordan had turned his charm on Marisa at the boxing gym. But it was because he hated to see his brother make the same mistake he'd made. It had nothing to do with being territorial about a teenage fling. He didn't do jealousy. Marisa was an attractive woman, but he was old enough to know the pitfalls of acting on pure lust.

As a professional hockey player, he'd always had easy access to women. But after a while it had started to lose meaning. When Jordan had joined the NHL, he'd given his younger brother *the talk* about the temptations facing professional athletes from money and fame. Of course, Jordan was a seasoned pro these days—but Marisa presented a brand of secret and stealthy allure.

He should know.

Cole tensed as he recalled how ready Jordan had been to succumb to temptation last week. Because his brother had been on the road for away games since then, with any luck he'd been too busy for Marisa to reach him.

Cole opened the unlocked front door and let himself in. The sounds of "We Open in Venice" hit him, and he wondered if his mother was again playing all the songs from Cole Porter's *Kiss Me, Kate*. She loved the musical so much, she had named her firstborn after its legendary composer.

Cole thought his life didn't need a soundtrack—least of all, that of the musical based on Shakespeare's *Taming of the Shrew*. Still, was it a coincidence—or the universe sending him a message? He had about as much chance of taming Marisa as of returning to his professional hockey career right now. Not that he was going to try. He was only going to make sure that he and any other Serenghetti were outside Marisa's ambit.

He made his way to the back of the house, where he found his mother in the oversize kitchen. As usual, the house smelled of flowers, mouthwatering food aromas…and familial obligation.

"Cole," Camilla said, pronouncing the *e* at the end of his name like a short vowel. "A lovely surprise, *caro*."

Although his mother had learned English at a young age, she still had an accent and sprinkled her English with Italian. She'd met and married Serg when he'd been vacationing in Tuscany, and she'd been a twenty-one-year-old hotel front-desk employee. Before Serg had checked out in order to visit extended family in the hockey-mad region north of Venice, the two had struck up a romance.

"Hi, Mom." Cole snagged a fried zucchini from a bowl on the marble-topped kitchen island. "Where's Dad?"

"Resting." She waved a hand. "You know all these visitors make him tired. Today the home-care worker, the nurse and the physical therapy came."

"You mean the physical therapist?"

"I say that, no?"

Cole let it slide. His mother had a late-blossoming career as the host of a local cooking show. Viewers who wrote in liked her accent, and television executives believed it added the spice of authenticity to her show. For Cole, it was just another colorful aspect of his lovable but quirky family.

"You beat me to the food. Did you taste the gnocchi yet?"

Cole turned to see Jordan saunter into the kitchen. Cole figured his brother must have driven up as soon as he'd entered the house. "How do you know she prepared gnocchi?"

Jordan shrugged. "I texted Mom earlier. She's perfecting a recipe for next week's show, and we're the guinea pigs. Gnocchi with prosciutto, escarole and tomato."

Camilla brightened. "I tell you? The name of the show is goin' to change to *Flavors of Italy with Camilla Serenghetti*."

"That's great!" Jordan leaned in to give his mother a quick peck on the cheek.

Cole nodded. "Congratulations, Mom. You'll be challenging Lidia Bastianich in no time."

Camilla beamed. "My name in the *titolo*. Good, no?"

"Excellent," Cole said.

Camilla frowned. "But I need to schedule more guests."

"Isn't that the job of the program booker at the station?"

"It's my show."

Jordan made a warding-off gesture with his hands. "Remember when you had me on last year, Mom? I made you burn the onions that you were sautéing. And Cole here wasn't much better when he was a guest."

From Cole's perspective, he and Jordan had been worth something in the sex appeal department, but his mother's show would never have mass crossover appeal to the beer-and-chips sports crowd.

Before he could offer to sacrifice himself again on the altar of his mother's show-business career, Camilla started toward the fridge and said, "I need somebody new."

"I'll put in a word with the Razors," Jordan offered. "Marc Bellitti likes to cook. And maybe a member of the team can suggest someone with better skills in the kitchen than on the ice."

Cole turned to his brother. "Speaking of ice, great game for you last night. You would have scored another goal if Peltier hadn't body-checked you at the last second."

Jordan grumbled. "He's been a pain in the rear all season." Then keeping an eye on their mother, as if to make sure he wouldn't be overheard, he added, "Guy needs to get laid."

At the mention of sex, Cole locked his jaw. "Has Marisa Danieli contacted you?"

Jordan cast him an assessing look. "Why do you ask?"

"She still needs a guinea pig for her fund-raiser. As I understand it, you're eager guinea pig material."

Jordan's lips quirked. "Being the test subject isn't half bad sometimes. Anyway, she wanted you."

"I told her no."

"Admirable fortitude. The guys in the locker room would be impressed."

"I'm asking you to tell her no."

"It hasn't come up."

Cole relaxed his shoulders. "She hasn't tried to reach you?"

"Nope. And quit focusing on the decoy. I'm a bad one. There's something else you'll find a lot more interesting."

Camilla set a big bowl of gnocchi on the counter and announced, "I'm goin' to check on your father and be right back."

"Take your time, Mom." Cole knew his mother was worried about his father's rough road to recovery. It had been several months since the stroke, and Serg still had not made a complete recovery—if he ever would.

When their mother left, Cole turned to Jordan and wasted no time in getting to the point. "What is it?"

"Word is that the job for the new gym at the Pershing School is going to JM Construction."

Cole's lips thinned. *She'd done worse than get Jordan on board for her fund-raiser.*

As far as jobs went for a midsize construction company like Serenghetti or JM, the new gym at the Pershing School was small-fry. However, JM would get the attendant publicity and goodwill.

Damn it. They'd been outbid twice in the past few months by JM Construction. Like Serenghetti, JM operated in the New England region, though both sometimes took jobs farther afield. Serenghetti's main offices were in Welsdale—at Serg's insistence—but they kept a business suite in Boston for convenience, as well as a small satellite staff in Portland, Maine.

"You know this how?" Cole demanded of his brother.

"Guys talking down at the Puck & Shoot. If you hung out there, you'd know, too. You should try it."

"A lot happens at the Puck & Shoot." Cole recalled that Marisa had found out how to run him to ground from a tip at the bar.

"The drinks aren't bad, and the female clientele is even better."

"I'm surprised you haven't spotted Marisa there."

Jordan snagged a cold gnocchi from the bowl and popped it into his mouth. "She doesn't look like the type to be a sports bar regular."

"A lot about her may surprise you."

His brother swallowed and grinned. "I'm sure."

"Jordan."

"Anyway, I was killing time. Someone brought up my recent ad campaign, so I mentioned an opportunity to do a little local promo for the Pershing School. I asked if anyone was interested."

"Putting in a good word for Marisa?" Cole asked sardonically.

There was laughter in Jordan's eyes. "Well, I knew you didn't want to volunteer. And you'd have my head on a platter if I did the fund-raiser."

"Good call."

"But I felt bad for her, to be honest. She was even willing to tangle with you in order to find a celebrity."

"She knows what she's doing."

"She seems like a good sort these days. Or at least her cause is a good one."

"Right." *Whose side was his brother on?*

"Anyway, you remember Jenkins? He graduated a couple of years after you did and played in the minors for a while?"

"Yeah?"

"He said the rumor was that JM Construction had the inside track on building the gym. So he thought it was curious I was mentioning the school fund-raiser to the Razors. He indicated it was mighty magnanimous of me to try to find a recruit for JM's cause."

"Oh yeah, it was." Cole resisted a snort. "Still feeling sorry for Marisa?"

The woman had more up her sleeve than a cardsharp.

Jordan shrugged. "She may know nothing about who's getting the construction contract."

"We'll see. Either way, I'm about to find out."

Life was full of firsts—some of them more welcome than others. Cole had been her earliest lover, and now he was giving her another first. Marisa stepped inside Serenghetti Construction's offices, which she'd never done before.

The company occupied the uppermost floors of a red-brick building that had once been a factory, square in the middle of Welsdale's downtown. The website stated that

Serg Serenghetti had renovated the building twenty years ago and turned it into a modern office complex. For years she'd felt as if she would never be welcome inside, but now she'd gotten a personal invite from Cole Serenghetti himself. It showed how life could turn on a dime.

Of course the actual call had come from Cole's assistant. But Marisa had taken it as a sign that Cole might be softening his stance. She was willing to hold on to any thread of hope, no matter how thin. Because as much as she'd bluffed, she had no Plan B. She hadn't tried to contact Jordan Serenghetti because it would be preferable for Pershing to have someone who'd graduated from the school as a headliner. Besides, she was sure Cole would block any attempt to recruit his brother.

In the lobby, Marisa tried not to be intimidated by the sleek glass-and-chrome design—a testament to money and power. And when she reached the top floor, she took a deep breath as she entered Serenghetti's spacious and airy offices. The decor was muted beiges and grays—cool and professional. The receptionist announced her, took her coat and then directed her down the hall to a corner office.

Her heart beat in a staccato rhythm as she reached an open doorway. And then her gaze connected with Cole's. He was standing beside an imposing L-shaped desk.

The air hummed between them, and Marisa steadied herself as she walked forward into his office. She'd dressed professionally in a beige pantsuit, but she was suddenly very aware of her femininity. That was because Cole exuded power in a navy suit and patterned tie. This was a different incarnation than his hockey uniform, or his hardhat and jeans, but no less potent.

"You look wary," Cole said. "Afraid you're in for a third strike?"

"You don't play baseball."

"Lucky you."

"You wouldn't have summoned me if you'd meant to turn me down again."

"Or maybe I'm a sadistic bastard who enjoys making you pay for past transgressions again and again."

Marisa compressed her lips to keep from giving her opinion. His office was devoid of personal items like family photos and as inscrutable as the man himself. She wondered if this room had been Serg's office until recently, or whether Cole had just avoided settling in by bringing mementos.

Cole smiled but it didn't reach his eyes. "So here's the deal, sweet pea. Serenghetti Construction builds the new gym at Pershing, no questions asked. I don't want to hear any garbage about handing off the job to a friend of a board member."

"What?"

"Yeah, surprised?" he asked as he prowled toward her. "So am I. I've been almost dancing with shock ever since I discovered you wanted me to be a poster boy for someone else's construction job. And not just anyone else, but our main competitor. They've underbid us on the last two jobs. But that's quality for you."

"I'm sure the construction would be up to code. We'd have an inspection," she said crossly.

"Being up to code is the least of your worries."

Marisa felt as if she'd shown up in the middle of the second act of a play. There was a context that she was missing here. "I have no idea what you're talking about. What friend of a board member?"

Cole scanned her face for a moment, then two. "It would figure they didn't let the teacher in on the discussion. Have you ever sat on a board of directors?"

She shook her head.

"The meetings might be public, but there's plenty of wheeling and dealing behind the scenes. It's you scratch my back, I'll scratch yours. We'll go with the headliner you want for the fund-raiser, but you'll back my guy for the construction job."

Marisa felt the heat of embarrassment flood her face. She'd thought she'd been so clever in her approach for Pershing Shines Bright. She hadn't even let Mr. Dobson know she'd talked to Cole because she'd thought her chances of success were uncertain at best. She'd wanted the option of persuading Mr. Dobson to go with someone else without the appearance that she'd failed.

Now she felt like a nitwit—one who didn't know what the other hand was doing. Or at least, didn't know what the school board was up to. She wanted to slump into a chair, but it would give Cole an even bigger advantage than he had.

"That kind of horse-trading is corrupt," she managed.

"That's life."

"I didn't have any idea."

"Right."

"You believe me?"

He made an impatient sound. "You're a walking, breathing cliché. In this case, for one, you're a naive and idealistic schoolteacher who's been kept out of the loop."

"Well, at least I've improved in your estimation in the last fifteen years." She dropped her handbag onto a chair. If she couldn't sit, at least she could get rid of some dead weight while she faced Cole. "That's more than you would have said about me in high school."

"At this point I have a good sense of when you're to blame," he shot back, not answering directly.

"Meaning you have plenty of experience?"

Cole gave her a penetrating look and then said, "Here's what you're going to do. You're going to tell the principal—"

"Mr. Dobson."

"—that you've got me on board for the fund-raiser, but there's one condition attached."

"Serenghetti Construction gets the job."

Marisa had been on a roller coaster of emotions since

walking into Cole's office. And right now elation that Cole was agreeing to be her headliner threatened to overwhelm everything else. She tried to appear calm but a part of her wanted to jump up and down with relief.

Cole nodded, seemingly oblivious to her emotional state. "Let Dobson deal with the board of directors. My guess is that the member with ties to JM Construction will have to back down. If Dobson plays his cards right, he'll marshal support even before the next board meeting."

"And if he doesn't?"

"He will, especially if I say Jordan will show up, too, even though he's not a graduate of the school. Pershing isn't a public school that's legally bound to accept the lowest bid on a contract. And giving the contract to Serenghetti Construction makes sense. The money that the school would save not having to pay a big name to appear at their fundraiser tips the balance on the bottom line."

She sighed. "You've thought of everything."

"Not everything. I still have to deal with you, sweet pea."

His words hurt, but she managed to keep her expression even. "Bad luck."

"Bad luck comes in threes. Getting injured, needing to take over a construction firm, you showing up…"

"We're even," she parried. "I've been cheated on, gotten dumped by my fiancé and had to recruit you for the fund-raiser."

He smiled, and she thought she detected a spark of admiration for her willingness to meet him head-on. "Not so diplomatic now that you know you have me hooked."

"Only because you're willing to be ruthless with your competitors."

"Just like your douche bag fiancé?" he asked. "How did you wind up engaged to Sal? Are you hanging out in sports bars these days?"

"You know from personal experience that I visit boxing gyms." She shrugged. "Why not a sports bar?"

His eyes crinkled. "You showed up at Jimmy's only because you were tracking me. You'd probably claim your appearance was under duress."

"I'm not going to argue."

"You're not?" he quipped. "What a change."

"You're welcome."

His expression sobered. "For the record, you don't know what to wear to a gym."

"I came from school dressed like a teacher," she protested.

His eyes swept over her. "Exactly. As I said, you're a walking cliché."

"And you are frustrating and irritating." She spoke lightly, but she sort of meant it, too.

"Talk to my opponents on the ice. They'll tell you all about it."

"I'm sure they would."

"It's nice to know I bother you, sweet pea."

Their gazes caught and held, and awareness coiled through her, threatening to break free. She wet her lips, and Cole's eyes moved to her mouth.

"Are you still pining and crying your eyes out for him?" he asked abruptly.

She blinked, caught off guard. She wasn't going to admit as much to Cole of all people, but she'd done enough pining and crying in high school to last a lifetime. Still, it would be pathetic if she'd met and lost the love of her life at eighteen. Her life couldn't have ended that early.

"For whom?" she asked carefully.

"Piazza."

"Not really."

She'd dated since graduating from Pershing, but nothing had panned out past a few dates until Sal. It was as if she'd needed to lick her wounds for a long time after high school—after Cole.

There'd been initial shock over Sal's betrayal, of course.

But then she'd gotten on with her life. She had a low opinion of Sal, and she was still angry about being cheated on. But she wasn't lying in bed wondering how she was going to go on—or wishing Sal would see the light and come back to her.

She'd been prepared to be hit by the despair that had assailed her after her teenage fling with Cole. So either she'd matured, or her relationship with Sal hadn't been as significant as she'd told herself. She refused to analyze which was the case.

Cole shrugged. "Piazza isn't worth it. He's a cheating a—"

"You've never cheated on a woman?" They were getting into personal territory, but she couldn't stop herself from asking the question.

Cole assumed a set expression. "I've dated plenty, but it's always been serial. And you never answered my question about how you met Piazza."

"Why are you interested?" she shot back before sighing in resignation. "We did meet in a bar, actually. Some teachers met for Friday night drinks, and I was persuaded to go along. He was an acquaintance of an acquaintance…"

Cole arched an eyebrow, as if prompting her for more.

"He was steady, reliable…"

"A bedrock to build a marriage on. But he turned out to be so reliable, he cheated on you."

"What do you suggest constructing a lasting relationship on?" she lobbed back. "A hormone-fueled hookup with a woman as deep as a puddle after a light rain?"

She didn't pose the question as if it was about him in particular, but he could read between the lines.

"I haven't even tried for more. That's the difference."

"As I said, Sal appeared steady and reliable…" And she'd been desperate for the respectably ordinary. All she'd wanted as an adult was to be middle class, with a Cape Cod or a split level in the suburbs and a couple of kids…and *no money worries.*

Sal had grown up in Welsdale, too, but unlike her, he'd attended Welsdale High School, so they hadn't known each other as teenagers. When they'd met, he'd been working for a Springfield-based sports management company, but was often back in his hometown, which was where they had gotten acquainted one night at The Obelisk Lounge. Sal traveled to Boston regularly for business, but he and his firm mainly focused on trolling the waters of professional hockey at the Springfield arena where the New England Razors played.

Cole looked irritated. "Sal is the sports version of a used car salesman—always preparing to pitch you the next deal as if it's the best thing since sliced bread."

"As far as I can tell, a lot of you sports pros believe you are the best thing since sliced bread."

They were skimming the surface of the deep lake of emotion and past history between them. Every encounter with Cole was an emotional wringer. You'd think she'd be used to it by now or at least expecting it.

Cole shrugged. "Hockey is a job."

"So is teaching."

"It's the reason you made your way back to Pershing."

"The school was good to me." She shifted and then picked up her handbag.

Cole didn't move. "I'll bet. How long have you been teaching there?"

"I started right after college, so not quite ten years." She took a step toward the door and then paused. "It took me more than five years and several part-time jobs to get my degree and provisional teaching certificate at U. Mass. Amherst."

She could see she'd surprised him. She'd gone to a state school, where the tuition had been lower and she'd qualified for a scholarship. Even then, though, because she'd been more or less self-supporting, it had taken a while to get her degree. She'd worked an odd and endless assortment of jobs: telemarketer, door-to-door sales rep, supermarket checkout clerk and receptionist.

She knew Cole had gone on to Boston College, which was a powerhouse in college hockey. She was sure he hadn't had to hold down two part-time jobs in order to graduate, but she gave him credit if he continued to work in the family construction business, as he'd done at Pershing.

"I remember you didn't have much money in high school," he said.

"I was a scholarship student. I worked summers and sometimes weekends scooping ice cream at the Ben & Jerry's on Sycamore St."

"Yeah, I remember."

She remembered, too. *Oh, did she remember*. Cole and the rest of his jock posse had hardly ever set foot in the store, but it had been a favorite of teenage girls. She'd waited on her classmates, and usually it had worked out okay, but a few stuck-up types had enjoyed queening it over her. Cole had stopped in during the brief time they'd been study buddies...

"And you worked summers at Serenghetti Construction," she said unnecessarily, suddenly nervous because they weren't squabbling anymore.

"All the way through college."

"But you didn't have to do it for the money."

"No, not for the money," he responded, "but there are different shades of *have to*. There's the *have to* that comes with family obligation."

"Is that why you're back and running Serenghetti Construction?"

He nodded curtly. "At least temporarily. I've got other opportunities on the back burner."

She tried to hide her surprise. "You're planning to play hockey again?"

"No, but there are other options. Coaching, for instance."

Her heart fell, but Marisa told herself not to be ridiculous even as she fidgeted with her handbag strap. She didn't care what Cole Serenghetti's plans were, and she shouldn't be surprised they didn't involve staying in Welsdale and heading Serenghetti Construction.

"How is your father doing?" she asked, trying to bring the conversation back to safer ground. News of Serg's stroke was public knowledge around Welsdale.

"He's doing therapy to regain some motor function."

Marisa didn't say anything, sensing that Cole might continue if she remained silent.

"It's doubtful he'll be able to run Serenghetti Construction again."

"That must be tough." If Serg didn't recover more, and Cole had no plans to head the family business on a permanent basis, Marisa wondered what would happen. Would one of Cole's brothers step in to head the company? But Jordan was having an impressive run with the Razors... She contained her curiosity, because Cole had been a closed door to her for fifteen years—and she liked it that way, she told herself.

"Dad's a fighter. We'll see what happens," Cole said, seeming like a man who rarely, if ever, invited sympathy. "He's joked about the lengths he'll go to retire and hand over the reins to one of his kids."

She smiled, and Cole's expression relaxed.

"How's your mother?" he asked, appearing okay with chitchat about their families.

"She recently married a carpenter." Ted Millepied was a good man who adored her mother.

Cole quirked his lips. "Where's he based? I may be able to use him."

"You don't believe in guilt by association?" The words left her mouth before she could stop them, but she was surprised that Cole would even consider hiring someone related to her by marriage.

Cole sobered. "No, despite what my cockamamie brother may have led you to believe about the Serenghettis and the labeling of relationships to the nth degree of separation."

Jordan's words came back to her. *Entangled by proxy? Engaged by one degree of separation?* In fact, there was no connection between her and Cole. She refused to believe in any. There'd only been dead air since high school.

"My mother is still in Welsdale," she elaborated. "She's worked her way up to management at Stanhope Department Store. In fact, she recently got named buyer for housewares."

She was proud of her mother. After many years in retail, earning college credit at night and on weekends, Donna Casale had been rewarded with management-track promotions at Stanhope, which anchored the biggest shopping center in the Welsdale area. The store was where Marisa's wealthier classmates at Pershing had bought many of their clothes—and where Marisa had gotten by with her mother's employee discounts.

Cole was looking at her closely, and she gave herself a mental shake. They had drifted deep into personal stuff. *Stop, stop, stop.* She should get going. "Okay," she said briskly, "if Pershing meets your terms about the construction job, will you do the fund-raiser?"

Cole looked alert. "Yes."

"Wonderful." She stepped forward and held out her hand. "It's a deal."

Cole enveloped Marisa's hand, and sensation swamped her. Their eyes met, and the moment dragged out between them... He was so close, she could see the sprinkling of gold in his irises. She'd also forgotten how tall Cole was, because she'd limited herself to the occasional glimpse of him on television or in print for the past fifteen years.

She swallowed, her lips parting.

Cole dropped his gaze to her mouth. "Did you mean what you said to Jordan?"

"Wh-what?" She cleared her throat and tried again. "What in particular?"

"Was he your Plan B?"

"I don't have a Plan B."

"What about regretting telling on me to Mr. Hayes in high school?"

The world shrank to include only the two of them. "Every day. I wished circumstances had been different."

"Ever wish things had turned out differently between us?"

"Yes."

"Yeah, me too."

A cell phone buzzed, breaking the moment.

Marisa stepped back, and Cole reached into his pocket. "Mr. Serenghetti?"

Marisa glanced toward the door and saw the receptionist.

"I've got it," Cole said. "He phoned my cell."

The receptionist nodded as she retreated. "Your four o'clock is here, too."

Cole held Marisa's gaze as he addressed whoever was on the other end of the line. From what Marisa could tell, the call was about a materials delivery for one of Serenghetti's construction sites.

But it was the message that she read in Cole's expression that captured her attention. *Later. We're not done yet.*

Marisa gave a quick nod before turning and heading for the door.

As she made her way past reception, down in the elevator and out the building, she pondered Cole's words about wishing things had worked out differently between them. What had he meant? And did it matter?

But there was more to puzzle over in his expression. *We're not done.*

It was more than had existed between them in fifteen years—or maybe they were just going to write a different ending.

Four

Marisa gazed up at him with big, wide eyes. "Please, Cole. I want you."

"Yes," he heard himself answer, his voice thick.

They were made to fit together. He'd waited fifteen years to show her how good it could be between them. He wanted to tell her that he would please her. This would be no crazy fumble on a sofa. When it came to sex, their communication had the potential to be flawless and explosive.

He claimed her lips and traced the seam of her mouth. She opened for him, tasting sweet as a ripe berry, and then met his tongue. The kiss deepened and gained urgency. They pressed together, and she moaned.

He felt the pressing need of his arousal as her breasts pushed against his chest. She was sexy and hot, and she wanted him. He'd never felt this deep need for anyone else. It was primitive and basic and...right.

"Oh, Cole." She looked at him, her eyes wide amber pools. "Please. Now."

"Yes," he said hoarsely. "It's going to be so good be-tween us, sweet pea. I promise."

He positioned himself, and then held her gaze as he pushed inside her. She was warm and slick and tight. And he was sliding toward mindless rapture...

Cole awoke with a start.

Glancing around, half-dazed, he realized he was rest-less, aroused—and alone.

He sprawled across his king-size bed, where damp sheets had ridden down his bare chest and tangled around his legs. Most of all, there was the feeling of being irritated and un-fulfilled.

Damn it.

He'd been fantasizing about Marisa Danieli. He'd itched to ride her curves and have her come apart in his arms. He worked hard to slow his pounding pulse and then threw off the sheets. A glance at the bedside clock told him he needed to be at the office in an hour. He hit the alarm before it could go off and then rose and headed to the shower.

The master suite in his Welsdale condo included a large marble bath and a walk-in closet. He'd bought the place—on the top floor of a prewar building in the center of down-town—in order to have a home base during his hockey career. Not to mention that like the rest of the Serenghettis, he was a keen real estate investor.

The condo had been a place where he could retreat dur-ing the off-season without becoming an extended house-guest of his parents. His brothers kept places nearby, while his sister preferred to stay at Casa Serenghetti—as the sib-lings sometimes jokingly referred to the family manse—when she was in town.

He opened the glass door to the shower stall and then stood under the lukewarm spray, waiting for it to cool him down before he grabbed a bar of soap and lathered up.

He told himself he'd been dreaming about Marisa only because he wanted to win. Sex was just a metaphor for crashing through her defenses. Then he'd have some relief from this frustrating dance that they were engaged in.

Certainly he didn't want a round two with her. He wasn't even sure he trusted her…

After dressing, he made the quick drive to his office at Serenghetti Construction. He'd just reached his desk when the receptionist announced that she had Mr. Dobson from the Pershing School on the phone.

Interesting. It appeared Marisa had spoken with Pershing's principal, and Mr. Dobson was wasting no time getting the wheels turning on his end.

Through careful questioning of his contacts, Cole had learned that a Pershing board member was golf buddies with the CEO of JM Construction. He didn't have solid evidence that JM Construction had been a shoo-in for building the gym, but it was enough. In the end, proof didn't matter anyway. He needed that job to go to Serenghetti Construction and not JM.

"Mr. Dobson, Cole Serenghetti here. What can I do for you?" Cole made his voice sound detached, even a bit bored.

Dobson engaged in pleasantries for a few minutes, as if he and Cole already knew each other and the call was an ordinary occurrence. Then without missing a beat, the principal thanked him for agreeing to headline Pershing Shines Bright, and invited Serenghetti Construction to submit a proposal for building the gym.

Cole leaned back in his chair. Since coming to his office last week, Marisa must have delivered the message at Pershing that the fund-raiser and the construction job were a package deal. Still, he needed to make sure there was no doubt about this understanding. He expected at least a handshake deal, if not a signed contract, before the school benefit took place.

Drawing on the business savvy that he'd gotten at an early age by observing Serg, Cole said, "I have an architectural partnership that I work with. I suggest setting up a meeting for next week where we can discuss the vision for the new gym as well as talk about costs and the timeline. Afterward, I'll submit contracts for your review."

Dobson paused a beat and then heartily agreed with Cole's suggestion.

"Feel free to invite any of the directors on your board to the meeting next week," Cole continued. "I want each and every one of them to be comfortable with the Serenghetti team."

There was another beat before the principal responded. "I can assure you that the board couldn't have been more pleased to hear the Serenghetti name mentioned in connection with both the fund-raiser and the construction of the gym. They need no reassurance."

Cole smiled, glad that he and Dobson understood each other. Clearly, the principal was savvy himself. He appeared to have done the math and realized that a *free* appearance by a hockey star or two was worth plenty to the school's bottom line. Cole made a mental note to call Jordan and tell him that *both* of them would be showing up for Pershing Shines Bright.

Thinking he needed to do Marisa a favor for keeping her word, Cole went on, "Invite Ms. Danieli to the meeting, too. If she's in charge of the fund-raiser, she'll need to be able to speak knowledgeably to potential donors about the building project."

"Excellent idea," Dobson concurred. "I will let her know."

As soon as his conversation with the principal had ended, Cole called his youngest brother and put him on speakerphone.

"Put the Pershing School benefit on your calendar," he told Jordan without prelude. "I'll email you the date and time when I get them from Marisa. You and I will be making an appearance in our best penguin suits or closest equivalent."

As he spoke, he opened a blank email and began drafting a message to Marisa. Did she have a black-tie event in mind? He hadn't concerned himself with the details up to now. He also needed to tell her that Jordan would be participating, too. He didn't pause now to analyze why he was relishing communicating with her, even if just by email, after the dead air between them since she'd shown up at his office.

Jordan's unmistakable chuckle sounded over the phone line. "First, you told me to stay away from Marisa, now you want me to attend her fund-raiser with you. Which is it? And more important, will you be a good date?"

Cole figured he should have expected Jordan's needling. "You wouldn't be my date for the fund-raiser, numbskull."

"Why, Cole," his brother cooed, "you do know how to break someone's heart. Did I lose out to Marisa, or is there another teacher who's gotten you hot under the collar lately?"

"Later, Jordan." Cole punched the button to end the call.

He finished his email, and then, after finding an address for Marisa on Pershing's website, fired it off.

Leaning back in his chair again, he allowed himself momentary satisfaction at cutting off JM Construction. Now all he needed to do was wait for Marisa to come calling with the details…

The second time wasn't as intimidating, Marisa thought, as she walked through Serenghetti Construction's offices on a Thursday afternoon.

Last week she'd sat in on a meeting between Mr. Dobson and Cole and his architectural firm to discuss the contract to build Pershing's gym. The talk had been about use requirements, building permits and environmental impact. Then there'd been a discussion of hardwood, maple grades, subflooring, HVAC systems and disability access. Marisa had jotted notes to keep up with the onslaught of details. She'd been aware of Cole's gaze on her from time to time as he'd talked, but she'd kept her head down and stayed in the background, asking only a couple of questions.

She was a teacher, not a builder, but she'd known as soon as the meeting was over that she would have to do some serious studying if she hoped one day to be an assistant principal. School administrators like Mr. Dobson had more on their plate than the curriculum. They were also responsible for the physical condition of the school buildings that they oversaw.

In fact, she had done a little online research this past weekend because today she had to deal with Cole all by herself. She was supposed to look at architectural plans and give her input to Mr. Dobson. The principal had asked her to look at the plans for other athletic facilities built by Serenghetti Construction.

She should be happy about her expanded responsibilities because maybe it was a sign that Mr. Dobson would consider her for a promotion. But instead, her thoughts were on Cole. Since their meeting last week, her communication with him had been limited. They'd exchanged brief emails about the time and place of the fund-raiser, and he'd signed off on the use of his bio and photo.

But her active imagination had filled in what had been left unsaid. She'd gone over every look and word that Cole had given her during their meeting with Mr. Dobson and the architect. She'd also replayed their last conversation at his office—especially the part about wishing their relationship had turned out differently.

She was grateful to him for agreeing to do the fund-raiser. And *vulnerable* and *attracted*…

Danger, danger, danger… She could never become involved with Cole. *Not with her family history.* She'd lived with the consequences of the past her whole life, even if she hadn't known the details until her twenties.

Bringing herself back to the present, she gave her name

to the receptionist, who directed her toward Cole's office with little fanfare.

When she reached Cole's door, he looked up, as if sensing her there.

"Marisa." He stood and came around his desk.

Her pulse picked up, and she stepped into the room, resisting the urge to hug her light blazer to her instead of leaving it draped over one arm. As usual, she was hit with an overwhelming awareness of him as a man. Today he was dressed in a suit but he had shed his jacket and tie. Still, even though he wasn't in full corporate uniform, he appeared every inch the successful and wealthy business executive.

Marisa shifted. She'd dressed in a striped shirt and navy pants—an appropriate and understated outfit in her opinion. She dared him to take note of her clothing one more time and call her a cliché.

Cole's eyes surveyed her as he approached, but he said nothing.

Did she imagine that he lingered at the V created by her shirt, his gaze flickering with heat for a moment? It was like being touched by a feather—light, and yet packed with sensation.

When he stopped in front of her, he asked without preamble, "What did you think of our meeting with Dobson last week?"

She resisted saying she thought of it as her and Mr. Dobson's meeting with *him*. "It went well."

Cole nodded. "Dobson wants you to see some older plans today. Every job is unique, but I'm guessing he wants to cover his bases and have you do some due diligence."

"In case he needs to account for the way the construction contract with Serenghetti came about?"

Cole gave her a dry look and inclined his head. "You'll be the one doing the explaining since you're here today. You're going to get a sense of what past clients have gone with."

"Okay." She really was in the hot seat. "Do you have plans for other gyms that Serenghetti has built?"

"One or two." Cole arched a brow. "You might as well get acquainted with the nitty-gritty of construction. Nobody plays around here. Least of all me." He pulled his office door open wider and indicated she should precede him out of the room. "You can leave your stuff here. We'll be back in a few minutes."

Marisa dropped her handbag and blazer on a chair and then walked beside Cole down the corridor and around the corner.

Stopping in front of an older-looking door, Cole retrieved keys from his pocket and opened two different dead bolts.

"I guess not everything at Serenghetti Construction is state-of-the-art," she remarked lightly.

Cole quirked his lips. "The new Pershing gym will be, don't worry. This building dates back to the 1930s, and we kept the old-fashioned storage room with concrete walls and dead bolts. It's where we keep confidential files and old documents."

He opened the door and flipped the light switch.

Marisa saw a small room lined with metal cabinets. A walkable strip down the middle extended about seven or eight feet into the room.

Cole moved inside, and Marisa watched as he scanned the cabinets.

"There must be a few decades' worth of files in there."

"Building rehabilitation is a substantial share of our business," Cole answered, glancing back at her. "We refer to these plans when we do renovations or additions to existing structures, either for returning clients or new owners."

"I see."

He looked amused. "Come on in."

Reluctantly, she let go of the door and stepped inside. She let her gaze travel over the cabinets because the alternative was allowing it to settle on Cole. The labels on the metal drawers were a mystery to her. "How do you know where to look?"

Then, hearing a click behind her, she turned to see that the door had creaked shut. Pushing aside a prick of panic, she said, "I'll, uh, step back out to give you more room to search for what you're looking for."

She grasped the door handle and tried to turn it. The door, however, didn't budge. She jiggled the handle again and pushed.

"Now you've done it."

She swung around, her eyes widening. "What do you mean?"

"You've locked us in."

She gave him an accusatory look. "You told me to step inside!"

"But not to let the door close behind you. There's a door-stop outside. Didn't you see it?"

"No!"

"Are you afraid of small spaces?" he asked sardonically.

"Don't be ridiculous." She had a fear of *Cole and small spaces*.

"Breathe."

"I don't want to suck all of the air out of the room."

He looked as if he was stifling a laugh. "You won't. Does this happen often?"

"It comes and goes," she admitted. "I'm not claustrophobic, but I'm not a big fan of tiny areas, either."

"Relax."

She sent up a prayer because she was in sensory overload right now, and his nearness in the closet-like space threatened to short-circuit her. "You're finding this amusing, aren't you?"

"Vasovagal syncope, claustrophobia… It keeps getting better and better with you."

"Very funny." She'd never put her best foot forward with him. She felt exposed, her vulnerabilities on display.

"You could scream for help," he suggested. "It might suck all the air out of the room, so think about whether you're willing to go for broke..."

"The only reason to scream is because you're making me crazy."

He stepped toward her, bringing them within brushing distance. "There's always your cell phone."

"I left it in your office along with my handbag." She perked up. "What about your phone?"

"Ditto except for the part about the handbag."

She lowered her shoulders. "How could you let this happen?"

"I didn't," he said with exaggerated patience.

She grasped at any topic she could in order to take her mind off her panic. "Did you ever think that Serenghetti Construction might be your second career after hockey someday?"

"No, but I have a construction background, thanks to working summers at Serenghetti Construction to earn money. I majored in management at Boston College, but I also took community college classes in bid estimating, drafting and blueprint reading that helped at the summer jobs."

"Because your father always wanted you to succeed him at Serenghetti Construction."

"Someone had to, but I never committed."

"And then your hockey dreams were cut short."

He gave her a droll look. "For a woman who doesn't like to confront uncomfortable topics, you sure don't mince words."

She frowned. "What topics don't I like to talk about? I'm just wondering whether it may have been hard to come to terms with your new situation."

He folded his arms. "Like you haven't come to grips with the past?"

"What do you mean?" *He was way too close.*

"Us."

"Some of us weren't lucky enough to have a Plan B that involved a job in the family business."

His gaze sharpened. "Oh no, you don't. I'm not letting you avoid the topic. Why did you go to Mr. Hayes with the story that I pulled the prank? Because I came from money and had a Plan B?"

"Please," she scoffed.

He was too close, too much, too everything.

The school assembly during their senior year had been named Pershing Does Good. It was supposed to have been video highlights of the Pershing community doing volunteer work. Instead, it had turned into a joke because Cole had inserted images of Mr. Hayes's head superimposed on a champion wrestler's body, and one of the principal seemingly dressed only in boxers and socks and posing next to a convertible.

It had been a brilliant piece of hacking, but Mr. Hayes had been in no mood to laugh.

Cole moved closer. "Or was it a way to get back at me after we'd had sex and I didn't shower you with pretty phrases?"

She made a sound of disbelief. "You didn't talk to me, either."

He paused, his eyes gleaming. "Ah, now we're getting somewhere."

"Where?" she demanded. "You've written a script about a jilted lover seeking revenge."

"Weren't you one?"

"I was a virgin."

"Okay, so I was the evil seducer who stole your virginity, and hell hath no fury like a woman scorned? That's a good story, too, except my recollection is that you were a willing participant."

She shook her head vehemently. "It had nothing to do

with sex. At least my confession to Mr. Hayes didn't. You were closer when you thought it had to do with money."

Cole's face hardened.

"Mr. Hayes called me into his office. He guessed there were seniors who knew more about the prank than he did." She fought to keep her voice even. "So he pulled in the person he thought he had something to hold over. Namely, me."

Cole scowled.

"You humiliated and embarrassed him in front of the whole student body. He was going to get to the bottom of it, come hell or high water. So he threatened to take away my recommendation for a college scholarship unless I confessed who did it." She swallowed. "I'd overheard you telling one of your teammates near the lockers that you'd managed to sneak into the school offices."

Marisa had known back then in the principal's office that Mr. Hayes's job was at stake. While working her after-school job sweeping hallways, she'd overheard conversations among the staff about the principal's contract maybe not being renewed by Pershing's board because there was debate about Mr. Hayes's performance. Cole's prank would further make it seem as if Mr. Hayes wasn't a good leader who commanded the respect of the school community.

Marisa had looked at Mr. Hayes, and in that instant, she'd read his thoughts. He was worried because his career might be on the line, and he had three kids to support at home. She had been able to relate because her mother had stressed about her job, too, and she'd had only one kid to worry about.

Cole's frown faded, and then his eyes narrowed.

"I was backed into a corner. I had no Plan B. I needed that scholarship money, or there would be no happy ending for me. At least not one involving college in the fall."

Cole's lips thinned. "It's unconscionable that the bastard would have twisted the arm of an eighteen-year-old student."

"I was on scholarship at Pershing. I was there on condition of good grades and better behavior. Unlike some people, I didn't have the luxury of being a prankster."

Cole swore.

"So you were right all along. I did sell you out, and I'm sorry." She felt the wind leave her, her words slowing after spilling in a mad rush. "If it helps, I was ostracized. People saw me go in and out of Mr. Hayes's office, so they guessed who ratted you out. After all, you got confronted by Mr. Hayes right after I was interrogated, so the rumors started immediately. My only defense was that if I hadn't kept my scholarship, I'd probably have struggled to make ends meet like my mother. I knew college was my ticket out."

She ought to stop talking but she couldn't help herself. The words had come out in a torrent and were now down to a trickle, but she couldn't seem to turn off the flow completely.

"Why didn't you tell me back then about Hayes blackmailing you into a confession?" Cole demanded. "He let slip your name when he confronted me, but he never got into details."

"Would you have been ready to listen?" she replied. "All you cared about was the Independent School League championship. My reasons didn't make a difference. You still wouldn't have been able to play the end of the season."

The old hurts from high school came back vividly, and she felt a throbbing pain in the region of her heart. She'd stayed home on the night of the prom. She and Serafina had watched Molly Ringwald flicks from the '80s. The high school angst on the television screen had fit Marisa's mood—because she'd been into self-flagellation. She'd discovered that Cole—his suspension ended—was going to the prom with Kendra Vance, a cheerleader. She'd cried herself to sleep long after Sera's head had hit the pillow, hiding her grief because she didn't want to invite questions from her cousin.

Marisa sucked in a trembling breath while Cole stared at her, his expression inscrutable. She realized she'd hurt him, and now he was still wary. But there was no way to change the past.

"How are we getting out of here?" she asked, reverting to her earlier panic—because, strangely, it seemed safer territory than the one she'd ventured into with Cole.

Flustered, she gestured randomly until Cole captured her hands. He gave her a look of such intensity, it stole her breath.

"Now would be the time to scream, I think," he said.

"Because we're out of options?"

"No. Because if I haven't made you crazy already, this will."

Then he bent his head and captured her mouth, swallowing her gasp.

Cole folded her into his arms. He kissed her with a self-assurance that sent chills of awareness chasing through her. She felt his hard muscles pressed against her soft curves. Her breasts tingled. *Everything* tingled.

He savored her mouth, stroking her lips until they were wet and plump and prickling with need. His tongue darted to the seam of her lips, and she opened for him. He moved his hands up to cup her head and thread his fingers in her hair. Then he stroked inside her mouth, deepening the kiss, and she met him instinctively. She sighed, and he made a sound of satisfaction.

She wanted him. She'd developed a crush on him in high school, and she still felt an attraction for him that would not be denied. Longing, nervousness and defenselessness mixed in a heady concoction.

Slowly, Cole eased back and then broke off the kiss.

Marisa opened her eyes and met Cole's glittering look.

"That did it."

"Wh-what?" she responded, her voice husky.

"You forgot about being panicked."

He was only partly right. She'd forgotten about the small space they were stuck in, all right. But she'd replaced that anxiety with a sexual awareness of him.

She took a small step back and felt the cabinets press up against her. Frowning, and seeking composure, she asked, "How can you kiss a woman you don't even like?"

"You needed a kiss right then."

She flushed. "What I need is to get out of here."

He moved past her and she tensed. One little push and she'd be back in his arms.

She turned and watched him grasp the door handle and turn it hard. At the same time, he shoved his shoulder against the door—once, twice… The door swung open.

Turning back, he smiled faintly. "After you."

She stepped into the hallway with no small relief. Still, she found herself tossing him an accusatory look. "You knew all along that it would open, didn't you?"

"I knew there was nothing stopping it, except maybe a little stickiness from age. Simple deductive logic. It would have occurred to you, too, if you hadn't been panicked and babbling."

"When I think I'm about to suffocate to death, the words flow." Now the only threat to her life was death by embarrassment. What had she confessed? And she'd melted into his arms… "I've got to go. I—I'm sorry. We'll need to reschedule."

"Marisa…"

She backed up a few steps and then turned and walked rapidly down the hall, not waiting for him to lock the storage room. She stopped only to grab her jacket and handbag from Cole's office as she made her way out the building and to her car.

She'd already consoled herself with chocolate cake—what was left?

Five

Cole perused the job site from where he was standing on a muddy rise. His mind was only half on the discussion that he needed to have with his foreman. The other half was on what he had to do about Marisa.

Unlike the construction project in Springfield where Marisa had waylaid him, this one was already at the stage where drywall and electrical had gone in. But he needed to get updates from his crew and hammer out remaining issues so they could come in under budget and on time. The five-story office complex outside Northampton was another one of their big projects.

"Sam is coming down now!" one of his construction crew called.

Cole gave him a brief nod before his thoughts were set adrift again.

He'd put in a call to Pershing's principal soon after Marisa had fled his offices several days ago. He'd covered for her by taking the heat for their meeting falling through. Hell, it was the least he could do after finding out the truth about fifteen years ago. And, he was willing to humor Pershing's principal to get the job done. Never mind that he thought reviewing the plans for prior construction jobs was a waste of time. Every job was unique; everybody knew as much.

Still, he hadn't been able to stop thinking about Marisa. All these years he'd hated her. *No, that wasn't right.* He'd built up a wall and sealed her off from the rest of his life.

Now he understood the choice that Marisa had faced in the principal's office. And yeah, she'd been right on target about the way he'd been in high school. He wouldn't have wanted to hear her confession. Because he'd been a callow eighteen-year-old to whom a high school championship had meant more than it should.

In contrast, Marisa had been an insightful teen. She'd shown that understanding when it had come to Mr. Hayes, and Cole had spurned her for it. But the truth was, Cole had fallen for her back then precisely because she'd seemed self-possessed and different. She'd stood outside the usual shallow preoccupations of their classmates. The truth was she'd been more mature—no doubt because she'd had to grow up fast.

Cole cursed silently.

Marisa had been wrong about one thing, though. *All you cared about was the hockey championship.* He'd cared about her, too...until he'd felt betrayed.

In the storage room, she'd looked at him with her limpid big brown eyes, and he'd stopped himself from touching her face to reassure her. He was sure that if he'd reached for her pulse right then, it would have jumped under his touch.

Then she'd rocked him with her explanation about being called to the mat by Mr. Hayes, and he'd kissed her. The lip-lock had been as good as he'd fantasized, and even better than his memory of high school. She had a way of slipping under his skin and making him hunger...

His pulse started to hum at the thought…and at the anticipation of seeing her again. He just needed to make it happen.

He took out his phone and started typing a text message. She'd called from her cell phone when she'd needed to set up the meeting at Serenghetti's offices to review construction plans, and he'd made note of the number.

Told Dobson our meeting cut short b/c I had other business. Let's reschedule. Dinner Friday @6. LMK.

As soon as he hit Send, he felt his spirits lift.

Spotting his foreman coming toward him, he slipped the phone into the back pocket of his jeans and adjusted his hard hat. There was unfinished business today, and there would be unfinished business on Friday. But first he had a meeting today that was a long time coming.

As soon as his consultation with the foreman was over, Cole drove to his parents' house. He made his way to the back garden, where he knew he'd find his parents, based on what his mother had told him during his call to her earlier.

Serg was ensconced in a wrought-iron chair. Bundled in a jacket and blanket against the nippy air, he looked as if he was dressed for an Alaskan sledding event. Because if there was one thing that Camilla Serenghetti feared, it was someone dear to her *catching a chilly*, as she liked to say. It came second only to the fear that her husband or one of her kids might go hungry. She hovered near a small round patio table littered with a display of fruit, bread, water and tea.

Cole took a seat and began with easy chitchat. Fortunately, the stroke had not affected his father's speech. The conversation touched on Serg's health before veering toward other mundane topics. All the while, however, his father appeared grumpy and tense—as if he sensed there was another purpose to this visit.

Holding back a grimace, Cole took his chance when the talk reached a lull. "I'm looking for buyers for the business."

Serg hit the table with his fist. "Over my dead body."

Cole resisted the urge to point out that it might well come to that—another stroke and Serg was finished. "We're a midsize construction company. Our best bet is a buyout by one of the big players."

Then Cole could get on with his life. Nothing had panned out yet, but there were coaching positions available, and he wanted to grow the business investment portfolio he'd begun to put together thanks to his NHL earnings.

"Never."

"It's not good for you to get upset in your condition, Dad." He'd thought he could have a rational discussion with his father about the future of Serenghetti Construction, because Serg was never going to make a one-hundred-percent recovery. So unless Serenghetti Construction was sold, Cole wouldn't just be a temporary caretaker of the company, but a permanent fixture.

"You know what's not good for me? My son talking about selling the company that I broke my back to build."

Camilla rushed forward. "Lie back against the pillows. Don't upset yourself."

"Dad, be reasonable." Cole fought to keep his frustration at bay. He'd waited months to have this conversation with his father. But now everyone had to face reality. Serg was not going to show more significant improvement. Maybe he could enjoy a productive retirement, but the chances that he'd be fit to head a demanding business again were slim. The discussion about the future had to start now.

"What's wrong with the company that you want to sell it?"

"It needs to grow or die."

"And you're not interested in growing it?"

Cole let silence be his answer.

"I heard you outmaneuvered JM to get the contract to build a new gym at the Pershing School."

Cole figured Serg had been informed about the gym

contract on one of his occasional phone calls to Serenghetti Construction's head offices. His father liked to speak to senior employees and stay clued in on what was going on beyond what Cole had time to tell him. Cole had told no one at the office about his bargain with Marisa beyond the fact that Serenghetti Construction had managed to stay a step ahead of its competitor JM Construction.

"Grow or die!" Serg gestured as if there was an audience aside from Camilla. "This company paid for your college degree and your hockey training. There's nothing wrong with it."

"Serenghetti Construction is not the little train that could, Dad." The company needed fresh blood at the helm in order to steer it into the future. Serg, like many founders, had taken it as far as he could. And if Cole wasn't careful, he himself would be captaining the ship for decades ahead.

"So what are you going to do instead that's more important?" Serg groused, shifting in his chair and nearly knocking over his cane. "Go be a hockey coach?"

Cole wasn't surprised his father guessed the direction of his thoughts. He'd interviewed for a coaching job with the Madison Rockets last fall, but having heard nothing further, he'd kept the news to himself. If a position materialized, there was no question that his time at the helm of Serenghetti Construction would need to come to an end because he couldn't keep jobs in different states—not to mention the travel involved in a coaching position.

Serg snapped his brows together. "Coaching is a hard lifestyle if you have a family and a couple of kids." He glowered. "Or is that something else you're planning to do differently from the old man? Another part of your heritage that you're planning to reject?"

"Getting married and having kids is hardly part of my heritage, Dad." More like a lifestyle choice, but Serg had jumped ahead several steps.

"Well, we damn sure don't speak the same language anymore! How's that for losing your heritage?"

"Serg, calm down," Camilla said, looking worried. "You know what the *dottore* said."

Camilla had always been the one to run interference between her husband and children. Cole also had a hunch that his mother had more empathy than his father about lifelong dreams and their postponement. His mother had her own second career as a television chef.

"The blood thinners will take care of me—" Serg harrumphed before shooting Cole a pointed look "—even if my children won't."

"I'll take care of you," Camilla said firmly.

Cole looked at his parents. "Well, this is a turnaround."

Serg frowned. "What? Stop speaking in riddles."

Cole wasn't sure his pronouncement would be welcome. "Suddenly Mom is the one with a career, and she's promising to support you."

"You always were a smart aleck," his father grumbled. "Maybe even a bigger one than your brother."

"Which one?" Cole quipped—because both Jordan and Rick qualified—and then stood up. "I'm going to let you continue to rest. I have a couple of calls to return for work."

"Rest! That's all anyone wants me to do around here."

Cole figured if he could rest, he'd be ahead of the game right now. But he had demands on his time, not the least of which was a certain wild-tressed schoolteacher who'd come crashing back into his life...

"Hi, Mom."

"Honey!" Donna Casale rushed forward, delight stamped on her face as she left her front door wide open behind her.

For Marisa, it was like looking at an older version of herself. Fortunately, the future in that regard didn't look too shabby. Her mother appeared younger than fifty-four. Donna Casale had maintained the shapely figure that had attracted male interest all her life—leaving her alone and pregnant at twenty-three, but also permitting her to attract a second admiring glance even after age fifty. And years in the retail trade meant she always looked polished and presentable: hair colored, makeup on and smile beaming. Of course, marriage might also have something to do with it these days. Her mother seemed *happy*.

Marisa felt a pang at the contrast to her own circumstances as she let herself be enveloped in a hug. Her mother and Ted had bought a tidy three-bedroom wood-frame house at the time of their wedding. Marisa and Sal had begun talking about buying a home themselves during their brief engagement, but those plans had gone nowhere.

When her mother pulled back from their embrace, she said, "Come on in. You're early, but I couldn't be happier to see you. You're so busy these days!"

Marisa *tried* to keep occupied. She'd plunged back into work after her breakup with Sal, taking on additional roles at Pershing in order to advance her career and keep her mind off depressing thoughts.

Donna closed the front door, and Marisa followed her toward the back of the house.

"I'm so glad you're staying for dinner," Donna said over her shoulder, leading the way down the hall.

"It's a welcome break, Mom, and you spoil me." Still, Marisa wanted to give her mother and Ted their space so they could enjoy their relatively new married life.

"Well, you're just in time to help me assemble the lasagna," her mother said with a laugh, "so you'll be working for your supper. Ted will be home soon."

When they reached a small but recently remodeled kitchen, Marisa draped her things on a chair, and her mother went to the counter crowded with ingredients and bowls.

Marisa's gaze settled on a framed photo of Donna and Ted on their low-key wedding day. Donna and Ted were all smiles in the picture, her mother clutching a small sprig of flowers that complemented a cream satin tea-length dress. Marisa had been their sole attendant, and one of their witnesses, because Ted had been childless before his marriage.

Marisa bit back a wistful sigh. She and her mother had always been each other's confidantes—the two of them against the world—but now her mom had someone else. Marisa couldn't have been happier for her.

It was just… It was just… An image of Cole rose to mind.

What had she been thinking? What had he? He'd kissed her in the storage room last week—and she'd kissed him back. And the memory of that kiss had lingered…replayed before she went to sleep at night, while driving to work and during breaks in the school day.

The teenage Cole had nothing on Cole the man. He'd made her come apart in his arms, and it had both shocked and thrilled her. She'd been under the influence at the time, of course. Panic and proximity—mixed with the confession of long-held secrets—had made a heady brew while they'd been locked in together.

Her mother glanced at her, her brows drawing together in concern. "You seem worried. Are you taking care of yourself?"

The question was one that Marisa was used to. Ever since she'd been born a preemie, her mother had worried about her health. She gave a practiced smile. "I'm fine."

"Well, you were a fighter from day one."

Marisa continued smiling, and as she usually did whenever her mother's worries came to the fore, she tried to move the conversation in a different direction. "Serafina found an apartment and is moving out tomorrow."

"I heard."

"I'll have my apartment to myself." Even before her cousin had moved in, she'd hardly felt as if she lived alone. She and Sal had been serious enough that he'd often been at her place or he'd been at hers.

"You should get married."

Marisa bit back another sigh. She hadn't succeeded in steering the talk to safer waters. "I was engaged. It didn't work out."

Ever since her mother had met and then married Ted, she'd viewed marriage in a different light.

"So?" Donna persisted. "He wasn't the right man. You'll meet someone else."

Marisa parted her lips as Cole sprung to mind. *No.* He was her past, not her future, even if he occupied her present. *Get a grip.* "Mom, I know you're still a bit of a newlywed, so you're looking at the world through rose-colored glasses, but—"

Her mother sobered. "Honey, how can you say so? I may be newly married, but I haven't forgotten the years of struggle…"

Donna's amber eyes—so like Marisa's own—clouded, as if recollections of the past were flashing by. Marisa wondered what those memories were. Was her mother recalling the same things she was? The years of juggling bill payments—staying one short step away from having the electricity turned off? The credit card balances that were rolled over because Donna was too proud to ask relatives for a loan?

"I know, Mom," Marisa said quietly. "I was there."

Donna sighed. "And that's part of my guilt."

"What?"

"I didn't shield you enough. Your childhood wasn't as secure as I would have liked it to be."

"You did your best." Wasn't she always telling her students to try their best? "I always felt loved. I graduated from a great school, got a college degree and have a great job."

"Still, I wish you had someone to lean on. I'm not going to be around forever."

"Mom, you're only fifty-four!" In that moment, however, Marisa understood. While she'd worried about her mother, her mother had reciprocated with concern about her.

"I wish I'd left you with siblings," her mother said wistfully.

"You could barely handle me!" Besides, she had cousins. Serafina for one.

"You were a good girl. Mr. Hayes at the Pershing School even came up to me on graduation day to tell me so, and that I'd done a great job raising you."

Marisa smothered a wince and then walked over to the kitchen sink to wash and dry her hands. Naturally, Mr. Hayes had thought she was one of the good guys. She'd ratted out Cole... Marisa had kept her mother in the dark about that part of her life. She hadn't wanted her mother burdened any more than she was.

"How is your job at Pershing, by the way?" Donna asked. "Are the kids taking a lot out of you?"

It wasn't the kids who were responsible for her current turmoil, but a certain six-foot-plus former hockey player. "I'm in charge of the big Pershing Shines Bright benefit in May."

"Ted and I will be there, of course. We want to support you."

"Thanks." Marisa eyed the pasta machine. "You've been busy."

"One of the benefits of having the day off from work. I made the pasta sheets for the lasagna from scratch."

Marisa picked up one of the sheets and set it down in a pan that her mother had already coated with tomato sauce.

"Is the planning going well?" Donna probed.

"It's fine." Marisa shrugged. "Cole Serenghetti of the New England Razors has agreed to headline."

Donna brought her hands together. "Wonderful. He's so popular around here."

Tell me about it. "He's not playing professional hockey anymore. He got hurt."

"Oh yes, I had heard that." Donna frowned. "He was such

a good player in high school... Well, until the incident that earned him a suspension."

Marisa kept her expression neutral. "He's running the family construction business these days, though I'm not sure how happy he is about it. His father had a stroke."

Donna's gaze was searching. "You do seem to know a lot about Cole."

"Don't worry, Mom," Marisa responded, setting down more sheets of pasta for the lasagna. "I also knew a lot about Sal before he dumped me. Once burned, twice shy."

"*Dumped* is such an ugly word," Donna said lightly. "*Fortuitously disengaged* is the way I put it for members of my book club."

"Are you doing ad copy for the department store circular these days?" Marisa quipped.

"No, but I did suggest to the book club that we read *Dump the Dude, Buy the Shoes*."

They shared a laugh before Marisa said, "You did not!"

Actually she thought the title might not be a bad one for the autobiography of her mother's life.

"No, I was joking. But I did tell everyone that I got promoted to buyer for housewares." Donna spooned a thin layer of ricotta cheese mixture on top of the layer of pasta that Marisa had created.

"They must have been thrilled for you." Before Marisa could say any more, she heard her cell phone buzz. Wiping her hands on a dish towel, she walked over to get the phone out of her handbag. When she saw the message on the screen, her heart began to pound.

Told Dobson our meeting cut short b/c I had other business. Let's reschedule. Dinner Friday @6. LMK.

"Is everything okay?" Donna asked, studying her.

"Speak of the devil," Marisa said, trying for some lame humor. "No, not Sal. The other devil. Cole Serenghetti."

Donna's eyebrows rose. "He's texting you? So you do know each other well!"

"First time. He must have a record of my cell number—" she paused to consider for a moment, thinking back "—because I had to call him to discuss something related to the fund-raiser and new gym." She was *not* going to mention to her mother that she'd visited Cole's offices. Because that might lead to mention of the incident in the storage room. And she was *so* not discussing that mishap. Especially with her mother. Even if she was thirty-three and an adult.

"Well?"

"He's invited me to dinner." As her mother's eyebrows shot higher, she added, "A business dinner."

She should go. She was grateful that he'd covered for her with Mr. Dobson. She was also relieved he was willing to keep dealing with her about the fund-raiser and construction project. It wouldn't look good if Cole announced he needed a different contact person at Pershing. And she had twenty questions about what he had to say—who wouldn't?

Dinner? Really?

Still, it wasn't as if they were having an assignation. As she'd told her mother, it was a business meeting. Pure business. The kiss last time notwithstanding. A blip on the radar never, ever to be repeated.

And now that Cole had agreed to the fund-raiser, she'd begun flirting with another idea—that is, until the storage room incident...

Donna continued to regard her. "Honey, trust me, I'm acquainted with the attractiveness of professional athletes."

Marisa knew they were no longer talking only about Cole. They'd both been burned long ago by another man chasing sports fame, except he'd been a baseball player. "This is purely business, believe me."

Marisa wished she could wholeheartedly believe it herself. So she and Cole had shared a kiss. Given the unusual circumstances—her panic and his need to reassure and, uh, comfort—they had an excuse. One that her mother didn't need to hear.

As her mother searched her expression, Marisa stuck to her best Girl Scout face and walked back to the kitchen counter.

Finally, seemingly satisfied—or not—Donna sighed. "We should find time to write that dude book together. Meanwhile, let's finish this lasagna, and I'll open a bottle of wine."

"What's this about, Cole?"

"Dinner. What else?" He looked bemusedly at the woman sitting to his left—the one who had bedeviled more of his nights and days than he cared to count. He'd chosen Welsdale's chicest restaurant, Bayart's on Creek Road, and she'd proposed meeting him there—much to his chagrin. He'd gone along with her suggestion, even though he saw through it as the defensive move it was, because he knew he was still treading on fragile ground with Marisa. He'd ordered a bottle of Merlot, and the waiter had already poured their wine.

Tonight she was in a geometric-print wrap dress that left no curve untouched. *My God, the woman is set on torturing me.*

"I mean the subtext."

He raised his gaze to her eyes. "Subtext? You were always a stellar student in English."

"And you spent your time in the last row, goofing around."

"Charlotte Brontë wasn't my thing."

"She was about the only female who wasn't."

"She was dead."

"Don't let that stop you."

He grinned. "That's what I discovered I liked about you, Danieli. You're able to serve it up straight when you want to. Back then, and now."

"I'm a teacher. It's a survival skill."

"I liked you better than you think, you know."

"Well, that's something, I suppose. Right up there with being someone's sixth favorite teacher."

He laughed because he liked this more uninhibited Marisa—one who felt free to speak her mind. "Still feeling the effect of your confession last time? You're letting it rip. It's—" he let his voice dip "—enticing."

She got an adorable little pucker in her brow and toyed with the stem of her wineglass. "It wasn't intended to be, but why am I not surprised you took it that way?"

"I really did like you," he insisted.

"You're just saying that," she demurred.

"Are you ready to talk about what happened in the storage room?" It was safer than focusing on the wineglass in her hand and imagining her fingers on him.

They could have been on a date, from outward appearances, because Bayart's candlelit interior invited intimacy. In keeping with the restaurant's formality, Cole was still in the navy suit that he'd worn to the office. And Marisa was probably expecting tonight to be all business...

"Wow, you're direct." Marisa blew out a breath. "Isn't it obvious? We're destined for close encounters in small spaces."

He smiled at her attempt at humor and deflection. "Try again." When she still said nothing, he continued, "I'll go first. I wonder what you saw in me while we were in high school. I was a jock and a jerk."

She joined him in smiling, and it was like the sun coming out. "That's an easy one. I admired you. You were willing to take risks. On the ice, you took chances in order to win. And off the ice, you skated on the edge with your pranks. I was meek, and you were confident. I was quiet, and you were popular."

"I was a jerk, and you weren't."

She blinked, and the curve of her lips wobbled.

"Fat lot of good it did me, too. I ultimately wound up

crashing and burning, on the ice and off." It was his offer of a mea culpa—accepting guilt and responsibility. Fifteen years ago she'd called a halt to his pranks. And if he'd been a jerk in the aftermath, it had been for nothing. He'd still gotten a professional career on the ice, and when it had ended, it had had nothing to do with Marisa.

"You know what they say. Better to have tried and failed than never to have tried at all…"

"You've never taken risks?" he probed.

"Well, I did recruit you for the Pershing benefit. I guess you bring out the daredevil in me."

"Yeah," he drawled. "The same way I tempted you to test out the theater department's prop during senior year."

Marisa looked embarrassed.

Before he could say more, the waiter came up to take their order. Marisa waffled on what to have, but settled on the Cobb salad.

"You can't choose a salad," Cole said with dry humor. "It's a sin in a place like this."

"It's not," she responded lightly. "I'm sure everything is delicious here."

Including her. He could tell she'd contemplated ordering a richer entrée, and he wanted to say he appreciated every inch of her lush curves, but he let it go. Maybe a salad was Marisa's go-to choice on a date—not that she thought of this as a date, but certainly dinner with a man. *Him.*

When the waiter had departed, the conversation turned to casual topics, but Cole was determined to shift gears back to what they had been discussing.

At a lull, he said, "It must have given you some satisfaction to see me taken down a peg or two in high school. After all, we did have sex, and then I avoided you."

"It hurt."

"I wasn't prepared to deal with what had happened between us. You were a virgin, and you caught me off guard. I might not have hurt you when we fumbled our way through sex, but I did in other ways."

She lowered her lashes. "We were both young and stupid."

"Teenagers make mistakes," he concurred.

She toyed some more with the wineglass, making him crazy. "It must have been an unwelcome surprise when we were first paired up to make a PowerPoint presentation in economics class."

"Not unwelcome," he replied, shifting. "You were an unknown quantity."

"A nonentity at school, especially among the jocks."

He shook his head. "Sweet pea, you may be a teacher, but you still have no idea how most teenage boys think. The only reason the jocks didn't know how big your breasts were is because you were always hiding them behind a bunch of books."

She stared at him. "You were looking at my chest?"

He smiled wolfishly. "On the sly. And I wasn't just looking. Do you think that whenever I brushed by you during our study sessions it was an accident?"

Her eyes widened, and her hand fell away from the wineglass.

"Definitely a C cup."

"I'm not a simple bra size!"

He reached out and covered her hand on the table, smoothing his thumb over the back of her palm. *Anything to avoid further arousal by her fingertips on a damn glass.* "You're right. I got to know the person beyond the teenage boy's fantasy, and you scared the hell out of me."

"I did?"

The look in her eyes was so earnest, it was all he could do not to lean in and capture her lips.

Instead, he nodded. "I started out a little intrigued and a whole lot bored when I was assigned as your partner in economics. But then I got near you, and the hormones kicked in. A few study sessions staring into your eyes, and I was toast. You were nice, smart and interesting."

"I had a crush on you even before we were paired up to do an assignment," she admitted. "All it took was some casual contact, and I was hooked."

"I didn't need a whole lot of convincing to ditch the books in favor of getting closer to you." They had progressed from kissing to more the next time they were together. And then after a few encounters, they'd really gotten intimate…

"But I bet I'm the first girl who got you involved with a theater department prop."

"I'll never forget that velvet sofa." As a scholarship student, Marisa had had a part-time job helping the custodial department clean the school, so she'd had access to a very convenient set of keys.

"They still have it."

He raised his brows. "Then you'll have to give me a tour when I'm at the school."

She parted her lips, but didn't take the bait, so he slid back his hand.

He angled his head, contemplating her. "You wanted me as badly as I wanted you, so I was surprised when it turned out to be your first time. Why did you do it?"

She shrugged. "I was hungry for affection and attention. I wanted to fit in."

"You were a virgin. You'd gotten under my skin and seen beyond the prankster and the jock. It was too heavy for me, so I did the only logical thing for an eighteen-year-old guy. I avoided you."

"Right, I recall," she said drily.

"You were the first woman to proposition me."

"But not the last."

"For professional athletes, propositioning usually goes with the territory."

"So women like Vicki the Vixen are always throwing themselves at you in bars?"

He bit back a smile at the moniker he was sure Vicki wouldn't appreciate. "I'm not a hockey player anymore. These days I'm a CEO…and Pershing School's knight in shining armor."

The waiter arrived with their food, and they dropped their conversation while plates were set before them and they exchanged polite niceties with their server. Then Marisa tucked daintily into her Cobb salad while Cole mentally shrugged and dug into his filet mignon and potatoes au gratin.

After several moments Marisa took a sip of her wine. "You called yourself Pershing's knight in shining armor." She paused. "And I, uh, have another way for you to shine."

He searched her face, and she cleared her throat.

"I have students who would enjoy a field trip to the Razors' arena as part of Career Week."

He sat back in his chair, his lips twisting with amusement. "It's one request after another with you."

"Since you seem to be more approachable these days, I figured I had nothing to lose."

"I don't come cheap."

"I know. Last time you got a construction contract out of the bargain."

He inclined his head in acknowledgment. Ever since their encounter in the storage room, he'd thought about how it would feel to cup her face in his hands again and thread his fingers in her hair. He'd bet her long curly locks fanned across his pillow would be spectacular—and erotic.

"So what's it going to be this time?" she asked.

He could think of a lot of things he'd like to bargain for. "An answer to a question. I'm curious."

She looked surprised and then wary. "That's it?"

He felt a smile tug at his lips. "You haven't heard the question yet."

She shifted in her seat. "Okay..."

"Why Sal? There are a lot of seemingly reliable, boring guys out there."

She stared at him a moment, eyes wide, and then took a deep breath. "Timing."

"I can appreciate the importance. Timing is everything, on the ice and off."

"Yes, and ours has never been great."

He had to agree with her there. "And Sal's was?"

"It was part of it."

"Which part?"

"My mother had just gotten married..."

"And Sal was available when you were vulnerable?"

"Something like that," she admitted.

"I can understand family responsibility, Marisa. Your mother getting married set you free and maybe even adrift."

She looked surprised by his insight. Hell, he was surprised himself. Where had that bit of pop psychology come from? Too much latent baggage from his own family floating to the surface?

Marisa wet her lips. "I guess I didn't want my mother to worry about me anymore once she was married."

"So Sal had it on timing?" *As opposed to a former hockey player?*

"He can also be quite charming when he wants to be."

"So is a used car salesman," Cole quipped. "So Sal laid on the charm...?"

"He was there, and the type I was looking for."

Cole quirked his lips. "You have a type? I thought your type was high school prankster."

She shook her head. "My goal was to marry someone not like my father."

"You knew him?" He didn't recall Marisa ever mentioning her father in high school except to say he'd died a long time ago.

"No, he passed away before I was born. But I'd always

thought my parents had meant to get married. In my twenties, I found out that wasn't the case…"

Cole said nothing, waiting for her to go on.

"My mother finally revealed my father had broken up with her even before he died in a car accident. He was out of the picture before she gave birth."

"So your father's side of the family was never involved in your life?"

Marisa nodded. "My father's only surviving relative was my grandfather, who lived on the West Coast. As for my father, he was pursuing a minor league baseball career, and a wife and baby didn't fit with his plans. He had big dreams and wanderlust."

"So you believed Sal was the guy for you because he wasn't bitten by the same bug."

"I thought he was the right man. I was wrong."

Cole suddenly understood. Marisa had thought Sal would never leave her. He wasn't a professional athlete whose career came first. In other words, Sal was unlike her father… and unlike Cole, who'd left Welsdale at the first opportunity for hockey.

Marisa had discovered the truth about her father long after she'd finished high school at Pershing. So if Cole's reaction after missing out on a potential hockey championship at Pershing hadn't soured her on athletes, then the truth she learned about her father in her twenties certainly would have.

As Marisa steered the conversation back to scheduling a student field trip to the Razors' arena, as well as setting up another time for her to review Serenghetti Construction's old architectural plans, Cole realized one thing.

He'd had his chance with Marisa at eighteen, but these days she was looking for something—someone—different.

Six

Marisa had never been inside the New England Razors arena, which was located outside Springfield, Massachusetts. The closeness to the state border allowed the team to attract a sizable crowd from nearby Connecticut as well as from their home base, Massachusetts.

Marisa had just never counted herself among those fans. She'd always felt that going to a game would be a painful blast from the past where Cole was concerned. The Razors' games were televised, but she could handle Cole Serenghetti's power over her memories—sort of—when it was limited to a glimpse of a screen in a restaurant or other public place.

Right now, however, she was getting the full Cole Serenghetti effect as he stood a few feet away addressing a group of Pershing high school students. He was dressed in faded blue jeans and a long-sleeved black tee. His clothing was casual, but no less potent on her senses. She was sensitive to his every move, and was having a hard time denying what it was: sexual awareness.

"Look," Cole said to the kids arrayed before him in a

semicircle inside the front entrance, "since it's a Saturday and this is a half-day field trip, we'll do a tour of the arena first and then some ice-skating. How does that sound?"

Some kids smiled, and others nodded their heads.

"And how many of you want to be professional hockey players?"

A few hands shot up. Marisa was glad to see those of three girls among them. Pershing fielded both boys' and girls' hockey teams, but the girls tended to drop out at a higher rate than the boys once they hit high school.

One of the students raised his hand. "Does your injury still bother you?"

Marisa sucked in a breath.

"It's important to wear protective equipment," Cole said. "Injuries do happen, but they're unusual, especially the serious ones."

The kids remained silent, as if they expected him to go on.

"In my case, I tore up my knee twice. I had surgery and therapy both times. After the second, I could walk without a problem, but playing professional hockey wasn't in the cards." Cole's tone was even and matter-of-fact, and he betrayed no hint that the subject was a touchy one for him. "I was past thirty, and I'd already had several great seasons with the New England Razors. I had another career calling me."

"So now you do construction?" a student piped up from the back row.

Cole gave a self-deprecating laugh. "Yup. But as CEO, I spend more time in the office than on a job site. I make sure we stay within our budget and that resources are allocated correctly among projects." He cast Marisa a sidelong look. "I also go out and drum up more business."

Marisa felt heat flood her cheeks even though she was the only one who could guess what Cole was alluding to.

A few days ago she and Cole had finally had their intended meeting at his offices to go over architectural plans for past projects. When she'd shown up this time, Cole had had the plans ready for review in a conference room. She must have appeared relieved that she wouldn't have to step back inside Serenghetti Construction's storage room, because Cole had shot her an amused and knowing look. Still, she'd gotten enough information to go back to Mr. Dobson with no surprises but some valuable input.

Fortunately, they hadn't had the opportunity to discuss their encounter in the storage room. Every time Cole had looked as if he was about to bring it up, they'd been interrupted by a phone call or by an employee with a question.

Cole scanned the small crowd assembled before him. "Today I'm going to show you career fields connected to hockey that you might not have thought of. Sure there are the players on the ice that everyone sees during the game. Their names make the news. But behind them is a whole other team of people who make professional hockey what it is."

"Like who?" a couple of kids asked, speaking over each other.

"Well, I'm going to take you to the broadcast booth, in case anyone is interested in sports journalism. We'll walk through the management offices to talk to marketing. And then we'll go down to the locker rooms, where the sports medicine people do their stuff. Sound good?"

The kids nodded.

"I'll stop before I show you the construction stuff," Cole quipped.

"Is that how you stayed involved with your old sport?" a ninth grader asked.

"Yup." Cole flashed a smile. "We repaved the ground outside the arena."

From her position a little removed from the crowd, Marisa sighed because Cole had a natural ability to connect with kids. He was effortlessly cool, and she was...not. Some things never changed.

Cole winked at her, shaking her out of her musings. "And if you're all good, there might also be an appearance by Jordan Serenghetti—"

The kids let out whoops.

"—who is having a great season with the Razors. But more important, in my opinion, he's having an even better life as my younger brother."

Everyone laughed.

Marisa thought Jordan would dispute Cole's assessment if he were there.

After Cole gave the kids a tour of the parts of the arena that he had referred to, he led the group to the ice rink.

As everyone laced up their skates, Marisa overheard a couple of the kids talking about her with Cole. When they mentioned to him that she was a fantastic cook, she felt heat rush to her face.

She hung back and skated onto the ice after everyone else. She was wearing tights and a tunic-length sweater so her movements weren't restricted, but she hadn't been on skates in a long time. She became aware of Cole watching her, hands in pockets, as the others glided around.

"I wasn't sure what to expect," he said.

She continued to skate at a leisurely pace, now only a few feet away from him. "I've had ice-skating lessons."

He arched a brow.

"It's New England. Everyone assumes you know how to stay upright on the ice."

To underscore her words, she did several swizzles, her legs swerving in and out.

"Looks like you did more than learn how to stay upright," Cole commented. "Where did you learn?"

"At the rec center outside Welsdale," she admitted, slowing. "It opened when we were kids, and they gave free lessons."

"I know. My father built it."

She stared at him and then gave an unsurprised laugh. "I should have guessed."

She thought a moment, concentrated and then gaining speed, did a scratch spin. Glancing back at Cole, now meters away, she shrugged and added, "I picked up a few moves."

She wasn't sure how many moves she could still do, but it seemed that as with riding a bike, some skills she'd never lose.

"So when did you change course from budding skating star to top-notch teacher?" Cole asked as he skated toward her.

She shrugged again. "We didn't have the money for me to pursue the sport seriously. It would have meant lessons, costumes and travel expenses. When I was accepted to Pershing, I had to concentrate on getting good grades in order to keep my scholarship."

She tensed as soon as the word *scholarship* was out of her mouth because they were close to the big bugaboo topic between them. Still, the truth was that Cole had gotten to play in the NHL while she'd received her coveted scholarship and moved on to teaching—a nice, stable profession rather than glitz and glory. He'd been able to afford his dreams while she hadn't.

"I was signed up for figure skating and ice dancing lessons as a kid—"

She laughed because she couldn't envision Cole doing the waltz—on the ice or off. He was too big…too male.

"—but they didn't take," he finished drily.

She bit the inside of her cheek, trying to school her expression. She was a lot better at keeping a straight face in the classroom.

"My mother was determined to make her sons into little gentlemen."

Marisa willed herself to appear earnest. *Instead Mrs. Serenghetti had gotten a bunch of pranksters.*

"You think this is funny."

She nodded, not trusting herself to speak.

"Here, I'll demonstrate," he said, approaching. "I remember a thing or two."

She blinked. "What?"

"We're here to show these kids careers related to hockey."

"Like ice dancing? I thought that branching out usually went the other way."

"Like if you sucked at ice dancing as a kid, you took up hockey instead?"

She raised her eyebrows.

"So now I'm a failed figure skater? Someone who couldn't hack it?" He rubbed his chin. "I have something to prove."

She didn't like the sound of that. But before she could respond, he reached for her hand and then slid his other around her waist, so that they were facing each other in dance position.

"What are you doing?" she asked in a high voice, caught between surprise and breathlessness at his nearness.

"Like I said, I have something to prove. I hope you remember your figure skating moves, sweet pea."

The arm around her was a band of pure muscle. He worked out, and it showed. The power he exuded made her nervous, so she didn't raise her gaze above his mouth—though *that* had potency enough to wreak havoc on her heart.

She and Cole skated over the ice, doing a fair facsimile of dancing together. His hands on her were warm imprints, heating her against the cold of the ice.

When she stole a peek at him, she quickly concluded he was still devastatingly gorgeous. His hair was thick and ruffled, inviting a woman to run her fingers through it. His jaw was firm and square but shadowed, promising a hint of roughness. His lips were firm but sensual. And the scar—oh, the scar. The one on his cheek gave character and invited tenderness. He was a catalog of sexy contrasts—a magnet for women in a much blunter way than Jordan. She lowered her lashes. *But not for me.*

"Are you ready for a throw jump?"

Her gaze shot to his. "What?" She sounded like a parrot but she couldn't have heard him right. "I thought we were just dancing! What about your knee?"

He shrugged. "It couldn't take repeated hits from a defenseman who weighs over two hundred pounds, but I'm guessing you don't weigh nearly as much."

"I'm not telling you how much I weigh!"

"Naturally." Cole's eyes crinkled. "Here we go, Ice Princess. Think you can land a throw waltz jump?"

In the next moment they were spinning around and Cole was lifting her off the ice.

"Ready?" he murmured.

She felt herself moving through the air. It was a gentle throw, so she didn't go very high or far. She brought down the toe of her right foot and landed her blade before extending her left leg back.

Cole grinned, and the kids around them on the ice laughed and clapped while a few chortled.

"A one-footed landing," Cole said, skating toward her. "I'm impressed. You've still got game, sweet pea."

She laughed. "Still, can you see me competing in the Olympics?" she asked, gesturing at her ample chest. "I'd have had to bind myself."

Cole gave her a half-lidded look as he stopped in front of her. "Now that would be a shame."

She'd walked into that one. Students glided by around them, and there were a few gasps as Jordan appeared. This was hardly the place for Cole and her to be having a sexually tinged moment.

"Relax," Cole said in a low voice. "Nobody is paying attention to us anymore."

Easy for you to say. She tingled with the urge to touch him again. "Cole Serenghetti, too cool for school."

"If you were the teacher, I'd have had my butt glued to my seat in the front row."

"You say that now," she teased, even as his nearness continued to affect her like a drug.

"I was a callow teenager who couldn't appreciate what you were going through."

"Callow?" she queried, still trying to keep it light. "Are you trying to impress the teacher with your vocabulary?"

He bent his head until his lips were inches from hers. "How am I doing?"

Oh wow. "Great," she said a bit breathlessly. "Keep at it, and you might even get an A."

It was the pep talk that she usually gave her students. *Keep trying, work hard and the reward will come...* The moral of her own life story, really. Well, except for her *love* life...

Cole's eyes gleamed as he straightened and murmured, "I've never cared about grades."

She didn't want to ask what he did care about. She'd guess his currency of choice was kisses—and more... Troublingly, she could seriously envision getting tangled up with Cole again even though she should know better...

Cole swiveled on his bar stool and looked at the entrance again.

This time he was finally rewarded with the sight of Marisa coming toward him. She was wearing jeans—ones that hugged her curves—and a mint-colored sweater. She had on light makeup, but it was a toss-up whether her curls or her chest was bouncier.

Cole felt his groin tighten.

He hadn't been sure she would show. His text had been vague.

Meet me at the Puck & Shoot. I have a plan u need to hear.

Ever since he'd upheld his end of the bargain by giving her students a tour of the Razors' arena, he'd been desperate to come up with another excuse to see her.

She stopped in front of him. "I heard women proposition you in bars these days."

"Care to make one?"

"How about a drink instead?"

"That's a start." He stood, closing the distance between them even further. "What'll you have?"

"A light beer."

Cole fought a smile. "Lightweight, are you?"

"Only in bars, not in the boxing ring."

"Yeah, I know." At the gym, she could pack a wallop in a simple dress that brought grown men to a standstill. But she wasn't too shabby in bars, either. She could still make him stand up and take notice. Without the baggage of her seeming betrayal in high school, he could acknowledge without reservation what a beautiful woman she was.

He signaled the bartender and placed an order.

She glanced around, as if uncertain. "This is my first visit to the Puck & Shoot."

"I thought you said this is where you got a tip about how to run me to ground at Jimmy's Boxing Gym."

"I wouldn't call it *running to ground*," she said pertly. "You were still standing when I left the boxing ring. Also, I didn't say I got the tip personally. My cousin Serafina has been moonlighting as a waitress here. She overheard some of the Razors talking."

"Like those at the other end of the bar?" Cole indicated with his chin. "The ones wondering what the status of our relationship is?"

Marisa tossed a glance over her shoulder. "Probably, but we don't have a relationship with a status."

He brought his finger to his lips. "Shh, don't tell. I like having them wonder why a gorgeous woman passed them over and made a beeline in my direction instead."

"You asked me to come here!"

He laughed at her with his eyes. "They don't know that, sweet pea." He reached out to smooth a strand of hair away from her face and remembered all over again how soft her skin was.

His body tightened another notch and she stilled, like a deer in headlights.

"I don't think Serafina likes the Razors very much…"

He settled his gaze on her mouth. "They can be a randy bunch."

"You included?"

"I'll let you be the judge," he responded lazily.

He wanted her. *Right now.* He'd dreamed about her again last night, and it had been his hottest fantasy ever.

"Jordan isn't the only joker in the family."

He handed her the beer that had just been set down on the bar and then watched as Marisa placed her lips on the bottle's long neck and took a swill. The woman was killing him with her sexual tone deafness.

"So where's Serafina?" he asked.

Marisa lowered the bottle. "She isn't working tonight. Wednesday isn't on her regular schedule, and she's about to quit for a better position."

"If this had been her shift, would you have met me here?"

"Maybe."

He smiled. "Or maybe not."

He took it as a good sign that Marisa wanted to keep their meetings on the down-low. It meant she cared what people thought about the two of them. *Like maybe there was something going on.* Which there was, whether Marisa would admit it or not. Still, she was skittish about the sexual attraction that still existed between them, and he needed to proceed carefully.

They were both adults, and he was itching to explore what had gotten cut short in high school. As long as he was indefinitely parked in Welsdale, there was no reason not to enjoy himself...

He let his gaze sweep over her. Besides the jeans and sweater, she wore black high-heeled Mary-Janes that showed off her shapely legs. She'd subverted the most school-marmish of shoes and made them sexy and hot...

Marisa raised her eyebrows as if she'd read his thoughts. "Why did you want to meet?"

Because he wasn't ready to share his sexy thoughts, he leaned against the bar stool behind him and gestured to the empty one next to him. "Have a seat."

"Thank you, but I'm fine."

Definitely skittish. Even leaning back, he still had a height advantage on her, but he had to admire her unwill-ingness to give an additional inch. Time to show some of his cards. "I noticed some of the kids on the field trip were interested in hockey. I'd like to give them a few pointers."

His offer, of course, was a pretext for getting her to meet with him again.

Marisa took her time answering, her face reflecting flit-ting emotions until it settled into an expression of determi-nation. "I don't just want you to give them a few pointers. I want you to run a hockey clinic."

Right back at you. He'd underestimated her. "That's a tall order. Giving a few pointers is one thing, and setting up a sports clinic is another. Let me clarify in case you don't understand—"

"Never having been a jock."

"—but training sessions involve drawing up practice plans and small area games—"

"So the kids will have others to play against."

"—and it's a big investment of time."

"You're up to the challenge," she ended encouragingly.

What he was up for was getting her into bed. "I'll tell you what. I'll start with informal coaching for a small group."

She nodded and smiled. "Now that that's settled, let's discuss the remarks you'll be giving at the fund-raiser."

The woman didn't miss a beat. But now it was his turn to hit the puck back at her. "If you search online, you'll come up with my past speeches. My talk to the sports group in Boston on working hard and realizing your dreams. My humorous anecdotes about my rookie year in the NHL—"

"You'll want to say something flattering about the Pershing School." She looked earnest as she said it.

"And my time there?" he queried. "How do I work in my suspension—" he leaned forward confidentially "—or the episode on the theater department's casting couch?"

She shifted. "I thought we'd established I didn't land you a suspension out of retaliation."

"No, but I still think of it as a...highlight of my high school career. How do I discuss my time at Pershing without mentioning it?"

"Stick to sports and academics," she sidestepped. "And it wasn't a casting couch. You're not a Hollywood starlet who had to put out for the sake of her career."

He grinned. "Yeah, but you were definitely auditioning me for the role of study buddy with benefits. How did I do?"

"Could have been better," she harrumphed.

"I am now, sweet pea. Don't you want to find out how much better?" He liked teasing her, and what's more, he couldn't help it.

Her gaze skittered away from his and then stopped in the distance, her eyes widening.

She looked back at him and flushed.

Before he could react, she leaned forward, cupped his face with both her hands and pressed her lips to his.

What the...? It was Cole's last thought before he went motionless.

Her lips felt soft and full, and she tasted sweet. Her floral scent wafted to him. He was surprised by the fact that she'd made the first move, but he was more than happy to oblige…

He parted his lips and pulled her forward.

She slipped into the gap between his legs, her arms encircling his neck.

He caressed her lips with his and then deepened the kiss. He stroked her tongue, tangling with her and swallowing her moan.

The sounds of the bar receded, and he brought a laser focus to the woman in his arms. He silently urged Marisa even closer so that her breasts pressed into him.

Come on. More…

"Talk about a surprise."

The words sounded from behind him, and Marisa pulled away.

Cole caught her startled, guilty look before he turned and straightened, and saw Sal Piazza's too-jovial expression. Vicki clung to Sal's arm, her face betraying shock.

Glancing at Marisa, Cole suddenly understood everything. He settled his face into a bland expression and forced himself back from their heated kiss.

Sal held out his hand. "I didn't expect to see you here, Cole."

"Piazza," he acknowledged.

Vicki's expression subsided from shock to surprise.

Sal dropped his hand as his gaze moved from Marisa to Cole. "You two are together."

It was a simple statement, but there was a wealth of curiosity behind it.

Cole felt Marisa go tense beside him and knew there was only one thing to do. He slid an arm around her waist before responding, "Yup. Not many people know."

Actually, it had been a party of two until seconds ago. And even then, *he* hadn't been sure what was up. That kiss had come out of nowhere and packed a punch even bigger than the one in the storage room.

Sal cleared his throat. "Marisa and I haven't been in touch since the break—"

"Lots of things can happen around a breakup." Cole made it a flat statement—and deliberately left the implication that he and Marisa had started getting acquainted at the same time that she and Sal had broken up.

Sal looked affronted, and Cole tightened his arm around Marisa as she shifted.

Sal twisted his lips in a sardonic smile. "Well, I—"

"Congratulations, I suppose," Vicki piped in with an edge to her voice.

Marisa smiled at the other woman. "Thanks, but we really haven't told many people about our relationship yet."

Cole kept his bland expression. Oh yeah, Marisa was with him. After this was over, though, he'd be quizzing her about their supposed liaison, including that kiss... Had she only planted one on him because she'd spotted Sal and Vicki?

Sal gave a forced laugh. "I guess a little partner swapping is going on."

Cole fixed him with a hard look.

Glancing at Marisa, Vicki narrowed her eyes and thrust her chin forward. "Be careful, sweetie. He's not one to commit."

"Which one?" Marisa quipped.

As Vicki's mouth dropped open, Cole found himself caught between laughing and wincing. They were a train wreck waiting to happen—or a hockey brawl.

"We're here for a corner booth and some dinner," Sal said grimly, his gaze moving between Marisa and Cole, "so we'll cede the bar to you two. Nice running into you."

Without a backward glance, Sal and Vicki headed toward the rear room of the crowded bar.

Cole figured that with any luck, he wouldn't catch a glimpse of the other couple again, which left Marisa and him to their own private reckoning...

Marisa slipped away from the arm around her waist, and her gaze collided with his.

"I'd hate to meet you in the ring," he remarked drily.

She sighed. "You already have."

"Yeah," he said with a touch of humor, "but that time Jordan was there to protect me."

Marisa compressed her lips.

"Well, this is an interesting turn of events," he drawled.

She seemed flustered and shrugged. "Who knew that Sal would show up with Vicki?"

"Since this is a sports bar, and he's a sports agent, not so far-fetched. Besides, it's not what I'm talking about, hot lips."

"I like *sweet pea* better," she responded distractedly. "Anyway, it seemed like a good idea at the time."

"I doubt thinking entered into it. Reacting is more like it."

"Well, making it seem as if we were involved was an easy shortcut answer to what we were doing in a bar together."

"How about the truth, instead?"

"Not nearly as satisfying."

"You got me there," he conceded.

They continued to stare at each other. She was inches away, emanating a palpable feminine energy.

"You know they're going to tell people," he remarked. "The news is too good not to share."

She looked worried. "I know."

He tilted his head, contemplating her.

"We'll have to let people wonder, and the gossip will fizzle out in time."

He shook his head. "Not nearly as satisfying."

She gazed at him quizzically. "As what?"

"As making it seem as if we really are a couple."

"What?"

Her voice came out as a high-pitched squeak, and he had to smile.

"Now that the cat is out of the bag, we'll need to keep up the ruse for a while in order to keep the fallout from hurting both our reputations."

"But I just explained it'll fizz—"

"Not fast enough. People are going to conclude we were trying to get back at our exes."

She looked stung, but then her expression became resolute. "All right, but we keep up the charade only until the fund-raiser. That should be enough time for this to pass out of public conversation."

He thought she was deluding herself about that last part, but he let it go. "Sal must really mean something for you to have pulled that stunt."

He wasn't jealous, just curious, he told himself.

She shook her head. "No, it's more about being dumped for someone who looked like a better bet."

"Vicki?"

"I can't believe you dated her," she huffed.

"Hey, you're the one who went so far as to get engaged—" he jerked his thumb to indicate the back of the bar "—to *that*."

"The correct pronoun is *him*. *To him*," she responded.

"Maybe for school, but not in hockey."

"Why do men—athletes—date women like Vicki?"

He flashed his teeth. "Because we can."

"Sal thinks he can, too."

He picked up his beer bottle and saluted her with it before taking a swig. "After that kiss, I'd say our relationship now qualifies as having a *status*."

Her eyes widened as the truth of his words sank in.

She was an intriguing mix, with the power to blindside him more than any offensive player on the ice. Back in high school and now.

And things were only going to get more interesting since she'd just handed him a plum excuse for continuing to see her...

Seven

He was in heaven.

A beautiful woman had just opened the door to her apartment. And delicious aromas wafted toward him.

Marisa, however, looked shocked to see him.

"What are you doing here?" she demanded.

She was wearing a white tee and a red-and-black apron with an abundance of frills. She had bare legs, and a ridiculous pair of mule slippers with feathers on them showed off her red pedicure.

His body tightened.

Hey, if she wanted to role-play, he was all for it. She could be a sexy domestic goddess, and he could be the guy who knocked on the door and…obliged her.

She was still staring at him. Devoid of any makeup, she looked fresh-faced and casual.

"What are you doing here?" she asked again.

He thought fast. "Is that any way to greet your newest—" What was the status of their relationship anyway? "Love interest?"

"We both know it isn't real!"

"It's real," he countered, "but temporary."

She looked unconvinced.

Ever since their encounter at the Puck & Shoot late last week, he'd been searching for another way to see her again. He'd decided the direct approach was the only and best option this time.

"People will expect me to drop in on my girlfriend." He arched an eyebrow and added pointedly, "And at least know what her place looks like."

She leaned against the door. "Our relationship isn't genuine."

"Everyone seems to think it is."

"We're the only two people that matter."

"How real did that kiss in the bar feel to you?" He wasn't sure how far the news had traveled—he hadn't gotten any inquisitive phone calls from his family *yet*—but sooner or later there was bound to be gossip. Sal and Vicki weren't the only witnesses to the kiss at the Puck & Shoot.

Marisa's brows drew together. "Shouldn't you be insulted that I used you for an ulterior motive?"

He shrugged. "I don't feel objectified. If a beautiful woman wants to jump my bones, she'll get no argument from me."

She tilted her head. "Why am I not surprised you wouldn't put up a fight?"

He gave a lazy smile, but he didn't miss the quick once-over she gave him from under lowered lashes. Her gaze lingered on the faded jeans he wore under a rust-colored tee and light jacket. Apparently, he wasn't the only one fascinated by clothing's ability to hide—and reveal.

"You're persistent."

"Is it working?"

Sighing, she stepped aside, and he made it over the threshold.

She locked the door behind him, and then touched her

hair, which was pulled willy-nilly into a messy knot at the back of her head. Strands escaped, including one that trailed along her nape.

He wanted to loosen the band that prevented her riotous curls from cascading down. There was a large mirror in a yellow scroll frame behind Marisa, so he got a great 360-degree view of her. Underneath the apron, she was wearing a pair of black exercise shorts that hugged a well-rounded rear end.

He needed divine assistance. "You look like you worked out or are about to."

He'd gone out on an early-morning run, but Marisa seemed to prefer to exercise after her school day was finished.

She looked uncomfortable. "I'm trying to get in shape."

She had a fabulous body as far as he was concerned. Her shape was more than fine. Still, if she wanted to exercise, he knew how they could get a workout in bed…

She wet her lips and turned. "Come on in."

He followed her from the foyer and down the hallway, deeper into the apartment.

"It's a prewar building, so this condo has a traditional layout. No open floor plan, like those renovated old factory buildings that you might be used to."

"Something smells delicious." *And someone looked delectable, too.* It was only four-thirty, but maybe Marisa liked to eat early. There was a living room off the hall, done in a flower motif—from plum-colored drapes to a damask armchair covered by a rose throw.

"Parent-teacher conferences are tomorrow night. The school usually has catered fare for the staff, but I got a request to bring my eggplant parmigiana."

They passed two bedrooms, but only the second looked occupied. It had aqua walls offset by white wicker furniture and a white counterpane. There was a mirrored dresser, and a vanity framed by floor-length window treatments.

At the end of the hall, they reached a bright but dated kitchen. The aromas stimulated his taste buds. If she'd been set on seducing him, she couldn't have planned it better.

"I didn't know you were going to show up," she said, as if addressing his private thoughts. "I was mixing the ingredients for cupcakes."

He was going down...but he adopted a solemn expression. "I understand. You're cooking for others."

She gave him a sidelong look. "Well, I did make an extra pan of the eggplant parmigiana to keep around. Would you like some? I just removed it from the oven."

"I'd love some," he said with heartfelt fervor.

Eggplant parmigiana was one of his favorite dishes, but ever since he'd moved out of his parents' house, he didn't often get a home-cooked meal. His specialty was grilling, not frying vegetables and creating elaborate baked dishes. His pasta came prepared from the gourmet market these days.

As Marisa retrieved a spatula, he spied an ancient-looking KitchenAid mixer on her countertop, right next to the fixings for cupcakes.

"Your mixer looks like it's seen better days."

"You mean Kathy?"

"You named your mixer." He was careful to keep his tone neutral.

She adjusted a baking pan on the range with an oven mitt and then glanced at him over her shoulder. "It belonged to my grandmother. It's an heirloom, so it gets a name. In fact, *Nonna* let me name it when I was six. Kathy KitchenAid."

He watched her cut a piece of the eggplant parmigiana for him. Then he hooked his jacket over the back of a chair and took a seat at the well-worn kitchen table. Moments later Marisa set a steaming plate before him and handed him a fork.

The mozzarella was still oozing, and the breaded eggplant peeked out in thin layers—like a delicate *mille fiori* pastry.

He swallowed.

"Would you like a drink?" she asked.

He doubted she had beer on hand. "Water would be fine, thanks."

As Marisa walked to the fridge, he dug in with his fork and took his first bite. Her eggplant parmigiana went down smooth, hot and savory. *Fantastic.*

Apparently, Marisa could cook in the same way that Wayne Gretzky could play hockey.

Cole was four bites in and well on his way to demolishing her baked confection when she returned with a glass of water.

"Not sparkling water," she said apologetically, setting down a tumbler, "but filtered from the tap."

He filched a napkin from the stack on the table, wiped his mouth and then took a swallow.

He was here to seduce her, but she was enthralling him with her culinary skills. Her dish was sublime, and he'd do anything for a repeat of that kiss in the bar. "Marisa, you make an eggplant parmigiana that can reduce grown men to a drool and whimper."

She lowered her shoulders, and her mouth curved. "Don't the Serenghettis have a family recipe?"

"This may be even better, but don't tell my mother."

"I'm sure it's been decades since your mother tried to bring men to their knees. But I'm also certain she wouldn't mind if it was her eggplant parmigiana that did the trick."

"Yeah, she takes pride in her cooking." The truth was that while Camilla Serenghetti used food to lure her sons home, she was a force to be reckoned with in other ways, as well.

Marisa touched her hair. "I'll let you finish your food. I'll, um, be back in a few minutes."

"Sure." Moments later he heard a door click.

Cole finished the food before him, savoring every bite.

When he was done, he got up and deposited his plate and glass in the sink—because if there was one thing Camilla Serenghetti had drilled into her sons, it was how to be polite and pick up after yourself.

Then he looked around and surveyed Marisa's place. It was unsporting of him, but he was willing to use any advantage to get to know more of her. Besides, he was curious about how she lived.

Walking out of the kitchen, he retraced his steps in the hallway. Marisa's bedroom door was closed. Beyond it, he entered the large living room. One corner held a desk, a bookcase and a screen that could be used to shield the nook from the rest of the room. A rolled-arm sofa upholstered in a cream-and-light-green stripe served as a counterpoint to the dominant flower motif. There were also several small tables that looked as if they could be hand-me-down family pieces—sturdy but with decades under their scarred chestnut tops.

From a builder's perspective, Marisa had done a good job sprucing up her prewar apartment without undertaking a major renovation. It was neat, cozy and feminine.

He walked over to a built-in bookshelf dotted with framed photos and found himself staring at a picture of Marisa the way she had looked in her high school days. She was laughing as she leaned against the railing of a pier. Wearing jeans and a sweatshirt, she appeared more relaxed and carefree than she'd been while roaming the halls at Pershing. With a sudden clenching of the gut, Cole wondered whether the photo had been snapped before or after the debacle of their senior year…

He glanced down at the books lining a shelf below eye level. Crouching, he tilted his head to read the titles. *Pleasing Your Man, Losing the Last 5 Lbs., The Infidelity Recovery Plan,* and last but not least, *Bad Boys and the Women Who Shouldn't Need Them.*

It didn't take a genius to make sense of the titles, especially since the final one seemed to be addressed to him personally.

Cole straightened. He'd never have guessed everything going on behind the facade of the normally reserved and occasionally fiery Marisa Danieli. He also couldn't believe his high school Lolita—edible as a sugared doughnut—saw herself as insufficiently sexy. Had ordering the Cobb salad at their dinner been about being thinner and more attractive? What about her exercise routine?

And what kind of jerk had she been engaged to? For sure, she'd had her ego bruised by Sal Piazza's horn-dog behavior. But if she thought Sal had strayed because she wasn't sexy enough, she was marching her feathered mules down the wrong school corridor. If Marisa could glimpse *his* fantasies lately, Cole was sure she'd overheat rather than doubt her sex appeal. He could happily lose his mind exploring her lush curves.

Hearing a sound behind him, he straightened and turned in time to see Marisa walk into the room, hair down and brushing her shoulders. "You've got an interesting collection of books."

Marisa's gaze moved from him to the bookcase, and she looked embarrassed.

"Sal wants to imitate the athletes that he represents," he said without preamble. "Sure he'd like to get his clients what they wish for, but he also wants to be them. That's why he wanted to bag Vicki. It wasn't about you."

"So don't take it personally?" she quipped.

"Those who can, do, and those who can't become sports agents instead," he responded without answering her directly.

"Like that saying about those who can, do, and those who can't, teach?" she parried. "Teaching is one of the hardest—"

"—jobs in the world," he finished for her. "I know. I was

one of those problem students who got himself suspended, remember?"

After a moment, she sighed. "Those who can't become sports agents, and those who can't become teachers. So I guess Sal and I were perfectly matched."

He sauntered toward her, shaking his head. "I'm going to have to detox you."

"Oh no, you don't." She sidestepped him. "You come in and eat my food and read my books, and I still don't know why you're here."

"Don't you?"

"No, I don't!"

"You're a great cook," he said, trying a more subtle maneuver. "I got a sample today, and a couple of your students at the rink last week mentioned it. The kids also said you've brought your homemade dishes to school functions in the past."

She looked surprised and then embarrassed. "And now you have a burning desire for eggplant parmigiana?"

He let the word *desire* hang there between them.

"Everything I know I learned from my mother," she added after a moment.

"Great. My mother has a cooking show on a local cable channel. She's always looking for guests."

Marisa held up her hands. "I don't like where this is heading."

He flashed his teeth. "Oh yes, you do." He was becoming a pro at the tit-for-tat game that they had going on between them. "If I'm going to do the rooster strut at Pershing's big party, then you can cluck your way through a televised cooking show. Fair is fair."

"We already struck our bargain," she countered. "You want to renegotiate now? You're already getting the construction job for the gym, no questions asked."

"I'm prepared to offer something in return for your appearance under bright studio lights," he said nobly.

"And that would be?"

"I'll expand my offer from informal coaching to running that hockey clinic that you want."

She looked astonished. As if he could never tempt her to appear on TV—but he had.

He was willing to coach the kids without receiving anything in return, but he wasn't going to tell her that. He'd created another opportunity to interact with Marisa, and she was going to find it hard to say no. He was brilliant.

"It's a big investment of time. I'd need a good recipe, and then I'd have to prep for the show. The hair and makeup alone will take two or three hours…"

His lips inched upward. "You're starting to sound like I did about the hockey clinic."

"My mother is the real cook in the family," she protested.

"Great. We'll get her involved, too. It'll take the pressure off you."

"No!" She shook her head. "How did we get here? I haven't even agreed to be a part of this crazy plan."

"We'll do a giveaway." He warmed to his subject. "A set of Stanhope Department Store's own stainless-steel cookware that retails for hundreds of dollars. You said your mother was the new housewares buyer, right? It'll be great promo. Move over, Oprah."

He was beyond brilliant.

"I'm busy right now. Parent-teacher conferences. The fund-raiser. The end of the school year… And I'm painting my kitchen cabinets before the weather gets hot because I don't have central air in this condo."

He glanced around them. "Yeah, you've got a retro vibe going."

"I like to call it modern vintage."

He wasn't familiar with the style but he was appreciating Marisa's '50s-style apron, and he had another great idea. "I'll help with the painting."

"You don't need to help. We're not dating."

He shrugged. "This isn't dating. This is an exchange of favors."

"Is that what you called your involvement with Vicki?" she parried. "An exchange of favors?"

He gave a semblance of a smile. "Oh, sweet pea, you're asking for it. Detox, it is."

"And you're going to provide the cure?" she scoffed. "It's pretty clear you're a womanizer."

"I enjoy women, yes. Therapy may be needed later, but right now I'm hung up on teachers with attitude."

"I know a great therapist," she said, her voice all sugar.

"And I've got a better idea for how to deal with our hang-ups."

She parted her lips, but before she could answer him, he pulled her into his arms and captured her mouth.

Marisa stilled, and then she kissed Cole back. She slid her arms around his neck, and her fingers threaded into his hair. He tasted of her baking, but underneath was the unmistakable scent of pure male.

One second she'd been fighting her attraction to him, and the next she'd been overwhelmed by it.

He held her firmly as his tongue stroked around hers. She pressed into him, her breasts yielding, and she felt the hard bulge of his arousal. Her mind clouded, waves of sensation washing over her.

Cole ended the kiss, and she moaned. But he trailed his lips down the side of her throat and then moved back up to suck on her earlobe. His breath next to her ear sent shivers chasing through her. Her breasts, and the most sensitive spot between her legs, felt heavy with need.

She tugged Cole back for another searing kiss. She felt the arm of the sofa behind her and realized that with one small tip, they could fall onto it.

He lifted his mouth from hers. "Tell me to leave now. Otherwise, this is going to end up where I want."

"And where would that be?"

He looked down at her clothes. "I'll be the guy who satisfies your inner domestic goddess."

Wow. His words served to arouse her further.

He gave a slow-burn smile and nodded at her ruffly apron. "I couldn't have dreamed of a sexier get-up if I tried."

"It's meant for cooking," she protested.

"Among other things." His hands settled on her waist, and he rocked against her as he bent and nuzzled her neck. "You didn't tell me to leave."

She couldn't. She tried to force the words, but they wouldn't come.

"You're beautiful and sexy and alluring. I want to be inside you, pleasing us both until you're calling out my name again and again..."

Oh. My. Sweet. Heaven. His words set her on fire. With Sal, sex had always been perfunctory. He'd never given her words...

Cole cupped her buttocks and lifted her, pressing her against him.

She cradled his face and kissed him again.

"Bed," he said thickly, "though the sofa would work, too."

"Mmm," she mumbled.

He must have taken her response for a yes because the next thing she knew, she perched on the back edge of the sofa.

Cole covered one of her breasts with his hand. He shaped and molded the sensitized mound and its taut peak. Then he trailed moist kisses down her throat and along her collarbone.

Releasing her breast, he tugged at the hem of her tee. She helped him, and then they both worked to slide the top over her head.

Cole's gaze settled on her chest, and she tried not to squirm. She'd always been self-conscious about her size.

"You're even more beautiful than I remembered," he breathed.

Then he bent his head and drew one tight bud into his mouth, bra and all, sucking her as if enraptured.

Oh. Oh. Oh. She didn't think she was going to last. She needed Cole now. She ached for him, already halfway to release even though he'd only put his mouth on her.

When he lifted his head, he blew against her breast, and if possible, her nipple grew tighter against its thin and wet covering. Marisa nearly came out of her skin.

Cole unclasped her bra and pulled it off her. He ducked his head and took her breast deep into his mouth, laving her with his tongue and then swirling it around her nipple.

Marisa pulled his head close. Sal had never given her body this level of attentiveness while Cole acted as if he had all the time in the world. Fifteen years ago she'd held Cole to her breast like this. But now he was all man—strong, capable and sure of himself. The scar across his cheek was pulled taught, and the stubble on his face was a gentle abrasion against her skin.

She gripped his head as he transferred his attention to her other breast. Her head fell back, and her eyes fluttered closed. With the world shut out, only Cole and his touch existed, with an even greater intensity than before.

Cole lifted his head, and his breath hissed out. "What do you want, Marisa?"

She opened her eyes to meet his. "You know."

"I want to hear you say it."

"You. I want you."

A look of satisfaction crossed his face. "Some things don't change, sweet pea. I can't keep my hands off you, either."

In response, she guided his hands back to her breasts, where they could both feel her racing heart.

"Marisa, Marisa," he muttered.

He was all appreciation, and it was like a salve to her

soul. She'd never felt like a goddess before, domestic or otherwise.

He gave her a gentle nudge, and she slid off the back edge of the sofa and onto the seat cushions, her legs dangling off one arm. Her mules hit the carpet with one muffled thud after another.

Cole pushed up her apron and then pulled off her biker shorts with one fluid movement. He stroked up her thigh, his calluses a shivery roughness against her skin—reminding her that he had a physical job as well as an office one.

"Ah, Marisa." Pushing aside her underwear, he pressed his thumb against her most sensitive spot while his finger probed and then slipped inside her.

She gasped. "What are you doing?"

"What does it seem like I'm doing?" he murmured, his thumb sweeping and pressing in a rhythm that made her tighten unbearably. "I'm going to make you breathless, sweet pea."

"Make me?"

It was the last thing she said before she gave herself up to sensation. Within moments she convulsed around him, her hips bucking. It was an orgasm born of a forbidden longing that had been brewing for fifteen years.

When she subsided, she realized Cole had satisfied her, but not himself. Her gaze connected with his, and she took in the intense expression stamped there.

"Yes," he said huskily. "It's going to be even better than before."

Better than before.

Marisa heard a knock at the front door, but in her sexual haze, it took her a moment to react. Then she froze.

Cole stilled, as well, apparently having heard the same thing.

There was the distinct sound of a key being slipped into the front door and the lock turning.

Marisa's eyes widened and fixed on Cole's.

In the next instant she was scrambling off the sofa—swinging her legs down and around and bolting to her feet.

Cole tossed her the biker shorts, but she had no time to do anything but stuff them under a pillow as she brushed down her apron.

"Marisa?" Serafina called. "Hello?"

Her cousin appeared in the entrance to the living room, and Marisa thought the whole situation could take the prize for *Most Awkward Situation in One's Own Home*.

Serafina blinked. "Oh…hello."

Marisa prayed her face didn't betray her. "Um, hi, Sera. I didn't know you were going to stop by."

"I overlooked a couple of small things when I moved out." Sera shrugged. "Since I still had the emergency key to the apartment, I thought it would be no problem if I showed up on my way to work. I did knock."

It was as if they were both pretending there wasn't a six-foot-plus sexy guy standing in the corner of her living room.

Marisa glanced at Cole, who was shielded by the high back of an armchair. She had no such cover. She hoped her apron was enough to disguise the fact that she was wearing only underwear. "Sera, you know Cole Serenghetti, don't you?"

Her cousin's gaze moved to Cole. "I thought I recognized you."

"Nice to meet one of Marisa's relatives."

Sera nodded. "I'm going to…go search the kitchen for my small blender."

"Sure, go right ahead," Marisa chirped. "I thought I saw it in there."

When her cousin turned and left, Marisa breathed a sigh of relief. Cole tossed the biker shorts at her, and she slipped into them while avoiding his eyes.

"I'll let myself out," he announced wryly.

"We shouldn't have done this," she blurted. *Nothing had*

changed. She was as easy a conquest for him as she'd always been. Willing to stop, drop and roll anytime, anywhere.

Cole ran a hand through his hair. "Get rid of the books on the shelf. You don't need them."

Marisa stared at him. It was a typical understated and sardonic Cole Serenghetti compliment. She wasn't sure whether to hug it close, or run for cover.

"I'll let you know the timing for the television show." Giving her one last significant look, Cole strode from the room.

Moments later Marisa heard her front door open and close for the second time. Taking a deep breath, she walked toward the back of the apartment. She found Serafina in the kitchen, opening and closing cabinets.

"I know that little handheld blender and juicer is in here somewhere…"

"Have you tried the cabinet above the stove?"

Serafina turned and gave her a once-over. "Well, you look fit for company again. At least the nonmale version."

"Cole came over because we had things to…discuss about the fund-raiser. And because he's looking for a couple of guests for his mother's cooking show, and I'm trying to get him to run a hockey clinic for the kids." *And I kissed him at the Puck & Shoot, and I hope the news doesn't spread…or hasn't already to you.* Fortunately, since she'd never been to the Puck & Shoot before last week, there was no reason for anyone to recognize her as Sera's cousin and make a connection.

Her cousin tilted her head. "And those, uh, discussions happened with your pants off?"

Marisa flushed. *Busted.*

Serafina lifted her eyebrows. "He's hot, for sure. And at least he doesn't have his brother's reputation for going through women as if he needs to spread the love."

"I—"

"You need a bodyguard. You obviously can't be trusted,

or he can't—or the both of you. I'm not sure which it is. It looks like he's forgiven you for high school and then some."

"It's not what you think." *It was pretend—or some of it was.* Sera seemingly hadn't gotten the bulletin yet that Marisa had kissed Cole at the Puck & Shoot, or her cousin would have mentioned it already.

"Wow, and we've descended into cliché, too. Give me a sec—I need to wrap my mind around this one. Maybe a bodyguard and a therapist? I can hunt up recommendations for you."

Marisa sighed. "C'mon, Sera."

"Well, you two have definitely got a thing for one another."

"We don't, really." The denial sounded weak, even to her own ears. *Ugh.*

"He wants you to appear on his mother's cooking show? That's serious."

"It's not as if I'm showing up as a member of the family."

"Just be careful. You two have a complicated past."

"I know."

"Great. Then that's settled." Sera gave an exaggerated sigh of relief. "Phew!"

"There's one tiny wrinkle."

Her cousin stilled. "Oh?"

"We're pretending to be a couple."

Sera's eyes widened. "That's not a wrinkle. That's a—"

"Really. We're faking it."

Sera jerked her thumb in the direction of the living room. "So you two were pretending to go at it in there?"

"No, yes…I mean, our relationship is fake!"

She filled in her cousin on what had happened at the Puck & Shoot, ending with her pact with Cole not to correct the perception that they were an item, at least until the Pershing Shines Bright benefit. Even as she told her story to Sera, Marisa admitted to herself that she had to try harder not to blur the line between reality and make-believe.

When she finished, Sera regarded her for an instant, head tilted to the side. "I wouldn't want to see you get hurt again."

"I'm not in high school anymore."

"No, but you still work there, and Cole has had another fifteen years to hone his lady-killer skills. Plus, he's admitted he wished things had turned out differently between you at Pershing."

"I told him I couldn't get involved. He knows the Danieli family history with professional athletes."

"If that's the reason you're hiding behind, go better. Cole is retired from pro hockey."

"Yes, but running the family construction business is a temporary sideline for him." She didn't want anything to do with someone who still had his hand in pro sports. She's made a good life for herself, right here in Welsdale.

"Well, you could become a temporary sideline to the temporary sideline. There's your reason to be wary."

Marisa threw up her hands. "You and Jordan should try Scrabble. Word play is your thing."

"What?"

"Never mind."

Eight

Marisa had done hard things in her life. Growing up, she'd sometimes been two short steps from foraging in a trash bin for food. But meeting Cole's family on the set of his mother's show, amid swirling rumors of their new status as a couple, trumped stealing away with a supermarket's barely expired eggs, in her opinion.

She hoped Cole had a good story to tell everybody about how they'd started dating.

"Relax," Cole said, giving her a quick peck on the cheek as she stepped onto the set. "It's fine."

"Then why is Jordan giving me a knowing look?" she responded sotto voce, nodding to where Jordan occupied an empty seat where the audience normally sat.

Cole caught his brother's bemused expression. "This situation is rife for humor, and he knows it." He frowned at Jordan, who gave a jaunty little wave in response. "Don't worry, I'll pound the jokes out of him in the ring next week."

Marisa turned away. "I'm going home. I can't do this."

Cole took hold of her arm. "Oh yes, you can."

"Cole, introduce me, please!"

Marisa swung back in time to see Camilla Serenghetti approaching them.

Too late.

Anyone could have guessed this was Cole's mother. Mother and son shared similar coloring and had the same eyes. Marisa had never had an opportunity to meet Cole's parents while she'd been at Pershing, but she'd glimpsed them in the stands at hockey games.

"Either she's the forgive-and-forget kind," she murmured to Cole, "or she's so thankful to see you in a relationship, she's willing to overlook anything."

Cole grinned. "Draw your own conclusions, sweet pea."

"Let's see, Italian mother, no grandkids…" Marisa was too familiar with the dynamics from her own family. "I choose the latter."

"She doesn't know about your part in my suspension," Cole replied in a low voice. "I did a good job of keeping her in the dark about my inner life as a teenager."

Marisa cast him a sidelong look. "So she doesn't know we—"

"—tested out the therapeutic properties of the theater department's couch?"

Cole arched a brow, and she flushed.

Cole shook his head. "No."

"Still," Marisa whispered back, "I know, and it's enough."

Cole's poor mother. First, Marisa had gotten her son suspended. And now she'd drafted him to star in a faux relationship. She could barely keep herself from cringing.

"Watch this," Cole said.

Marisa looked at him questioningly as he bestowed a broad smile on his mother.

"Mom, meet Marisa. She makes an eggplant parmigiana that rivals yours."

Marisa took a deep breath. *Well.* "I learned everything from my mother."

Camilla clapped. "Wonderful. I'm so glad she's comin' on my program, too."

"She should be here any minute. And my mother has seen your show, Mrs. Serenghetti. In fact, both she and I have watched numerous episodes."

She was a glutton for punishment. She avoided Cole's eyes, but heat stained her cheeks. She was a pushover for cooking shows. The fact that the host of this one was Cole Serenghetti's mother was beside the point. At least that was her story, and she was sticking to it. She purposely hadn't sought out news of Cole over the years, but when she'd stumbled upon an episode of *Flavors of Italy* more than a year ago, she'd been hooked.

"Please, call me Camilla. I've been trying to get Cole and Jordan to come back on the show for a long time."

Marisa looked inquiringly at Cole. "You don't want to be on your mother's show again?"

He'd been on the program at least once—how had she missed that episode? It must have been one of the early ones. She should be glad she missed it, so why did she feel disappointed?

Cole raised an eyebrow. "I can only work on saving one parent at a time."

Oh right—the construction company. Marisa could relate—how often had she worried about her mother? Family ties could bind, but they also had the potential to choke.

"You live in Welsdale, Marisa?" Camilla asked.

"Yes, I have my own condo on Chestnut Street."

Camilla looked perplexed. "You live alone?"

"My cousin Serafina was my roommate until recently."

Cole's mother appeared slightly mollified. "Well, is something."

"My mother thinks living alone is wrong," Cole said drolly. "We had lots of relatives on extended stays with us when I was growing up. You could say my mother never got out of the hotel business, even after marriage."

"Cole, don't be fresh."

"What? I'm wrong?"

"Your cousin Allegra is coming to visit with her family this fall."

"And I rest my case," Cole said.

Camilla adopted a slightly wounded look. "My children moved out. There's room."

Marisa was saved from saying anything, however, by the arrival of her own mother.

The family party was just getting started... Jordan Serenghetti, for one, had graduated from looking entertained to outright amused.

Donna Casale glanced around the set and then walked to where Marisa was standing with Cole and Camilla Serenghetti. Scanning the empty audience chairs, she said, "I must be early. There's hardly anyone here. Oh well, at least we can nab the best seats!"

Marisa stepped forward. "Actually, Mom, there isn't going to be an audience." Unless you counted Jordan's avid spectating. "This isn't a taping."

Donna looked confused.

"We're not going to be part of the audience, we're going to be guests on the show." She added weakly, "Surprise!"

Jordan guffawed.

Marisa fixed a smile on her face, willing her mother to go along. She hadn't said anything about their guest appearance because she'd wanted to avoid too many questions. Plus, she figured the element of surprise would work to her advantage because her mother wouldn't have a chance to get intimidated and say no.

Donna's eyes widened. "We're going to be on TV?"

Marisa grabbed her hand. "Yes! Isn't it great?" She needed all the enthusiasm she could muster in order to keep nerves at bay. "Let me introduce you to Camilla Serenghetti...and her sons."

Introductions were made, and Marisa was relieved that

everyone seemed to relax a little. Her mother actually started to appear happy at the prospect of making an appearance on a program that she watched.

Marisa cleared her throat. "And Cole has this great idea that we can do a giveaway on air as an advertisement for Stanhope Department Stores. What do you think, Mom?"

Her mother looked at her speculatively and then smiled. "I'll bring it up with management at work, but I'm sure they'll be thrilled."

Marisa lowered her shoulders, but Cole seemed bemused.

"You didn't tell your mother that she was about to become a star?" he murmured.

"Stop it," she responded in a low voice.

"Mmm, interesting. The first time you've asked me to stop." The sexual suggestion in his voice was unmistakable. "The words never crossed your lips in the storage room, or at the bar...or in your apartment, come to think of it."

"St—" She caught herself and compressed her mouth. "You're enjoying this."

"There are a lot of things I enjoy...doing with you."

Marisa felt a wave of awareness swamp her. Fortunately, their mothers appeared to be deep in their own conversation, because she could barely look at Cole. She grew hot at the memory of what they had done on her couch, which she'd now taken to referring to as Couch #2—never to be confused with the chintzy Couch #1 that still resided at the Pershing School. Whenever the student theater group had used #1 in a play over the years, Marisa could hardly keep her mind on the performance.

And right now Cole looked primed and ready for another round. Except she wasn't about to defile his mother's TV set sofa, no matter how hungry and frustrated Cole was.

She suppressed a giggle that welled up from nowhere and forced her mind back to the topic at hand. Camilla and her mother were engaged in a brisk discussion about whether to make a *tiella* or a *calzone di cipolla* on the air. The potato-

and-mussel casserole and the onion pie were both dishes of Puglia, the Italian region of Marisa's ancestors.

"The calzone is a traditional Christmas recipe," Donna said. "Like plum pudding in England. And since this show is going to air in the spring, I think the *tiella* would be better."

Marisa had told her mother to bring a couple of recipes along today, and had discussed them with her in advance. Her little white lie had been that the show planned to enter audience members in a raffle giveaway if they brought along a recipe.

"Donna, *cara, siamo d'accordo!*"

Cole's mother's enthusiasm and agreement were apparent no matter what the language spoken. Still... *Donna, cara?* When had her mother and Cole's progressed to being bosom buddies?

"You will be *perfetto* on the show, Donna. You and the *bellissima* Marisa."

Marisa felt Cole lean close.

"I'm surprised she isn't suggesting you become a bottle blonde," he murmured sardonically, "like the rest of the hostesses on Italian television."

"This is not an Italian show, Cole!" His mother fixed him with a look that said she'd overheard. "My hair is brown, and I speak English."

"Some people would debate the second part."

"Uh-oh," Jordan singsonged from his seat in the front row. "Cole's gonna be barred from the lasagna dinners."

"Exactly what is your role here?" Cole shot back.

Jordan grinned. "Comic relief. And Mom invited me." He looked around. "Hey, where's the popcorn? The drama's been good up to now, but the concessions leave something to be desired."

Cole ignored his brother and turned toward Marisa and her mother. "What my mother means is that she thinks Mrs. Casale has the personality for television. It's important to engage the audience on the small screen."

"Yes," Camilla agreed. "And dress in bold *colori* but not too much zigzag or *fiori*."

"Chill on the patterns," Jordan piped up.

"Makeup—more is better."

"I'm so glad we're doing this," Donna remarked with enthusiasm. "Marisa has loved to cook and bake since she was a little girl."

"Cole loved to eat," Camilla confided.

"Marisa was born a preemie, so I spent the first few months making sure she put on weight!"

Marisa bit her lip. "Oh, Mom, not that story again." Her mother had a terrifying habit of bringing it up in public situations.

"Scrappy, that's what I've always called her."

"Cole was nine pounds. Was a long labor," Camilla put in.

"Why doesn't anyone think of sharing those types of details on a date?" Cole quipped to Marisa.

"Maybe because you're too busy admiring your date's inner domestic goddess?" she shot back in a low voice before she could stop herself.

Cole gave her a half-lidded look. "Yeah...there's that distraction."

"Your mother is hilarious," she sidestepped.

"Larger than life. It makes her perfect for television."

As if on cue, his mother interjected, "Marisa, *bella*, you will come to the party in two weeks, *si*?"

What? What party?

"Ah...yes." She gave the only answer she could with three pairs of Serenghetti eyes on her.

"I ask your mother already, but she's going to a wedding tha' day."

"Ted's cousin's daughter is getting married," Donna explained in response to Marisa's inquiring look.

"Right." How could she forget? And now it seemed as if she was going to be flying solo with the Serenghettis.

"*Grazie per l'invito*, Camilla," Donna said. "Another time."

"Your mother speaks Italian?" Cole asked.

"She grew up in an Italian-speaking household," Marisa responded distractedly because she was still dwelling on the invite to the Serenghettis' domain.

Camilla perked up. "Cole knows Italian. We did *vacanze in Italia* when he was young."

Marisa figured that explained why Cole hadn't been in her Italian classes at Pershing.

"You speak *italiano*, Marisa?"

"*Abbastanza.*"

Camilla clasped her hands together, and shot a glance at her eldest son. "Enough. Wonderful."

Marisa could swear her expression said *she's perfetto*, but Cole just looked droll.

Fortunately for her, the show's producers interrupted at that point, and the conversation veered in another direction. But once the details of their guest appearance had been hammered out—and the appropriate forms and releases signed for the show's producers—Marisa moved toward the exit.

Unfortunately, Cole stood between her and the door.

"What are you doing this weekend?" he asked without preamble.

"Why do you ask?" she hedged, even though they weren't within earshot of Jordan or their mothers, who remained engrossed in conversation on the studio's stage.

"This weekend I'm having the first meeting of that hockey clinic that we talked about," he said. "But I prefer the rest of my time not be spent with a bunch of teenagers."

"You'd never make it as a teacher."

"I think we've established that," he responded drily. "But I pegged you for one who'd be teaching economics."

"After high school, I knew I'd never really understand economics."

"You seemed to be doing okay to me."

"Right. As if you were in a good position to judge."

He smiled. "We were both distracted back then, but I'm not going to apologize for being a major diversion for you. Speaking of which, how about dinner at Agosto at seven this Saturday?"

"I'm painting my kitchen cabinets."

"You're kidding."

She shook her head.

"I've been turned down for dates before—"

She feigned astonishment.

"—but never because someone needed to paint the kitchen cabinets."

"This relationship has been a land of firsts." She could have bitten her tongue. Of all the firsts, him being her *first* lover was at the top of the list. And from his expression, the thought had hit him, too.

"You, me, a can of paint. I can't think of a kinkier combination."

She rolled her eyes even as she tingled at his words. He'd switched gears smoothly from suggesting dinner at a fine restaurant...to making painting seem adventurous.

"I hope you chose a red-hot shade. Make Me Magenta. Or Kiss & Cuddle Coral."

"You know, I'd never thought of the building business as sexy, but now I see how wrong I've been. Just buying paint must leave you breathless!"

A slow smile spread across his face. "If you invite me over, you can find out what else leaves me breathless."

"I was planning on painting the cabinets by myself."

He looked her over. "Why bother when you have a sexy construction guy to do it with?"

She was starting to feel hot again—and very, very breathless. Damn him. He knew what he was doing, but he was also keeping a straight face. "I don't have the money to hire someone. That's why I was planning to do it alone."

"For you, sweet pea, I come free."

"The kitchen cabinets are a little dreary," she said unnecessarily, trying to cool things down.

"Add color to your life."

She'd paint *him* red—he was definitely a red. "The cabinets are going to be yellow. Unblemished Sapphire Yellow."

He cut off a laugh. "I guess I shouldn't be surprised."

"I've already bought the paint supplies."

"Great. When do we start?"

"I start on Saturday morning." She hoped she sounded repressive enough.

"I'll be there at eight."

When Marisa opened the door to her apartment on Saturday morning, Cole was holding a container with coffee cups and assorted add-ins. He grasped a brown paper bag with his other hand.

"Doughnuts," he announced. "A construction industry morning tradition."

"Thank you," she said, taking the bag from him.

She stepped back so he could enter the apartment, and her heartbeat picked up. He was strong, solid and masculine. And yummy. *Forbidden, but yummy.* He looked great in paint-stained jeans, work boots and an open flannel shirt over a white tee.

By contrast, she'd dressed in a green tee and an old pair of gray sweats. She'd used a scrunchie to pull her hair back in a ponytail. With no makeup or jewelry, she hardly felt sexy—though she still itched with need at the sight of him.

"I'd show you to the kitchen, but we'll be working in there, not…eating." A sudden image flashed through her mind of Cole slipping his hands under her tee and up her midriff, moving ever closer to her breasts…

Wow, it was hot in here.

She led the way into the living room and then turned back toward him.

"Let me take the coffee from you," she said, intending to set the coffee carrier down on the wood tray that covered a rectangular ottoman.

Their fingers brushed, and her eyes flew up to meet his. They both stilled, and then he leaned in and touched her lips with his.

"You're welcome," he said in a low voice as he straightened.

"I thought we'd keep up the pretense about painting at least until nine." She set down the coffee and faced him again.

"Sex first thing in the morning is great," he responded, "and I've been saving it all for you."

"I thought sports guys abstained from sex before a big game in order to keep their edge." If he was going to expend a lot of effort today on painting, wasn't it a similar situation?

"Sweet pea, I don't play professionally anymore, and you'll never see a better painter after this," he responded with heartfelt enthusiasm.

She gave a nervous laugh—because he did make her tense. And aroused. And crazy. It was hard not to be thrilled with a guy who lusted after her even when she looked as if she was going to haul out the garbage. Even if her mind told her she shouldn't.

He stepped forward and cupped her face, his fingers threading into her hair and loosening her ponytail. Gazing at her mouth, he muttered, "You know, I used to steal glances at you when we were working on that presentation for economics class. Just for the sheer pleasure of looking at you."

"Really?" she breathed.

He nodded, and then gave her another light kiss.

When he straightened, she swallowed. "I could tell you were staring at me sometimes…I thought I had a food smudge or a blemish, or you were wondering why my face wasn't completely symmetrical—"

His eyes crinkled. "Marisa?"

"Yes?"

"Adolescent boys think about one thing, and it's not about looking in the bathroom mirror for hours and searching for flaws."

"Oh, and what do you think about?" she asked, even though she had a good idea.

"This."

He claimed her lips for a deeper kiss. He traced the seam of her mouth and then slipped inside. She breathed in his warm, male scent and then met his tongue, leaning into him. The power of the kiss seeped into her.

She followed his lead, meeting him again and again, until she was in a pleasant languor, her head swimming. When they broke apart, she bent her head, her forehead coming to rest against his lips.

He settled his hands on her waist and then slipped them under the bottom of her sweatshirt. He kneaded her flesh, caressing her back and rubbing up to her shoulder blades. With a deft move, he unclasped her bra and she spilled against him.

Raising his mouth a fraction from her forehead, he muttered, "Marisa."

"What?" she asked dreamily.

"I've fantasized about your breasts."

"Now?"

"Now. High school. Forever."

"Mmm."

He pulled the sweatshirt over her head, and she took out the scrunchie holding her hair, shaking her head to loosen the strands.

Gazing down at her, he said, "You still have the prettiest breasts I've ever seen."

"And on a schoolteacher, no less. Go figure," she joked.

"Luscious Lola. You live up to your nickname."

"What?"

He raised his eyes. "You didn't know? It's what the guys

in the locker room called you. But we couldn't agree on how big your breasts were because you had a habit of hugging books to your chest."

Her eyes widened. "You're kidding."

He gave her a teasing smile. "Nope. The nickname Luscious Lola was sort of tongue-in-cheek. The imaginations of teenage boys can outstrip reality." His look turned appreciative. "Not in this case, however."

"I didn't even know I existed in the jocks' locker room!"

"Oh, you existed, all right."

"You gave out nicknames?" She still couldn't believe it. She'd thought she'd been invisible in high school—well, at least until the end.

Cole shrugged.

"Well, you eventually found out how big my breasts were. But I couldn't figure out why you didn't broadcast the news…"

He sobered. "By that point, it was too heavy to share. I'd started thinking of you as my personal Lolita. The girl who slew me and led to my destruction."

"And now?" she asked, curious and a little wary, even as she adopted a tone of mock reproach. "Am I still just a sex object with big breasts?"

He looked into her eyes. "And now you're the woman I've been fantasizing about. *Ti voglio.* I want to make love to you, Marisa."

When he held out his hand, she went weak and then put her hand in his. If she was honest with herself, she'd admit this moment had been inevitable ever since Cole had announced he'd help her paint. The last time he'd been in her apartment, they'd ended up tangled together on her living room couch until Sera's unexpected arrival. She could have done more to avert this moment if she'd wanted to, but in the secret recesses of her heart, she knew she'd always wanted to deal with the unfinished business between her and Cole.

Cole threw some pillows on the floor and tugged her

down to their makeshift bed, where they both kneeled and faced each other. He gently pulled her into his embrace, and then he kissed her, one arm anchored around her waist, the other caressing her breast.

Marisa moaned, her scruples evaporating. Cole's thumb toyed with her nipple, causing sensation to shoot through her and pool between her legs.

"Cole," she gasped, her fingers threading through his hair, "please."

"Please, what?" he asked gutturally.

"Now, more…"

"Yes."

She lay back against the pillows, and he pulled off his shirt and then tugged the white tee over his head.

Marisa sucked in a breath. He was *built*. Bigger and broader than in high school, but solid muscle nonetheless. He might have left the ice, but he seemed as toned and ready for action as ever. He had flat abs, and sculpted muscles outlined his upper arms. She'd gotten a partial look at Jimmy's Boxing Gym, but unclothed, he was even more spectacular.

He gazed at her with glittering promise. Then he grasped the waistband of her sweatpants and pulled them off, taking her panties, socks and canvas lace-ups with them.

Tossing her clothes aside, he moved back to her and stroked a hand down her thigh. He raised her leg, flexed her foot and placed a kiss on the delicate skin behind her knee. "You've got a fantastic figure, sweet pea. Made for loving."

She'd dreamed about this moment in the past. She'd wondered what would have happened if things had turned out differently—if her relationship with Cole had survived to become a real adult one.

For his part, Cole looked like a man who'd reached an oasis and wasn't going to hold back. He stood and pulled off his shoes and then stripped off the rest of his clothes. When she held out her arms, he came down beside her.

He claimed her mouth again, and she ran her hands over

his arms, feeling his muscles move and flex beneath her fingertips. His erection pressed against her, cradled between her thighs.

How many times after high school had she replayed their one time together? The truth was she'd never completely put him behind her.

When the kiss broke off, she touched his cheek. "You explained the knee injury that stopped your career with the Razors. But you never said how you got the scar."

Cole's look turned sardonic. "Simple. Another player's blade connected with my mug."

She frowned and then traced the long, white line bisecting the side of his face. "Have you ever thought of getting it fixed?"

"Nah…and have my good looks marred by cosmetic surgery?"

Impulsively leaning up, she trailed featherlight kisses along his scar. When she was finished, Cole looked as if he'd been undone.

"Ah, Marisa," he said gruffly. "That was…sweet."

"Women would die to have your nonchalant attitude about their physical appearance." She paused. "Women would die to have you, come to think of it."

He gave her a lopsided grin. "After our first time in high school, I used to think about ways to make the experience better the next time."

"You did?"

He nodded. "Yup. I still have a game plan filed away that I never got to use."

She sighed dreamily.

He stroked her arms. "Close your eyes, Marisa. Just feel."

When her eyes had fluttered closed, Cole began to massage her back, loosening her muscles and making her relax. Slowly, she came away from the edge of nervous arousal to something deeper and more soul-stirring.

Cole kissed her and then trailed his mouth down the column of her neck. He paused, blew on her nipples and then laved one with his tongue. When she jerked, he shushed her, gentling her with his hands. Then he drew her other breast into his mouth.

Awash in pleasure, Marisa threaded her hands in his hair, holding him. She felt fantasy merge with reality. Cole was here, making love to her. How many times had she dreamed about it? It was like her fantasies, but better in many ways... He was sure of himself, confident in his ability to please her. The full adult version of the teenager she had known.

"We'll never use a real bed," she murmured.

Cole stifled a laugh. "All in good time, including the kitchen, eventually."

She opened her eyes. "I cook in the kitchen."

"Me, too."

"Not that type of cooking."

"Ah, Marisa." He moved downward and kissed one inner thigh and then the other. Then he pressed his lips against her moist core. He found her with his mouth and caressed and swirled her with his tongue.

She moaned, and her hips rose, but Cole held her to him, his hands under her rear end.

She turned her head to muffle her moans against a pillow as sensation swamped her. But it was too much. Panting, she gave in, and let the world explode as she bucked against Cole's mouth.

Seconds later, spent, she collapsed back against their makeshift bed.

Cole came back up to face her. "It's not over until you're completely sexually satisfied."

Oh. "I need a moment." Her heart was racing, and she could still feel his arousal against her. "You have incredible staying power."

"In hockey and in business, it's about self-control. Like life, generally." He smiled, smoothing her hair. "But don't sell yourself short. You have wonderful stamina yourself."

"You've always had a lot of self-control around me." She knew she sounded wistful, but he'd been able to turn away from her so easily fifteen years ago...

"No, I don't," he corrected on a growl. "Let me show you."

Standing up, Cole withdrew a foil packet from the pocket of his jeans and sheathed himself. Tossing her a rueful grin, he said, "Wishful thinking, but I came prepared."

Marisa licked dry lips. With Sal, it had always been plain-vanilla sex—on a bed, at night and over quickly. She was unprepared for Cole's lustiness, though she'd be lying to herself if she said she didn't like it.

In the next moment Cole flipped her on her stomach and grasped her legs, spreading them as he pulled her to the edge of the pillows. He leaned forward, bracing himself over her, and his erection probed her entrance.

"You are so hot and slick," he breathed beside her ear. "So ready for me."

She felt him slide into her without any resistance and cried out at his possession, while Cole gave a labored groan behind her. He thrust into her once, twice, three times, and she called his name.

He set up a rhythm for them, pumping into her. "Marisa."

She could feel him tightening, and could tell he was close to finding his climax. She clamped down around him, and he cursed. Then they were both spiraling, the air filled with the sounds of their release.

She cried out as she crested on a wave of sensation so pure and beautiful—its power building for fifteen years—that tears stung her eyes.

After a moment, Cole slumped on top of her. Then he kissed her ear and rolled to his side, bringing her with him into the shelter of his body.

Marisa waited for her heart to slow down. Cole had given her one of the most spectacular experiences of her life. She was caught between joy at the wonder of it and embarrassment at her uninhibited response.

"Was that the game plan that you had filed away for fifteen years?" she asked.

He gave a helpless laugh. "Part of it."

There was more? Still, she managed, "It was so much better than on a regular bed."

He smiled against her hair. "I told you it would be better with a sexy construction guy."

Nine

If Marisa had any doubt that she and Cole had grown up in very different circumstances, they were erased when she entered his parents' house—a Mediterranean villa set amidst beautiful landscaping with a stone fountain at the center of a circular drive. She could almost believe she was in Tuscany, which she'd backpacked through one summer.

Still, she'd been nervous about this party ever since Camilla had issued her invite. She'd debated what to wear and had settled on a shirt and short skirt. Cole had driven to her apartment building, and she'd met him downstairs in the entry, not trusting the two of them in her condo alone even for a few minutes. Seeing him in a shirt and khakis, she'd been reassured that she'd at least dressed appropriately.

Thanks to Cole, her kitchen had gotten a wonderful face-lift. After their romantic interlude, they had gotten on with the job of painting, and she'd discovered Cole knew much more about the intricacies of stripping old paint and dealing with molding than she did. Her kitchen looked great—and he'd worked magic on her, too.

Marisa followed Cole through gleaming rooms decorated with a bow to the Serenghettis' Italian heritage to the back of the villa. When they reached his parents' backyard, she took in the impressive outdoor kitchen, blue-stone patio under a striped awning and wrought-iron furniture. It was an unseasonably warm day in May, and the Serenghetti party was mostly an outdoor affair. People milled about, glasses in hand, and platters of food had been set out on most flat surfaces.

Marisa looked over at her construction guy. Though when she'd started thinking of Cole as hers, she couldn't quite say. It was a telling slip that was *dangerous*. They'd had spectacular sex that had transported her from her comfort zone to an area where she was vulnerable, exposed and swamped with emotion and sensation. But still, she couldn't—shouldn't—attach too much importance to it. She had once in high school, and she'd fallen flat on her face. She also hoped it wasn't obvious to everyone that they'd recently become lovers for the first—no, second—time.

Cole placed his hand at the small of her back, and Marisa glanced at him. He wasn't trying to be subtle about their connection—though which of the two of them was a fraud was hard to tell. Weren't they supposed to pretend to be a couple? It was getting so confusing...

Cole bent for a quick kiss. "I'm glad you're here."

"There are more of you Serenghettis than I've ever seen in one place," Marisa responded, wondering how many people had seen that peck on the lips.

Cole laughed. "Don't worry, they don't bite—" he bent to murmur in her ear "—unlike me."

On her quick intake of breath, he straightened, his eyes gleaming.

Quelling the sudden hot-and-bothered feeling, Marisa scanned the crowd. She had known in high school that Cole had three younger siblings, but she hadn't been friends with any of them. She'd heard a bit about Jordan over the years

because his hockey career and endorsement deals had kept
him in the public eye. And before they'd arrived at the party,
Cole had mentioned that his sister, Mia, the youngest, was a
designer based in New York, and his middle brother, Rick,
traveled the world as a stuntman on movie sets.

"Come on," Cole said. "I'll introduce you."

Marisa bit her lip. "Uh…sure."

The Serenghettis had been a colorful lot so far. She took
a deep breath and followed Cole as he made his way toward
a lithe and attractive woman who obviously possessed the
Serenghetti genes.

"Mia, this is Marisa Danieli."

Cole's sister was beautiful. Her hair was longer than
Marisa's, and wavy, not curly. Her almond-shaped eyes
tilted slightly upward at the corners, hinting at Slavic or
Germanic ancestors—not an uncommon story for those
with roots in Italy's north.

"I remember you," Mia said, stepping away from the
serving table next to her.

Yikes. In her case and Cole's, recollections of the past
couldn't be a good thing. Still, Marisa couldn't fault Mia if
the other woman wanted to size up Cole's newest girlfriend
and be protective of her brother. Mia hadn't yet reached
high school when she and Cole had been seniors, so Marisa
placed her at close to Serafina's age.

Mia tilted her head. "You were the smart girl who
brought down the high-and-mighty hockey team captain.
Come to finish him off?"

Marisa felt heat flood her cheeks. Still, Mia's tone was
surprisingly neutral, joking even. Cole's sister had faulted
her brother for his arrogance in high school and called
Marisa smart.

"Mia—"

Before Cole could say more, Marisa found her voice.
"No, I need him too much to polish him off. He's the head-

liner for the Pershing fund-raiser." She cast a quick glance at Cole. "Besides, he's shaped up to be a decent guy."

Mia's shoulders relaxed a little. "That's what I think." She smiled. "And you're not his typical fashion-model type."

"Thanks for the endorsement, sis," Cole said drily.

"You could be a model yourself, Mia," Marisa interjected, knowing it wasn't just flattery to get into Mia's good graces, it also happened to be true—Cole's sister was a knockout.

"I was a leg model for a while," Cole's sister admitted, her tone rueful as she pushed one of her chestnut locks over her shoulder. "I didn't like it, but I thought that if I wanted to be a designer, it would help to know the fashion industry from the leg up, if you know what I mean. I did a lot of hosiery ads."

"Yeah," Cole cracked, "I tried to get her to insure her legs."

His tone was jesting but there was also an element of brotherly pride. And Marisa felt a sudden pang at Cole's easy bond with his siblings. She had her cousin Serafina, but they'd always lived in different homes, though sleepovers had made up for some of that distance.

"Hmm," Mia said, considering. "Well, don't count me out on the insurance. I may need to continue to model my own clothes, and from the leg up if it comes to it. Designers starting out have to make do with what they have."

"I've got some helpful advice for you," Cole teased. "Put Jordan in drag. If he's a hit with underwear, he'll rock a strapless dress."

While Marisa smiled at the image, Mia laughed. "Jordan is going to throttle you for suggesting it."

"Don't worry, you've got plenty to hold over him. He'll come cheap."

Marisa warmed to Cole's sister, who obviously had a self-deprecating charm. She could also identify with a woman who was trying to get a career off the ground and running.

Cole looked down at her. "Can I get you a drink?"

"Yes, please," she said, realizing a glass would be a good prop to help disguise her nervousness. "A diet soda would be great."

"I think you need something stronger," Cole teased. "You still haven't met all the Serenghettis."

"I'm going to check in with Mom in the kitchen," Mia announced, stepping back. "Knowing her, she's in a frenzy of activity."

When Cole and Mia had moved off, Marisa found herself alone and looked around. The crowd had thinned—some people heading indoors—and she spotted Serg Serenghetti sitting in a chair near the outdoor kitchen. The family resemblance was unmistakable—she'd have recognized him even if she hadn't seen pictures in the local paper from time to time over the years.

He beckoned to her, and she had no choice but to walk toward him.

Serg's hair was steel-gray mixed with white at the sideburns, and he shared some of his eldest son's features—not to mention Cole's imposing presence, even though he was seated.

When she'd neared, Serg waved a hand to indicate their surroundings. "You're a teacher, Marisa. Based right here in beautiful Welsdale, my wife says. Not like those model types…"

How much had Serg been told about her? "Yes, I've been teaching at the Pershing School since I received my teaching degree. Cole has been generous enough to help with our fund-raiser."

"Pstcha," Serg retorted. "It's not generosity. Cole wants you to keep seeing him."

Marisa had stopped listening at *Cole wants you…*

Serg tilted his head in imitation of his daughter. "Smart guy." Then he adjusted the blanket covering his lap and frowned. "My wife likes to keep me bundled up like an Eskimo facing a blizzard even though spring has come early this year."

Cole returned, drinks in hand. "I see you've met the *pater familias*." Handing Marisa a wineglass, he added, "He's curmudgeonly in a teddy bear sort of way. I trot him out to make a good impression on the girlfriends."

"Ha!" Serg replied. "I give thanks every day that your fancy schools at least taught you some Latin."

Cole quirked an eyebrow. *"Acta est fabula, plaudita."*

The drama has been acted out, applaud. Marisa hid a smile. She'd studied Latin, too.

"At least I know how to entertain," Serg grumbled. "Smart-ass."

"Chip off the old block."

Serg made some more grousing noises before glancing at Marisa again. "Beautiful woman based right here in Welsdale. Perfect."

"You'd think so," Cole remarked drily.

"Get Marisa to take you on, and you're set. Then you can stay put and run Serenghetti Construction."

"Right."

What? Cole's mocking tone was undeniable but Serg surely couldn't be serious. Marisa felt as if she'd landed in the middle of a family drama that she didn't totally understand.

Serg shook his head. "I had a stroke but I can still understand sarcasm."

"I'm the best you've got. Jordan and Rick are worse."

Camilla appeared and came forward to fuss over her husband, and both Marisa and Cole stepped back.

Serg looked up from under lowered brows. *"Vade in pace.* Go in peace. Latin was required in my day, too, you know."

As she moved aside, Marisa bumped up against something—or rather, someone—and turned around.

A tall, good-looking man smiled down at her. "Hi."

Cole sighed resignedly. "Marisa, this is my brother Rick.

The prodigal son back from a film set at the edge of the Earth."

"Don't listen to him," Rick said with a lazy grin. "I'm the movie star. But I've been trying to get Cole here to play one of the bad guys for a long time. With the scars and all, don't you think he looks menacing?"

What Marisa was thinking was that Cole made her heart go pitter-patter...

"You're a stuntman and you've been a body double for Hollywood's A-list," Cole replied. "Still doesn't make you a movie star."

"A fine distinction."

Marisa had to concede that Rick had movie-star looks. Closest in age to Cole, he was also rough-hewn. But he'd been a wrestler, not a hockey player, in high school. That much she knew.

"So word is you two are an item." Rick looked at Cole, his expression droll. "Hot for the teacher?"

Marisa heated to the roots of her hair. She took a sip of wine to fortify herself.

"You can always count on a brother to embarrass you for no reason," Cole said drily, though he didn't look greatly perturbed.

"Your taste in women is improving. What's to be embarrassed about?"

"You."

"Payback." Rick grinned. "So what happened? Marisa clobbered you in high school, and now you're moonstruck?"

Marisa observed the back-and-forth between the brothers, a nervous and self-conscious smile on her lips. Still, it seemed as if Rick was willing to be open-minded about her relationship with his older brother—whatever it was.

Cole, on the other hand, looked as if he was praying for patience. "Mr. Hayes made her 'fess up about who doctored the PowerPoint presentation, smart-ass. She was going to lose recommendations for a college scholarship."

"No, really," she interjected, "I think that explains my behavior but doesn't excuse it."

"You had a good enough reason for doing what you did," Cole replied.

"I shouldn't have cared about Mr. Hayes's embarrassment." She shrugged. "Chances were good he'd keep his job regardless. You paid a big price."

"I had it coming. Everything worked out eventually."

Marisa wanted to argue further, but then she caught Rick's amused expression.

"What a love-fest," Rick remarked, looking back and forth between them. "I should get out of the way while you two fall all over yourselves making excuses for each other."

Marisa clamped her mouth shut. Something had been changing between her and Cole. She felt as if there were silken ties—a lingerie robe sash came to mind—binding her to him. For his part, Cole seemed as if he couldn't wait to be alone with her again…

Cole linked his hand with hers. "Come on, there are other people I want to introduce you to."

Rick stepped back. "Have fun. I have my hands full avoiding Mom. She wants to capitalize on my rare family appearance."

Murmuring a nice-to-meet-you to Rick, Marisa allowed herself to be led away. Cole introduced her to one group after another until Marisa found it hard to keep track of so many family members, friends and associates. In between, she ate Camilla's delicious food, and Cole had a burger and hot dog while taking his turn grilling.

When they finally reached a lull, Marisa checked her phone and realized they'd already been at the party for three hours.

Cole glanced down at her. "Let's get out of here."

She looked around. "But the party isn't winding down yet."

He gave her a heavy-lidded look. "Right. It's the perfect

time to go. People will understand we want to be alone. It'll keep up the appearance that we're a couple."

Nervous anticipation spiraled through her. "Where are we going?"

Taking her hand, Cole raised it to his lips. "My place is closer."

She sucked in a breath. "Okay."

She'd never been in Cole's apartment, and it occurred to her that they were crossing another threshold...

The drive to Cole's was quick. They made their way through the understated lobby and ascended in the elevator to the top floor.

When he let them into his loft, Marisa glanced around. The penthouse was like the home version of Cole's office. Masculine and conveying muted power. Everything looked state-of-the-art—from the electronics that she glimpsed in the living area to the appliances visible in the kitchen.

In the next moment Cole backed her against the exposed brick wall for a searing kiss.

When they broke apart, she said breathlessly, "We have to stop this. We're in a pretend relationship."

"This is helping us pretend better."

"I don't follow your logic."

"Then don't. Just go with the flow."

He was making her feel too much. She was afraid...and yet she couldn't resist taking the plunge.

He touched her face. "I want to take you on a bed this time. I want you to cry out my name as I come inside you."

She placed unsteady fingers on the top button of her shirt, and Cole zeroed in on the action.

"I've been glimpsing your lacy bra all night. The peekaboo effect has been driving me crazy."

"You've been staring at my breasts?" How many guests had noticed? And how had she not been aware of it? Probably because she'd been too nervous and overwhelmed by her surroundings.

"Yeah," Cole said thickly, "and Rick caught me at it, too. I haven't bumbled so much since high school."

A girlfriend would have told her that her bra was showing so she could fix the problem. *Not Cole.*

"Think of it as foreplay." He braced a hand on the wall next to her and leaned in to trail kisses from her lips to the hollow behind her ear.

She shivered, and her fingers fumbled with the buttons of her shirt. When she finally finished, she tugged her top out of the waistband of her skirt and opened it wide. The cool air hit her skin, raising goose bumps.

"So pretty," Cole murmured, trailing a finger from her jaw, down her neck and to the swell of her breast.

Marisa lowered her eyes as the back of Cole's hand grazed over the top of her breast...again and again. Her breath hitched. She couldn't wait to experience what Cole wanted to show her—and do with her—this time.

He slid one hand up her thigh and under her skirt, and she leaned against the wall for support. He nuzzled her neck, and then found her with his hand, delving inside her welcoming moistness.

She tangled her hands in his hair. "Cole."

"Yeah?" he said thickly.

"Tell me this isn't in the playbook."

"No, but this is." He crouched and moments later used his tongue at her most sensitive spot.

Her knees nearly buckled, and she sank her fingers into his hair, anchoring herself in a world flooded with sensation. "Cole, please."

"Please, what?" he muttered. "Keep going?"

She was so aroused that she couldn't breathe right. "Oh..."

"My pleasure."

Minutes later her world splintered, coming apart like a kaleidoscope exploding, and she sagged against the wall.

Cole straightened, bracing himself with a hand against the wall near her face, his eyes glittering.

"You're going to ride me," he said huskily. "You're breasts are going to bounce and drive me crazy...and then after you scream for me, I'm going to come inside you in one long rush."

Marisa parted her lips. She'd never been so turned on in her life.

"Bed. Now," she gasped.

"The magic words," he responded, grinning.

He swung her into his arms and strode down the hall. The bedroom was at the end, on the right.

It was an enormous room, with skylights and glass doors opening onto a terrace.

When he set her feet down, they both stripped, their fingers working quickly on more buttons. He beat her to the finish—naked when she still had on a bra and panties.

He prowled toward her with purpose. *He was perfect.* All muscle and sculpted maleness. Not an ounce of softness, but still, she was prepared to be cosseted.

He cupped her breasts, kissed the top of each one and then claimed her mouth. With a deft move, he undid her bra and she spilled against him.

He pushed down her panties until they pooled at her feet. And then he was laying her down on the bed and stretching over her. He fanned her hair out across the pillow.

"What are you doing?"

He gave her a crooked smile. "This is the way I've fantasized about you. Your hair spread across my bed...entangling me."

"I thought I was going to be on top."

"You will be," he promised before he kissed his way down her body.

When he was ready, he flipped her on top of him.

She straddled him, and then sank onto him until they were joined. They both groaned, and he helped her set up a rhythm that they enjoyed.

When she finally crested on a wave that was pure and beautiful, she heard her own gasps of pleasure as if from a distant place. Cole's face was contorted with effort until he found his own release and spilled inside her in one long thrust.

Marisa sagged forward against him, and he caught her, their hearts racing.

"I don't think I can survive much more of you, Marisa."

"You don't need to," she murmured. "I've given you all I have."

It was true—and also what she was afraid of. Cole had her body and soul. She only hoped she wasn't just another score…

"Cole, come on up and taste Marisa's cooking."

Cole smiled for the camera. Which producer had come up with this stunt? Or had it been his mother's idea? His mother was looking excited and decidedly innocent. Never mind that the dish to be sampled had more accurately been a joint production of Marisa *and* both their mothers.

If Marisa hadn't been looking so horrified—but how many of her students tuned in to local television in the middle of the afternoon?—he might have suspected her of having a hand in the making of this made-for-TV moment. As it was, he wanted to laugh. He hadn't expected to be an extra in this episode of his mother's show.

When he reached the stage, he said gamely, "I'm sure it's delicious, but I'm not a connoisseur."

Camilla gave Marisa a spoon with a sampling of *tiella* on it—bits of rice, onion, potato and mussels mixed together—and nodded expectantly.

When Marisa turned, she made to hand off the spoon to him.

"No, no, Marisa," Camilla said laughingly. "I always raise the spoon to the *bocca* when I ask my family for an *opinione*."

The audience laughed along gamely, and even Donna smiled at Camilla's exuberant admonishment.

Cole could read the defeat in Marisa's eyes as she realized there was no way out. Unlike him, she wasn't used to being on camera. But they both knew everyone—the audience, their mothers and the producers—was waiting for her to feed him.

Slowly, she raised the spoon, cupping her other hand under it to prevent spills. He locked his gaze on her face, and at the last second, took hold of her wrist in order to guide it. She gasped softly, the moment between them becoming molten even before the food touched his mouth.

The seafood dish was delicious. She was delicious. He wanted to start with the *tiella* and then have his fill of her until he was satisfied—though he had no idea when that would be. He'd always thought she was edible, but a taste wasn't enough. Their two trysts had just whetted his appetite. He wished he could say he was sorry for roping her into an appearance on his mother's show, but the truth was he looked forward to any opportunity to be around her these days.

Marisa finally pulled away, lowering the spoon and looking flustered.

Camilla clapped, her expression expectant. "So?"

Cole swallowed and cleared his throat, raising his gaze from Marisa. "Mmm…fantastic. You could tell it was prepared with love."

He didn't know where he was dredging up the words. He figured he was having an out-of-body experience since he couldn't ever remember being this turned on without having a blatant physical sign of arousal—which would have been an inconvenient turn of events right now, to say the least, even with a kitchen counter providing camouflage from the cameras.

His mother turned to address the audience, saving him from the spotlight. "And now for another special surprise. We are giving away a set of Stanhope Department Store's own brand of stainless-steel cookware today, thanks to our guest, Donna Casale. You can try yourself today's recipe with your own new cookware!"

To much applause, a producer lifted the top of a big, white box to reveal a ten-piece set of gleaming stainless-steel pots and pans.

"Please look under your seats!" Camilla announced. "The person with the red dot is the winner!"

After a few moments, a middle-aged woman stood up excitedly and waved a disc.

"Auguri!" Camilla called, clapping. "Come down to look at your gift."

When the audience member arrived to inspect her prize, Camilla put an arm around her and turned to the camera. "If you like the Danieli family recipe, please go to our website."

She paused for what Cole knew would be a voice-over, and the appearance onscreen of the recipe and web address when the episode aired. Then Camilla thanked her guests and the audience members for coming. "Until next time. *Alla salute!*"

When the camera lights turned off, signaling the end of filming, Marisa visibly relaxed.

"Good job, Mom," Cole said.

Camilla gave him a beatific smile. "Thank you for *l'assistenza.*"

If he wasn't saving one parent, he was saving another. Though he doubted his father would think Cole was saving anything when he heard there was finally a buyer interested in Serenghetti Construction. He'd received an offer earlier in the week but hadn't shared the news yet with anyone.

At the moment, though, he had more pressing concerns.

As the audience began to rise and disperse, he cupped Marisa's elbow.

"Are you okay?" he asked in a low voice. "You looked as if you were about to have a swoon-worthy moment back there."

"Only for your legion of female fans," she replied, blowing a stray hair away from her face.

He suppressed a laugh. *That'a girl.*

His mother and Donna were approached by a couple of audience members, so he and Marisa had relative privacy.

"Looks as if you might have gained some admirers today, too," he remarked.

She eyed him. "Including you?"

"I've always been a fan."

"Of my cooking?"

"Of everything, sweet pea."

Marisa waved a hand in front of her face. "You do know how to turn up the heat."

He gave her an intimate smile. "We haven't done it in the kitchen yet."

At her wide-eyed look, he bit back a grin. He admitted it—he loved flustering Marisa.

"There are other people here," she replied in a low, urgent voice.

He leaned over to whisper in her ear. "Your kitchen or mine?"

She sucked in a breath. "I—I have to show out my mom."

He gave her a lingering look, but nodded. Sooner or later, he'd have another chance to fan the flames with Marisa. He figured he'd survived the last fifteen years only because he hadn't known what he'd been missing...

As Marisa walked out of the television studio with her mother toward the exit that led to the parking lot, she kept her thoughts to herself.

"So what am I not supposed to know?" Donna asked lightly.

Marisa threw her a sidelong look. "I don't know what you mean."

"Hmm…it looks like it's more than just business between you and Cole Serenghetti."

Marisa felt a telltale wave of heat rise to her face. "Just doing a favor to thank him for participating in the fundraiser," she mumbled. "Besides, I thought it would be fun. You love cooking shows. Didn't you have fun?"

"Yes, I did," Donna agreed, "and part of it was the enjoyment of watching you and Cole interact. He looked as if he couldn't wait to be alone with you."

"Mom!"

Donna turned to face her. "You're a beautiful, desirable woman, Marisa. I know what a prize my daughter is. Cole would be foolish not to be interested in you."

There was the problem in a nutshell. She wasn't sure where she and Cole stood—where pretending left off and reality began. And whether they were just hooking up with no possibility of a future together.

"Camilla Serenghetti, for one, believes something is going on, and she couldn't be happier about it. She said she's heard rumors around town…" Donna sighed and then gave her a long-suffering look. "The mothers are always the last to know."

Marisa sighed herself, not having the heart for further denials. "Cole and I have a complicated past."

"All relationships are complicated, honey. But what I saw in there was Cole eating you up with his eyes."

"Mom, please!" she protested, because she wasn't used to such frank talk from her mother.

Donna laughed. "Honey, I'm acquainted with the attractiveness of pro athletes."

"Of course you are."

Her mother looked at her probingly. "I hope your hesitancy about Cole doesn't have anything to do with what happened between me and your father."

They stopped at the closed door leading out of the building.

When Marisa didn't say anything, Donna added, "Oh, honey, if baseball hadn't broken us up, something else would have. We were too young."

Yup, Marisa could identify with the tragedy of young love. She and Cole had been there themselves.

Still, she was surprised by her mother's toned-down reaction. Ever since Marisa had discovered the truth in her twenties about her parents' relationship—that her biological father was out of the picture even before an accident had claimed his life—she'd assumed her mother would be averse to professional athletes and their lifestyle.

Sure, her mother had been matter-of-fact when she'd finally detailed the circumstances around her pregnancy, but Marisa had assumed her mother had adopted that attitude for her daughter's sake. Marisa had vivid memories of exactly what sacrifices had been involved in her upbringing, and she figured her mother did, too, and despite hiding it well, couldn't help but be infected with some bitterness.

It appeared she was wrong—at least these days.

"You know, Mom," Marisa said jokingly, "marriage really has changed your outlook on life."

"Older and wiser, honey," Donna replied. "But the events in my life that you're referring to also happened a long time ago. I had time to move past them and get on with it. And I have never, ever regretted having you. You were a gift."

Tears sprung to Marisa's eyes. "Oh, Mom, stop."

Donna gave her a quick squeeze and then laughed lightly. "Enough about Cole Serenghetti, you mean? Well, let me know what happens there. Sometimes mothers would like to move up from last on the totem pole!"

Ten

Marisa looked around the glittering ballroom where the Pershing Shines Bright fund-raiser was being held. The Briarcliff was a popular event venue on the outskirts of Welsdale. It was also one of the locations she'd scouted for her wedding to Sal.

That last thought made her realize how much had changed—how much *she'd* changed—in the past several months. The man uppermost in her mind was Cole, not Sal.

Because tonight was bittersweet. She was relieved the fund-raiser had come together as a nice event. Thanks to Cole, they'd sold more tickets than she'd ever hoped for, and Jordan was a hit, as well. But even though she and Cole had not talked further about it, after this evening they were scheduled to drop their charade about being a couple.

She looked across the room at where Cole stood talking to Mr. Dobson, and her heart squeezed.

Cole looked beyond handsome in a tux. She knew he'd have no trouble attracting female interest again once people no longer thought that he was dating her. In fact, more than one woman tonight had thrown him an appreciative look or had hung on his words and giggled at something he'd said.

Marisa sighed. She should be focused on other things. Her mother and stepfather were here to support her. And after this evening, she might have proved herself enough to become assistant principal at Pershing. Mr. Dobson had asked her last week to submit her résumé.

The principal had given no indication that he was aware of her relationship with Cole—and she certainly hadn't broadcast it at school. In fairness, however, she'd casually mentioned that she and Cole had begun to see each other, having become reacquainted over preparations for Pershing Shines Bright. Marisa figured it was best the principal got the news from her first. And if Mr. Dobson had been a fan of *Flavors of Italy with Camilla Serenghetti*, he would have seen the episode with her and Cole that had aired two weeks ago, a few days after taping.

Cole glanced her way, and their gazes locked, his look appreciative.

He made her feel beautiful. She wore a green satin dress with a black lace overlay covering the sweetheart neckline, and chandelier earrings. She'd chosen her outfit with him in mind.

In the past couple of weeks, she'd seen more of Cole than she would ever have imagined. They'd attended a Razors game together to cheer on Jordan, where they were even nabbed on the Jumbotron sharing a quick kiss. She'd attended his second hockey clinic for Pershing students, and she'd teased him about making a teacher out of him yet. They'd also bonded in the kitchen, where he'd helped her make some of her signature Italian dishes.

She heated at the thought of what else they'd recently done in the kitchen…

Marisa had known then, if she hadn't before, that she'd fallen in love with him. Because heartbreak was her middle name.

"My God, he only has eyes for you."

Marisa jumped, yanked from her reverie, and turned to see Serafina behind her. "You sound like a bad advertisement for a women's hair-care product."

Serafina shook her head. "It's not your hair that I'm talking about."

"Ladies."

She and Serafina swung in unison to see Cole's youngest brother.

Jordan's eyes came to rest on Serafina, and his smile was enough to melt ice. "Marisa didn't tell me she had an even more perfect relative."

"Oh?" Serafina responded and then glanced behind her. "Where is she?"

Cole's brother grinned. "I'm looking at her, angel. I'm—"

Serafina scowled. "My name is not Angel, and I know who you are."

"Cole's brother," Jordan supplied, still unperturbed.

"The New England Razors' right wingman and leading scorer."

Jordan's smile remained in place. "You watch hockey."

"Leading scorer on and off the field," Serafina elaborated, her voice cool. "I read the news, too. And I've been moonlighting as a waitress at the Puck & Shoot."

"I know, and yet somehow we've never been introduced."

"Fortunately."

Marisa cleared her throat. She was happy she was no longer the focus of Sera's attention, but it was time to step in. "Jordan, this is my cousin Serafina."

"Named for the angels," Jordan murmured. "I was right. Must be divine kismet."

"In your dreams."

"It's where you'll be tonight…unless you also want to join me at the bar later?"

"My God, don't you stop?"

Marisa knew Serafina didn't like players, but she'd never known her cousin to be rude.

Sera's scowl deepened. "How did you know Marisa and I were related?"

For the first time, Jordan's gaze left Serafina for a moment. "Same delicate bone structure, and smooth cocoa butter skin. What's to mistake?"

"Unfortunately nothing, I suppose," Serafina allowed reluctantly.

"You're lovely."

"You're persistent."

"Part of my charm."

"Debatable."

Jordan grinned again and then shrugged. "The offer still stands. The bar, later."

"You're going to be lonely," Serafina replied. "At least for my company."

Jordan kept his easy expression as he stepped away. "Nice to meet you... Angel."

Serafina waited until Jordan was out of earshot and then fixed Marisa with a look. "A professional player."

"Cole is one, too."

"He's retired from the game. At least the one on the ice."

And then with a huff, her cousin turned and marched off, leaving Marisa speechless.

Cole appeared next to her. "What happened?"

She shook her head. "Actually, I don't know, except your brother and my cousin did not hit it off."

Cole frowned. "Surprising. Jordan is usually able to charm the—"

"—panties off any woman?" she finished bluntly for him.

Cole smiled ruefully.

"I think that's Serafina's issue with him."

Cole leaned in close, nuzzling Marisa's hairline. "The only woman I want to use my charm on is you."

Marisa's pulse sped up. "We can't here."

"We're supposed to be a couple."

One that would soon be *uncoupled*. "We're supposed to be professional, too."

She looked away, and then froze as she spotted a familiar figure across the room.

Cole's brows drew together. "What's wrong?"

He followed her gaze, and then he stilled, too.

Mr. Hayes. The former principal had been invited tonight because he usually was for major school events. She just hadn't thought of apprising Cole of the fact. And she'd sort of ducked the issue by not checking with the administrative staff about whether Mr. Hayes had said he would be attending.

She hoped a meeting fifteen years in the making wouldn't spell disaster...

"Cole Serenghetti and Marisa Danieli," Mr. Hayes hailed them.

Cole looked at Marisa but she was avoiding his eyes.

"Mr. Hayes," she greeted the other man. "How nice to see you. You look wonderful. Retirement agrees with you."

Retirement would have agreed with the sour Mr. Hayes fifteen years ago, Cole thought sardonically. Of course, the old codger would be here tonight. He was grayer and less imposing than when he'd held Cole's fate in his hands, but he still had the same ponderous personality from the looks of it.

Cole gazed at Marisa, and she implored him with her eyes to make nice. Tonight was important to her, so he was willing to go along. He gave her a slow smile. *You owe me, and I'll collect later, in a mutually pleasurable way...*

Mr. Hayes glanced from Cole to Marisa. "I understand you two are a couple these days. Congratulations."

Marisa smiled. "Thank you."

"I bet you're surprised," Cole put in.

Marisa appeared as if she wanted to give him a sharp elbow.

"Not really," Mr. Hayes replied.

Cole arched an eyebrow. "I turned out better than you expected."

"Well, naturally—"

"I understand there'll be a video retrospective tonight. Might want to withhold judgment until then."

Marisa widened her eyes at him, and Cole smiled insouciantly back at her. He was willing to play along, but he could still tweak Mr. Hayes's nose and have some fun in the process.

Mr. Hayes cleared his throat. "Speaking of video presentations, I would like to set the record straight on one issue. When Marisa was called to my office that day, and I asked—"

"Interrogated, you mean?"

"—her about the prank, I could tell she cared about you."

Cole tamped down his surprise.

"At first, she was very reluctant to say anything. And then when she revealed your connection to the stunt, she was worried about what would happen to you."

Cole felt Marisa's touch on his arm.

She'd cared about him in high school, and even Mr. Hayes had been able to see it. Cole wondered why he himself hadn't, and realized it was because he'd been blind to anything but his sense of betrayal.

Cole met and held Mr. Hayes's gaze. "I learned a lot from that episode in high school. It was the last school prank I ever pulled." He covered Marisa's hand with his. "But everything ended well. More than fine. I'm lucky."

Marisa went still, and Cole figured she was wondering whether he was playacting for Mr. Hayes's benefit. She probably thought he was highlighting their relationship in order to rub the former principal's nose in it.

But he wasn't acting. He was dead serious. The realization hit him like a body check on the ice.

He wanted Marisa in his life. He *needed her* in his life.

Sooner or later, he was going to make her see she needed him, too.

Two days after the fund-raiser Marisa opened her door to the last person she expected to catch on her threshold again. Sal.

Since Pershing Shines Bright, she hadn't had a chance to see Cole again, though he'd congratulated her by text on a job well done. She'd been on duty the night of the fund-raiser, so she'd departed after everyone but Pershing staff had left. After a quick peck on the lips, Cole had regretfully excused himself because he had an early-morning work meeting.

She was left in a crazy-making limbo about where she and Cole stood, wondering whether the meeting was an excuse because he remembered, too, that the clock on their relationship was due to strike midnight at the end of the fund-raiser.

Still, the morning—or two—after, she hadn't expected Sal.

She reluctantly stepped aside so he could make it over the threshold. "Sal."

"Marisa, I need to talk to you."

Closing the door, she turned to face her former fiancé.

"Vicki left me," Sal said without preamble.

"I'm sorry."

Well, this was an interesting turn of events. Marisa wrapped her arms around herself. In some ways, she should have predicted Sal and Vicki's breakup. They appeared to have little in common, except perhaps for their joint affinity for sports stars.

Still, what did Sal want from her? A shoulder to cry on? She needed consoling herself about Cole.

Sal grimaced. "It was for the best that Vicki made for the door. I've been acting like an idiot."

Marisa couldn't disagree, but she said nothing, not wanting to hit someone when he was down.

Sal suddenly looked at her pleadingly. "I'm done with the high-flying lifestyle of pro athletes, Marisa. I thought I wanted it for myself, but I've tendered my resignation at the sports agency. I'm taking a job with a foundation that brings sports and athletics to underprivileged kids. I want to make a difference."

She couldn't argue with the admirable impulse to help kids. She worked with children every day. It was exhausting but exhilarating work. Still, while she was happy Sal appeared to be in a better place, she wondered about the road he'd taken to get there. "And Vicki leaving you led to this epiphany?"

He had the grace to look sheepish. "She wasn't you, Marisa."

"Of course not. Wasn't that why you were attracted to her?"

"I was an idiot," Sal repeated. "But I've done a lot of thinking in the past few days."

She waited.

"Marisa, I still have feelings for you."

She blinked and dropped her arms to her sides.

Sal held up his hand. "Wait, let me finish. I know it'll be hard to regain your trust. But I hope it won't be impossible. I'm asking you to give me another chance." He reached for her hand. "Marisa, I love you. I'm willing to do anything, whatever it takes, to have you back."

She didn't know where to begin. "Sal—"

"You don't need to say anything." Sal gave a half laugh. "There's nothing you can say that I haven't already thought of. I've called myself every name in the book."

She snapped her mouth closed.

"The thing is, I got cold feet with our engagement." He shrugged. "You could say it took Vicki to make me realize the person I really want. You, Marisa."

As a heartfelt declaration, it wasn't half-bad. But she was no longer sure he was the right man for her.

Sal had made a mistake, by his own admission. But otherwise he was safe and predictable and what she'd thought she always wanted—until Cole had come back into her life.

Still, Cole had never shown any indication of settling down. And while she'd been falling in love with him, he hadn't given any sign that he returned her feelings.

She cleared her throat. "Sal, I—"

"No," he interrupted. "Don't say anything. Think about it. I know I've laid a lot on you."

"Really—"

He gave her a quick kiss, startling her. It was as if he was determined to prevent a knee-jerk rejection. "I'm going to check in with you again soon."

With those words, Sal turned and was out the door as quickly as he had come.

Cole had just gotten off a conference call at work when his assistant put through a call from Steve Fryer, an acquaintance from his days on the ice.

Cole looked at the papers strewn across his desk. He was already pressed for time, his morning occupied with meetings, but Steve had no way of knowing that.

Cole also itched to be with Marisa. He hadn't seen her since the fund-raiser a few days ago. He'd had a busy schedule with a couple of work emergencies, and today was looking no better.

"Cole, I've got good news," Steve announced. "The coach for the Madison Rockets has decided to take the job in Canada after all because the sports advertising agency there agreed to meet his contract terms." Pause. "We'd like to offer you the coaching position."

Cole leaned back in his chair, his world coming to a screeching halt. This was the opportunity he'd been waiting months for. The Rockets were one of the best minor league teams in the American Hockey League. The job would be a good launching pad for an NHL coaching position. Rather than starting as an assistant coach in the NHL, he could prove himself as the head of his own team.

"Great news, Steve. I think the Rockets made the right decision."

Steve laughed.

"I'll get back to you," Cole said, eyeing the jumble of papers on his desk. "As you can imagine, there are things to sort out at this end." He expected Steve would assume he needed to contact his agent—or former agent, to be more accurate—to begin the process of negotiating a suitable employment contract.

Only Cole knew his complications were bigger. He needed to disentangle himself from Serenghetti Construction, for one. He thought again of the offer to purchase the company—it was now or never. And then there was his relationship with Marisa...

"Take your time," Steve responded. "We'll talk next week."

"You'll be hearing from me." Cole gave the assurance before ending the call, his mind buzzing.

The wheels were moving in the direction he wanted, but in the past year he'd become more encumbered than ever in Welsdale. Marisa was chief among those ties...

He'd suggest she move to Madison with him.

A weight lifted as his mind sped up. There would be plenty of teaching jobs there for her. If she had the potential to advance at Pershing, then she certainly had the qualifications to be an attractive hire at other schools. She might even decide that moving someplace else was the better bet—she hadn't yet gotten a promotion at Pershing, and one might never materialize. Another school might start her out in administration from the beginning.

He could make this situation work—for the both of them. He *would* make it work.

But first he needed to tackle a dicier situation. It was time to tell Serg about the offer to buy Serenghetti Construction.

Cole picked up his jacket off the back of the chair and told the receptionist he'd be out and reachable on his cell. After texting his mother, he made the quick drive over to Casa Serenghetti, where he figured he'd find Serg in one of two moods: grumpy or grumpier.

When he stepped inside the house, he greeted his mother with a peck on the cheek and then followed her to the oversize family room, where his father was ensconced in a club chair.

Cole sat in a leather chair and braced his elbows on his knees, his hands clasped between them. Camilla took a seat on the sofa, and there was small talk about the weather and how Serg was feeling. But Cole could tell his father was suspicious about this unexpected visit. Serg regarded him from under his customary lowered brows.

Cole took the bull by the horns. "Someone's offered to buy the company."

"Offered?" Serg shot back in his rumbling voice. "Like someone came banging on your door? Or you solicited a buyer?"

"Does it matter? It's a good offer from a bigger outfit with operations in the Northeast." Cole knew they couldn't expect better.

Serg grumbled, his eyes piercing. "I'm going to have another stroke." Then he bent his head and grimaced.

Camilla shot to her feet. "Madonna. Serg! Where does it hurt?"

But Cole had a better question. "Right now?"

Serg cracked one eye open. "Does it matter when? You've killed me, either way."

"Serg, please," Camilla exclaimed, throwing Cole an exasperated look.

Cole was used to drama from his family. He'd had a lifetime of it.

"You fought hard to get the contract to build the Pershing gym, and now you're planning to sell the company?" Serg asked accusingly. "I was starting to think you had my competitive business instincts."

Cole was ready. "I do, and that's why I believe selling the company is the best thing."

"Camilla, bring me my meds," Serg instructed at the same time that he waved Cole away. "I need to rest."

"The offer is a good one," Cole said again, and then stood because he'd known before he'd arrived that he needed to let Serg get used to the idea. "Let me know when you're ready to hear more of the particulars."

One meeting down, one to go. On the way out the door, Cole texted Marisa to meet him at the Puck & Shoot after work…

Eleven

When Marisa walked into the Puck & Shoot, she was nervous. Cole had asked her to meet him, and she knew she needed to mention Sal's visit.

She slipped into the booth and sat opposite from Cole, not giving him a chance to rise at her entrance. A waitress appeared, and at Cole's inquiring look, she ordered a light beer.

Cole's cell phone buzzed, and she was saved from having to say anything more. Apologizing for having to take a work call, he stood up and walked a few feet away.

The last time she and Cole had been at the Puck & Shoot, she'd thrown herself at him when Sal and Vicki had appeared, and their charade as a couple had started. How fitting would it be if they buried their faux relationship here, as well?

When the waitress returned and set her drink before her, Marisa took a swallow. She was nervous, and she sensed something was up with Cole, too.

Cole slipped back into the booth, pocketing his phone. Marisa felt her pulse pick up. She wanted to slide into the booth beside him, sit in his lap, twine her arms around his neck and brush his lips with hers. But she no longer knew whether she was allowed to. She didn't know where they stood. Neither of them had talked about anything substantial since the end of the fund-raiser days ago.

As if reading her mind, Cole stared at her intently. "We've done a good job pretending to be a couple."

"Yes." It was the pretend part that she'd had trouble with.

"I've been offered a coaching job with a hockey team in Madison, Wisconsin."

Marisa's heart plummeted.

Cole, however, looked pleased. Could their relationship—okay, their pretending—have meant so little to him? She wondered why he'd brought up the coaching job right after mentioning their charade. It seemed like a non sequitur...unless this was Cole's way of breaking things off? *It's been good, but now I'm moving on, sweet pea?*

"Sal wants to get back together," she blurted.

She knew it was a defensive move, but she couldn't help herself. Cole hadn't said he was taking the job in Wisconsin, but...he seemed happy. And he knew she was tied to Welsdale and her job at Pershing School—not that he'd said anything about having her move with him.

Her mind was racing, but she just couldn't bear to hear the words *it's over, baby.* She'd been dumped by Sal and had survived, but she wasn't sure she could pick up the pieces after Cole. He meant too much. Still, she couldn't blame Cole for leaving. The fund-raiser was finished, and she'd been the one to insist their pretend relationship would end with it.

Cole blinked, and then his face tightened. "Don't tell me you're considering giving that jerk a second chance."

No, but right now she needed her walls up where Cole was concerned. She had to keep him at a distance. She'd fallen in love with him, but he'd never given any indication that he felt the same way about her. In fact, he was leaving.

Cole nodded curtly. "If you go back to Sal, you'll be playing it safe."

"I'm a teacher. It's a nice, safe profession."

He leaned forward. "If you think you're not passionate and daring, you're wrong, sweet pea. I can tell after our time together."

She wasn't passionate, she was greedy. She wanted it all, including Cole's unwavering love and attention. But Cole had never shown any inclination of settling down, and as far as she could tell, he wasn't starting now. "You're passionate about hockey. You should pursue the dream."

It hurt to say the words. She felt a heavy weight lodge in her heart. But if there was one thing she'd learned from the past, it was that it was futile to stand in the way of dreams.

Cole said nothing, but his hand tightened on his beer.

"Sure your parents would love to have you in Welsdale," she continued. "That's why they liked that we were a couple. But we both know it was pretend." Just saying those words made her ill.

Cole's mouth thinned. "Are you forgetting how we got into a fake relationship?"

Yes, it was her fault. She heated but stood her ground. "And now we're uncoupled."

He gave a brief nod. "There's nothing else to say then. A bargain is a bargain."

Marisa wanted to say a lot of things. *I love you. Don't leave. Stay with me.*

Instead, she nodded in agreement and reached for her handbag beside her. She fumbled for bills to pay her tab.

"Leave it," Cole said, his voice and face impassive. "I've got it."

She nodded and slid out of the booth without looking at him. "I've got to go. I squeezed in a detour to the Puck & Shoot when you texted, but I've got papers to grade tonight."

She would not meet Cole's gaze. It would be her undoing. "Thanks for the beer."

She headed toward the door on autopilot. *Please don't let me faint. Please let me survive this.*

The next night Cole found himself at the Puck & Shoot again. Anyone with a morbid sense of humor would say he enjoyed wallowing in misery by returning to the scene of the crime.

He still knew which way was up, but he hoped to correct the situation soon, starting with the drink before him. He'd never been turned this inside out by a breakup with a woman, and it took some getting used to.

On top of it, he was questioning his plans for Serenghetti Construction. If that wasn't evidence that he needed his head examined, he didn't know what was. Without his knowing it, the family company had grown on him in a sneaky way. It didn't seem right to sell it.

He grimaced. He could handle only one breakup at a time.

"What are you doing? Drinking yourself silly?"

Cole turned, surprised at his brother's voice. "Your powers of observation are impressive, Jordan."

Cole figured he should have chosen a bar other than the Puck & Shoot if he'd wanted to be left alone. At least Marisa's cousin Serafina wasn't working tonight. Unfortunately, however, Jordan had decided to show up for a drink.

"Well? Where's Marisa?" Jordan looked around the bar. "It's Saturday night. I thought you two lovebirds were joined at the beak these days."

"She decided she prefers another guy."

Jordan raised his eyebrows. "Sal?"

Cole didn't answer.

"And you're conceding the field?"

"She made her choice," he responded.

Jordan shook his head. "Man, you are pathetic—"

Cole grabbed a fistful of his brother's shirt and got in Jordan's face. "Leave it alone." Then he thrust his brother away and took another swallow of his scotch. He needed something stronger than a beer tonight.

"You can't see what's in front of your eyes."

Cole propped a hand up in front of him on the bar and spread his fingers. "I'm not that far gone. Yet."

"You want her bad."

"There are other women."

"Vicki."

"Hell, no. We're through."

"So you aren't willing to settle for any—"

"She is." He didn't need to elaborate who the *she* was. *Marisa.* She'd been in his thoughts nonstop. "She's willing to take the horn-dog back."

"Has she said so?"

"She's considering it."

Jordan looked around. "I thought she'd be here."

"Why the hell would she be here?"

"She texted me earlier. She's looking for you. She said she had something of yours to return—"

Probably his heart.

"—and I told her I had no idea where you were, but the Puck & Shoot was worth a try."

Great. There was no way he wanted his brother—and who knew how many others—to witness his final denouement. "She knows how to break up with a guy."

"Too public?" Jordan guessed. "Why don't you go to her apartment then and beat her to it?"

Brilliant idea. The last thing he needed was for Marisa to find him at the Puck & Shoot, nursing a drink like a lonely lovesick puppy. If he seemed pathetic to Jordan, he didn't want to think how he'd appear to Marisa.

If she was looking for him, best to get this over with. He'd save her the hassle of finding him. At least that was what he told himself. He ignored the way his pulse picked up at the thought of seeing her again.

Cole straightened off the bar stool and tossed some bills on the counter for the waiter.

"I'll get you a cab," Jordan offered.

Cole twisted his lips. "Because I'm not fit to drive?"

"Because you're not fit for public consumption. You look like hell, and something tells me you were that way even before you got to the Puck & Shoot."

The ride to Marisa's apartment was swift.

When Cole reached Marisa's door, it was open a crack. He heard voices and pushed his way inside without invitation.

The scene that greeted him made his blood boil. At the entrance to the living room, Sal and Marisa were locked in a tight embrace, Sal's lips diving for hers. It would have been an arresting tableau even without his appearance as the spurned ex-lover, Cole thought, but his unexpected arrival had turned this into a spectator sport.

"Sal, no!" Marisa tried to shrug out of Piazza's grasp.

The scene before him took on an entirely new cast. Cole sprang forward and yanked Sal away, shoving him up against the wall. He put his face in the sports agent's surprised one.

"She said no," he said between clenched teeth.

"Hey, man…"

Cole gave Piazza a rough shake. "Understand?"

"We were just—"

He slammed the other guy back against the wall. "You were just leaving."

Sal struggled. "Get off me. I have every right to visit my girlfriend."

"Your former girlfriend," Cole corrected.

"Same goes," Sal retorted. "You sports guys think you can have whatever you like whenever you want it. How does it feel to be dumped for a change?"

Cole glanced over at Marisa. He was at a disadvantage

because he didn't know what she had said to Sal and what she hadn't.

She looked at him mutely for an instant, as if dumbfounded, and then stepped closer. "Cole, don't hurt him."

Cole turned back to Sal, staring down the red-faced sports agent.

"I'll sue you," Sal said.

"That's what it's always been about," Cole said. "You hankered for the money and the women, and the other baggage that comes with a pro athlete's life. Is that why you want Marisa back, too?"

Marisa gasped.

Sal gave a disbelieving laugh. "I've wised up. You're on an ego trip, Serenghetti."

"Not as big as the one you're on, Piazza."

Marisa came closer. "Cole, let him go. Sal, you need to leave now."

The threat of violence hung in the air even as Cole dropped his hold and stepped back.

Sal shrugged and straightened his collar. Then he ran his hand through his hair before settling his gaze on Marisa. "You know where to reach me, honey. I'll leave you to give Serenghetti his walking papers. He must have had trouble reading them the first time."

Cole tightened his hand into a fist, but he let the sports agent make his exit without further incident.

When the door to the apartment clicked shut, Marisa turned toward Cole. It was quiet, and they both seemed to realize at the same time that they were now alone to face the charged emotions between them.

"What are you doing here?" Marisa asked.

"Thank you, Cole, for saving me," he replied in a falsetto voice.

"I can take care of myself."

"Right." He still wanted to break Sal in two. "Here's the

better question. What was Sal doing here, and if he wants you to take him back, why were you resisting?"

"Sal and I aren't back together."

Despite himself, Cole felt better. She hadn't taken Sal back *yet*, and from the looks of things, Sal may just have ruined his chances.

"But I told him the reason wasn't because you and I are still together."

"So he saw his opportunity to press his case?"

Marisa sucked in a breath. "Next question. Why did you show up? You couldn't have known Sal was here."

"Jordan said you were trying to track me down."

She shook her head. "No."

Cole clenched his fist. Either his brother was misinformed, or Jordan had duped him into going to Marisa's apartment. If he hadn't agreed to go, would Jordan have tried to lure Marisa down to the Puck & Shoot instead? One thing was for sure—he was going to do physical violence to his brother, upcoming hockey playoffs or no.

First, though, he needed to get one thing straight. "Fine, you weren't trying to track me down. I've still got something to say."

Marisa stared at him without saying a word.

"You're a beautiful woman. You're ambitious and passionate and worthy of whatever life throws at you. The two of us might be finished, but don't settle for Sal."

He wanted to grab her and kiss her, but that would put him in Piazza's league. Instead, he forced himself to turn and walk out the door.

Marisa expected the senior play to be the last big event on the school calendar at Pershing. She didn't think, though, that the seniors' swan song would also be the place she ran into Cole again—maybe for the last time before he left Welsdale.

Ever since he'd left her apartment last week, she'd been

thinking about him. She wasn't about to take Sal back just because Cole intended to leave town for a coaching job in another state. Sal had only been a convenient smokescreen when Cole had announced he was moving to Wisconsin—and yet the realization that Cole may have been misled had done nothing to ease her heartache...

She also had no idea why Jordan would have told Cole that she was looking for him. Maybe Jordan had been misinformed—or maybe he was trying to get the two of them back together. No, the latter was wishful thinking.

She stole a look at Cole, who was sitting across the aisle in a different section of the auditorium. Would she ever stop yearning where he was concerned? She assumed Cole had been invited to the play by Mr. Dobson because he was a famous alumnus intertwined with the school's plans for the future.

Even with the space separating her and Cole, however, she had trouble concentrating. Even more depressingly, Pershing's seniors were staging *Death of a Salesman.* And as the scene opened, her heart rose to her throat. Because there it was...

The sofa where she had lost her virginity to Cole. Right there on stage. She burned to the roots of her hair. She stared ahead, not daring a glance at Cole. Out of the periphery of her eye, however, she thought she detected a movement of his head in her direction...

Marisa didn't know how she made it through the rest of the play. The sofa...the memories... Cole. She longed to race up the aisle, through the doors to the auditorium and all the way home...where she could console herself in private.

She loved Cole, and he didn't love her in return. It was a replay of high school. And like her mother, she was getting burned by a pro athlete who wanted to pursue his dreams.

Somehow she made it through the whole play. She breathed a sigh of relief when the curtain came down and the student actors took their final bow. Any moment now, she could duck out.

But when the audience finished clapping, Mr. Dobson headed to the stage.

After complimenting the students' efforts, the principal cleared his throat. "I'd like to make some final remarks, if I may. It's been a wonderful year for Pershing School. Our fund-raiser was a huge success, and we are constructing a new school gym." Mr. Dobson paused at the round of applause and cheers. "Great thanks go to Cole Serenghetti and his company for donating construction services. I'm also extremely pleased to announce the new gym will be called The Serg Serenghetti Athletic Building."

Marisa's gaze shot to Cole, but he was looking at Mr. Dobson, clapping like everyone else.

No one got a campus building named after them without making a major monetary donation. In all likelihood, Cole had made a significant cash pledge in addition to donating construction services.

But why?

She'd worked so hard to overcome his resistance to helping with Pershing Shines Bright. The only reason he'd agreed to participate was because of the lucrative construction contract. But now even that profit had evaporated because Cole was making a hefty donation to the school.

Mr. Dobson waited for the audience to settle down. "I'd also like to take this opportunity to welcome our new assistant principal starting next year, Ms. Marisa Danieli."

Marisa blinked, shocked. She hadn't expected that announcement tonight. Caught by surprise, she felt flustered, her heart beginning to pound. Most of all, she felt Cole's eyes on her.

"Ms. Danieli earned her undergraduate and master's degrees from the University of Massachusetts at Amherst. She has been a beloved teacher at Pershing for almost ten years, and a tireless and invaluable member of the school community. Marisa, please come up here, and everyone, join me in congratulating her."

Marisa felt a squeeze on her arm as one of her fellow teachers congratulated her, and then she got up and walked to the stage on rubbery legs. The audience applauded, and there were hoots and hollers from the student body.

The minute Marisa was on stage, she sought out Cole with her eyes, but he was inscrutable, clapping along with everyone else. Had he played a role in her promotion? Had he put in a good word for her, as the school's current and likely most valuable benefactor?

She felt the prickle of tears.

Mr. Dobson was looking at her expectantly, so she cleared her throat and forced herself to speak. "Thank you. I'm thrilled to be Pershing School's new assistant principal. Almost twenty years ago, I walked through the front doors here for the first time. I was a scholarship student, and Pershing changed my life." She paused. "You could say I've gone from being called to the principal's office to having the room next to the principal's office. The distance is short, but the road's been long!"

There was a smattering of laughter and a lot of applause.

"I'm looking forward to my new role." Marisa smiled and then shook hands with Mr. Dobson.

As she stepped off the stage and made her way back to her seat, the principal wished everyone a good night, and the audience began to stand and gather their things.

Marisa hoped she could make a quick escape. She needed to get her emotions under control and to take time to process everything that had happened. But she was waylaid by congratulations, and by the time she was finished, Cole stood at the end of her aisle.

Cole's expression gave nothing away. She, on the other hand, was crumbling.

She pasted a smile on her face and took the initiative— she was the new assistant principal, after all. "Congratulations. You must be thrilled about the new building being named for your father."

"He's excited about the honor."

They stared at each other.

She clasped her hands together to keep from fidgeting. It was either that or give in to the urge to touch him. "So you're ready to embrace your alma mater?"

"That's one way to interpret a large donation."

"Thank you."

Cole still looked indecipherable. "Are you speaking in your role as the new assistant principal?"

"Yes." *And as the woman who loves you.*

He nodded curtly.

"Did you put in a good word for me?" she asked impulsively, knowing she might not get another chance. "Did you pull strings?"

"Does it matter?"

"Did you?" she persisted against all reason.

Cole shrugged. "It turns out my endorsement wasn't needed. You were the overwhelming favorite for the job."

She swallowed. "Thank you."

"You worked hard. You got what you wanted."

Not quite. She didn't have him. She'd never have him.

Just then, a Pershing board member came up to them. "Cole, there's someone I'd like to introduce you to."

Marisa was thankful to be saved from any additional awkwardness with Cole. Murmuring her goodbyes, she turned and fled down the aisle, head bent. She was sure anyone who saw her face would be able to read the raw emotion on it.

Tears welled again, and she made for the exit nearest the stage. Everyone else was streaming toward the doors at the back of the auditorium, which led to the street and parking lot. But she needed a moment alone before reaching her car. She didn't know if she could manage even a small blithe lie to explain away why she was crying.

In the hall beyond the exit, she made a beeline for the closest door, and found herself in the theater department's dimly lit prop room. Furniture was stacked everywhere, some of it covered by drop cloths.

Hearing footsteps outside, she reached behind her and turned the lock on the door and then leaned against the frame.

Someone tried the knob. "Marisa?"

Cole. She said nothing—hoping he'd go away.

"Marisa?" Cole knocked. "Are you okay?"

No, she wasn't. He didn't love her. He was leaving. Nothing was okay.

"You looked upset when you said goodbye. Let me in, sweet pea."

Why? So he could leave her again? She didn't think she could stand it. She strangled a sob and hoped he didn't hear it.

She heard Cole move away from the door, and irrational disappointment hit. Moments later, however, she heard the click of a lock, and then the door was creaking open.

She stepped back and turned to face Cole. "Underhanded and sneaky."

He pocketed a Swiss Army knife. "I learned to pick locks in the Boy Scouts." Then he looked around the room. "We have to stop meeting this way."

"We're safe. The sofa is still onstage."

Cole searched her face and then quirked his lips. "Depends on how you define safe."

Marisa's heart clenched. No, she wasn't safe...and yet she felt like she was home whenever she was near him. "Is there anything you do that doesn't involve bulldozing?"

"Not if I'm going to continue to be the CEO of Serenghetti Construction."

Her eyes went wide. "Is that what you want?"

He gazed at her and then slowly stepped forward, his

look tender. He lifted her chin and brushed a thumb across her cheek. "I want you. Marisa, I love you."

She parted her lips and sucked in a tremulous breath, her world tilting.

"I've never said those words to a woman before." He glanced around the storage room before his gaze came back to hers. "And this isn't the way I was envisioning things, but the word at the Puck & Shoot is that you told Sal you wouldn't take him back. Give me a chance, sweet pea."

"You're leaving," she said in a wobbly voice.

"No, I'm not. I'm not taking the job in Wisconsin. I'm staying here to run Serenghetti Construction."

She rested her hand on his arm. "You were angry at me in high school because I interfered with your hockey dreams. I'm not going to make the same mistake twice."

"You're not," he said affectionately. "I'll be coaching here in Welsdale. I'll be teaching teenagers who want to improve their game for a shot at a college scholarship or even the NHL." He paused. "Because I know how life-changing those college scholarships can be."

Her heart swelled. She adored this man.

"The more time I had to think about selling Serenghetti Construction, the more it didn't seem right. I had to acknowledge that construction is in my blood." He tilted his head. "Besides, I've got some ideas, including growing the business into a real estate development firm."

Marisa smiled. "Face it, Serenghetti Construction is just another arena for you to be competitive. That's why you were so set on winning over JM Construction. And who knows? The kids you're coaching may give you another chance at a hockey championship."

"Sometimes, Marisa, I swear you know me better than I know myself." He brushed her lips with his.

"Hang on to that thought because I plan to be around a lot." Cole was good, strong and hardworking. He also happened to be able to make her feel like the sexiest woman alive. He was the person she'd always been looking for.

"You're marrying a construction guy."

"Are you proposing?"

He twined his fingers with hers and raised her hand to his lips. "Damn right."

"I'm ratting you out, Cole, and this time I don't care who finds out." Her voice grew husky with emotion. "I'm telling everyone that you confessed your undying love for me. That you proposed!"

He kissed her. "You forgot *he can't keep his hands off me*, *he talks dirty to me*, and *he gets hard just thinking about me*."

"That's right."

"I'm in love with you."

"Good to know. I love you, too."

She sighed, and he kissed her again.

Epilogue

If they pulled this off, it would be Cole's biggest prank ever.

Leave it to her soon-to-be husband to involve her in the ultimate practical joke. Around her, guests mingled while waitstaff circulated with hors d'oeuvres. Everyone was unaware of what was to come next.

Marisa rubbed nervous palms on her column dress and then brushed aside the curls of hair that caressed her naked shoulders. As she did so, the diamond ring on her finger caught and reflected the light of the chandelier in the main ballroom of the Welsdale Golf & Tennis Club.

At the dais, Cole cleared his throat and called for attention, wineglass in hand. When everyone quieted, he said, "Thank you for joining us tonight. Marisa and I wanted to throw a big party to celebrate our engagement, so there are over two hundred of you here. Big love, big party—"

There was a smattering of laughter and applause.

Cole straightened his tie. "As some of you know, Marisa and I have had more excitement on the way to the altar than most people witness in an NHL game."

Their guests grinned and laughed.

"I had a crush on her in high school." He paused. "And I know what you all are thinking. Pershing's super jock and practical joker thought he had a chance with the beautiful, smart girl who sat in front of him in economics class? She had a mind and a body that turned him into brainless teenage mush."

Marisa swallowed against the sudden lump in her throat.

Cole shrugged. "So I did the only logical thing. I hid how I felt and told no one. Flash forward fifteen years. I got lucky when my fantasy woman skated onto my rink again. This time I knew I wasn't going to let her get away. I asked her to marry me."

Marisa blinked rapidly. Everything Cole had said was true, and yet, he'd cast it in a light that she'd never seen before.

Cole extended his arm. "Marisa, I love you."

A path opened for Marisa as people stepped aside. On shaky legs, she walked toward Cole, who gazed at her with love in his eyes. She placed her hand in his, and raising the skirt of her dress with the other she stepped up onto the dais.

Their friends and family hooted and clapped.

"That was quite a speech," she murmured for Cole's ears only. "I nearly ruined my makeup."

He grinned. "You would have looked gorgeous for the photos anyway."

"You're blinded by love."

"I wouldn't have it any other way, sweet pea." He gave her a quick peck on the lips before turning back to their audience, keeping his hand linked with hers.

"Save the PDA for the honeymoon," Jordan called from the side of the room, to much laughter.

"Thanks for the great lead-in," Cole answered. "Because Marisa and I are getting married. Tonight. Right now."

There were audible gasps, and people looked at each other.

The officiant she and Cole had chosen stepped forward from the side of the room.

"Surprise," Cole announced, and then he pulled Marisa into his embrace for another kiss.

When Cole had first suggested the idea of a surprise wedding, Marisa had thought he was kidding, but she couldn't have asked for anything more. She felt like a bride in every sense. She'd paired an embroidered lace-and-ivory gown with high-heeled gold sandals. And of course, she'd marry Cole anytime, anywhere.

There was a flurry of activity as their guests allowed themselves to be shepherded out of the ballroom and into one that had been secretly set up for a wedding ceremony. A photographer would be documenting the festivities, and a florist waited nearby to hand Marisa a tightly packed bouquet of white roses.

Marisa felt her heart swell, and then caught Cole's grin. Suddenly struck with an idea, she bit back a mischievous smile.

"Oh, Cole, this has been so overwhelming. I think…I think…" She closed her eyes and pretended to swoon melodramatically.

Cole wrapped strong arms around her. "Marisa?"

She opened her eyes and said teasingly, "I'll be falling into your embrace for the rest of our lives."

Cole grinned. "I'll always be here to catch you."

And they sealed their bargain with a kiss.

* * * * *

COMING SOON!

We really hope you enjoyed reading this book. If you're looking for more romance, be sure to head to the shops when new books are available on

Thursday 29th November

To see which titles are coming soon, please visit **millsandboon.co.uk**

MILLS & BOON

LET'S TALK
Romance

For exclusive extracts, competitions
and special offers, find us online:

- **f** facebook.com/millsandboon
- 🐦 @MillsandBoon
- 📷 @MillsandBoonUK

Get in touch on 01413 063232

For all the latest titles coming soon, visit
millsandboon.co.uk/nextmonth

Maureen Child writes for the Mills & Boon Desire line and can't imagine a better job. A seven-time finalist for a prestigious Romance Writers of America RITA® Award, Maureen is an author of more than one hundred romance novels. Her books regularly appear on bestseller lists and have won several awards, including a Prism Award, a National Readers' Choice Award, a Colorado Romance Writers Award of Excellence and a Golden Quill Award. She is a native Californian but has recently moved to the mountains of Utah.

Elizabeth Bevarly is a *New York Times* bestselling, RITA® Award nominated author of more than seventy novels and novellas who recently celebrated the twenty-fifth anniversary of signing her first book contract—with Mills & Boon! Her novels have been translated into more than two dozen languages and published in more than three dozen countries, and someday she hopes to visit all the places her books have. Until then, she writes full-time in her native Louisville, Kentucky, usually on a futon between two cats. She loves reading and movies and discovering British TV shows on Netflix. And also fiddling around with soup recipes. And going to farmers' markets with her husband. And texting with her son, who's at college in Washington, DC. Visit her website at www.elizabethbevarly.com or find her on Facebook at the Elizabeth Bevarly Reader Page.

USA TODAY bestselling author **Anna DePalo** is a Harvard graduate and former intellectual-property attorney who lives with her husband, son and daughter in her native New York. She writes sexy, humorous books that have been published in more than twenty countries and has won the RT Reviewers' Choice Award, the Golden Leaf and the Book Buyers Best Award. For the latest news, sign up for her newsletter at www.annadepalo.com.